NO LIGHT

WERELOCK  EVOLUTION

ISBN: 978-0-9973429-9-4

Join my newsletter mailing list to hear about new releases, author giveaways, and ARC opportunities!

http://bit.ly/HettieNews

ABOUT THIS BOOK

Although *No Light* is book number four in the Werelock Evolution Series, please note it may be read as a standalone within the series. It is not necessary to have read *Werelock Evolution: The Complete Trilogy* prior to reading *No Light*.

That said, having read the trilogy that precedes this book may enhance your enjoyment, as those who are familiar with the earlier books in the timeline will pick up on a few jokes and references that will be lost on new readers.

Please be advised that Hettie Ivers has a tendency to see satire and irony everywhere, and she has never met a foul word or raunchy euphemism she didn't like. *(With the exception of "baby batter"—which remains a hard limit for her.)* This book contains violence, foul language, adult content, and a lot of over-the-top werelock characters. If such material offends you, please do not read. *(Or read it and be offended, if that's your bag.)*

PROLOGUE

Avery

They said Bigfoot wasn't real. Neither was the Boogeyman.

Werewolves. They were supposed to be myth as well.

They weren't.

I'd watched one claw my beloved fiancé's chest open in broad daylight. I'd witnessed it murder my best friend and dismember her husband before any of us had time or thought to reach for the rifle that lay just inside our camping tent.

And I'd felt the cruelest burn of defeat I'd ever known deep in my abdomen as the unholy, monstrous animal shuddered and climaxed between my battered thighs while I bled out from the gash its teeth had made in my throat.

A normal person might've prayed for death as their body lay broken in the dirt, violated by an unnatural, beastly aberration.

I'd never aspired to be normal.

My life didn't flash before my eyes as I fought for my final breaths. All I saw was that Rock River AR-15 rifle in my mind's eye. Even as I felt my heart stopping, my very essence draining, my spirit disconnecting from the pain radiating throughout my damaged being—I wanted that rifle above all else.

My fourth foster mother had often told me I was too stubborn for my own good. She'd thought to beat that stubbornness out of me. She'd failed. I was the kid who took a blow and came back swinging with both fists. Every single time.

That I couldn't get back up now was inconceivable. That I'd never exact revenge on that wolfman creature who had just taken from me everything I valued most in life was beyond enraging. The farther I drifted up and away from my body, the more unthinkable it all was.

I was dead?

Fuck me. There was something beyond after all. Because I was dead yet still part of something bigger. It should've reassured me.

It didn't. I wasn't done swinging. I wanted back inside of my broken body. Already I missed the pain that said I was still alive, the agony that meant I hadn't stopped fighting.

I wasn't ready to be this orb of light floating through the ether, farther and farther away from the smell of fresh blood mixed with earth where my body would soon begin its inevitable process of decomposition.

If only I could get back up one last time. *If I could wrap my fingers around that rifle …*

Other light orbs surrounded me, some unknown, some achingly familiar. Their energy pulled me farther away from where I wanted to be. I felt Marcus next to me, pulling at my soul strings, his gentle spirit telling me not to be afraid to move on.

Marcus was the love of my life. He was everything I'd ever wanted. We could be together for eternity now, safe from the pain and strife that had always followed me.

I'd lived a very full thirty-two years. I'd beaten every single odd that had been stacked against me since birth. I'd proven every self-serving foster parent, hypocritical social worker, and naysayer wrong and made more of myself than any of them had made of their own sorry lives.

And I wasn't done. I still imagined the sensation of my fists clenching, my body readying for battle. I'd never quit anything before. I didn't know how.

Marcus was tugging harder now, urging me to surrender to the inevitable and let go … to leave the world of the living behind and be with him in whatever spirit realm lay beyond for us. I sensed my best friend Sloane's spirit circling and embracing me, reassuring me that everything would be fine.

Sloane's radiant energy proved harder to resist. Sloane was family. From the moment we'd met at sixteen, I'd sensed we shared some deeper cosmic destiny that defied the fact we came from worlds that couldn't have been more different. She'd accepted me with a love that was absolute, and I'd fancied myself her sworn protector throughout our college years, knowing she was too sweet and too sheltered to recognize the darkness that lurked in the hearts and minds of most men. But I'd failed her this time. And still she loved me unreservedly, calling to me with her tinkling laughter and sparkling, indefatigable optimism, tempting me away from thoughts of rifles and revenge, luring me farther from the pull of gravity and into the unknown where she and her husband, Garrett, and my beloved Marcus were rapidly flying.

Reluctantly, I followed, letting their energy carry me higher until the earth was but a speck of lint suspended in space below. As we joined other light orbs, I began to feel even more weightless. Boundless. I saw Marcus, Garrett, and Sloane's energy balls burn brighter than before. I felt their elation, their uncompromising joy. I tried to let it in—to feel what they felt, to become the oneness that they were morphing into.

But another energy source caught my attention. There was a dark energy swirling amid the orbs of light. It looked lost. Out of place amongst the celebratory beams of light energy dancing about. *It was searching for something.*

How I knew a random, dark celestial matter was looking for something was beyond a living mind's ability to fathom. But my soul—or whatever this was that was left of me—simply knew.

As it got closer, I realized it was so much more than dark energy. There were shades of grey. Color, too. And within the slivers of color were the faintest streaks of light.

They were barely noticeable at first, but the longer I observed them, the more those faint streaks fascinated and called to me until they appeared to burn brighter than all that was dark and ugly within the black orb. *Glimmers of hope.* My existence on earth had often been sustained by less.

And I knew. It was looking for a way back. Just like me. It wasn't finished yet either.

I perceived its overwhelming yearning for revenge, as well as its long-harbored hope for salvation. But more than that, I sensed at its core it was looking for something to nurture it … someone to love it and believe in it despite the darkest shadows marring its very nature. It needed … a mother. And it had chosen me.

Or maybe, we'd chosen each other.

Marcus and I had been trying to conceive, hoping to start a family shortly after our wedding set for next month. Thoughts of being the kind of mother I'd always wanted drew me closer to the curious dark orb, even as vibrations from Marcus and Sloane's energy grew stronger, more anxious to keep me with them.

But I was captivated by the dark energy the closer I drew to it. It was as powerful as it was needful, bursting with a strange brand of magic beyond anything I'd ever encountered. An inexplicable enchantment surrounded and saturated it, rendering it a nearly indestructible force of being.

And yet, it was nothing without a host. It needed a willing vehicle through which to return—someone strong enough to care for it, while sensitive enough to nurture the faint light within struggling to emerge.

If I followed Sloane, Marcus, and Garrett, I knew I'd find peace and certainty. Whereas fear, anger, unprecedented confusion, violence, and struggle lay within the dark, mystical matter poised before me. It was a road that would lead me back into the arms of danger—and likely far more peril than ever before.

But it would lead me back.

Powerful as my will had always been, the bait of hope amid the worst stack of odds was a drug I'd never had strength enough to decline. It called to me like no other poison. And it was those thin rays of hope I glimpsed in the dark orb that tipped the scales in its favor, drawing me closer and closer while all of the other light orbs merged and shied away from it.

The energy of Marcus and Sloane grew frantic behind

me. I could almost hear their human voices again, telling me this wasn't my fight, pleading with me to walk away from this challenge—as they had so many times in life. I heard Sloane's sweet, loving voice of reason, urging me to understand that I couldn't save everyone, that it wasn't my responsibility to change the world.

But the hope within the dark matter believed otherwise. And I did, too. Together, we could.

I focused my energy on Sloane and Marcus, imploring them to understand what I needed to do. Marcus's energy was devastated, yet resigned. I felt waves of his love wash over me as slowly he let me go.

Sloane emanated an odd mixture of wistful yet mirthful comprehension as her inner light observed mine for the last time. She knew me too well. She knew I wouldn't have the strength to leave her. I felt her final thoughts and emotions reverberate through me like a weary sigh as she relinquished me to the dark matter with a forceful shove of gravity that sent us both barreling back toward earth like a lightning bolt.

"If you have to go, go now. And Avery? Make it hurt."

It was the oddest sentiment she'd never spoken. So not a Sloane thing to say or think. And I knew it would both mystify and delight me to the point of watery giggles every single day that I lived on without her and remembered.

Regaining consciousness within my wrecked body was far more painful than I'd estimated. Everything hurt. I felt the sting of flesh melding together, skin and tendons knitting and healing themselves within my torn throat. Deep inside, my cervix burned as if it'd been grated and doused in saltwater, even as I felt a foreign, welcome magic healing my abused vaginal canal.

I heard my heart pumping, slowly at first, then rapidly, as a life-giving surge of adrenaline shot through my veins once more. Experimentally, I flexed my fingers, leisurely grazing over the dirt and leaf litter they rested upon, until a feral grunt to my right sent my eyes flying wide.

I was alive. And viewing the world in Technicolor, judging by the scenery that assaulted my senses as I stared up into the changing fall foliage above against the backdrop of a bright blue sky.

I'd never been praised for possessing patience, and not even experiencing death was meant to alter that, it seemed. Because it took every ounce of forbearance I possessed to slowly test my limbs and arise as stealthily as possible once I saw, from the corner of my eye, the animal shift into its full humanoid form and abandon the cooler of food he'd been rummaging through in favor of sniffing and licking at Sloane's dead body.

The wind picked up, swirling leaves and rustling branches. In my heart I imagined it to be the spirit of my departed best friend, helping to conceal the sound of my movements, because her lifeless body provided whatever further distraction was required, enflaming the beast's temporarily abated lust once more and causing him to claw at her clothes and tug her shorts to her ankles.

It seemed to take an eternity before I reached the tent that stood a scant few feet away. And I hardly allowed myself a breath until I had Marcus's AR-15 nestled against my right shoulder. A rage blacker than anything I'd ever felt was the only thing that prevented me from screaming and vomiting my guts up when the werewolf mounted and began to violate the prone, motionless body of my best friend.

I was a crack shot. I could've blown the mongrel's head off the first time I fired. But that was more than it deserved. The first bullet I fired into his shoulder, startling and knocking him off balance more than injuring. I knew it from the way stunned yellow eyes flew over his shoulder to glare at me in disbelief.

"Get off of her!" My throat felt raw. The order emerged garbled.

He snarled. I fired again, taking his ear clean off and disfiguring the side of his face. He howled and leapt from Sloane, spinning around to charge me.

The next bullet blew through his right knee, causing him to stumble sideways when he pounced in my direction. The fourth hit his left thigh, sending him flailing to the ground at my feet. And the fifth ... the fifth shot took out his privates.

With great effort, I forced myself to pause, to breathe in and out through my nose and remember my own rules of engagement. I needed information first. *Then I would make it hurt.*

Unfortunately, I would discover that crazed, rogue werewolves weren't the easiest source of useful intel on the species. Eighteen minutes and twenty-six bullets later, the most critical things I'd gleaned were (1) I was going to turn into a werewolf in seven days, (2) I wasn't likely to survive that transformation, and (3) werewolves were damned tiresome to kill.

By the time I was certain he was dead, there wasn't

much left of him that hadn't been riddled with bullets. But I figured it was enough for a team of scientists to begin their process of dissection and discovery. It would have to do. Because there was no way I'd have ever allowed that *thing* to live. And by the time I found my phone and dialed 9-1-1, my entire body was shaking something fierce and I'd thrown up the contents of my stomach. Twice.

I held it together while I told the authorities everything that had happened, carefully omitting several key parts—such as the part where I'd been raped by a rabid animal, died, met up with a dark orb, and then come back to life with the assistance of said magical orb as it healed my torn neck and vajayjay.

I mean … I'd just handed them a monster straight out of *Grimm's Fairy Tales* on a silver platter. No need to pique their interest to the point that they felt the need to dissect and investigate *me* next for being some kind of walking dead creature. I left out the interrogation part of my story as well, letting them think I'd simply gone nuts unloading the rifle in self-defense.

Cautious as I believed I was being, the greatest mistake of my life had already been made.

And no, it actually wasn't getting killed by a werewolf and coming back to life harboring a soul attached to a magical, revenge-greedy dark matter that would soon become my unborn werewolf fetus.

As it turned out, my greatest mistake of all was alerting the authorities to the incident in the first place. I might've fared better in the years that followed had I simply tattooed a giant red target on my forehead and ass.

CHAPTER 1

Alcaeus

Almost a decade later in Los Angeles, CA

I NEEDED PUSSY. BADLY. MY COCK FLEXED AGAINST THE seam of my jeans as I inhaled the buffet before me.

Not even the stench of alcohol, marijuana, and cheap perfume melding with the sweat emanating off of the human bodies filling the bar could mask the underlying scent of freshly washed, neatly landscaped, eager-to-be-fucked human pussy wrapped in lace undies and crammed into too-tight pants and skirts.

"Wallet," Kai's voice demanded, halting me midstep.

I turned to find my oldest friend and Beta with his hand outstretched, a harassed look on his face.

I frowned. "Forgot yours?"

"No. I don't see why we should make a poor Omega search dirty alleys and public restrooms to locate yours later on when you can give it to me now for safekeeping."

"Such a dutiful wife," I muttered, fishing my wallet from my back pocket. "Remind me when it's our anniversary to get you something nice." I slapped the wallet into Kai's awaiting palm.

"Like a divorce? Remind me why we're here again?"

My knuckles cracked as my fist clenched at my side. "Because Los Angeles is a city of loners. It's the perfect hiding spot for a rogue."

And because we'd already searched everywhere else across the U.S. for most of the past decade. *More or less.*

"I was referring to this bar." His tight smile was one of condescension. "Don't you think a rogue werewolf might be inclined to avoid the L.A. party scene?"

"Have a drink, Kai. Talk to a woman." I added the weight of authority to my words. "That's not a suggestion."

"We're wasting time, Al. Our mission here is done. The *Rogue* obviously isn't in the States."

I shook my head. "We're going to find him here. It's only a matter of time. The best seers all said—"

"The same seers who are all dead?" He raked a hand through his hair and lowered his volume as he continued. "Future events shift as circumstances change. You and I have lived long enough to know that."

"Too long," I mumbled, scanning the crowd for my next escape. I felt like I would fly out of my skin at any moment if I didn't ground myself. It'd been days since I'd killed anything. I needed to walk away from Kai before I said something I really wanted to.

He and I were both in our fifth century. I'd begun to think that maybe that was what was wrong with us. I'd grown tired of the empty look in the hazel eyes that stared back at me through the mirror each time I caught my own reflection. And I was beyond sick of having to face Kai's comatose features each day over the past decade that we'd coexisted on our *Rogue* mission in America—to the point that I largely avoided eye contact with him anymore. It was too damned depressing.

And infuriating.

"The pack needs you."

Bullshit. I laughed outright, my eyes rolling away from the blonde blatantly checking me out across the bar. "The pack's doing better than ever without me. Everyone knows it."

"It's got nothing to do with your absence. And it doesn't mean that Milena doesn't still need or want your help. Besides ... Jussara misses you." He took aim below the belt. "It'd be good for you both to spend some time grieving togeth—"

"Jussara's fine," I snapped. "She and I talk every week."

"Really?" His brow arched. "A week is still measured as a period of seven days, you know."

"You want to go back to Brazil? Go. I'll be fine carrying on the mission without you."

"Ha! What mission? If I weren't here to keep the team on track, this would be nothing but a nonstop sex tour of the United States."

"Not true." I threw my pointer finger in his face. "We've eliminated scores of rogue werewolves over the past decade."

"Which any peon werewolf can do. Come on, Al, you were a real Alpha once."

"And you were a man once!"

Fuck. I shouldn't have said—*shouted*—that. I ran my palm over my face as people sitting at the bar nearby turned to stare at Kai, who was subtly shaking his head at the ceiling—that all-too-familiar pinched look of open dis-approval lining his face.

For a century throughout the Reinoso pack, Kai had been known as the "pack priest" because of his longstanding celibacy. But in the past decade while on our mission in America, the guys and I had taken to calling him "pack eunuch."

I might've started it.

"I gotta go," I said rather than apologize. "Have a drink and talk to a woman," I ordered again before striding off in the direction of the hot blonde.

Some things never got old no matter how long I lived or how dead inside I became: like the sight of my dick sliding balls deep inside a beautiful pink pussy and gliding back out again dripping wet. That visual *never* got old.

Nor did the sounds a woman made while getting properly filled and fucked, her skittle played just right.

I had needed this. It'd been far too long—since yesterday.

Besides fighting and killing, sex was the only thing that grounded me anymore, pulling me out of my head and reconnecting me to my wolf.

Kai had labeled it an avoidance addiction. But to me, it was the opposite. It was the only time I felt present. Alive. Sensate.

And it was more than the primal, physical sensation of my cock dragging in and out of a velvety-smooth, gripping wet channel that did it for me; more than the inevitable release. It was the scent of a living, breathing, and warm and willing human female—even if it would forever be the wrong scent.

The wrong human female.

And I'd fucked hundreds—*okay, more like thousands*—of wrong human females over the past decade. After centuries of largely abstaining from sex with the fragile species, I was sure I'd become more proficient at handling them than even my human-harem-keeping stepbrother, Remy.

In the beginning, it was to prove to myself that I could. That I could take a human female sexually without breaking her. God knows why. I guess I felt the need to punish myself with that knowledge—the knowledge that I'd been a coward for fifty years.

The knowledge that maybe if I'd done something differently ... if I'd forged more of a physical, sexual connection with—

"Oh, God! Oh, oh, oh *fuck!*" The wrong human female squealed, clenching hard around my thrusting cock. Her spine arched and her nails clawed the bathroom countertop she was bent over.

Orgasm number three for the blonde, and I still wasn't anywhere near reaching my own. Nowhere near feeling grounded enough.

Damnit.

I shut my eyes and focused on her human scent, on the sensation of soft skin and smooth, feminine curves beneath my exploring fingertips. After a moment, I started to lose myself in the desperate, pleading sounds she began to make as my fingers pinched and rolled over her clit. I felt my wolf rising to the surface at last as I gripped her hips more forcefully, my dick swelling and my balls drawing up—

"And to think the pack rumors were kinder than reality for once."

My eyes flew open at the sound of my brother Alex's supercilious words to find his reflection in the mirror, standing a few feet away, dressed to the nines in a dark silk tux. He looked almost comical against the backdrop of the dirty bar restroom, his patent leather wing-tip shoes so shiny I could probably catch the reflection of my dick in them. But there was nothing funny about him teleporting in on me and thwarting my impending ejaculation.

"What the fuck are you doing here?"

"Trying not to inhale, at the moment," Alex said from behind his palm, taking in his surroundings with un-abashed disdain.

Sonofabitch.

I rammed hard into the blonde one final time, inadver-tently setting off her fourth orgasm. *Great.*

I groaned and covered her mouth with my hand as she began shrieking.

My Beta was a dead wolf. Kai could barely stand my little brother, Alex. Those two had never gotten along. If he had called him here for the petty sake of trying to rat me out, then things were far more strained between us than I'd thought.

"Kai called you?" I demanded, angrier than ever at hav-ing to endure my dick being squeezed in the best possible way while being unable to chase my own release.

Alex shook his head. "No. You have your own idiocy to blame for the fact that I just left a perfectly dignified function—which, by the way, I happened to be enjoying immensely with my wife—to come here and witness your sad descent into"—he waved his hand about, his nose scrunching up—"E. coli-ridden debauchery. You Alpha-commanded him to talk to a woman. You of all people should know by now there are only two women on the planet with whom Kai converses anymore if he can help it."

Jussara and Milena.

Of course Kai had called Milena. It was doubly annoying to acknowledge that Alex was right: I should've anticipated that the pack eunuch would find any excuse to avoid socializing with a member of the opposite sex in a bar setting. God forbid he remembered what attraction and arousal felt like.

"As often as Milena reminds me that it's only a small man who would celebrate another's misfortune"—Alex winced, sucking air through his teeth as the asshole grin he'd been struggling to withhold broke across his face—"I must admit … it's *really* taking all of my self-restraint right now not to throw one of your own windbag know-it-all lectures back at you."

Her orgasm waning, I released my hand over the blonde's mouth. When she turned her head, she started beneath me as her half-mast eyes landed on Alex, realizing for the first time that we had company.

"How rude of me." Alex held his hands up in a poor imitation of shock and contrition. "I didn't realize my brother had company in here. I knocked, but … I guess you two were indisposed." He shrugged, then gifted the blonde with a phony smile of sympathy. "You must be so distressed. I'm sure you never imagined such an embarrassing scenario occurring when you snuck in here for a quick fuck."

That was my baby brother. No matter how much everyone believed that my sister-in-law had changed him, Alex was pretty much the same prick he'd always been.

The blonde frowned, accurately deducing that he was insulting her. But then Alex winked and flashed his phony megawatt smile, and I watched in disgust as her face lit up.

And she blushed.

Ugh. I felt my penis shrinking in revulsion as I pulled out of her. *You're welcome for the four orgasms.*

Her eyes flitted back and forth between the two of us as she straightened her undies and skirt. I disposed of the condom and tucked my blue balls into my jeans.

"Wow," she said on a breathy exhale.

"Wow, indeed." Alex's voice dripped sarcasm. "You'll have to excuse my brother for failing to properly introduce us. He was literally raised by wolves, I'm afraid." He threw an impudent smile my way, prompting an introduction. The little shit was banking on me not knowing her name.

And he was right.

"Oh, we agreed no names." The blonde unwittingly jumped to my rescue. Alex's cocky smile slipped. She shrugged. "I mean, you know … why complicate a good thing?"

And this was why I loved American girls—particularly the New York City and Los Angeles variety.

"So I'm not normally into threesomes, but if you two …" She left the invitation hanging in the air as she bit her lip and made eyes at Alex.

Jesus, what was it about my brother that women always went for? It defied the laws of logic and self-preservation.

"Flattering," Alex said in a tone that suggested he was more repulsed than anything else. "But not interested." He held his left hand up and wiggled his ring finger, showing off his wedding band. "However, there is a friend of ours sitting at the bar who I'd love for you to chat up." He flashed her his cheesy grin again, and I found myself stifling laughter, knowing that he was about to charm her into hitting on Kai without even needing to use compulsion.

"Did you hear what I said?"

Disregarding my brother, I leaned back in my stool chair and took a leisurely sip of beer. He was standing next to the high-top table where I was seated, having judged the stool chairs as beneath his ass to sit upon, no doubt. "Why are you really here, Alex?"

"I've told you. Milena's worried about you."

"Me? Don't you mean Kai?"

"Eh … sure." Alex's lip curled with distaste. "Him, too, I suppose." His eyes shifted to where Kai was seated at the bar about twenty feet from us. Kai's posture was ramrod straight and awkward as he engaged in forced conversation with no-name hot blondie. A satisfied, sadistic smirk returned to Alex's mouth, relaxing his tense features somewhat. "Lately she fusses more over you. Anyway, she wants you both to come back and help with the *Rogue* search in Europe."

I shook my head. "Tell her to quit worrying."

"Like that'd work."

"It should. I'm a grown fucking man. I survived four centuries without your wife worrying about me."

"Yes, I've assured her that dumb luck has long been on your side. It failed to assuage her concern."

"Knock her up and give her a baby to fuss over. What are you two waiting for anyway? I'd like a niece or nephew sometime before I turn half a millennia."

Alex's jaw tightened. It was a sore subject and I knew it. I smiled into my glass of beer as I tipped it back. My brother was beyond eager to impregnate his mate. But Milena was dead set against bringing a baby into the world until the *Rogue* had been eliminated.

Centuries ago, during my late father's tenure as Alpha, seers had foretold that a mythical *Rogue*—the firstborn of a new and errant breed of werewolf—would rise to power during the time of the second vessel. As the second vessel, Milena had been prophesied to be "the key to the *Rogue*."

She was widely regarded within our pack as being our best shot at both finding and eliminating the abomination. Few took the task of rogue hunting more seriously than Milena did. Not even me—and I'd been playing at hunting the creature for most of my damn life.

"Look, I'm not saying *I* want you or Kai to return—yet. I'm asking you to come for a visit. Check in with her. You haven't been back since …" Alex hesitated, but only for a breath before going for the open wound few dared to poke. "Since Lupe's death."

I ignored it. "I'll order Kai to return. He spends all his time on the phone with Milena anyway," I provoked right back.

Alex's coal eyes turned steely. "I'm aware." His gaze returned to Kai and the blonde at the bar. "If he wasn't the pack eunuch already, I might make him one for real." The open bafflement and underlying pity in Alex's eyes as he studied Kai's behavior with the blonde mirrored that of every man who tried to wrap his brain around the anomaly of nature who was our permanently celibate pack doctor. "But we all know you need Kai. I wouldn't dream of leaving you to rely solely upon public transportation."

I rolled my eyes at his juvenile jab at the fact that I couldn't teleport. As far as we knew, there were only a handful of werelocks on the planet who could teleport. Within our Reinoso pack, Kai was one of them. Alex and my sister Alessandra were also capable of teleporting. Among our enemies, we knew of two other werelocks who possessed the gift.

"I'll manage. My mission in America isn't over."

"Oh, come on! You know I can't stand it when she gets that sad, distressed look on her face. And then she does that—that thing …" He gestured to his mouth. "That little thing with her lip."

"Stop. I'm gonna be sick."

"I'm serious. It's fucking heartbreaking, that lip thing." He rubbed his palm against his tuxedo shirt. "My chest gets tight and I can't breathe when she does it."

I didn't doubt it. Alex had been a virtual slave to Milena's emotional projections ever since the moment they'd met. It was as if his long-arrested sense of empathy had finally been awakened through their mate connection. Years later, he was still very much like a baby discovering his own hand and learning how to use it when it came to emotional intelligence.

"Not my problem, Alex."

"I can make it your problem."

I laughed. Alex had reigned as Alpha of the Reinoso pack for longer than I ever had before him, yet he'd somehow never gained the ability to command me. We both knew he couldn't order me to do shit. And while I wasn't as confident of my odds against him in a fight, I was willing to risk it.

"Go ahead and try—"

"Damnit, Al!" He smacked his hand against the table, sloshing his untouched glass of scotch everywhere. "I promised Milena I wouldn't resort to violence. It's *one* family visit."

"Wait a minute … you're asking me for a favor?" I mocked. "Oh, wow, I'm sorry. I failed to catch that fact based on the way you blew in here cock-blocking and insulting me. Apparently those pack rumors about how well Milena has housebroken and taught you basic human manners were exaggerated."

He bit the inside of his cheek, looking put out and disgusted, his stubborn eyes all but pleading with me not to make him say the magic word Milena had finally succeeded in teaching him to use at the ripe age of one hundred forty-one. Finally, he cast those eyes to the ceiling. "Fine. Will you *please* come back to Morumbi for a visit?"

"Of course," I merrily agreed. "I've been hoping for an invitation." I waited a few seconds for the set of his shoulders to relax minutely before adding, "And an opening to ask for a few favors of my own."

CHAPTER 2

Avery

"**C**YN-THIA?" I PEERED OVER THE RIM OF MY DARK glasses at the polished man seated across from me. He'd made an effort to dress down this morning. And still, even amid the backdrop of the tacky, twenty-four-hour, empty dive diner we'd met in, he'd managed to pull off a look that said casual Armani chic.

"You do this to fuck with me, don't you?" I drummed my fingers against the Formica tabletop, staring at my new passport. "And ... Pressley? I'm supposed to pass for a Cynthia *Pressley* Blackwood? Tell me that's not the name of some bitch you banged in boarding school."

"She left a lasting impression," he deadpanned over the pen in his mouth as he proceeded to shuffle through the tidy stack of papers, manila envelopes, and folders inside the briefcase balanced on his lap. "Sign these." He tossed a folder onto the coral pink surface in front of me, prompting me to reach forward and borrow the pen from his mouth.

"Full signature by all green markers, please. Initials only by all blue."

"I have a Ph.D., you know."

"Copy that. Not as Cynthia P. Blackwood, you don't."

I worked the pen, doing my best to replicate the signature on the passport. "Putting 'black' in a name doesn't make it a black girl name, Wyatt." I glanced up in time to catch his pink lips parting, his white teeth revealing themselves, softening his anxious features.

"No? And here I'd hoped to offend your Latina heritage this time."

"Who says you didn't?"

"Navajo, too?" His grin broadened, but it was forced.

I groaned. "Hellfire, you smell nervous. You should come out with it before I start imagining something worse than whatever your bad news is."

"Coffee?" a pitchy female voice interrupted. A matronly server in a fuchsia apron approached with a fresh pot in hand.

"Yes, please. She'll take it black," Wyatt informed the waitress, his eyes on my face as the woman proceeded to pour my cup. "She'll also have eggs Benedict over an untoasted muffin, with one side of hash browns and a double side of bacon."

Wyatt was the only man alive whose balls I wouldn't take for ordering on my behalf.

"Thank you," he said with a smile once she'd finished dispensing coffee and scribbling down the order. He issued a perfunctory nod of appreciation in the woman's general direction that somehow managed to charm her to the point of blushing, when in reality it was classic Wyatt body language for "you're dismissed."

As she departed, I shook my head at him and muttered, "I hated guys like you growing up."

"Excuse me? Guys like me?"

"Why aren't you eating?"

"It's almost two a.m., *Cyn-thia*. I ate earlier—closer to midnight—while I was waiting. Don't change the subject. What guys like me?"

"Right. Sorry about that …" I shifted my position on the sticky vinyl bench seat. I'd forgotten how late I was. "Got held up at the airport." I cleared my throat. "With things."

His brow arched. "How many *things?*"

I brought my coffee mug to my lips and blew. "Eight."

He made a noise of irritation in the back of his throat and ran long, shapely fingers through his full head of brown locks that were beginning to show signs of grey. "Where?"

"C terminal. Rogue hunter welcoming committee."

"Fuck. They knew you were coming then."

Not a question. So I ignored it. I decided not to mention the surprise attack on the light-rail ride from the airport.

Within werewolf society, rogues had long been universally demonized. *And annihilated without exception.* Given that my initial werewolf encounter had been with a rogue who had slaughtered the closest thing I'd ever had to a family, I should've been inclined to agree with the popular werewolf society assessment. But if my years of scientific study had taught me anything, it was that not everything that deviated from nature was abhorrent. I still believed in positive genetic mutation.

And while I may not have been a rogue in the true werewolf sense, as far as the species' spectrum of "normal" went, I wasn't exactly within range either. My daughter was off the charts completely.

"Ever play anymore?"

"What?" Wyatt snapped, his composed demeanor cracking.

"Piano," I clarified, my eyes on his long fingers that were now yanking distractedly at the roots of his hair. "Ever play?"

"No." He frowned. "Never. Why would you ask?"

"No reason. Just something I've wondered about. I always mean to ask you—"

"Stop. You're a terrible subject-changer. Avery, we can't keep thi—"

"Am not. I was admiring your hands, asshole. Remembering the way they used to look when you played that summer I—"

"Wait—*admiring* my hands?" he pressed with a bemused grin. "As in … finding them attractive?" He held them out in front of him over the table, flipping them back and forth, palms up and down, making a great show of inspecting them. And proving once again that the same old tricks still worked on him. "By God, I believe you've accidentally complimented me, Ms. Blackwood. You know, 'guys like me' do tend to have damned fine hands."

"'Course you do." I pushed the last of my signed paperwork into said hands. "Make them useful and put that away before I change my mind and demand a cooler identity."

"Copy that," he said with a laugh. "By the way, you'll find a backpack for Ms. Cynthia Pressley Blackwood under your seat."

"Mmmm … I knew I smelled overpriced leather. Very nice …" I mumbled as I recovered the hidden treasure beneath my bench seat. "Ms. Blackwood hauls around a men's black leather Louis Vuitton backpack? Interesting touch. And ... wowza!" I gasped as I began to rifle through the fancy backpack. "Baby, you shouldn't have," I gushed as I took inventory of the weaponry, gadgets, and stacks of cash. "I love it when you go all Bruce Banner on me."

"You mean Bruce Wayne. And you're welcome."

"Who? Oh, thank God," I exclaimed upon spying a ziplock bag of pill bottles amongst the goodies Wyatt had brought me. I was nearly out of my supply of ovulation suppression hormones. "Wait a minute ..." I lowered my sunglasses to the tip of my nose in order to better peruse the contents of the bag on my lap. "Is that a hush puppy? Dr. Banner, you know I don't do silencers."

"It's *Wayne*. You mean Bruce Wayne. This is the city, Avery," he lectured, speaking just above a whisper. "If you're going to use a gun, you need a silencer."

"It fucks my aim, Banner. Isn't this still a red state?"

"*Wayne*. Banner is the Incredible Hulk's alter ego. Purple. Colorado is still a firmly purple state."

"Whatever. Either Bruce. Doesn't matter; this is all awesome. But I'll never use the silencer."

"Either Bruce? Doesn't matter? Aside from being completely different superheroes, one's out of Marvel Comics and the other's DC."

"So?" I shrugged. Taunting him.

"So?" he parroted, eyes widening with exasperation. "So they're entirely different comic universes."

I'd long ago discovered the fun of watching mature, sensible Wyatt become rankled over my professed ignorance of comic books—his one sophomoric obsession. It was a game we played that never got old.

The truth was I knew a lot about comic book superheroes. Because during the darkest week of my life, while

I was chained up inside a cage in the basement of Wyatt's Connecticut estate awaiting the initial change that would classify me as an X-files creature forevermore, Wyatt had relayed story after story to me about every single super-hero and supervillain he knew of.

He'd stayed by my side through it all—even through the final three days of the disgustingly vile, excruciatingly painful transformation that should have killed me—*safely on the other side of reinforced metal bars and holding a tran-quilizer gun, of course.*

I grinned and reached across the table to pinch his cheek. "Whichever one has cool gadgets and secret spy shit and tosses around wads of cash is the one you remind me of. Thanks for the backpack of goodies and the new iden-tity, Daddy Warbucks."

"Daddy Warbucks?" His hand flew to his heart. "The crotchety bald billionaire from *Little Orphan Annie* is not a superhero, and you fucking know it."

I grinned in the face of his feigned outrage as our server arrived with my order. I thanked her, even as I eyed my plate with apprehension.

"Better than it looks," Wyatt assured me once she was beyond earshot. "Presentation's not their strong suit at this particular establishment."

With a snort at his use of "establishment," I dug in. I was famished. To my delight, I found that he was correct. "Not bad."

"See? When have I ever led you astray, my Orphan Annie? Trust me, you need that silencer."

"Now who's the bad subject-changer?"

"Certainly not me. I just made a perfect segue from 'I'm right about this diner's food' to 'I'm always right about everything,' and therefore you should listen to me with regard to the silencer."

"Can't believe you're still single," I managed over a mouth stuffed with eggs Benedict. "Do you list 'expert know-it-all' on your date-a-billionaire-dot-com profile?"

He gave me a tight-lipped smile and leaned forward on his elbows atop the table. "Well, *Cyn-thi-a,* between my busy schedule of constantly covering your tracks, not to mention your daughter's very existence, altering your crime scenes, and bribing countless witnesses and officials, there's not been much time for dating."

Ouch. "Point taken. I'll use the silencer. I'll be less conspicuous and try to blend in more—" I started to promise, until a shout of disbelief from the opposite side of the table halted me. "What?" I huffed. "I will!"

Wyatt bent closer and said, "Avery, you couldn't 'blend in' *before* you were the shape-shifting mother of an unholy berserker who the entire supernatural world is determined to destroy."

"She is not an unholy berserker!" I admonished in a whisper-shout.

"No, 'course not. Speaking of which, so sorry I missed little Sloane's ninth birthday celebration. If the police statements, fire department reports, insurance claims, and five lawsuits are any indication, the party was an incomparable success."

My gut knotted. Wyatt had tried to tell me the party was a bad idea.

"About that ..." I withdrew my sunglasses completely in order to look my only friend in the eye as I prepared to eat crow.

To my surprise, he was already smothering laughter

behind his fist, his blue eyes bright, awash with humor. His laughing countenance took years off his face. It also made him look like his late little sister, my best friend, Sloane.

"Wait—" I shook my head, my body settling in relief. "You're really laughing about this? Wyatt, I swear to you, I didn't know before that pizza party that Sloane could start fires with her thoughts," I spoke truthfully of my daughter, who was his late sister's namesake.

"No?" He chuckled, canting his head to the side and bestowing that whimsical grin that had given me butterflies as a teenager. "Can't imagine why you wouldn't just assume that at this point? Pretty sure our little supernatural problem child could unleash a nuclear explosion with her thoughts were she so inclined."

I ignored the way my heart warmed at his use of "our." I knew it to be a slip of the tongue rather than a proprietary claim. Wyatt had never cared for my daughter—had pleaded with me to abort her in the womb. But Wyatt loved me. And he loved his late sister Sloane. *Two things I shamelessly continued to use to my advantage where my daughter Sloane was concerned.*

"In any case, I own what's left of that entire strip mall now if she ever feels the need to practice her pyrokinesis skills again."

"I'll pay you back every penny—"

"Ha!"

"I will! How much are strip malls in Cleveland going for nowadays?"

"Stop being absurd and eat." He gave me his stern big brother look that meant the conversation was over. "You might not be hungry after what I have to tell you."

"Ah. See? I knew you had fun news coming." I tapped the side of my nose. "Canine olfactory never lies. So what'd you find out down in South America about this breed of superbeasts coming for me?"

CHAPTER 3

Alcaeus

THE OSTENTATIOUS HOMECOMING RECEPTION AND extravagant evening feast held in the renovated banquet hall of the Reinoso pack's palatial estate in Morumbi was exactly the type of event I'd spent the past ten years avoiding.

The memories of what had happened the last time I'd been inside that dining hall were still too fresh. Too painful.

But as soon as I saw Jussara and Milena rushing toward me, tears in their eyes and arms outstretched, I felt like the world's greatest coward for avoiding it for so long. If they could move past the horrific events of that fateful day nearly ten years ago in that hall, then surely so could I. And seeing them both standing there in the space that had haunted me was worth the painful reminders of it that had kept me away.

It'd been over a year since Milena and Jussara had last visited me in the States, and it was good to see them again. I was happy to see Milena so happy. Happier still to see how close she'd become with Jussara—who seemed to be doing well, too, near as I could tell. Unlike Milena, who wore her heart on her face, Jussara had always been a tough read. *Like her mother.*

Aside from my disappointment at my sister Alessandra's absence, it was a fine affair. Sure, there were moments throughout dinner when seeing Alex sitting there at the head of the table looking so calm, so utterly content in his domesticated bliss made me want to punch his head through the nearest stone wall. But that was likely to remain a normal, knee-jerk impulse where my bratty baby brother was concerned for at least another century, given all the bullshit he'd put me through since becoming my responsibility when he was five.

In truth, I was genuinely happy for him. Not to mention grateful and happy for myself that he was finally settled and no longer a constant cause of worry to me. Settled with a hall-monitor type with a solid moral compass, no less. Evidencing once again that sometimes the fates really did get it right when it came to the whole mating bond business. They'd done us all a solid by pairing Alex with Milena.

"What's her fixation with Europe?" I asked my stepbrother Remy as we strode through the woods later that evening, following behind a small group of guards and other higher-ranking Betas headed to witness some grand display of Milena's new abilities that Alex had been bragging about.

"Fixation? Whatever do you mean? I don't think Jussara cares for Europe any more than she does the States."

Jussara? "I'm talking about Milena," I said with impatience. "Milena's fixation with searching for the *Rogue* in Europe."

Why would Remy assume that I was speaking of my

ward Jussara? And how the fuck would he know her feelings on Europe or the States, for that matter?

"Oh, right. Of course you are," Remy said with an anxious chuckle, his face coloring in a way that alarmed every
protective instinct I possessed for Lupe's daughter. "Not
sure. But you make a good point. I suppose Milena has
been somewhat focused on scouring Europe. Particularly
the western countries," he continued to ramble at a fast clip,
further rousing my suspicion and concern about his initial Jussara presumption. "Although, she did just complete
a tour of the eastern countries. But then she's planning to
search France *yet again*." He laughed harder than necessary
at whatever joke he thought he was making. "You know,
I was saying to Alex the other day that I think she must
simply love the food there, because I can't imagine there's a
rogue left to be found in all of France at this point."

I was suddenly gripped by a strong instinct to wrap my
hand around Remy's throat and remind him that Jussara
was off-limits, when the object of my concern turned from
where she'd been strolling ahead of the group with Milena
and Alex, to call back at me.

"Tio, come on!" Jussara's face was alive with excitement
as she dashed over, inserting herself between Remy and me
and linking her arm with mine. "I've been dying for you to
see this. You're not going to believe how amazing Milena's
abilities are," she gushed, pulling me ahead and away from
Remy. It mollified me to note that she hadn't even spared
him a glance.

I should've known better than anyone that Milena was destined for greatness. My father and I had once met the powerful werelock whose legacy of incomparable blood power she'd inherited. Hell, I'd even personally held that blood power for her for a brief period of time during her initial transformation.

Yet nothing could've prepared me for how well Milena had managed to develop and expand upon her given abilities in the short years that I'd stayed away from Brazil.

My initial jubilance over her demonstration swiftly waning, I stared, dumbfounded, as the angry sky opened up above me, my eyes unblinking even as electricity lit up the night and drops of water fell to cloud my vision.

"He who controls the weather will control the world."

This couldn't be real.

Milena couldn't possibly have developed some power of empathic hydrokinesis. Or electrokinesis. Or was it called meteorokinesis? Fuck, whatever it was called, it was big.

I forced my eyes from the heavens and glanced around to gauge the rest of the group's reactions. Kai's face reflected awe. Alex looked like he was trying to calm an erection.

"Way to go, Miles," Jussara cheered, bouncing on the balls of her feet in excitement.

"Thank God she's on our side, right?" Remy muttered next to me, beaming like a proud mother hen.

I nodded slowly in agreement as I felt my own smile fade. "Right."

Chuckling, Remy leaned closer and confided, "Sometimes I fantasize about instigating a nasty marital row just to witness the supernatural ass-whooping Milena would unleash on Alex now."

"Second that," Kai deadpanned without hesitation.

I nodded absently again as I watched the spectacle of thunder and lightning, an unsettling feeling gnawing my gut. Remy was right. I wasn't sure my brother Alex would be able to best his wife Milena—our pack's most treasured, well-prophesied, perpetually sweet and adorable vessel— anymore either.

That knowledge shouldn't have bothered me. Except it meant that Milena's power and abilities had surpassed all of ours at this point.

And somehow I'd managed to ignore this growing development despite Alex's incessant bragging and the regular reports on Milena's progress from both Remy and Jussara.

"Wait till you see her manifest a twister," Remy said before moving closer to the action, going to stand next to Jussara.

Too close to Jussara.

My frown deepened when Jussara turned and smiled up at Remy.

What. The hell?

Jussara was the closest thing I had to a daughter. Remy knew that she was off-limits. He wouldn't cross that line. *Would he?* What's more, Jussara had always hated Remy. What the fuck had changed between them while I'd been away?

"I believe Alex intends to work her up to a tsunami next," Kai's amused voice spoke in my ear, drawing my attention back to Milena's grand display. When I didn't react, Kai pressed, "She's incredible, right? You thought I was exaggerating."

I forced myself to smile. "Tsunami, huh? So we're

turning our cherished vessel and savior into a WMD? That the plan? Or are we planning to use her to reverse global warming? I'm sure that our ancestors would be proud." My words came out infused with more bitterness than the teasing tone I'd aimed for.

Kai didn't miss a beat. "You make a face that reminds me of Antonio when you get jealous."

I snorted and clapped him on the back, struggling to shake off the foul mood encroaching. "Well, that's good to hear. Dad was a handsome SOB."

Who was Kai kidding? He checked in with Milena near constantly. He raved about her accomplishments nonstop. He was her biggest fan and supporter. If anyone was jealous of Alex's relationship with Milena, it was Kai. I was pretty sure Alex was getting in the way of Kai's girl-time bonding with Milena.

"Hey, who wouldn't be jealous of Alex and want to be the one in his shoes right now, eh?" I acknowledged good-naturedly, gesturing to the happy, power-hoarding couple practicing their natural disaster-making skills.

It was close enough to the truth. My baby brother Alex had always seemed to reap more than his fair share of luck in life. Even before Milena had become a supernatural powerhouse to be reckoned with, she had been covet-worthy as a mate. More than easy on the eyes, Milena was also a consummate sweetheart and do-gooder. A quiet, effective leader who led without trying to lead. She'd done more to unite our pack in the past decade than my brothers or I had managed in our lifetimes.

"I wasn't referring to Alex."

The full implication of Kai's words sank in as I watched his retreating form jog over to a grinning Milena.

"Did you see that?" she exclaimed.

"Sure did. You were magnificent!" Kai praised.

"She still can't teleport," my sister Alessandra's voice drawled from behind me, unabashedly rife with the envy Kai had just accused me of harboring.

My chest exploded with laughter at my sister's most welcome presence in that moment and her characteristically critical assessment of our sister-in-law.

It was true. Despite her tremendous power and skills, Milena couldn't teleport. And Alessandra had clearly done just that—expertly, too—because I hadn't heard a sound or felt so much as a ripple of magic at her entry.

"Lessa!" I spun around and engulfed her in a hug, lifting her off her feet and twirling her around. "Just the old bitch I was hoping I'd see today."

"I am not old."

Eleven years my junior, Lessa was my only full-blooded sibling, and the only contemporary of my generation besides Kai within our pack. She hated being reminded of her age. The bitch designation, however, was one she relished.

"Put me down, you big cur," she protested. "You're going to get me all mussed."

I knew she was teasing, but I set her down just the same, rounding on her in a hushed voice the moment that I did. "I'll muss you all I want. What the hell has been going on around here, anyway? Why didn't you tell me about this?"

"What? Why of all—I did! We all did. You've been dick deep in American pussy so long your brain is fried."

"Did Kai say that? Who told you that? And I prefer the term balls deep."

She punched me hard in the chest.

"Ouch." Lessa had never in her life hit like a girl. Not even when she'd been a little girl.

"More like who *didn't* tell me that."

"Eh, whatever." *Fucking pack rumors.* "How's she doing it? How's Milena controlling weather elements?"

"First of all, it's *they*, not she." Lessa jutted her chin in Alex and Milena's direction. "Alex likes to give Milena all the credit, but I know he's helping her. Controlling the end result. Alex has always been the master of physical elements, as you and I well know."

Huh. She was probably right. I wasn't sure if that made me feel better or worse about this unique power development. "Okay, so how are *they* doing it?"

"Not here. Let's walk and talk." Lessa latched onto my elbow and turned us away from the group.

I hesitated. "I should probably say something to Milena first—"

"There's no time," Lessa insisted, and in a blink she'd teleported us and was dragging me along the deserted cobblestone quay along the Seine.

"This is over the top, Lessa. Even for you. And kinda cliché, don't you think? Paris? Really? What is it—midnight here, too?"

"Shut up and walk."

"Fine. But start talking so we can get back before Milena notices I bailed. I don't want to hurt her feelings that I left without even saying anything about her grand thunderstorm show."

"Oh, for God's sake. Milena and her fucking feelings! I swear that's all anyone in this pack cares about anymore. Is it any wonder it's come to this?"

"I am one hundred percent lost," I admitted, turning around and jogging backward on the path so that I could face my sister while staying ahead of her brisk walking pace.

"She's an endless font of emotion, and Alex is her magnifying conduit. That's how they do it." She threw her hands in the air as if she was stating something that should be obvious to any idiot.

But not this idiot. "Still not following, sis."

"Milena's always been a virtual bottomless spigot of emotions, right? I mean, the girl cries more than any living creature I've ever met." Her hazel eyes caught the moonlight as they rolled. "And Alex ... we know Alex inherited his mother Renata's empathic abilities, and yet he never even realized he had those powers because he only found his emotional awareness after the living spigot came into his life."

Wow. "So you're totally having a hard time with Milena being Alpha, huh?"

"Turn!" she ordered at a shout, her long brown hair flying behind her with the force at which she pivoted. Her heeled feet clicked noisily against the stone as she stomped a path away from the water.

I followed behind her, noticing for the first time the prim blouse and calf-length skirt she was wearing once I was staring after her back.

"Hey, why're you dressed like a schoolteacher?"

She threw the middle finger over her right shoulder and kept stomping.

"All right, look, I'm sorry I stayed away so long. It wasn't you I was avoiding."

She groaned and threw up another finger at me.

I couldn't help but laugh as I jogged after her to keep

up with her long, angry strides. "Oh, come on, don't be like that. I've missed you. I said I was sorry. I just needed some time away from—"

She stopped abruptly and spun around to face me, her eyes flashing amber beneath her raised brow. "Do you think I'm Alex? You think I don't know why you had to stay away? You think I don't understand? Or that maybe I need Milena to fucking explain it to me?"

It was the wrong time to bust up laughing, but I couldn't help it. Lessa never made fun of our baby half-brother like this. She had always praised and doted on Alex to a fault, much to my annoyance, as well as our stepbrother Remy's, who had also shared in the burden of raising Alex. Lessa had consistently defended Alex, always taken his side in every disagreement—even all five times that he'd burned my house to the ground as a kid. Milena's presence had obviously put a strain on their relationship.

"I'm sorry," I apologized again, choking up with laughter. The stress of my day had caught up with me. "It's not you. I swear."

She rolled her eyes and shook her head.

It felt damn good to be in my sister's presence. Arguably the pack's best fighter, Lessa could terrify the bravest of men. Smart as a whip, she could rattle the most confident. She was also vain and selfish and sometimes embarrassingly shallow. And there was no one on earth I'd known and loved longer than my little sister.

I realized where she'd taken us. In a few more steps we'd be standing next to the stone archway that read: "Cimetière des Chiens."

Lessa hadn't brought me here to talk about Alex or Milena.

"You wanted to talk to me about the *Rogue* in private?"
She nodded.

"Why?"

"Because I've found the *Rogue*."

I swallowed, curiosity replacing the mirth I'd basked in a moment ago. "I'm listening."

Her fingers fiddled with the bow-tie neckline of her silk blouse. I still didn't understand why she was dressed like a schoolteacher.

"There are … complications. I need your help."

"Why don't you want Alex or the others to know?"

She squared her shoulders. "The *Rogue* was always our quarry, Al." Her hazel eyes, so similar to mine, dared me to disagree. "You and me. Dad said it was our mission."

I nodded. I decided not to point out that she'd gotten bored with that mission eons ago and hadn't done much to help me with it since Dad's passing. She was clearly on a competitive streak with Milena right now.

"Okay. I'll help you, Lessa."

"And you'll keep this between us? You won't even tell Kai?"

"Yes." As the word left my mouth, I knew I'd probably live to regret it. But I might've been a little competitive myself. And it was kinda fun feeling like Lessa was on my side again after so many years of her going against me for Alex's sake.

She smiled. "We're going to need to break a few pack laws."

CHAPTER 4

Avery

"It's too many prophecies and curses," I complained, pinching the bridge of my nose. "I can't keep track, Wyatt. I need a chart ... maybe a Venn diagram."

Among the first things I'd learned upon joining the underground world of supernatural beings was that werewolves clung to their lore and way of life with four paws. They took occultism seriously, and they were superstitious as hell. So much so that any gobbledygook out of the mouths of supposed seers, oracles, prophets, clairvoyants, necromancers, and the like was upheld as gospel. What's more, drastic actions were often taken based on outdated prophecies and rampant paranoia over *alleged* future events.

"Oh, come on, it's not as bad as that," Wyatt said as he typed something into the notes on his iPad. "You're just tired. When was the last time you slept?"

"When I was human."

He gave me a sympathetic smile and glanced at his watch. "How far do you need to drive still tonight—erm, this morning—to reach Sloane?"

"Far enough. Let's keep going."

"Speaking of, you'll find a set of keys in your backpack to an old black Audi A4 parked on level three of the structure on Blake Street. You know the one?"

"Sure do. RiNo's my old hood—sorta." I rubbed my temple. "You were saying something weird and obscure about the decade of no light," I prompted helpfully.

He set his iPad down and removed his reading glasses. "Listen, Avery. Lately, I've been thinking, maybe I should know Sloane's whereabouts? You know ... in case anything ever happens to Azda while you're away ... and you need me to relocate Sloane to another safe house—"

"No. Uh-uh."

"But she's old and half-blind—"

"Wyatt, no. Azda's fine. It's too risky."

He looked a little offended by how quickly I'd shut him down. But it couldn't be helped. "Avery, I would never—"

"It's not about that. I just think it's safer for everyone this way. I know you'd never betray us." Not intentionally. Or without excessive torture at least. My hunch was that silver-spoon-fed white guys didn't hold up well under torture. "Let's get back to that prophecy about the decade without light."

He sighed. "Right. Almost ten years ago, and nearly overnight as the story goes, every important seer, clairvoyant, and necromancer across the globe mysteriously fell dead, thrusting the supernatural world into a state of figurative darkness."

"Who killed them all?"

Wyatt shrugged. "No one knows. They just ... croaked." He gave me a half-grimace, half-grin, trying his best not to give in to the humor we invariably injected into these sessions. Because really, we had to laugh so we wouldn't freak out.

"That's preposterous. They all just dropped dead on the spot? At the same time?"

"Yep." He bit his lip and rubbed at the back of his neck. "Allegedly so."

"O-*kay*." I reached for my cold coffee mug. "Let's just suppose for argument's sake that actually happened. I still don't get why it would spawn so much excessive rogue hunting. What's this great panic over killing every possible rogue left on the planet before the decade of no light's end?"

Wyatt shook his head.

"You think maybe, absent the 'perceived' second sight they'd come to rely so heavily upon as a society, they just … I dunno … flipped their collective supernatural wig, so to speak? And they've been runnin' around killing rogues to work off steam while awaiting further instruction from the silent ether ever since?"

"Mmmm … perhaps …" Wyatt's lips curled and his eyes crinkled with humor. "It's a good enough theory, anyhow, given the voodoo-loving set we're dealing with."

We knew the supernatural world had been hunting for a powerful *Rogue*-with-a-capital-*R* who was prophesied to usher forth the birth of a new breed of werewolf species that would be unbeholden to the pack mentality and way of life to which all werewolves presently adhered. But that was a centuries-old prophecy. It didn't explain the more recent rogue-killing frenzy.

Slipping his glasses back on, Wyatt raised his iPad and resumed reading through his notes, his finger scrolling over the screen. "An oracle foretold something about a war sparked by the death of a guilty innocent caught between two rival packs."

"The ongoing fighting between the Brazilian and the Portuguese super-werewolf packs Perry told us about, right?" I took a sip of cold coffee and pulled a face. "The stolen eye prophecy?"

He nodded, then read from the screen: "The stolen eye no number of wrong eyes would make right. The unforgivable sacrifice destined to unearth a wrath so black as to obliterate night. Ushering forth the war of the century, the rise of a blind warrior, and the dawn of a decade without light."

"You think the original seer or oracle who came up with that one really made it a rhyme?"

"Doubtful." Wyatt grinned. "That one's from the seventeen hundreds, I believe. Most likely someone turned it into a dumb nursery rhyme after the fact and it's lost something in translation as a result."

"Fuck it all." I pushed my coffee mug aside. We were losing time and getting nowhere with deciphering the prophecy nonsense. *As usual.* "How 'bout I just keep torturing rogues for intel?"

Despite being a believer of positive genetic mutation, I'd tortured and killed a fair share of rogue werewolves over the years in my quest for information on my new species. I rationalized that every single one of them had been mad and headed for demise anyway—deranged and warped as they all inevitably became from lack of sufficient contact and communion with other wolves.

"Works for me," Wyatt readily agreed.

"Great. Let's move on to the South American super-werewolves."

"This is Alex Reinoso."

"Daaamn." I rummaged blindly through my new back-pack and tried to control my drool reflex as Wyatt flipped through photos of a gorgeous Brazilian god. "I feel a heat cycle coming on. Where are those pills?"

"Him?" Wyatt squinted at the photos. "Ugh, don't tell me you go for that type?"

"You mean the perfectly hot type? The tall, dark, hand-some Alpha type? Definitely. Please tell me that beautiful man's not coming to kill me."

"He's coming to kill you."

"So unfair. I hate killing the hot ones. Too dangerous to fuck first?"

"Yes. Too dangerous to attempt to kill as well. But he's only part of the problem." Wyatt flipped through more photos on the iPad before stopping on a series of shots of a waiflike young brunette with long, wavy hair, bright blue eyes, and delicate, angelic features. In the photos, she was getting out of a Bentley SUV, surrounded by big, beefy hotties on all sides—more super-werewolves, no doubt. "This is Alex Reinoso's better half, Milena Caro-Reinoso." Wyatt's manicured forefinger tapped the screen. *"She* is en-emy number one."

"She's the Alpha bitch?" I grabbed the electronic note-pad from his hand. "This little girl here? The one who looks like she's just come off of a peace and love bender at Burning Man?"

"She'd just come off of a rogue killing spree in Eastern

Europe when this was taken, actually." Wyatt gave me a pointed look devoid of humor. "Word is she calls the shots and runs the show these days within the Reinoso stronghold. And that the pack both respects and adores her as their fearless leader." He scratched his chin. "She's also referred to as the *vessel*. But I haven't figured out yet what that means or which prophecies it relates to."

"*She's* the Alpha of the Reinoso pack? The pack that includes this breed of super-werewolves? Alpha of one of the oldest, largest, most powerful werewolf packs on the planet?"

"Not one of," Wyatt corrected, "*the* largest, most powerful known werewolf pack. And the ones with the extraordinary magical capabilities are known as *werelocks,* not super-werewolves or superbeasts. The werelock subspecies originated from the union between a powerful warlock and a werewolf back in the first quarter of the sixteenth century."

"You're pulling my leg with this. She doesn't even look Brazilian."

"She's not. She's American. From the surfer town of Santa Cruz, California, as a matter of fact."

"NoCal flower child turned rogue werewolf killer?" I shook my head. "We're being set up. This can't be right."

"Avery, you of all people should know a person may be far more than what they appear on the surface."

"Spare me the afterschool special message. I'm serious." I proceeded to flip through photos, pausing on one where the flower child had gone from walking from the vehicle to being sprawled out on the pavement with multiple beefy hotties hunkered over her. "What happened here? Gunfire? Were they attacked?"

"No." Wyatt coughed into his fist. "She ah … tripped and fell, I believe."

"Oh, good Lord." I offered the pad back to him. "Shall we move on to that French pack of superbeasts in Alsace? Got any pics of 'em eating croissants you wanna try and terrify me with?"

"Very funny." He snatched the iPad from me and began searching through photo folders. "So she's a little clumsy for an Alpha werelock. That doesn't make her any less dangerous."

"True." I signaled our server for a coffee refill. "Suppose I'm unable to trip her?"

"Haha," he deadpanned. "Avery, you need to take these werelocks seriously. Especially this Alpha Milena."

"Believe me, I do. Come on, a cute, privileged white girl everyone adores? That's a rival the likes of which I've never seen before."

"You're impossible."

"You're laughing on the inside."

"That's beside the point."

"Just show me photos of the easy pack target with the weird name that you told me about so I can go and practice my tripping skills."

He opened another folder of photos and flipped the iPad around for me to see just as our waitress approached with my refill.

"Sweet Jesus!" our server's high-pitched voice rasped, taking the words straight out of my mouth as she and I both shamelessly eye-fucked the dark, hunky stranger in the photo filling up Wyatt's screen.

CHAPTER 5

Alcaeus

"WHICH PACK LAWS WOULD WE NEED TO BREAK?" I asked Lessa as we entered the pet cemetery. "Aside from the one about keeping secrets from our Alpha, that is."

"The one about executing minors."

"What?" I halted in my tracks.

"Just hear me out," she appealed, lifting her chin as she stopped and turned to face me. "When you and Dad enacted that law centuries ago forbidding the persecution and execution of the underage family members of our enemies, I don't think any of us ever contemplated that the *Rogue* might be discovered while it was still a child."

"Because it can't be a child."

"Of course it can," she insisted.

I shook my head and resumed walking along the path lined with tombstones. "Lessa, never once throughout our species' history has anyone reported encountering a rogue werewolf who wasn't an adult."

"Right. That's because the run-of-the-mill rogue were-wolf becomes one more or less by choice," she reasoned as she kept pace with me. "But it makes greater sense that the *Rogue* prophesied to beget all rogues would be *born* as such."

She had a point. It was indeed a possibility, if however improbable, that the *Rogue* might be found as a child. Which only raised more questions. "It's too early developmentally to determine something like that in a child. What if a young werewolf was abandoned and forced to go rogue? Or abused by its parents or pack? We'd have to at least try and assimilate an underage wolf displaying rogue characteristics before we could determine—"

"Suppose we already knew?" she countered. "What if its own mother knew what it was and chose to hide it from the supernatural world?"

"How can it be considered a rogue when it's still with its mother?"

"Because she's still a child, Al," Lessa insisted, impatience bleeding into her voice as she withdrew the phone that was vibrating in her skirt pocket and silenced it. "Think about it. Imagine a mother realizes that her daughter isn't normal and can't connect like other werewolves. That doesn't mean that mother would give her child up. Least not if she had any spark of maternal instinct whatsoever."

"She? You think the *Rogue* is a girl?" I failed to keep the disbelief from my tone.

Lessa's eyes narrowed in a way that reminded me of our mother. "Why not? Who said the *Rogue* has to be a boy? None of the seers ever specified that it would be male. They largely referred to it as an 'it.' Everyone just assumed it would be male." Her upper lip curled. "As with most things labeled powerful and dangerous."

"You're right," I appeased. "The *Rogue* could very well be female." I'd learned centuries ago that it was wiser—certainly less painful and time-consuming—to agree with Lessa when it came to such things in order to keep her on topic. "But how do you know this girl you've found is the *Rogue*? Where is she? How much have you interacted with her? When and how did you discover this? How old is she?"

"She's American." A smile stretched Lessa's mouth. "Just like we always thought the *Rogue* would be." Her grin turned triumphant—more than a little smug. "Milena's been wasting the pack's time searching every corner of Europe." She huffed. "And Alex has just been going along with—"

"How *old*, Lessa?" I pressed her to the point.

She inhaled a beat and released a sighed, "Nine."

"Nine?" I stopped abruptly. "You're talking about us executing a *nine-year-old*? A little girl who probably hasn't even shifted for the first time yet?"

Lessa's phone went off again, momentarily distracting her as she stopped as well. "Look, I'm not happy either about that part. But put it in perspective, Al. We either exterminate one little girl or allow the entire human race to be slaughtered by an uncontrollable, malevolent rogue species destined to overrun the planet."

"No. Absolutely not." A child *Rogue* was a scenario I'd never contemplated.

Lessa groaned. "Stop pacing; you're trampling the daisies. And mind your tells."

Shit, I was pacing. And pulling on the back of my neck—an anxious "tell" of mine that our mother had often called me out on. It was always more irritating when Lessa did it.

"We are not killing a child, even if it is the *Rogue*," I said as I continued to pace and yank at my neck. "*If* it is determined that the child in question truly seems destined to become the *Rogue*, we'll simply have to take her and her mother captive and attempt to assimilate them into our pack. There's no way we can definitively determine until after the girl hits puberty and shifts whether she's actually going to be the *Rogue* in the true sense of the prophecy."

Lessa shook her head, scowling down at whatever message she was reading on her phone. "It could be too late by then," she said absently as she rapidly thumbed a response. "The little girl is already powerful. Far more advanced than she should be, given what I know of her werewolf parentage. She hasn't even shifted yet and she can start fires with her thoughts! Just like Alex could as a child."

The memory of how powerful and destructive our little brother Alex was by age nine was enough to give me pause to reconsider that Lessa may have a valid point about an exception to our pack law needing to be made. "How do you know all of this? How much have you interacted with the girl?"

"I haven't. I've only seen the child through the eyes of a human man who is friends with the *Rogue*'s mother. All of my information on the girl and her mother I've gleaned directly from his memories." She continued to thumb away on her phone. "He financially supports the mother and helps to keep her and the daughter hidden, but even he doesn't know their actual whereabouts." She looked up from her phone at last. "I need to be somewhere. And you need to get back. We'll continue this later."

In classic Lessa fashion, she teleported me back to Morumbi as fast as she'd whisked me away. Then she

immediately teleported herself elsewhere, being intentionally vague about where she needed to be and when she'd
return, leaving me in the lurch and still reeling from the
confusing, incomplete information she'd just shared about
her alleged child *Rogue* discovery.

I caught up with Milena and Alex back at the main estate. After extending the appropriate amount of praise to
Milena for her impressive new abilities, I went on to grill
them both for as many details as possible as to how she was
accomplishing it. Alex was every bit as evasive as I'd expected he would be. And Milena was as forthcoming and
eager to talk about it as I'd banked on.

Lessa had been right. Alex was partially helping to
harness and magnify the supernatural powers of nature
that now flowed from Milena as readily as her emotions
always had.

When Alex excused himself to take a call that had
come in on Milena's phone, leaving the two of us alone in
the sitting room adjacent to her office, Milena proceeded
to share more than I had expected.

"I was so angry for so long about Lupe," she confided
to me in a quiet voice, her blue eyes growing bright with
unshed tears. "One day, I was reflecting on it while in the
woods in wolf form chasing the scent of a rogue that I'd
been tracking. It had just begun to storm when I spotted
him. I started sprinting. And I was imagining Maribel as I
chased him down—as I've often found myself doing whenever I'm hunting a rogue."

Her cheeks colored at her confession as her frank eyes bore into mine. I knew that this was something she probably had never shared with Alex before—possibly not with anyone.

"You know … since Maribel's parting message to me when I last saw her in between worlds was about the importance of destroying the *Rogue* before the decade of no light's end," she elucidated unnecessarily in a weak attempt to put a politically correct spin on her previous revelation.

While her rationalization was truthful and factual, we both knew it wasn't why she liked to envision Maribel whenever she was hunting rogues. I knew that Milena and I were a united, albeit largely silent, minority within the pack in that neither of us embraced the popular pack point of view concerning Kai's deceased mate, Maribel, and her widely-praised-as-heroic actions ten years ago that had led to Lupe's death. I couldn't deny that I had on more than one occasion, myself, envisioned tearing Maribel apart as I'd torn into rogues.

"As I got closer to him, I was channeling so much of that hurt and rage," she continued. "And suddenly, I felt the ground splitting open beneath my paws as I ran. I heard the sky crack with thunder." She shook her head, taking her lower lip between her teeth as those guileless blue eyes of hers seemed to beseech the depths of my own for some greater understanding. "I didn't realize that it was me who was conjuring the storm or causing the ground to split until lightning had struck the rogue for the third time."

She brushed an errant tear from her cheek. "I stood over that rogue's dead form and I just knew, Al. My emotions had always been the key—the impetus for so much throughout my life." She shrugged. "It made twisted sense to me that they would ultimately manifest as my greatest source of power, I suppose."

I leaned forward in my chair, nodding my understanding and silent approval as words failed me. I didn't want to talk about Lupe. Or Maribel. But I appreciated that Milena could. More than that, I appreciated knowing that she still quietly despised Maribel just as much as I did, even though this was the most we'd ever spoken of it.

"I worry that we're running out of time." Her brow wrinkled, and she did that distressed lower lip thing that castrated Alex every time. I knew Milena well enough to know that it was an unconscious mannerism and not an attempt at manipulation. I was just thankful it didn't work the same way on me as it did my brother. "The decade of no light will be over in a few months. Maribel was very clear that it would be vastly harder to destroy the *Rogue* once second sight was restored to the world—when the next generation of seers emerged."

"Believe me, I know."

"We've done all we can to unite the world's most powerful packs against the idea of the *Rogue*. But there are still those who would protect it. Gabriel Salvatella continues to gain traction in the East. His Beta has somehow managed to charm the Saint Petersburg pack"—she cast her eyes to the ceiling—"despite barely speaking passable Russian."

I noted she was still refusing to refer to Gabriel's Beta—her brother, Raul—by name. I knew from Kai that she and Raul hadn't spoken at all in the past decade. Not since Milena's recovery immediately following the incident in the dining hall.

"I know, Milena. But we can only do so much. Don't worry, we'll find it in time."

"I really wish that you would come back and help us here. Kai and I think the *Rogue* isn't going to be found in America after all."

Alex reentered the room, smelling as annoyed as I'd felt at the mention of Kai a moment ago. I was thankful for the interruption as Alex grumbled under his breath and poured himself a glass of scotch.

"What's wrong?" Milena asked. "Is Bethany okay?"

Alex huffed. "Gregg has asked Bethy to marry him." He and Milena shared a disgusted look.

"And she said yes?" Milena deduced with a wince.

"You need to talk to her." He handed Milena her phone as he took the seat next to her on the couch. "Convince her he's an asshat. Get her to call it off before it's too late. For now I've convinced her they should have a long engagement." He turned to me and announced, "We don't like Bethy's boyfriend, Gregg." He tossed half his scotch back in one gulp. "At all."

"Yeah. Caught that." I couldn't help but smile as I marveled at how protective Alex had somehow become of Milena's childhood best friend. Maybe my little brother was a bit housebroken after all.

"There's just something *off* about Gregg," Milena said to me, scrunching her nose up. "I can't put my finger on it, but he doesn't seem entirely trustworthy."

"He spells his name with three g's, for fuck's sake," Alex proclaimed, as if it were the ultimate character indictment. Which it pretty well was. "I can't understand what she's thinking. We're going to have to intervene."

"No, we are not, Alex. It's none of our business. Bethany has to make her own choices in life."

Alex rolled his eyes. "Fine, then I'll anonymously send

her incriminating photos of Gregg's penis engaging with other women's vaginas so that she can better make the *right* choices in life." He turned to me directly. "He cheats on her. I've seen it in his head."

"Alex!" Milena gasped. "You said you wouldn't."

It was my cue to bail. "I'm gonna get going." I stood. "Jussara's probably waiting up for me back at the house."

"Oh, no, I forgot I was supposed to tell you," Milena piped up. "Jussara got called away for a ... a thing." Her eyes darted nervously at Alex. "She won't be back to the house until tomorrow morning. So ... so you have the place to yourself," she said with an overly bright smile as Alex cough-laughed into his fist.

Fuck. Milena was a terrible liar. Always had been.

"I mean—unless you don't want the place to yourself?" she rambled. "Because you could ... you could just stay here, too. You're more than welcome—"

"I'm good," I said, my scowl directed at my laughing brother. "You wouldn't happen to know where Remy is tonight, would you?"

"*Remy?*" Milena squeaked, causing Alex's shoulders to quake anew as he covered his face with his hand.

"Yes. *Remy.* You know, that stepbrother of mine who has never gotten along with my ward, Jussara."

"Oh, *that* Remy." Alex beamed at me, enjoying my growing ire as he wrapped his arms around an increasingly distressed-looking Milena. "I believe he got called away for *a thing* as well. Didn't he, love?"

Milena jammed her elbow into his ribs, and Alex laughed all the harder, successfully wrestling her into his lap even as she scolded and threatened him with lightning bolts.

I felt my eyes shifting, my blood boiling at the thought of Remy's hands on Jussara. I still remembered the way she'd looked as a newborn. Remembered how big and delighted her little girl smile was whenever I'd come home at night and she'd run halfway down the stairs before jumping the rest of the way into my open arms. And I remembered the way Lupe would laugh so joyously at the sight of us in those moments before composing her features and yelling at me to take my fucking shoes off.

Milena's eyes on me were sympathetic as her words penetrated my somber reverie. "I think it'd be good if you and Jussara talked more, Al."

This couldn't be happening. I'd only been away for ten years. I was imagining things, and Alex was using my paranoia to mess with me, like he always did. There was no way something was going on between Jussara and Remy.

"Where's Kai?" I found myself asking. I wasn't sure why. Kai's patronizing face was the very last I wanted to see right now.

"I believe he's at the infirmary," Milena answered. "Or perhaps the lab. He said he'd be by later. I'll tell him you were looking—"

"No need. I'll talk to him in the morning."

Milena nodded. "I'll walk you out."

CHAPTER 6

Avery

"**C**AN I FUCK THIS ONE FIRST?" I ASKED OF THE SUPPOSEDLY "easy target" Reinoso pack werewolf once our server was out of hearing range.

Wyatt's eyes rolled. "I think it'd be best if you simply killed him."

"You're no fun." And I hadn't gotten laid since I'd been human. "What's his name again?"

"Alcaeus."

"Al-kay-*huh?*"

"Think 'Al' plus 'chaos'—Alcaeus. Alcaeus is the name of Perseus and Andromeda's son in Greek mythology."

"Wow, they really excel at teaching useless subjects in private school. Why's he an easy target?"

"Perry said he's more of a scout and informant for the Reinoso pack than a rogue hunter. Apparently Alex and Milena have had him searching across America for signs of the capital *R* rogue for the past decade. Supposedly, he's on his way to Denver next to meet with some of your old friends."

Ah. "Well, can't risk that happening." I raised my fresh coffee cup in salute. "Kill him it is then."

By "old friends," Wyatt referred to the local Colorado pack I'd gotten acquainted with during my early werewolf days. Prior to Sloane's birth, I'd felt the irrepressible, innate pull to belong to a pack, so I'd sought out and attempted to integrate with several. Unfortunately, in my ignorance as a new wolf, I'd done more to expose and endanger myself. As a result, I still had packs across the country hunting me to this day—in addition to all the rogue hunters I'd pissed off over the years.

With the first werewolf pack that had taken me in— the one here outside of Denver—I'd foolishly revealed surviving a rogue attack. That's when I'd learned that humans didn't survive rogue attacks. More importantly, humans didn't survive the initial werewolf transformation. *Ever.* In fact, even half-weres born of human and werewolf unions rarely survived. I was quickly labeled an abomination by the pack elders and ordered killed.

Regrettably for that first pack, they lost big time picking a fight with me, because I wound up burning their entire Highlands Ranch gated community to the ground. I was a bit hormonal during my pregnancy, oddly obsessed with fire, and given to violent impulses that seemed to come out of nowhere at times.

After that I went on the run, pissing off several more packs along the way, before fabricating an acceptable backstory about myself in order to get a nice, God-fearing pack in North Carolina to take me in just prior to Sloane's birth. I played the sympathy card by making up an abusive ex-boyfriend werewolf who'd knocked me up. It was a good thing my backstory worked because I couldn't very well give birth at a hospital. And I wasn't keen on giving birth by myself—or, heaven forbid, with Wyatt assisting me.

All was going well enough with the North Carolina pack and my luck was beginning to look up, but then my daughter, Sloane, was born utterly *scentless*—to everyone but me. Stranger still, I ceased having any sort of smell to anyone but myself and to Sloane the moment that Sloane was born.

Scent meant everything to wolves. They trusted their sense of smell above all other senses. The fact that my daughter and I suddenly had no discernable scent whatsoever was considered an aberrant horror on the scale of demonic possession.

So I went on the run again. And fortunately for me, the drive to belong to a pack had vanished along with my scent the moment that Sloane was born. Despite no longer needing a pack, I knew that I wasn't a rogue in the true sense—at least not in the *Rogue*-with-a-capital-*R* sense. Because if I went too long without seeing Sloane, I experienced the same ill effects that other werewolves did when they attempted to go rogue. As long as I spent enough time with Sloane in between hunting rogue hunters, I was fine. Sloane, however, was another matter.

"So what about the Reinoso sister? Where's her dossier of glamour shots? I expected more photos of her than anyone else."

"What sister?"

"The sister. Perry said there was a sister who had also headed the family for ages."

Wyatt's brow pinched.

"*Alex's* sister," I clarified when Wyatt continued to give me a curiously blank look. "We talked about her before you went out there. Did she turn out to be a cousin or other relation then?"

"No …" He rubbed his temple. "No, there's no sister. I'm sure I never said there was a sister." He frowned. "Did I?"

"Yes. You did. You even mentioned her when you called me from Brazil."

His frown deepened. He shook his head. "I couldn't have. There was no sister."

I felt my own forehead crumpling. It wasn't like Wyatt to be forgetful. "You said she was the most gorgeous woman you'd ever seen," I pressed. "You joked that you'd probably taken more photos of her than was necessary. God, what was her name? Alexis? Alexandria? No, that's not it, but something close to that. Ugh." I tapped my fingernail against the rim of my coffee mug. "It was like the female equivalent of Alex, but not Alexandria … It was …"

"You're mistaken." His voice sounded sure, but his eyes were still squinting with confusion and doubt. "I must've been talking about Milena, the Alpha."

"Nope." I shook my head and stood my ground. "Definitely not. Innocent-looking hippie waifs have never been your type. You fuck power-drunk, high-society stuck-up-bitch types who take no prisoners, both in the bedroom and in the boardroom. *That* is your type."

"Ha! As if!" he balked. "That is *not* my type. And that is positively the most antifeminist sentiment I've ever heard out of you. I happen to like women who are comfortable with their sexuality and equally confident navigating a man's world."

"A man's world?" I scoffed into my coffee cup. "And I'm antifeminist?"

"You know what I meant."

"Suuure."

"It's easy enough to settle this." Wyatt retrieved his phone from his pocket and set it on the table. "I'll just message Perry and ask him if he ever gave me information on a Reinoso sister."

He was thumbing through his contacts when the phone began to vibrate atop the Formica surface. The name "Lessa" flashed across the screen. As soon as it did, Wyatt's face lit up like the Dow Jones had just gained five hundred points.

Whoa. "No time for dating, huh? Who's Lessa?"

A vacuous, dreamy grin overcame Wyatt's features as he snatched his phone up. "Ah ... no one," he said absently, beaming down at the vibrating device in his hands. "Just a new acquaintance."

But his heart rate had spiked and his thumb hovered anxiously over the "talk" button a few moments too long before declining the call to voicemail for Lessa to be no one.

"You make a face like a twelve-year-old girl at a Justin Bieber concert anytime no one important calls you?"

He made a "pfft" noise of dismissal and quickly composed his features before tucking his phone away. "Don't be absurd. Bieber hasn't toured in years."

"Seriously? *That's* the joke you're gonna go with as your defense here? What happened to calling Perry?"

"Who? Oh, right." He whipped his phone back out, emitting a nervous chuckle.

I'd never seen Wyatt flustered like this. Giddy wasn't part of his normal repertoire.

"How long have you been seeing no one?"

"Really, there's nothing to share. It's all very recent. Lessa was seated next to me on my flight back from São

Paulo, actually. And then we ran into one another at a fundraising event in Manhattan a few days later."

"Wow." I nodded slowly, feeling my eyebrows strain for my hairline. "And you've decided this was kismet, huh? Not … strategic coincidence?"

"Avery, she's no one."

"*No one* who just happened to be on the same flight as you from Brazil? And then at the same event days later?"

"Trust me, she's not connected to all this in any way. True coincidences do still happen."

His phone vibrated, and "Lessa" flashed across the screen once more. He shrugged sheepishly at my withering look.

"So you ran a background check and she came up clean?"

"Yes—I mean, no. But I will." He tugged distractedly at the roots of his hair. "Look, there's nothing to be concerned about, all right? The woman's an angel. Involved in charity work for kids and homeless seniors—"

"Don't need details." I held my hand up. "Just run the check, please."

"Of course." Apologetic blue eyes cut back and forth from me to his phone. "I think … I think maybe I should get this. What if it's important?"

I pointed to the clock on the wall. "It's ten to three a.m., Wyatt. Who rings their new fling at this hour? Does she not know how to text?"

"She texts. She's just old school," he said defensively. "Besides, she's in New York. It'd be five a.m. her time."

Ignoring the unblinking, are-you-fucking-kidding-me stare I leveled at him, he answered the call, and a look of gleeful innocence erupted over his face in a way I'd never seen before. "Hi, there." He cradled the phone close to his ear and arose from the table, well aware of my supernatural hearing abilities.

An awful sense of dread settled in my gut. I needed Wyatt, and I couldn't afford for him not to be focused. It was selfish of me, I knew, but I didn't have a choice. I needed his help more than ever right now with this were-lock situation unfolding. Wyatt was the only ally I had.

I tasted both jealousy and contrition as I watched him pace in place on the opposite side of the diner—his face alight with happiness. It was hardly the first time I'd felt a sense of guilt over the knowledge that involving him in my werewolf problems had probably prevented him from having a normal life and starting a family these past ten years. I liked to rationalize that he'd long been a workaholic playboy who'd steered clear of settling down anyway, but Wyatt was pushing fifty now. And he was on track to be a Brad Pitt or Dylan McDermott kind of fifty—still hot and getting hotter with age.

He came back over to the table and rifled through his briefcase, giving me another apologetic look and mouthing something about Lessa needing a contact he'd promised her.

I couldn't deny I felt threatened by another woman stealing his attention. It wasn't that I had romantic inclinations toward him. Sure, he was good-looking and charming, and admittedly, I'd had a fleeting schoolgirl crush on him as a teenager, but he'd quickly become a big brother figure in my life, and that's where he'd remained. We enjoyed one of those rare male-female relationships where, despite any inherent romantic appeal, we understood one another well enough to know that we'd always be best suited as friends. *And that was before I'd turned into another species.*

"I need to run out to the car," he whispered to me, holding the phone to his chest. "I'm sorry. It'll only take a second." Still searching through his briefcase as he pushed the diner door open with his foot, he missed the baleful look I gave him as he went off in search of whatever it was Ms. Needy so desperately required at this hour.

I was so wrapped up in my thoughts as I watched Wyatt bound across the street to his parked rental car that too late I noticed the prolonged absence of our server and the scent of freshly spilled blood coming from the kitchen. It was the telltale scent of C-4 that caught my attention just seconds before the rear wall lining the kitchen exploded.

CHAPTER 7

Alcaeus

I THOUGHT MY TORMENT WAS OVER AFTER MILENA AND I had parted ways with my immature asshole of a baby brother and she was leading me out through the back terrace. But when I went to say goodnight to her, Milena linked her arm in mine and asked if we could take a brief walk, saying that she wanted to talk to me about Kai. It was on the tip of my flippant tongue to tell her to talk to Kai about Kai, but Milena had always been too sweet to say no to.

It occurred to me that perhaps I wasn't much more immune to her emotional influence than Alex was. I used to think it was because she was our vessel or because she was my little brother's mate that I felt so protective of Milena and somewhat beholden to her every whim whenever I was in her presence. Yet now I wondered if it had been Milena's special brand of Alpha pull at work all along, quietly wrapping us all around her little finger. *Well, all of us but Alessandra.*

I realized the evidence of Milena's influence was every-where I looked as we strolled through the gardens. Human pack members now resided in the main house if they wanted to. There were more female soldiers and guards than we'd ever had before. Abuse of power was frowned upon and swiftly punished under Milena's reign.

I knew she had enacted a law forbidding werelocks within the Reinoso pack from invading the minds of their lower-ranking fellow werewolf and human pack members. And while I was certain Alex was still actively violating that one, I couldn't deny that under Milena's influence my little brother and former Alpha was arguably more subdued and well behaved than he ever had been.

In fact, the many pack members I'd interacted with throughout the day all seemed pretty darn happy and far more … settled. The whole energy of the place was different. There was less infighting between the higher-ranking Betas within the pack. And it seemed as if everyone unanimously adored Milena and was eager to get on board with whatever she asked of them. *Aside from Lessa,* I once again qualified inside my mind.

"Kai seems to be doing fine with teleporting still," Milena broached conversationally. "He hasn't mentioned ever having anymore episodes—err—visions … least not to me," she fished. "Everything going okay as far as you know? I mean, he's still reliable for you and the team as transportation on your missions in America, right?"

Interesting. "Yep. Totally fine." Aside from being a giant, ticking time bomb of suppressed emotions and sexuality, a consummate wet blanket, and a general pain in my ass. But there was no need to burden Milena with any of that. "He's great. No issues teleporting that I've noticed."

She exhaled audibly. "Thank goodness. I'm so glad to

hear it. I hate to pry with him, you know? I understand how hard it is for him to talk about her."

By "her" and "visions," Milena was referring to Maribel—my least favorite topic and seemingly the only one Milena wanted to talk and pry with me about tonight.

"Alex tells me Kai still doesn't really ... interact ... with females yet," Milena continued to probe.

"Nope. Still celibate." Still pining after a dead bitch.

"Do you think he still feels some sort of connection to Maribel?" Milena lowered her voice to a whisper as she slowed her pace. "I mean, do you suppose that's why he hasn't been able to move on or consider anything with other women?"

Duh. "I dunno. Maybe."

Was this awkward stroll over yet? We were practically to the tree line.

"Are you saying you think Kai's mate connection to Maribel was never fully severed in the official sense? Or that he's simply still grieving?"

"Milena, I don't know." I tried not to sound as aggravated as I felt when she pulled us to a stop.

I was pretty sure Kai topped the list right after Alex of pack members eager to do Alpha Milena's bidding. I had no doubt he would've told her anything she'd wished to know. Lucky for me, Milena was too kind-hearted to risk upsetting Kai by asking him directly. *So she was torturing me instead.*

"The last time I saw Maribel in the ether, it was awful, Al," she confided softly. "She was *warped*. Demented. She'd done too many horrible things. She'd long passed the point of redemption, and she knew it. There was nothing left within her that was remotely worthy of Kai anymore."

Milena's eyes were glassy with emotion as she looked up at me. For the briefest moment, though, I glimpsed something more than sadness and empathy in their blue depths. But she glanced away, and the flicker of whatever it had been was gone before I could identify it.

"It was a mercy that Kai was severed from her." The harder lilt of Alpha had permeated Milena's tone, and when her azure gaze returned to me, streaks of green had bled through the blue, revealing how close her wolf was to the surface. "I'm afraid that if Maribel somehow weren't already gone, I'd stop at nothing to find a way to end her, to prevent her from harming Kai and the rest of our pack again."

I nodded mutely, awed and a little unnerved by the snap, dynamic shift of energy that had passed over her. I realized then what it was I'd glimpsed before: Zero hesitation. Zero remorse. Zero compassion—*for Maribel.*

But just as quickly, her voice was as gentle as the slight, sad smile that raised one corner of her mouth as she told me, "I don't know that Kai would ever understand. I don't know if Alex could. But I believe you do."

I nodded. I did understand. And yet … I suddenly had the strangest sense of being in the dark.

"There's something I never told you before, Al. When I met Maribel in the ether all those years ago, she … well, she asked me to give you her condolences." Milena squeezed my hand in hers as she winced up at me. "She said that one day you'd understand. I never said anything to you before because at first I hadn't understood what she'd meant. And once I realized that she'd meant Lupe, I … I'm so sorry …"

Classic fucking Maribel.

"It's fine, Milena." I nodded stiltedly through the red

haze enveloping me. "I understand why you didn't want to mention it before."

I wished that she had never mentioned it at all. It was an awful misery not being able to strangle someone because they were already dead. I'd spent enough time over the past decade grappling with that. It wasn't as if I needed another reason to despise Kai's dead mate.

"I'll never be able to fathom how Maribel managed to do all the awful things she did," Milena contemplated out loud. "But then again, I suppose I'll never realize the merits of the consequentialist point of view, either," she remarked with an embittered, dry laugh.

When I gave her a questioning look, she expounded, "Maribel thought that one day I would understand her reasoning. That I would even come to embrace the merits of the consequentialist point of view." She shook her head. In a blink, her eyes had turned a shade of cold, glowing green beneath the moonlight. "She was so morally lost, you see, that she honestly believed the end justified her means, vindicating all the evil she'd 'had' to do in the name of love."

I kept my expression carefully neutral as I digested Milena's words, remembering a time when I, too, had interfered in the path Milena's life would take, mere days before Maribel had.

I'd never wondered before whether my interference had been the right decision. I did now. Because Milena didn't seem to recognize the ways in which she had already come to embrace the merits of the consequentialist point of view.

CHAPTER 8

Avery

I DUCKED BENEATH THE TABLE AS A SECOND, CLOSER explosion blasted my eardrums and debris rained down all around me.

Don't shift. Don't shift.

I couldn't smell how many there were with all the noxious fumes and drywall in the air, but I knew I had mere moments before whoever had orchestrated this attack would be upon me. Judging from the location of the explosion, they were either terribly incompetent assassins or aiming to take me alive. I had a bad feeling it was the latter.

I yanked my backpack down from the bench seat and dug through it. I took the silencer off the gun and double-checked that it was loaded before securing it in the outer pocket. I snagged one flashbang and two hand grenades and inserted earplugs before zipping the bag up. When two more seconds went by without another explosion, I wrapped the fingers of my left hand around the iron base of the table. Holding the two grenades in my right hand and leaving the stun grenade positioned at my feet, I swung the table up and straight back into the diner's street-front window alongside my bench seat with all my might as I sprang upright.

Releasing the table as the glass window shattered, I quickly crouched back down, pulling the pin from one of the grenades as I did so, and tossed it over my shoulder through the broken window front while I began counting off seconds in my head. I'd flung it just far enough to clear the sidewalk but not reach too far into the street.

Thank fuck Wyatt's needy fling had caused him to be all the way on the opposite side of the street when the kitchen had exploded. I hoped that as soon as he realized what was going on, he'd be smart enough to know that he could best help me by staying away and taking cover right now. I kept him out of these attacks as much as possible. Helpful as he might try to be, the few times he'd been present he'd only proved a liability. Wyatt was simply not cut out for active duty.

At the count of two seconds, I pulled the next grenade pin out. I couldn't see for shit, but I knew that if anyone was still alive in the kitchen, it wasn't anyone I wanted to survive, so I threw the second grenade straight into the cloud of smoke and debris still billowing from the destroyed rear wall of the restaurant. At four seconds, the grenade outside detonated.

Drawing my gun, I looped my arms through the backpack straps so that it was loosely secured to my front over my chest, snatched up the flashbang grenade, and withdrew the safety pin at seven seconds—right after the kitchen grenade went off.

At nine seconds, I felt the vibration of heavy footsteps pounding against the sidewalk outside just before the glass front door shattered. I threw the flashbang toward the shattered front door a second before I jumped through the broken window front.

I hit the concrete sidewalk rolling and gained my feet crouched behind the cover of a parked car.

Five huge, armed werewolves in human form were on the sidewalk outside the diner, illuminated by the glow from streetlamps. They were all teetering on their feet from the effects of the stun grenade—which I could count on to disrupt their equilibrium and disorient them for only five to ten seconds. I shook my earplugs out and encountered the grating sound of multiple car alarms going off as I took aim and rapidly fired at ankles, faces, kneecaps, and nuts.

A civilized shot to the chest often took hours to kill a werewolf. I went for immediate pain and incapacitation.

"Over here!" I heard Wyatt call to me from his car across the street.

Oh, Jesus, no. I ducked down and stole a glance in time to see him waving at me—motioning for me to run over and get in his car—as if we could make so easy a getaway right now. He was going to get himself killed.

I turned my aim on him and shot out the back window of his car, hoping he'd get the clue to bail and that I could somehow fool the wolves into assuming he was just some idiot good Samaritan I didn't know.

A bullet hit the car I was ducked behind, drawing my attention back to the front of the diner as three more disoriented wolves filed out of the broken entryway. Eight total. Nice. It seemed it was to be my lucky number of wolves per attack today.

Disoriented and disabled as the first five should have been, some of them were already firing back—albeit poorly—which was a very bad sign. Upon closer inspection, I realized it was because two of them hadn't been injured at all by the shots I'd immediately delivered. In fact, the blond one I specifically recalled shooting in the face didn't appear to have so much as a scratch on him—which was impossible. I knew I hadn't missed.

Wyatt had learned abroad that werelocks were a virtually indestructible form of werewolf. I had an unsettling feeling that I was staring at my first werelock opponent in the flesh. But I had to be sure.

I had three bullets left before I'd need to insert a new clip, and just a few more seconds before the effects of the stun grenade would wear off. I shot the same blond wolf in the face again, just as he was taking unsteady aim in my direction. To my horror, he jerked his head only slightly as the bullet hit his cheek ... and *bounced right off*. Then he swatted the air in front of him as if he were shooing at a fly.

It was time to run.

I dove across the sidewalk and took off at a sprint down the alleyway adjacent to the diner. Behind me, I caught the sound of squealing tires peeling away from pavement. I prayed it was Wyatt regaining his common sense.

Five blocks. I could make it five blocks to the parking structure. I was a fast runner. The werewolves would be slower, recovering from the flashbang. And they couldn't scent me. Two of the first five were most likely werelocks, which was bad news. I didn't know the status of the other three yet.

My canines extended as I ran, as did my claws.

Don't shift.

Don't drop the gun.

I didn't have a change of clothes, and I desperately needed the contents in my backpack that was still strapped to the front of my chest. Although it was night and few humans were about, shifting would complicate everything.

I cut down a side street before racing through another dark alley in an effort to throw them off. Three more blocks. I would make it.

The growl coming from the three-story building above me said otherwise. As did the claws that raked down my back a moment later as a werewolf descended from above and attacked—not in human form.

My leather jacket was shredded like paper as claws sliced the skin from my back. I ignored it. Barely felt it. The burning pain was all but blocked by the rush of adrenaline coursing through me. I knew my back would heal. The more pressing issue was the paw now morphing into a hand that was squeezing around my neck as the wolf who had jumped me regained his humanoid form and took me to the ground.

The contents of my backpack slammed unpleasantly into my ribs and stomach as I hit the pavement, facedown.

I still held my gun, though. And the awkward positioning of the backpack gave me the leverage I needed to twist my arm behind me as my assailant attempted to flatten and restrain my limbs against the ground. I only had two bullets left, but I couldn't afford to waste time on perfect blind aim with my airway blocked. I pressed the end of the barrel into whatever flesh on my attacker's midsection I could reach and fired before he had a chance to wrest the weapon from me. He made a grunted noise of pain and surprise, and his grip went slack around my throat.

Hallelujah. He was a werewolf, not a werelock.

I threw my head back into his face. A crack sounded as my skull connected with his nose. Not enough to break it, but enough to distract him further and allow me to throw him off my person and regain my feet as multiple sets of both feet and paws beat swiftly against the pavement in our direction.

The blond werelock was in the lead and coming toward me as I stood. I had one last bullet in the current clip. So I shot at the blond werelock's nearest companion running in wolf form beside him, banking on that one being a common werewolf and not a werelock. I aimed between the eyes, but the wolf jerked aside and I caught him in the shoulder instead.

He skidded to the ground with a howl of pain, proving my werewolf assumption right. One more momentarily down. Three more standing: two in humanoid form and one running on four paws.

We common werewolves were fastest and strongest in our canine form, so it stood to reason that werelocks were perhaps so strong and fast already that they relied less on fighting in wolf form—particularly when faced with inconvenient human territory settings. It was a fair bet the two in human form were both werelocks.

I'd no time to ponder it further, though, because the blond werelock raised his gun at me and fired. I dove to the side too late to avoid the bullet, so I was surprised when I didn't feel the pain of a bullet wound radiating through my chest as I hit the ground.

Rejoicing in my unbelievable good luck, I looked up from the ground and caught sight of the true bearer of said "luck"—a young man standing a few paces in front of where I'd stood a moment ago. The bullet that had been meant for me bounced to a stop on the pavement next to a pair of large men's feet encased in Vans black loafers.

What the—? Where the hell had this guy come from? It was as if he'd materialized from thin air, given how fast he had to have moved in front of me to block the bullet.

More bullets fired from the blond werelock's weapon, only to bounce off of my would-be savior.

Great. Another werelock.

The newcomer werelock stood at six foot three, possibly taller. Densely packed muscle covered what was visible of his lean physique beneath the threadbare T-shirt and ripped jeans he wore. His short brown hair had wisps of curl to it where it was slightly overgrown on top, and his smiling jaw was covered in a layer of dark scruff. It was only that scruff and the subtle, underlying air of authority and vibration of anger emanating from him that prevented him from looking like some harmless, pretty boy-band member who'd stumbled into the wrong alleyway.

"Fifteen against one starts to look a little desperate, don't you think?" His deep, American-accented voice was self-assured and infused with humor as he addressed the blond werelock, who seemed to have run out of bullets at last. "She's either a very important mission for you"—he tilted his head in my direction—"or Alessandra must be paying soldiers in sexual favors again."

Alessandra! That was it—the name of Alex Reinoso's sister that I hadn't been able to recall before. *Wait—fifteen?* There'd been eight total outside the diner, and I was down to just three plus two partially injured werewolves now.

But as I quickly recounted them in my head, more werewolves that I hadn't scented before leapt down from the three-story building above and into the alleyway to surround the newcomer. *Ten of them.*

Shit.

Strangely, the newcomer appeared indifferent, perhaps entertained by this development, whereas the blond werelock smelled increasingly anxious, his eyes locked squarely on the casually dressed werelock opponent in front of him. An opponent who looked as if he'd just strolled off a beach somewhere to join in this supernatural alley brawl. In fact, I was pretty sure he had done exactly that somehow as I caught the faint scent of saltwater clinging to his hair and skin. Along with … was that surfboard wax I smelled?

"A word of advice," the pretty-boy surfer werelock told the blond one. "I'd retreat now if I were you. Her majesty's cunt never quite lived up to the legend that preceded it for me. Certainly, it's not worth dying for, my man."

Internally, I rolled my eyes. Maybe I'd get lucky and just this once it wouldn't be about me at all. Maybe they'd all end up fighting over the "legend" that was this Alessandra's cunt.

The blond werelock laughed. It was more of a scoffing sound. He was nervous as hell, and there was no hiding it. I decided the surfer-slash-boy-band werelock was now the greater threat to me.

While the rest of the alley was distracted by the showdown brewing between the blond werelock and the newcomer, I opened my backpack and quickly rummaged for a fresh bullet clip.

I was not dying today.

CHAPTER 9

Alcaeus

THE HOUR WAS LATE BY THE TIME I PARTED WAYS WITH Milena. I ran in wolf form through the woods to let off steam. I only bothered to conjure new clothing for myself as I entered the old cabin on the off chance that I might find Jussara waiting for me there—on the hope that she hadn't been called away for some nebulous "thing" that may or may not have involved a "thing" with Remy.

At first glance, the home that I had lived in for over a century looked about the same as I'd remembered it. Of course, it would never be the same again without—

I stopped cold in my tracks when I noticed what appeared to be an altar lined with flowers, candles, and photos of Kaleb in my—Jussara's—living room. I'd turned ownership of the house over to Jussara before I'd left for America. Reminding myself that it was Jussara's home now to do with as she wished and not mine was maybe the only thing that quelled the instantaneous urge I felt to tip one of those altar candles over and let the whole place go up in flames.

I took a deep breath and toed my clean, newly conjured shoes off. *Knowing that Lupe would've wanted me to.*

My shoeless feet carried me upstairs. I didn't go to her bedroom. I went to her little sitting room instead; the one where she used to spend hours immersed in her favorite telenovelas. I'd sat through a few of them with her from time to time over the years, mostly to tease her and make her laugh with my commentary and humorous storyline predictions.

It was ultimately an excuse to spend time with her. To hear her laugh and see her shake her head and smile that wry grin of hers that said she didn't give a fuck what I thought of her shows. Nor did she care how long I'd been alive or how much I thought I knew, for that matter. She was going to watch what she damn well wanted to watch. She didn't require my approval or anyone else's.

Her lingering scent was strongest in this room. So much so that I half-expected to hear her cackle fill the space at any minute, to see her familiar form reclining on the old sofa. For a few stolen moments, it felt as if I'd never left.

As if she'd never left.

I'd never understood what appeal those cheesy soap operas held for Lupe. I popped a well-worn *Avenida Brasil* DVD in and pressed play. Six hours and a gallon of cupuaçu ice cream later, I still didn't have a clue.

"You have ice cream all over your face, Tio."

I tore my zombie eyes from the television screen to find Jussara standing in the shadowed doorway. I'd been so engrossed in my own thoughts I hadn't even heard her enter the house. I smiled and scrubbed blindly at my mouth and chin with the back of my hand. "Thought you weren't coming back here until morning?"

"It is morning." She crossed the threshold and plopped

down on the couch next to me. "Change of plans for the day. Milena and I are leaving for Alsace. Came to say good-bye." She licked her thumb and swiped it across my cheek-bone. She repeated the action several more times on my chin and jawline. Her nose wrinkled. "You need a shave. And a shower."

I frowned. "Alex going with you? You two aren't going alone, are you? I don't trust that pack. Even Milena's charm has its limits."

She laughed. "Did you not see yesterday afternoon what Milena is capable of? I don't think we'll need to rely on her 'charm' to get us out of there safely if our peace meeting takes a wrong turn."

"She can't teleport," I reminded her, "and neither can you."

Her eyes rolled. "Yes, Alex is going."

"Is Remy going?"

"Not sure. I know Yuri and Diogo are going, and several others," she evaded, turning her head toward the television screen where the characters had begun arguing. Her smile was nostalgic. "I always loved this episode. Mom loved it, too."

She was avoiding my Remy question.

"Well, I don't get it." My voice sounded surly and petulant to my own ears. "These shows are God-awful. The storylines implausible, the characters shallow. Why did she like them so much? And what's up with the creepy memorial to Kaleb in my living room downstairs? The only thing that's missing is a damn chalk outline. How can you stand to live here? I don't think it's healthy for you to live here."

What's going on between you and Remy?

"Geeeez!" She burst out laughing. "You sound like

a grumpy old dad. Hard to believe the stories Kai tells of your wild exploits in America right now."

"It's none of Kai's business to be sharing that kind of stuff with you."

She snorted. "That kind of stuff? You mean sex? Remember when I turned fifty-nine this past year?"

"That's beside the point," I snapped. "Fuck." I dropped my head in my hands. "I'm sorry. It's your house now. You can erect whatever memorials you want. I just … don't understand any of it."

I felt her slim arms go around my shoulders and squeeze. "I know, Tio."

"I don't understand why she did it."

"I know." Jussara sighed and pressed a kiss to the side of my bent head. "I didn't understand either at first. But I think … she just wanted a choice for once."

The last statement I'd spoken more to myself. I hadn't expected her to answer. I lifted my head and turned to face her as she continued. She still looked like a teenager to me. Her face was too youthful to house such wise, jaded green eyes.

"She wanted a say in her own final destiny. When Nahuel killed my grandparents, he robbed her of the only world that she knew. Then she came here, and Alex took her future choices from her when he forced her to stay and be part of his pack."

She'd obviously given this a lot of thought. Maybe more than I had over the years.

"This room"—she looked around the small space—"those videos … it was the only environment she felt she could control. She watched the same stories again and again." Jussara's eyes, so much like her late mother's, grew bright as they misted with tears. "She knew all the endings by heart. I think there was a comfort in that because her own ending had become her worst looming fear. The telenovelas—they were safe."

"But she was safe here with me. From the very first day she arrived. I *always* kept her safe."

"You did. I know you did. And she knew it, too." She cupped my cheek in her hand. "I used to think it was all about me, too. That she'd done it to try and save me from a connection to the Salvatella pack. And maybe in part she did. For so long, I held onto such guilt over it. Until I realized, she came here to the Reinoso compound for me. She stayed and carved out an important place within this world for me." She dropped her hand from my cheek and slapped it against her knee. "Hell, I think the only reason she never slept with you was because of me. But leaving this world—she did that for herself."

What? Jussara was the reason Lupe had never slept with me?

"Maybe it helped for her to rationalize that she was doing it to save me from a connection to Nahuel's family and to save Milena from a faulty blood curse, but in the end, those things were only to justify the first arguably selfish move that she'd made since her parents' murder." She clasped my hands in hers. "She knew how much it would hurt all of us. Especially you. And she did it anyway. Because she had to put her own needs first in the end."

I shook my head. "I could've found another way. She shouldn't have had to resort to help from Maribel. I could've—"

"No, Tio. You couldn't have." She bit her lip. As her eyes overflowed with tears, I had the worst sense that they were for me. "You did everything right by her. By us. What's done is done. You have to let it go. You have to let *her* go."

I felt his telltale trail of magic invade the house seconds before Kai teleported into the hallway outside Lupe's sitting room. He hadn't yet mastered my sister's finesse for teleporting.

I knew Jussara had felt Kai's entry, too. She'd begun wiping at her tears and composing herself before he knocked on the doorjamb to announce his presence.

"Sorry for the intrusion. I wanted to catch you before you left."

"It's fine," she told him with a smile. "I do need to get going," she said to me. She threw her arms around my neck and gave me a good squeeze. "Try and remember, it was her choice, okay? She just wanted a choice for once. We have to honor that."

I hugged her tightly back, wishing that we had more time, that Kai wasn't in the room with us, and that I wasn't such an emotionally bereft dolt at a loss for what to say to her where her mother was concerned.

She gave Kai a hug, too, promising that she and Milena would visit us in America next if we didn't come back to Brazil soon.

Uncomfortable silence descended upon Lupe's sitting room after Jussara left. Kai stood there awkwardly, just a few feet within the doorway, while I pretended to be watching the telenovela on the screen.

"You still want to head back later today, right?" he asked at last. "Because we have that meeting in Denver tomorrow."

I nodded.

"You sleep at all?"

I shrugged.

He turned his attention to the episode playing on the television. "I don't think I ever saw this one."

"Why would you have?"

My snap reply had come out sounding like I was accusing him of something, so it shouldn't have surprised me when he huffed and returned defensively, "Why *wouldn't* I have? I watched every single episode of *2-5499 Ocupado* on rerun with Lupe during the summer of eighty-nine, thank you very much."

I racked my brain a moment and recalled that 1989 was the summer I'd been away on a mission with Kaleb. At my request, Kai had stayed behind to look after Lupe and Jussara while I'd been gone.

"I remember the ongoing arguments Lupe and I had over the implausibility of Emily and Larry's relationship like it was yesterday," Kai said with a chuckle. I felt myself scowl as I watched a stupid, wistful grin spread across his face. "I mean the absurdity of that entire storyline was beyond measure. Did you ever watch that one with her? The one about the woman in prison who was a telephone operator?"

It was one thing to wax nostalgic with Jussara. It was another thing to do it with Kai. I didn't want to share memories of Lupe with Kai. Not even the ones that were already his—as irrational as it was. As he began to reminisce aloud about other ridiculous telenovela plotlines he'd debated with Lupe over the years, I cracked.

"Hey, I got an outlandish, over-the-top storyline for you," I cut off his sentimental musings. "Remember that time when my best friend's dead mate who wasn't all the way dead killed the only woman I ever loved?"

"Okay." Kai held his palms up and backed out through

the doorway. "My apologies for interrupting your tele-novela. We'll talk later."

Fuck. "Kai, look, I'm sorry," I called after him. "I didn't mean to say it like it was your fault." *Except I did.*

I definitely did.

He leaned his shoulder into the doorframe and nodded slowly at the floor. "You know, you're not the only one who lost Lupe."

He was right. But it was the last thing I wanted to hear. From him in particular.

I nodded. "I know."

"It's been almost ten years, Al."

As if I didn't know? God, there he went with his conde-scending tone again.

"I really think … maybe it's time you stopped mourning your loss with meaningless sex and channeled that grief into something more constructive. I think Lupe would've—"

"You know what Lupe would've wanted?" I was sud-denly standing. And shouting. His arrogance and pre-sumption had finally eroded whatever thin restraint I'd been clinging to. "Lupe would've wanted you to get your dick wet just once this fucking century! Did you ever think that maybe I feel compelled to fuck enough pussy for the both of us? To make up for how you've mishandled Lupe's sacrifice?"

His eyes widened. Then they narrowed. "Mishandled her sacrifice?" He looked affronted.

Good.

I tossed my arms in the air at his endless pompous ig-norance. "Lupe died for your mated dick's freedom. She made a deal with the devil so that you wouldn't have to stay tied to a psycho undead bitch for all eternity."

"No." Kai's jaw tightened. "She died to free herself from an eternity with Nahuel. It's like Jussara said. She wanted a choice for once."

"A choice? Oh, please, that psychobabble bullshit sounds like just the sort of thing Remy would say to put a positive, empowering spin on things for Jussara's benefit in order to try and get into her pants." I leveled my pointer finger in his face. "And by the way, I will fucking kill him and all the rest of you if I find out that he has gotten into those pants and you guys have been keeping it from me."

"Do you hear yourself? Jussara's pushing sixty. And she's not your daughter."

"She might as well be!"

"I'm going to go now. I'll come back later when your ice cream hangover has worn off."

"Lupe was manipulated, and you know it. She was preyed upon. *Used.*" I hissed the word at him. "Misled by that demon undead bitch of yours that you're still actively pining over even after everything that you know she's done."

His eyes flashed bright blue, and I tasted a moment's satisfaction knowing that at least I'd gotten a reaction out of the wolf, if not the man, as he growled, "She is still my mate."

"Really? Well, I don't see a mark on you anymore." I shrugged. "And there's a body count over ninety-eight years long to show for how hard she worked to be rid of you. Maybe you should think about that fact the next time you're stroking your dick to her glorious memory."

The sound of fabric rending was instantaneous, and the white wolf was on me before I'd managed to shift—having wasted a half-second relishing the victory of his wolf's reaction.

CHAPTER 10

Avery

WHEN IN DOUBT, THROW A FLASHBANG.

I think I read that advice off a fortune cookie once. Or maybe it was my cell wall at juvie. Those little buggers had saved my ass more than a few times—both before and after turning werewolf.

So when one of the werewolves broke from the group fighting the surfer werelock to lunge in my direction as he saw me fishing through my bag, I grabbed the next best thing to the fresh clip I'd been searching for, pulled the pin, and threw the stun grenade at him before closing my eyes and plugging my ears at the last moment.

I was on my feet as soon as the flash behind my closed eyelids settled. I opened my eyes as the same werewolf stumbled into—onto—me, swearing his annoyance at the effects of the flashbang as he knocked me back to the ground. I jerked my knee into his groin at the first opportunity, but he still managed to get a decent, if awkward, hold on me. I had the right angle and leverage to head-butt him in the throat, so I went for it, but my head met cool air as he was torn off me.

"Someone needs new moves." The surfer werelock was standing above me, wearing an affable grin as he extended a hand to help me up. "You're kinda predictable." He tilted his face in profile, showcasing an earplug he was wearing.

"Sonofa—"

Two huge, growling wolves jumped onto him before I could finish that thought. They looked like they were fresh to the party, too, not at all disoriented by my stun grenade like the rest of the group in the alley was—aside from the cocky surfer, of course, who had just morphed into a giant, black and white wolf.

I grabbed my bag and ran while I still had a chance. I hadn't sprinted more than thirty feet before a bullet whizzed by my head. I threw my shoulder into the next building rear door I came upon, intending to cut through whatever business or residence it might be. The door didn't budge. I tried kicking it in. No dice. Fuck. Since when had RiNo become a secure, safe neighborhood?

Another bullet hit the brick wall next to me. I bobbed and proceeded to sprint, weaving an unpredictable pattern as I went. I was almost to the next block, where I'd be able to slip down another street. But as I reached the corner, a muscled forearm came out of nowhere and hooked around my waist.

Before I could give in to my instinctive response to kick and fight free from whoever had grabbed hold of me, a bizarre nothingness encompassed me. Literally, my form ceased to exist. I was nothing but air, surrounded by darkness, lacking even the lungs to scream my panic.

But in the next moment, I was standing on Blake Street—two blocks from where I'd been grabbed.

Jesus Christ. That had not just happened.

What had just happened?

"You okay?"

I gulped air into my lungs and swayed on my feet as the arm released me. I inhaled the faint aroma of sea salt and surfboard wax. And ... *magic*—a rare fragrance I recognized only because my daughter carried a similar, albeit more faint, underlying scent.

"This the right parking garage?"

Wide-eyed, I met the nonchalant features of the surfer-boy werelock standing next to me. He jutted his chin at the parking structure beside us—as if this were all perfectly normal and he'd just transported me here on his skateboard rather than by violating the laws of matter and energy.

I was in deep shit. I had to get away from this guy.

Unsure of how I should answer, I simply shook my head and went with, "I don't know."

"You got a ride somewhere on Blake Street, though, right?"

Again, I shook my head. Who was this superbeast? How did he know?

"Who are you?" I couldn't stop myself from asking aloud.

"I'm a friend," he said with a smile. He sniffed the air and squinted up at the structure. "I think there are a few more up there." He scrubbed a hand over his chin. "I'd tell you to wait for me, but I know you won't." He glanced at me, then up at the structure, like he was deliberating something. "Okay." His eyes leveled on mine. "Watch your back in there. I'm gonna take care of the ones left in the alley. Then I'll be back to help you clear the structure, all right?"

In the next breath, he was gone—*vanished into thin air.*

Maybe there'd been a hallucinogenic in my eggs Benedict.

I shook my head. It was all crazy. *But so was my life.* I didn't have the luxury of time to wonder why.

I entered the structure and ran inside the nearest stairwell. Taking the steps four at a time, I didn't scent anything beyond urine-soaked concrete until I was racing up the last flight before level three. *Shit.* Why hadn't I inserted a fresh clip when I'd had the chance?

My hand dove frantically into my bag just as I reached the third floor landing. But a heavy boot landed a kick to my stomach as a male werewolf burst through the open entryway to the parking area, sending me flying backward down the stairwell.

My body smacked hard against the concrete landing below. Pain radiated through my hipbone that had borne the brunt of my fall. My eyes shifted; my claws emerged. *Don't shift. Don't shift.*

The guy who'd kicked me called out, "I've got her." He had an accent. European. German maybe. "Get the van!"

So they wanted to take me with them. Alive or dead was the critical question. I placed my bet on alive and rolled the dice.

"My knee," I cried out. "I can't move it." I groaned and made a show of being injured as the booted beast jumped to the landing next to me. I scanned his body and caught sight of a weapon strapped to his midsection, beneath his left arm. *Booyah.*

"Don't hurt me, please," I said in as frightened a voice as I could manage, casting my best helpless girl eyes up at the beefy blond stranger looking down at me.

His hard blue eyes softened just a fraction. I scented no

magic on him like I had on the surfer guy, so he was likely a normal werewolf. He looked young. And uncertain—like he was suddenly unsure of his mission or why I was his prey. He probably wasn't that bad of a guy when it came down to it—just another rogue hunter blindly following his pack leader's marching orders.

But that was enough for me. It was his life or Sloane's.

I shifted my hips and cried out in agony, curling inward and clutching my leg just above the knee. "I think it's broken."

When he foolishly crouched down next to me, I made my move. Pretending to be terrified, I shrieked, "Don't hurt me!" and jerked my body away from him, leading him to lean in closer, at which point I flailed forward again, head-butting him in the nose, grabbing the gun from his holster, and shooting him twice in the chest and once in the leg.

Despite his injuries and the shock of my attack, he fought back, clawing at me as I put him in a chokehold, flipped him over my shoulder, and hefted him up and over the open outer concrete ledge of the stairwell, letting his big body drop to the sidewalk several stories below.

I wiped his fresh blood coating my hands on my jeans so that his gun wouldn't slip from my fingers, checked my new weapon's bullet count, grabbed my backpack, and headed back up the stairs, prepared to take on whoever he'd told to get the van as tires screeched to a stop inside the garage.

The ache in my hipbone from my fall was bad. Even the adrenaline fueling me didn't prevent me from hobbling a little as I went, hugging the wall and holding my gun at the ready as I approached the entryway door to the parking area. I'd be in trouble if I needed to run.

I heard a car door open and steadied my grip as I listened to the footsteps coming closer. One guy. Was that possible? It seemed too easy. Unless I was missing something? They seemed to want me alive based on the other guy's reaction. But that didn't mean this guy wouldn't hesitate to injure me—especially when I attacked.

The footsteps stopped. I heard the metallic click of a magazine locking in place. Shit. *Do or die, Avery.*

I was about to go for it when the surfer werelock materialized out of nowhere, his broad back facing me and blocking the doorway I'd been about to charge through.

"Hey, bro," he greeted whoever was on the other side.

The sound of a semi-automatic weapon firing was instantaneous as bullets blasted my would-be savior werelock's chest and strays nicked the doorframe. I ducked and backed up so fast I nearly fell backward down the stairwell again. After what seemed like forever and a gratuitous number of bullets, I heard the inevitable empty clicking sound, signaling that the attacker was out of ammo.

Surfer boy didn't miss a beat. "Got any jumper cables I can borrow?"

I heard the sound of metal clanking to the concrete, followed by rapid, retreating footfalls.

"Aw, seriously? Why would you run? I just asked for cables," the indestructible werelock taunted from the doorway. Then he turned and threw over his shoulder at me, "Don't get any ideas. You and I need to talk."

Awesome. He was warning me not to run. Of course, I'd figured all along I was the prey that he was ultimately after when he'd first shown up and interfered in the alley fight. But his warning caused my heart rate to skyrocket nonetheless.

How did one run from a person capable of disappearing and reappearing themselves in places?

"Come on, man, let's see what you got for me," he called out to the fleeing werewolf.

Swallowing my inner panic, I stood and followed him at a cautious distance as he strode into the parking level, past an abandoned van and the discarded M16, until we were standing near the center of the dimly lit lot.

Surfer werelock did no more than crook his fingers, and the dark-haired werewolf sprinting for his life across the half-empty parking garage levitated in the air and floated back to us. The werewolf shrieked in panic, his arms and legs flailing wildly.

Fuck. Me. How was I supposed to fight this guy?

"I don't know anything!" the terrified werewolf shouted when he was a scant few feet away from the werelock who was somehow holding him levitated and immobilized at whim.

I cringed internally. I couldn't help but feel a flicker of pity for the werewolf—even knowing he probably would've blasted me to pieces with that semi if given the chance. At the same time, my self-preservation instincts kicked into high gear. I scanned the sparsely filled lot and spotted the black Audi A4 parked about forty feet to my right, in the opposite direction from where the werewolf had run.

"Perfect," the cocky werelock responded with a laugh, "because I wasn't planning to waste time interrogating you. I'll just ransack your memories."

"Wait, no—no, I *do* know things."

Ransack memories?

The man fell to his knees—whether by force of magic

or of his own volition, I couldn't say—and proceeded to desperately babble and bargain. The surfer whipped the threadbare T-shirt he was wearing over his head and held it up for the pleading man to see how well the front had been riddled by bullets.

"You ruined my favorite T-shirt. I've had this one forever. And you weren't planning on being very nice to my friend here, either." As he said it, he stepped aside, allowing the kneeling werewolf an unobstructed view of me.

"No—no, I wasn't going to hurt her. I was sent to capture her."

"And bring her to Alessandra Reinoso," the shirtless werelock concluded, turning around to me to ensure I'd heard that part of the plan.

I stared blankly back at him as his captive blathered on in confirmation. My eyes lowered to his shirtless chest. Surfer werelock was ripped. More importantly, he hadn't sustained so much as a scratch on his chest despite his bullet-ridden T-shirt.

"Okay, we're done talking now," he announced, turning his attention back to the ill-fated werewolf on his knees. "I'm interested in seeing the things Alessandra didn't allow you to remember."

"No, no, please, not my mind—"

The werewolf's pleas were cut short and his eyes rolled back in his head as the werelock's own eyes closed in concentration.

This was some serious, creepy shit.

I inched a side step to my right, then another.

I had to make a run for it. Even if I didn't get far, I had to try.

And I didn't get far. Because a force of gravity knocked

my ass to the petroleum-stained concrete two retreating steps later.

My lungs felt compressed and I struggled to take in air as I witnessed the scary-powerful werelock employ some sinister, invasive magic to seemingly pull information from the werewolf's mind.

The surfer werelock's face was a mask of concentration, until suddenly his mouth broke into a devilish grin, and he muttered, "Oh, *hel-lo*."

I suspected he'd found whatever secrets he was looking for, because in the next moment, the werewolf made a terrible sound of agony and clutched his head with both hands before collapsing face first to the dirty concrete. *Dead.*

His silenced heartbeat made my own racing heart sound that much louder.

The gravity force that had been holding me down and constricting my lungs abated as the shirtless werelock turned to me with a smile, shaking his head and tsking. "I told you we needed to talk."

Hellfire, things were dicey. He hadn't even broken a sweat this whole time, and I was still panting on the ground, covered in blood and filth, my hipbone throbbing.

I jumped to my feet and took a step back. "Who are you?" When all else fails, keep the enemy talking.

"Told you, I'm a friend."

I retreated another step. "Right. Where I come from a friend is someone you know, not a scary stranger you just ran into in a parking garage fight."

"What?" He made a mock pouty face. "I get no brownie friend points for saving your life, Avery?"

"How do you know me?" I asked before my rattled

brain had a chance to realize my mistake. "I mean … how do you think you know me?" I stupidly corrected, knowing from the smile growing on his face that he wasn't buying any of it. "You have the wrong person. My name's Cynthia, not Avery."

"Well, Cynthia," he played along, stalking closer and extending his hand out to me in offering, while I continued my awkward retreat, "it's a pleasure to meet you. My name is Raul."

I didn't take his hand. It took the last shreds of my floundering dignity and the logic that it wouldn't help me anyway to stop myself from continuing to back away.

"How'd you do that? How'd you kill him? How'd you survive those bullets?" I pelted questions at him. "What do you want from me?"

Wow. I so needed that silencer. For my mouth.

"May I have your backpack, please?"

"Huh?"

"Your backpack, Avery."

"You want to rob me?"

He laughed. There was a warmth and sincerity inherent to the sound that I'd not expected as it echoed through the parking structure. "Nah, silly," he teased as if we truly were old chums. "I want to program my contact information into your phone in case you need to reach me."

"For serious?" I squawked. "You did all that because you wanted to give me your number?"

"Will you hand me your phone already? Please?"

With fumbling fingers, I rummaged through my backpack and managed to locate my new phone for him. Then I stood staring like a mouth-breather in headlights as he thumbed in his information.

"There. I've programmed myself under both 'Scary Stranger' and 'Friend' so however you choose to remember me, you'll have my digits."

I accepted the phone back with a bewildered, "Right."

"If you need me, I'll be a phone call away. Anytime. Anywhere. Understand?"

I knew I should just shut up and be thankful he hadn't killed me with that silent mind death trick yet, but my willful tongue often had designs of its own.

"How'd you move without moving before?"

He opened his mouth to reply, then paused before answering, "Let's just say I'm a student of Darwinism."

Clearly. "Caught that much. Why'd you help me?"

"Because some would say I'm also an active proponent and purveyor of Darwinism."

I shook my head. "A true proponent of Darwinism would have left me to fend for myself. Natural selection and all that." *Why was I arguing this point?*

"Look, Avery …" He exhaled, and a deep, disconsolate chasm creased his brow, making him suddenly seem far older than his otherwise youthful appearance. And making me curious to know the hidden pain that had etched its way into this man's soul.

"I know who you are and what you're hiding. I understand better than you do the odds you're up against, because I know the rogue hunter who's coming for you. The one your friend Wyatt told you about. Milena Caro-*Reinoso*." His features contorted as he forced out the last three syllables of the Alpha female's hyphenated surname, saying "Reinoso" like it was a disease. "You need to understand, Sloane is in grave danger."

My pulse sprinted at the mention of first Wyatt's and

then my daughter's name—at the realization that this powerful stranger knew far, far more about us than he should. I knew he heard it, but I schooled my features nonetheless.

Muttering a dismissive, "Thanks for the tip," I turned my back on him and headed for the rental car. Whatever his game was, he didn't want me dead. *Least not yet.* Or I would've been dead already.

"I'm the only one who can stop her," he called out from behind me. And then he was standing smack-dab in front of me, blocking my path.

"Jesus!"

"Milena's not like the other rogue hunters you've taken out," he proceeded calmly while I stood clutching my backpack to my racing chest. "You won't win this fight. Not alone."

I couldn't suppress the growl that escaped me at his rude assertion. "Are you finished?"

"Don't let your pride dictate your daughter's fate."

"Pride?" Oh, that got my canines out. Claws as well. "My pride has nothing to do with this. This is about me protecting my child from hunters and supernatural opportunists alike. I will die before I tell you where she is, so either kill me or get the hell out of my way, pretty boy."

He stepped aside, making a sweeping, gentlemanly gesture with his arm for me to pass.

I did. Maneuvering around him as quickly as possible.

"You're still limping from a fall you took a full ten minutes ago," he pointed out, raking my last nerve as I fished through my backpack, willing the car keys to materialize. "I took at least eighteen bullets to the heart five minutes ago, and I'm standing here without a scratch."

"You want a fucking ribbon?" I threw back over my shoulder. *Ass.*

He laughed. "I want you to understand that we're on the same side."

I kept walking. *Where the fuck were those keys?*

I heard a throat clear behind me, along with the sound of keys jingling. I stopped. My eyes shifted, and I had to take a calming breath before turning to face him.

He was grinning from ear to ear as he tossed me the car keys. He looked more like a harmless, prankster frat boy than the dangerous supernatural killer that I knew him to be.

"Sorry, swiped 'em for fun. Figured a woman with your juvenile rap sheet would've caught on sooner."

Nice segue. He'd read my criminal file. Those were sealed records. Wyatt's father had seen to it. But I supposed nothing was off-limits to a guy who read minds. Which made me wonder …

"You read that wolf's mind back there?"

He nodded.

"Have you read mine?"

"No."

"Would I know it if you had?"

He hesitated before answering, "Most humans and werewolves don't remember. I'm careful to cover my tracks and erase the memory of my invasion."

Or simply kill them. "You didn't answer my question."

"Because I don't know the answer, Avery. I can't access your mind like I can other werewolves. If I could, I wouldn't be standing here, because I'd already know where Sloane is."

My stomach flipped. He was telling the truth. I could

smell it. It made the reality of his words scarier, and yet reassuring. "What makes me different?"

His brows shot up, and he laughed like it was an absurd question. "What makes you different?" He shook his head. "Oh, I dunno … everything? You gave birth to the *Rogue* of rogues." His gaze was assessing. "I don't believe fate picked you by accident, either."

A chill swept over me. It was the adrenaline rush let-down. *And the fact that he for sure knew as much as I'd feared.*

He took a step closer and stage-whispered, "Don't think it's escaped my attention that you have no scent. I'm assuming it's the same for Sloane?"

I didn't respond. But my heart rate answered for me despite my intentions. I needed to get home to my daughter. *Without him following me.*

"So how's this gonna work?" I cut to the chase. "You'll pretend to let me go so you can follow me?"

A slow, easy smile spread across his face. "I think I like you, Avery."

"Enough that you won't melt my brain and leave my body in a parking garage?"

He chuckled. "Odds are definitely in your favor on that."

"Yay me," I deadpanned. I slung my backpack over my shoulder and crossed my arms over my chest. "Again … how's this gonna work?"

"I am going to let you go. And I won't follow you … *if* you agree to one condition."

"Ah, this should be good."

"Pick any other car in this parking lot and let me start it for you. I'm not okay with you taking one that Wyatt secured."

"Seriously? You think I can't hotwire a car on my own? I'm offended."

"How many times have you been attacked in the past six hours? Think about it. Your attackers were one step ahead of you every single time. How often has that happened before today? What's the common thread?"

I raised my pointer finger at him. "No dice, mind-bender."

"*Wyatt.* You know that it's Wyatt."

I rolled my eyes and turned on my heel, heading for the Audi.

"Look, I'm not claiming Wyatt has or would betray you on purpose. But his mind has been compromised by a powerful enemy werelock: Alessandra Reinoso. He no longer has a choice in the matter."

I kept walking, even though I scented no lie in his words, clicking the unlock button on my car key. Raul materialized in front of my ride as I approached it, leaning against the driver-side door.

"Trust me, I know her well." His smile was bitter. "Know firsthand what it's like to be seduced and manipulated by her without the added use of mind control that she's employed with Wyatt. Lessa is a conceited, power-hungry, opportunistic bitch, Avery. She'll stop at nothing to get what she wants. And right now your daughter is the trophy she's set her sights on."

Fuck. *Lessa.* The chill in my veins turned to ice as the pieces clicked into place.

Alessandra Reinoso, Alex's sister—the werelock Wyatt had mysteriously forgotten about—and Lessa, the needy new fling Wyatt was so smitten with, were one and the same bitch.

CHAPTER 11

Alcaeus

I'T'D BEEN YEARS SINCE KAI AND I HAD SCUFFLED—I mean really tussled. We sparred all the time for sport, but we hadn't truly fought since we were kids.

I went down fast in human form, then shifted to my wolf form just as Kai's maw tried to clamp onto my shoulder. When his footing faltered slightly with the shift, I reared up and threw him.

There was a crashing sound as Kai's canine form flew into the TV console. It should've stopped me, knowing that I was destroying Lupe's most treasured things—her sacred space within the home we'd shared for fifty years. But somehow that realization egged me on, heightening my anger and fueling my need for vengeance.

It was the same vengeance that taunted me daily. Hourly. One I could never quench. Never deliver to the proper source.

I chased a retribution that I would never be able to exact from that undead supernatural cunt of the century who had deliberately, callously targeted and ensnared my Lupe within her warped scheme to skirt the laws of the cosmos

The fact that Maribel had sacrificed Lupe to save my best friend, and that she'd also arguably "saved" Milena and the rest of us from the flawed Salvatella blood curse in the process, didn't make her a saint in my book. Nor did it make accepting her actions any easier.

It made her a sick fucking bitch as far as I was concerned.

Because how was I supposed to reconcile the loss of Lupe against the deliverance of Kai? I could never value Lupe's life above Kai's. Neither could I hold Kai's life above Lupe's.

And it was no accident that Maribel had set it up that way.

No, the scenario was just the sort of fucked-up shit that the Maribel I knew and remembered—in all her demented "genius"—would've quietly, proudly contrived. *While professing to have no other choice in the matter, of course.*

Before I knew it, we'd torn Lupe's old sofa to shreds. The more we destroyed, the more enraged I became. Rationally, I knew it wasn't Kai's fault what Maribel had done in the name of her twisted love for him.

But it *was* his fault for being too stupid to seize the second chance at life that he'd been given as a result.

We'd destroyed the entire sitting room and crashed through the floor to the living room below before I registered my sister Alessandra's shrill voice yelling at us to stop. And I only ultimately heard her because her words were accompanied by a blast of magic that pulled Kai's wolf body and my own apart, as Lessa sent Kai's body flying through the front bay window of the house.

Lessa rattled off the plans she'd set in motion for tomorrow as she cleaned up the last of the drywall dust and debris that had settled on Kaleb's altar photos when Kai and I had fallen through the ceiling. The other areas of the room that had been impacted were still a mess, as was the upstairs sitting room.

Kai had yet to return to the house since being thrown from it. It was for the best. He and Lessa hadn't gotten along very well in the past century.

I felt numb inside as I sat on the couch watching my sister tidy up Jussara's creepy Kaleb alter when she hadn't seen cause to clean or straighten up anything else in the living room. I guess I'd known that Kaleb had been one of Lessa's favorite soldiers—and sometime lover. If I hadn't realized it before, it was apparent from the way that she was fussing over his photos and relighting his altar candles, just how dear a friend he'd been to her.

Yet Lessa had somehow been able to overlook her friend Maribel's role in Kaleb's murder. In fact, she'd more or less led the brigade to canonize Maribel for her brilliance and heroism in defeating Nuriel Salvatella and fixing Milena's flawed blood curse ten years ago.

I dropped my head in my hands. *I'd destroyed Lupe's sanctuary.* There was no salvaging what was left of it. Pack members were on their way to help repair the other damage I'd done to Jussara's home. But I didn't know what I was going to tell Jussara about her mom's beloved sitting room when she got back from Alsace.

"Are you listening?" Lessa asked, snapping her fingers above my bent head to get my attention.

I fucking hated it when she did that. I raised my chin and gave her a hard look in response.

"I need your head in the game, Al." She planted her hands on her hips. She was wearing another prim blouse and skirt outfit. And her hair was in a weird twist on top of her head.

"I'm listening, damnit."

Her back straightened. "What did I just say then?" she challenged.

My eyes rolled to the gaping hole in the ceiling above my head. "Kai and I are supposed to meet with the Highlands Ranch pack tomorrow night at the designated bar in Denver," I told her through clenched teeth. "But I'm to order Kai to stay at the hotel at the last minute and go to the meeting alone."

She nodded and motioned with her hand for me to continue.

I sighed. "Being the supremely clever bitch that you are, you've set the *Rogue's* mother up to crash the meeting and attempt to assassinate me. My job is to capture the mom, flee the scene, and then get in touch with you without Kai knowing anything that happened."

"Perfect. The *Rogue's* mother is constantly switching her name and identity, but you'll be able to recognize her easily enough since she's a werewolf with no scent. And based on the fact that she'll be trying to kill you. If there's any doubt as to her identity, everyone in the Highlands Ranch pack who will be there for the meeting should be able to confirm it. Now let's talk about the complication."

"I thought Kai was the complication."

She made a disgusted face and threw a dismissive hand gesture my way. "Kai's an inconvenience and a consummate annoyance. He's not relevant enough to be a complication."

"Never gonna let that incident go, huh?" I goaded just to razz her. "If it makes you feel better, he can't get a boner for any woman these days."

"It has nothing to do with that. And you've no room to talk. Look around at the destruction you just caused if you think I'm the only person who has issues with that freak of nature."

"All right, all right." I held both palms up. *Sheesh, she was touchy.* "Bad joke." Worse timing. "Pray continue." I mimicked the same hand gesture she'd given me a moment before.

"Look," she huffed as she proceeded to fiddle with her fancy-weird bow-tie neckline, "the thing is … I—I'm seeing someone new. Who is … um … special to me."

Huh. "And he has a thing for teachers?"

"What?"

"That why you're dressed like a teacher?"

She looked down at her outfit with affront. "I am not dressed like a teacher."

"Well, whatever that look is." I waved my hand up and down the length of her person. "You've been dressing a bit differently than normal."

"What do you know about the way I normally dress?"

"Aw, come on, I notice stuff."

She made a "pfft" noise and sank down onto the couch beside me, slumping low against the seat cushions in what was a very uncharacteristic posture for Lessa.

"I'm in love, Al," she announced in one quick exhalation of breath. "And it's awful. I don't know how I'm supposed to act or even dress anymore." She covered her face with her hands. "I feel like my makeup and hair is never right no matter what I do. I'm exhausted by the whole thing, and it's only been three weeks."

My jaw popped open. "You're shitting me! Who's the lucky victim?"

Her arm swung out and her fist connected with my face before I could block it. It did nothing to curb the idiot grin of elation I was wearing. Plenty of men had come in and out of Lessa's life over the past four centuries, but never had I heard her profess to be in love with any of them before.

"Lessa, this is amazing! Why didn't you tell me sooner?"

She groaned, covering her face with her hands again. "It's not amazing. It's a mess. I say stupid things to him all the time. I end up constantly having to erase from his memory the embarrassing things I've done and said. But then I can't always remember the things I've erased or which alternate memories I've implanted, or which background story I've told him about myself—"

"*Whoa*—back up, sis. I'm no expert, but I'm pretty sure you're walking a short plank to relationship suicide with that level of deception. What are you doing? Who is this guy?"

He had to be a common werewolf if she was able to manipulate his mind that easily. I wasn't sure how I felt about that. It wasn't exactly what I'd pictured for Lessa—to the extent I'd ever contemplated a mate for her over the years at all. Lessa had always been a tough one to imagine mated and settled, period.

"You don't understand. It's complicated. I've been second-guessing myself ever since I met him."

I went from being elated to pissed. "It sounds like he's all wrong for you. Who is this loser who's making you doubt yourself?"

"He's not a loser. He's perfect in every way. He's smart, he works hard, he does things to help other people—to the point of risking his own safety."

She sounded irritated—almost jealous—about that last part. I liked the idea of this guy less and less.

"Well, I don't like him for you."

"And he's gorgeous," she proceeded to gush, ignoring my comment entirely. "But he's that annoyingly natural kind of gorgeous nerd type where you can tell that he kinda-sorta cares but doesn't really care how he looks, you know? I mean, he's letting his hair go grey and everything, and it still looks super-hot on him."

Gross. "Thanks for that detail. The first thing I wondered about was his hair. Is this silver fox of yours wheelchair-bound or can he get around with a cane at least?"

She straightened enough to whack me in the shoulder.

"What?" I balked. "How the fuck old is this geezer? I'm trying to remember at what age normal werewolves go grey, but I can't recall the last time I actually saw a grey-haired werewolf."

"He's human, you idiot."

"He's *what?*" My jaw dropped once more. "You're fucking with me. Wait—is this about your rivalry with Milena and Alex?"

"What rivalry with Milena and Alex?"

"Oh, come on, Lessa. Why would you go after a human guy? Human men have never been your type." *Aside from her poor lapse of judgment with Raul.*

"Well, tell it to my wolf! This wasn't something I planned on, Al."

"Wait a minute, are you saying you found your true mate? And he's human?"

She nodded.

Oh, shit. "You're positive?"

"Yes."

"You're absolutely sure? One hundred percent—"

"Al!"

"That's awesome," I proclaimed with a forced smile. "I can't wait to meet him."

I knew she knew I was full of shit from the glare she leveled at me.

"Fine. I'm not thrilled about this 'complication' of yours. But I'm sure I'll feel differently after I've met him. How old did you say he was again?"

"Forty-eight. And his humanity isn't the complication."

"Forty-eight? That's all?" I heaved a sigh of relief. "Forty-eight's perfect for you, Lessa." I grabbed her hands in mine and gave them a squeeze. "I mean, let's look on the bright side: he'll always look older than you are despite your three-hundred-and-fifty-year age gap," I said reassuringly.

She groaned and yanked her hands from my grasp.

Fuck, that was the wrong thing to say. Where was Remy when I needed him? I was terrible at this stuff.

"Have you told anyone but me yet?"

She shook her head, looking like she might cry.

I'd never seen my sister like this. We needed to get a handle on the situation before one of our enemies found out.

"Okay, where is he now?" I stood from the couch. "Let's do this right away. We can get his werewolf transformation process started before lunchtime." Best to do it as soon as possible, before my mind ran rampant worrying that the idiot who had shredded my sister's confidence would die of sudden heart failure or get hit by a bus and inadvertently get her killed via their mate connection.

"Sit down, Al. We can't turn him yet."

"Sure we can. There's no time like the present. C'mon, if we move quickly, we can freeze the aging process before his jowls drop another millimeter."

"He doesn't know, Al."

"That's okay. We'll tell him all about it as we're guiding his first shift."

"You're not hearing me. He can't know yet," she insisted, her voice rising in panic. "My mate, Wyatt, is the human friend of the *Rogue's* mother that I told you about before. That's the complication. I can't turn him or reveal who I am without compromising our *Rogue* mission. But until I do turn him, he's in near-constant danger because of his affiliation with her." Her hazel eyes filled with unshed tears. "And when he finds out that I've betrayed him in order to capture his friend and her daughter, he might hate me forever and not even accept me as his mate."

Oh, Jesus. "Are you serious? Your true mate's named *Wyatt?*"

CHAPTER 12

Avery

"**W**HAT HAPPENED NOW?" I ASKED, TAKING IN THE CHARRED sofa and the discarded fire extinguishers littering the floor next to Azda's rocking chair.

"What is the Caribbean?" Azda said in response to the *Jeopardy* answer at play on the television screen before telling me, "Another Red Vine incident."

I pinched the bridge of my nose. "Azda, we talked about this. I bought you guys two huge containers last time so this wouldn't happen."

"Who is Jefferson Davis?" she told Alex Trebek on the screen before giving me a shrug. "She finished hers on the drive and wanted mine."

I let my backpack drop to the wooden floor with a thud. "So just let her have them, for God's sake." I was exhausted, filthy, and out of patience.

"I did." Her tone became defensive. "I agreed to *share* mine with her. But she wanted me to keep the lid off. She likes them stale; I don't. And they were my Red Vines—"

"Who cares? She's *nine*. It's just cheap candy. You're the adult. C'mon, you know how much soft Red Vines set her off."

"What is the Guggenheim?" she said in answer to the television screen, then gave a celebratory fist-pump when Alex Trebek confirmed her answer as correct and the contestant's response as incorrect.

"Azda, memorizing the answers to rerun *Jeopardy* shows doesn't count. It's not the same as guessing it right the first time."

She huffed. "Says who?"

"Common sense and Alex Trebek, for starters."

"Bah," she shooed a dismissive hand at me. "I am a *Jeopardy* champion."

"We can't afford to keep destroying every house we rent. Aside from the cost, we risk drawing attention."

Her milky eyes cut to me. "The darkness grows in that child, Avery. Avoiding parenting her isn't going to stop it."

"Avoiding—" My mouth fell open. "Do you have any idea what I go through in any given day just to keep her safe?"

"Sloane cannot get her way in everything. Your job is to shepherd her, not simply protect her."

"I'm trying, damnit!"

"I am blind, not deaf. You must try harder. It's like our ancestors say: when your fingers are frostbitten and your toenails have fallen off from herding, only then do your sheep belong to—"

"She's not a sheep," I said through clenched teeth. "She's a *child*. I don't need a sheep-herding analogy from you right now, okay? I've got superbeasts wielding crazy-scary powers coming to kill me. I need to shower, sleep, and plan. I don't have energy to debate sheep-herding or stale Red Vines with you tonight."

I stomped to the kitchen, snagged a beer from the

fridge, and guzzled half the bottle before returning and plopping down onto the ruined couch. Seven a.m. was as good a time as any for a beer, right?

Azda remained silent through the next several *Jeopardy* questions, even forgoing the daily double as her milky pupils stared unseeingly at the television screen, her rocking chair creaking against the wooden floor. She was half-blind from glaucoma and cataracts—which she refused to see a real doctor about. But she didn't miss much. It was one of the reasons I trusted her with Sloane.

I knew she was right. I just didn't know how to fix it— how to fix Sloane. *Or my relationship with her.*

Azda had been a close friend of my late paternal grandmother. She was the only link to my biological parentage that I had. The irony was that she'd come looking for me in order to fulfill some mysterious promise she said she'd made to my dying grandmother—a promise that Azda had never to this day revealed. She said it was because it didn't translate from the Navajo language to English in a way that I'd understand it.

When Sloane was almost two years old, Azda had come knocking on our door. *Literally*. Where supernatural rogue hunters had failed, an old, half-blind Navajo woman who'd lived on a reservation for most of her life, and who'd barely understood how to use the Internet or a phone at the time, had managed to locate us and show up on our doorstep. That alone had earned her props in my book.

Sloane had also tolerated Azda's presence from day one far better than she did anyone else's—almost better than she tolerated *my* presence at times. So I'd decided Azda's involvement in our lives might prove useful, particularly given the Navajo connection it afforded us. The ability to hide out on a reservation when necessary was a valuable perk of my heritage indeed.

The transportation logistics that had come with having a half-blind caregiver for my toddler had been tricky to navigate at first, but Azda and Sloane managed to get around by car on their own for the most part these days when they needed to. I'd found a guy to help me jerry-rig an autonomous Mercedes-Benz a few years ago so that Sloane was able to program it. Sloane and Azda had driven up from Arizona by themselves two days ago—and had consumed too many Red Vines on the way, apparently.

"I'm sorry," I said, breaking the silence between us. "I didn't mean to yell at you."

"Yes, you did."

"Maybe I did," I admitted with a dry chuckle. My eyes lifted from my beer to meet her milky pupils. "I just don't know what to do anymore. I don't know how to reach her."

"Dark and light energies exist all around us, Avery. Influences not of this world, and not of the next, call to each of us." She halted her rocking chair. Abruptly, her eyes flicked back to the television screen, and she answered, "What is Istanbul?" before continuing. "But for Sloane, the dark energy lives inside of her. It breathes every breath with her. It speaks to her constantly. You are her mother. You must speak louder than the darkness, or you will lose her forever."

I nodded and pushed up off the couch as Alex Trebek recaptured Azda's attention.

The truth was I barely knew how to nurture the light within myself, much less foster it in another person. That was the problem. I was good for punching darkness in the face with more darkness—that was my greatest talent.

I'd been a fool to think that the three years of decent parenting I'd received from my eighth foster mom could prepare me to be a mother myself.

I found Sloane in her new room, sitting atop the bed. I noted that the little Disney suitcase I'd gotten her for her ninth birthday last month was laying open on the floor by the dresser, but she hadn't unpacked anything yet. She was probably wondering how long we'd really be here. She'd been living on the run and out of suitcases for most of her short life.

She was talking to herself. Only she wasn't speaking; it was more like humming. And not a tune, either. She would often vocalize hum-like sounds and moans in varying inflections for hours, nodding her head and responding with facial expressions as if she were having an internal back-and-forth dialogue—or perhaps multiple conversations. Her eyes often remained blank as she did this, drifting listlessly or staring into space.

Sometimes she'd unexpectedly burst into tears. Other times, she'd start screaming for seemingly no reason at all. Most recently, she'd started setting things around her on fire. *With her mind.*

She never allowed me or anyone else to comfort her when she cried. She didn't want anyone to touch her when she started screaming either, but the contact was often necessary in order to physically silence her—particularly when she awoke screaming from one of her recurring nightmares.

I feared she'd somehow developed this new ability to telekinetically set fires in an effort to create even more distance between herself and the few people she was forced to be in contact with.

I'd held her near constantly as an infant. Nursed her for almost a year until one day she'd stopped—refusing to latch on or take any interest anymore. It had seemed abrupt to me at the time, but I knew babies were supposed to wean when they were ready, and mothers were supposed to take cues from their babies, so I did.

That was the beginning. The void between us had continued to grow ever since, morphing into an abyss the breadth of an ocean.

She stopped hum-talking to herself, and her amethyst eyes settled on me in the doorway, taking in my bedraggled appearance and bloodstained clothing with a quiet apathy that belied her youthful innocence.

At nine, my daughter had the makings of a great beauty already—with her midnight black hair, olive complexion, high cheekbones, stubborn chin, and regal, upturned nose. But it was those eyes—the unusual hue of those strangely vacant yet all-seeing eyes—that had always caused people to take notice, to stop and stare.

"I was hoping you wouldn't come back this time, Avery."

Her words were spoken without malice or scorn—without any emotion at all. I didn't think she said them to be hurtful. She said them every single time I returned home as if simply confessing a fact.

And even though I was prepared, it somehow gutted me just the same.

Every time.

She'd stopped calling me mom at age three, when she realized that Avery was what everyone else called me. It bothered me a little, although I tried not to let it. I rationalized that it was better to be called by my given name than something rude and random—like what Sloane had recently begun calling Azda.

"Well, of course I came back," I said with a practiced smile. "Moms always come home."

"If you were smarter, you wouldn't," she told me, her expression frank. She really believed it.

That was the toughest part to reconcile. That and the fact that she spoke like a twenty-year-old already at times. Still, I attempted to respond to her as if she were a preteen— as if I didn't realize her IQ was already higher than mine.

I shrugged and teased, "Maybe I live to disappoint you. I hear that's what moms are for."

"You won't live much longer if you keep coming back." She tilted her head in indication of my bloodstained clothing as I fought the lump forming in my throat, knowing what she was going to say next.

I nodded mechanically as I tried to emotionally prepare myself. I had yet to manage a good response to this line of conversation we'd been repeating lately.

"You're going to die when they come for me," she announced. There was no emotion in her violet eyes as she said it. There never was. "I've seen it. It happens that way in every dream." She was simply reciting the facts, as she knew them. "You always die. I can never stop it."

I nodded. The tears slid down my cheeks as she stared stoically back at me. It was the statement of fact that she spoke at the end that always made me cry: *I can never stop it.*

She said it with zero emotion, yet the meaning was there: *In her dreams, she had tried to stop me from dying.* More than once. Perhaps in every dream.

My daughter didn't want me dead. For a little girl prophesied to be the ultimate *Rogue,* it was as strong of a profession of love as I could ever expect to get. It filled me with hope. Hope that Sloane *could connect.* That she *could love.* Maybe in a way that would always be different than what the world wanted from her, but it still counted.

It fucking counted. And I would make the world see that it did.

"I wasn't supposed to be born. I was a mistake." More statements of fact.

"No." I shook my head, wiping my tears away. "No, it wasn't a mistake, Sloane." I forced an easy, gentle smile as I took a few steps into the room, careful not to come too close. Getting too close to her physically too quickly often set her off. "I wanted you to be born. And your … soul … wanted to come here," I faltered. I'd never been religious, and I still struggled with the concept of souls, even though I'd felt firsthand the part of me that had survived death. "So we could be here together on earth … and have fun … adventures together."

She gave me a dubious look that called bullshit. I couldn't blame her. We didn't really have a lot of fun. Hiding and running for your life all the time got tiresome fast.

"I can't have fun, Avery. I can only do bad things. The voices know. If you could hear them, you'd know, too."

"What!" I laughingly shrieked, while inside, her words eviscerated me. "Are you kidding me? You were born to have fun! My mission in life is to have fun. It's impossible for my daughter not to be fun, too."

"You don't know that. You just like to believe it. You and the old blind spot like to pretend you see good in me so you can sleep better."

I took another step closer, reminding myself that I needed to ask her at some point why she'd started calling Azda "the old blind spot."

"Look, Sloane, I did some … not-so-nice things as a kid. Most of the adults around me all thought I was … well, pretty much evil, and that I was destined to only do bad things in the world. I heard them tell me so for years, and their voices stayed in my memory, playing in my head long after those adults were no longer around. But they were wrong."

"I was supposed to die," she continued as if she hadn't heard me, her eyes drifting to a corner of the room. "I was supposed to take the voices with me and stay dead. It was a mistake when I was born."

How I despised those voices in her head. I wished I could strangle every one of them. "It wasn't a mistake, Sloane. I was there. I wanted you to be born. You're the best thing that ever happened to me."

It was the truth. Sloane was my greatest love and life purpose. If I had a soul mate, she was it for me. More so than Marcus had ever been. I hadn't realized it until my death—when I'd experienced how easily I'd been able to separate from Marcus. I'd loved my fiancé very much. He and I had shared a strong connection, but it wasn't the same. It wasn't enough to hold me to him in death. I'd had a stronger bond with my best friend, Sloane, and even that hadn't been enough to keep me from my baby, Sloane.

She was my reason for being. I had come back to life for her. And I would never give up on her.

"That's what you have to say." She shrugged at the empty corner of the room as she dismissed my words. "You won't think I'm the best thing that happened to you when you're killed because of me."

"Yes. I will, baby. I'll still think it." I knelt on the floor by the edge of her bed, trying to catch her line of sight. "*If* it happens that I have to leave you because I leave this world, you'll still be worth every moment I've gotten to spend with you. You'll always be the best thing that ever happened to me."

She didn't make eye contact with me, and she began hum-talking to herself once more. I stayed and watched her for a while. Watched as she became more engrossed in her strange, internal discussion, as she shut the world around her out until her entire focus was inward—on the darkness that lived and breathed inside of her.

Unlike the rest of the supernatural world, I refused to accept that it was an indomitable darkness borne of magic or prophecy. Although, sometimes I felt that might've been easier for me to face.

My greater fear was that this was a darkness I already knew. One I had seen and faced ... and lost to before.

"Peter has always reminded me of my most delicate garden flowers."

I snorted, eyeing the old bat's grandson with disdain where he sat on the swing set all the way on the opposite side of the yard—too scared to come near me. His head hung low, and his long, auburn bangs blew across his face, partially concealing it. I could still make out the black eye I'd given him the day before, though, and I couldn't help but smile a little.

Poor kid. He was already weak enough. The last thing he needed was a grandma who compared him to a fucking flower. He probably got his ass beat daily at school. I would find out soon enough when I started going with him in a few days.

"Do you know why I picked you, Averhilda?"

I was about to say the extra cash from the state that I knew foster parents got, but instead, I went with, "Don't really care." I gave her my best bored, "fuck off" face that got me slapped by most adults. When she didn't hit me, I sassed, "My name's Avery. Remember it if you want me to answer."

She smiled and nodded. "Okay. Avery, then." Her white hair was streaked with dirt. She even had dirt smudged on her face.

I missed the smell of the city already.

"I chose you because you are not a flower," she told me.

Oh, boy. I had a live one here.

"Flowers are beautiful, but fragile," she continued to ramble. "They can be temperamental. Their existence fleeting." Her eyes crinkled at the corners despite her smile as they darted a glance at her loser grandson. "You remind me of a lovely, stalwart garden weed, Avery. The kind of weed that grows strong and proud despite less than favorable soil conditions."

I rolled my eyes as she bent to pat more dirt around whatever she was planting. I decided I'd hit her grandson every chance I got until she sent me back. Anything was better than hanging out in Bumfuck with a gardening old lady and a boy too slow to block a punch.

"A weed that can survive even when it's starved of light and water. A weed that has managed to thrive even though it has received no love at all." She paused in her dirt patting to look up at me. She smiled and bit her wobbly old lip, looking as if she might cry. "Because your power is sourced from within, child."

Aw, crap. "Gardens suck," I interjected. Lame comeback, Avery. Her weird, emotionally charged gardening lecture was making me uncomfortable, though, giving me this terrible hollow feeling in my chest.

She laughed like I'd said something hysterical. "Hellfire, Avery, gardens are life. And the weed is the hardiest, most enduring plant in any garden." She looked around her ugly garden full of random weeds and flowers and dying tomato plants like it was some kind of paradise to take pride in, before returning her gaze to me.

"We live in a world filled with delicate flowers. It's a rare gift to be born a weed. Be glad of it. You were meant to rule the garden, dear. You may choose to be a weed who overpowers and strangles the delicate flowers around her, or you may choose to protect them." Her eyes cut to Peter. "Maybe even teach them to be stronger flowers."

Now we were getting somewhere. The awful hollow feeling in my chest fell away the minute I knew the score. Gardener Granny was speaking my language now.

"You want me to keep other kids from bullying Peter," I concluded. "Because he's a weak flower who gets beat up by weeds like me." Why hadn't she just said that?

Her brow wrinkled and she nodded. "That's right, Avery." The sad yet hopeful look in her blue eyes suddenly made me feel powerful. Less than forty-eight hours in and already I owned these country hicks.

The old lady could think me a weed if she wanted to. A scrapper was what I was. Some had used the term "hustler" before. There was no great mystery to how the world worked. You figured out what people were after and then figured out how to give it to them in exchange for what you wanted. It was that simple. And I was good at it.

I looked over at pathetic Peter, then at his pathetic grandma. "Yeah, I guess I can do that," I told her with a shrug. "But it's gonna cost you."

She nodded and bit her lip again, only this time it looked like she was trying to hold back laughter rather than tears. "Okay." She held her soil-coated hand out for me to shake. "Let's cut a deal then."

I took her bony, wrinkly white hand and gave it a firm shake, our palms mashing the soil between them.

The deal I struck with Grandma Ellie at age eleven was a momentous turning point in my childhood. Being placed with Ellie resulted in one of the most important shifts of my life. My happiest childhood memories were of the three years I spent befriending Peter while living at Ellie's home.

I protected Peter from bullying kids at school. And I grew to love him like he was my own brother. But he remained a delicate flower. Try as I might, I never managed to strengthen him. Not while Ellie was alive, and not after her death that would thrust us both back into the state's care.

I pressed the heels of my palms to my eyes as the warm shower spray rained down on me, blocking the memories of the years that followed Ellie's death from my mind as I washed away the sins of my day.

Sloane wasn't Peter. She never would be. No matter

how much she spoke of death, she didn't mean it. She didn't understand what she was saying.

My daughter was a stalwart weed. Like me.

She was destined to grow and thrive and weather any storm. I'd known it from the moment our souls connected: *She was a weed like me.* I wouldn't accept otherwise.

Weeds didn't give up. Weeds clung to life even when the delicate flowers around them they loved most withered and died.

Peter wasn't the first or last fragile soul to enter and leave my life. But he remained my deepest loss and greatest regret.

There had been times when I'd hated him for being weak. Resented how easy it had seemed for him to give up. *To leave me behind.*

But that would always be the hardest part about being a weed: Seeing the fragile flowers around you give up and fade away. Not understanding why they were made that way—why they couldn't seem to change. Watching the inevitable, dark storms brewing within them and not being able to stop it.

Knowing you'd always be the one left behind, because it was written in your DNA to survive.

CHAPTER 13

Avery

THE LANDSCAPE OF DENVER HAD SURE CHANGED OVER the past decade. Between the expansion of the light-rail and the birth of the aerotropolis, the city was swarming with aging, entitled hipsters. And they all seemed to have congregated in uber-gentrified LoDo on this Monday night, filing out of their boozy art and guitar classes to hit the shittiest formerly-condemned-brick-building-turned-cool-urbanspoon-nightspot that they could find.

Ironically, they made for a convenient addition to the trendy shithole setting in which my former werewolf pack was supposed to be convening with my easy-target Reinoso informant.

As embarrassing as it was to admit it, I was able to blend in with the hipster crowd fairly well. I was a cute, hip, indistinguishable ethnic girl whose appearance fell within what I liked to think of as that "safe" mix of nebulous races that urban white people felt cooler just for being seen with.

With my slouchy beanie firmly in place, I launched into a debate about the restrictiveness of teaching music theory amid the upsurge of creative autonomy in the modern music scene. Within two minutes, I was able to blend into the background of the hipster group at the bar as they ran with the debate, while I covertly kept an eye on the seven members of the Highlands Ranch pack sitting at a table in the corner. They were awaiting their Reinoso pack guest, I presumed.

Several of the pack members I recognized from the brief time I'd spent with them prior to burning their community to the ground—like the one who'd always had bad breath even though as a werewolf his temperature ran high enough that it should've killed the offending bacteria in his mouth.

I shuddered internally in remembrance of my time with those idiots. It truly was a blessing that I hadn't felt the need to belong to a pack for very long. And luckily, those idiots had known me when I was pregnant—before I'd lost my scent. Without a werewolf scent to tip them off, I was banking on them simply dismissing me as another clueless human who had come to hang out in the dimly lit, former-eighteen-hundreds-era-brothel-turned-bar tonight. They were too self-absorbed to look very closely anyway.

Twenty minutes of nauseating urbanite conversation went by while I nursed my shitty craft whiskey with the cutesy label. I was beginning to think the Reinoso informant wouldn't show, when suddenly, the next time I glanced over, a tall, sexy, dark-haired wolfman was standing by the corner table, shaking hands with none other than the bad-breathed redneck.

He must've come in through the back, because he sure as hell hadn't walked in through the street entrance. I would've noticed him. He was standing in profile to me, and damn if he didn't look good. From his fine, jean-clad ass to the dark scruff covering his jaw, he was basically edible.

It appeared he'd come alone tonight. Which made him a stupid hottie, but a hottie, nonetheless. From what I could view of his face in profile, he definitely resembled the werewolf in the photo that Wyatt had shown me. He ordered a beer and sat down at the table with my former pack. His face was still partially obscured to me.

I watched.

And waited.

It was difficult to hear very much of what was being said over at the table. Not with the hipsters now vying for my attention as they squawked ignorant platitudes at me about the contributions of Native American culture. After the music theory debate had settled down, I'd started one on the plight of the Navajo Indian. In truth, I knew very little about my Navajo heritage, but that had never stopped me from capitalizing on my one-quarter Native American blood just to incite political debates about the Long Walk before.

Finally, after about a half hour of tense torment, the Reinoso informant got up from his seat. He stopped a busboy, and I heard him ask where the bathroom was. *Geez*, he hadn't even bothered to learn the layout of the place before coming to meet with these turkeys. Informant hottie was going to be an easy kill, indeed.

Fortunately for me, I *had* learned the weird layout of this renovated old brothel. So I knew that the men's bathroom was located downstairs—in a section of the bar that was reserved for live performances, and otherwise closed off on a Monday evening.

Luck was on my side tonight.

I waited until my werewolf target descended the stairs, and then I pretended to take a call on my phone, giving me the excuse I needed to leave the bar in order to find a quieter spot. Grabbing my backpack, I meandered down into the basement.

As I pressed my ear to the bathroom door to confirm that he was preoccupied, the door opened a fraction. *No way.* The fool hadn't even locked it?

I was doing him a favor then. He was too stupid to live. I went inside.

As soon as I drew my gun and flipped the bathroom lock into place, it hit me: his scent.

Exotic. Spicy. Clean as ocean air. Earthy and pure like mountains and pine. But … complex. Strangely alluring. Surprisingly appealing, in fact.

And old.

As. Dirt.

Old and *powerful.* I caught the now-recognizable scent of magic on him—the same underlying scent I'd picked up on Raul—differentiating him from a normal werewolf and classifying him as a superbeast.

In an instant, I knew I'd been set up. My "easy" werewolf target was anything but. He was a *werelock.*

Wyatt would never betray me. Which meant that Wyatt had been set up to set me up. *Or his mind had been compromised by a powerful enemy werelock—as Raul had claimed.*

He looked enormous standing in the small space of the bathroom at the lone urinal. His back was to me, but the moment I'd entered and flipped the lock, his head had turned ever so slightly to the side, his nose tilted in the air to sniff out the intruder.

The fact that he wouldn't be able to scent me could possibly buy me a few seconds of additional time—if he was the curious type. Or it might get me killed faster. Because despite the fact he couldn't smell *me*, I knew he would definitely smell the weapon in my hand.

Still, I hesitated, my composure shaken by the shock of his scent, of the perfect male beauty of his sculpted, naked ass cheeks on display—and the knowledge that I was fucked.

It was too late for retreat. I'd never make it out the door and back up the stairs if this guy was capable of the things I'd witnessed Raul do.

And if he was anything like Raul, no amount of bullets would stop him anyway.

As I watched, his body visibly stiffened.

Shit.

I aimed my gun, yet remained otherwise frozen as he inhaled a second time—his upper back expanding, his shoulders rising as his lungs filled with air.

Pull the trigger, Avery.

Now.

Do it.

I'd never had any qualms before about shooting a target in the back when his pants were down. I wasn't big on heroism or sportsmanship; I stuck to ease and efficiency. But something was stopping me now. Something in his scent felt too … right … to be ended.

And some foolish part of me wanted to see his face. I told myself it was to confirm that he was the one from the photo, to make sure I had the right target.

Slowly, he turned.

Damn.

He was gorgeous.

His hazel eyes burned bright gold as they took me in—brazenly looking me up and down, his jaw agape.

The gun grew heavy in my hand. I felt my own eyes shifting to that of my wolf as they traveled from chiseled, ruggedly handsome, seemingly awestruck facial features, down a thick neck that caused my canines to extend and salivate, over a T-shirt-encased chest and abdomen that my hardening nipples were demanding to rub up against.

Fuck.

My inner bitch hadn't been this excited by a male since …

Ever.

My captivated wolf eyes wandered over beautiful, tanned skin covering densely corded arm muscles, down to a well-formed, huge hand that held … an even huger dick.

That was lengthening and expanding before my eyes.

My mouth watered. I could've sworn my vaginal muscles actually jumped.

Mine.

My inner bitch's excitement was suddenly overwhelming. I had a mad urge to drop my gun and leap right on him.

But my daughter's life was at stake. So I forcibly shut my she-wolf down.

And I shot him instead.

The quiet plink sound of the brass casing hitting the tiled floor was horrifying on multiple levels. My wolf was horrified that I'd actually fired at our—*this*—man. And I was horrified that the bullet hadn't so much as scratched his skin.

I glanced down and noted his erection was even bigger than before.

Maybe Wyatt hadn't been set up to set me up. Maybe this guy was like the "Dopey" werelock of his pack, and that made him an easy target?

I fired again.

My she-wolf howled in protest. I pulled the trigger a third time.

I'd hit my target dead in the heart, as evidenced by the burnt hole I'd made in his shirt. But the man—super-beast—beneath was perfectly fine. He reached up and fingered the hole, his glowing eyes never leaving my face. He ceased gaping and an indulgent, lopsided grin stretched his luscious mouth.

Then he chuckled—a rich, masculine sound that caused pure feminine need to pool between my thighs.

He whipped his T-shirt over his head and tossed it aside.

Fuck, that chest.

Those abs!

I didn't even try not to look. I openly ogled him—my sex pulsing to life against the seam of my jeans.

He took a step toward me. A step that was made awkward by the fact that his jeans were around his ankles. He glanced down briefly, taking note of the issue. A second later, his pants were gone. *Vanished.*

Fuck. He was one hundred percent for sure a werelock.

A dead-sexy, one hundred percent naked werelock with a massive erection.

That curved.

The right way.

There was a predatory gleam in his eyes as he took

another step closer. But it was also playful. Scary. Yet fun—like he was daring me to do something.

Claim him, my she-wolf chanted.

Bite him.

Submit him.

I shook her aside. *Kill him*, I countered.

To my ever-loving shame, I actually bit my lip and winced the fourth time I pulled the trigger, aiming the barrel of my gun at his perfectly beautiful, flawless, naked chest. I had the worst sense that it had somehow hurt me more to pull that trigger than it had him.

I was right. This time, he groaned as the bullet bounced off of him and the casing clinked to the floor. It was a groan of pure pleasure. Of carnal lust.

"Fuuuck." His bass spoke directly to my nether lips. "You. Are perfection." His words caused my heart to flutter as they echoed softly off the tiled walls. The sound of his voice felt oddly familiar. Warm. Safe.

No.

Werelock, I reminded myself.

Not safe.

A cold sweat broke out over my skin. The gun had begun to shake in my hand. I steadied my arm and adjusted my aim. This was the craziest I'd felt since turning into a crazy *Grimm's Fairy Tale* creature a decade ago.

He kept talking, saying something about how beautiful I was and remarking on my mixed heritage. He may have asked a question, but I couldn't be certain with the way the blood was pounding in my ears now. My ancestry had always intrigued and stumped everyone.

He seemed so genuinely enthralled, his eyes moving over my face as if cataloguing every tiny detail. There was a dazed intensity to his gaze that was throwing me off kilter—making me feel sensations in places I shouldn't have, calling forth emotions that were foreign.

Conjuring feelings that were supposed to be dead.

"Stop." My mouth began to work. "Mistake." *And not very well.* "Wrong bathroom—I mean—bar ..."

What was I saying? *Why was I out of breath?*

He kept coming.

Why did he have to smell so damn good?

I swallowed. He was almost directly in front of me. And I was just standing there. Doing nothing. I felt my heart rate spike, and I caught the scent of my own fear—something I rarely gave off anymore.

Suddenly, he stopped. His head tilted and his nostrils flared. His Adam's apple bobbed in his throat. He frowned. His wolf eyes glowed a shade brighter.

Crap. He'd likely caught onto my nonexistent scent.

Another swift move and he'd placed himself at arm's length, allowing the silencer extending from the barrel of my gun to press against the impenetrable muscle of his chest, directly over his heart—as if the weapon wasn't in any way a threat.

It wasn't, I guess.

"I'd never hurt you." He spoke as if the very notion were anathema to him.

Huh?

He pressed himself closer, crowding me against the door and forcing my arm holding the gun to bend at the elbow and retract. *But not before I'd fired another bullet ... straight at his heart.*

As before, it did nothing to injure him. But his eyes widened and his frown deepened.

"Fuck. I'm sorry." Huge warm palms were suddenly framing my face. Heat washed over me at his touch, battling the cold fear that had me in its embarrassing grip.

What the—? Had he … apologized?

After I'd shot him?

He gently tipped my face up to his, his fingertips caressing my jawline in a manner that managed to feel at once familiar and reverent. It was as if he'd touched me like this a million times before. As if he cupped my face in his hands daily and still somehow it was the most important thing he did in any given day.

He leaned in, slanting his lower body away from me—his massive erection standing at attention between us. "I didn't mean to scare you."

Sure enough, his mouth was moving. He was speaking to me. Apologizing. *For scaring me.* Saying something about how he would never harm me. I had difficulty processing his words as the scent of his precum assailed me.

Mine.

I felt my backpack strap slip from my fingers. Vaguely, I registered the sound of it hitting tile floor below. The mad pounding in my ears was nearly deafening, but I could've sworn I heard him reassure me that he wasn't going to take my gun away as long as I kept it aimed at him.

"I'll have to take it from you if it looks like you might hurt yourself," he explained.

What?

Hurt myself?

His casual slight—the inference that I was ill-equipped to handle my own firearm—was enough to raise my human hackles, if not my she-wolf's, momentarily jarring me from the mesmerizing effect he was having on me.

"I'm a crack shot."

One corner of his mouth lifted at my proclamation, and the most annoyingly adorable twinkle lit his eyes. *Smiling eyes.* Great. He was one of *those.* The kind who managed to look like they were laughing at the world, seeing humor everywhere they went—delighting in some never-ending private witticism. The confident type who rejoiced uninhibitedly regardless of whether anyone else in the room got the joke. *Not our type,* I projected to my excited inner wolf.

"I believe it. You haven't missed me yet. But I'd feel better if you pointed the gun at my head," he told me with a wink.

An actual. Fucking. *Wink.*

I was so gobsmacked I didn't resist as one of his hands traveled from my face down to the wrist of my hand that held the gun between us and brought it up alongside his head.

"If I do anything you don't like, just shoot, all right?" He repositioned my aim so that the end of the silencer was pressing against his temple.

That settled it. He was for sure the Dopey of his pack.

"You make the funniest faces," he observed with a giddy, boyish chuckle. His hand returned to my face, his long fingers slipping into the hair behind my ear to rub away at my eroding common sense. I realized he'd removed my beanie at some point.

"Fuck, this is just like my dad said it'd be. But nothing like I ever imagined." He bit his smiling lip. "He would've liked you. My mom would've loved the fact that you shot me straight out of the gate."

I couldn't follow his crazy talk. Yet I felt an inexplicable tightness in my throat at his words. Maybe because he sounded so sincere. He even *smelled* sincere.

Or maybe it was because I couldn't remember when anyone had ever looked at me with quite so goofy-happy an expression. Certainly not at first sight, and not anyone who looked and smelled so good. The man was just so … incredibly … *fuckable.*

But not our type, I reminded my wolf.

"Have to get going," I mumbled, evidently at a loss for more intelligent speech. My voice came out breathy again, too. Not at all convincing.

He nodded. "'Course." His face inched closer. "Whatever you want." His tongue swept his bottom lip as his heavy-lidded gaze fell to my own lips.

My God. He was seriously going to fucking kiss me. *After I'd just shot five bullets into his chest.*

"May I?" he asked faintly as his mouth descended.

Slow and tentative as they first brushed back and forth, his full lips felt soft against mine. *Sweet.* It might've been the most innocent kiss anyone had ever given me. Definitely not what I had expected, given how turned on I knew he was.

Oh, hell. This was ridiculous.

I drew his lower lip into my mouth and bit it.

I swallowed his groan of surprise as my mouth attacked his, my tongue dipping inside to taste the powerful male essence that had been taunting me. *And fuck, was it heady stuff.*

When I sucked his tongue into my mouth, all bets were off. His lips became firm and demanding. His tongue assumed control, stroking deeply as his hands found my breasts … my ass … the juncture of my legs.

I reveled in his touch, pushing my breasts up against him, grinding my center into his palm when he cupped me between my thighs.

"May I?" he murmured thickly as his fingers made quick work of the clasp and fly of my jeans.

I didn't say no. Didn't protest. Not even when I felt his big hand wedge its way down the front of my jeans and slip inside my undies as he announced, "Need to touch you, okay?"

In fact, I was so far gone I think I nodded—even as I gripped the butt of my gun tighter and steadied the aim of the barrel pressed to his head.

CHAPTER 14

Alcaeus

S*HE WAS WET.*
Thank fate and all that was holy, my fingers found a dripping wet, hot heaven as they glided down between my mate's smooth lips. Oh, *fuuuck*.

Mine.

Slow, I ordered my wolf. *Gentle*, I told him.

Remember to ask her name soon, I reminded myself.

I focused on her panted breaths, on the sound of her heartbeat, and on the scent I'd waited my whole life to inhale.

My mate was a werewolf, not a werelock. This made her more fragile. I had to remember that—especially with a gun still in her hand. She also smelled quite young in were-wolf years. Young and confused. I wasn't sure if she understood the meaning of what had happened between us. She'd clearly felt something, though. She'd been startled enough to shoot me. Five times.

She was definitely into me. And absolutely adorable. Gorgeous. Dark and exotic—the most exquisite combination of beautiful races.

"Oh, God," she moaned as my thumb rolled over her slippery, swollen nub and my middle finger sank inside her.

My balls tightened painfully and my teeth raked down the side of her neck, even as I forced myself to go slow—slower than I sensed we both wanted. My dick jerked, leaking more precum. I'd never felt so desperate to bury myself inside a woman before.

Because this was no mere woman. She was *my* woman. *My mate.*

My mate who was rolling her hips into my hand, riding my thumb and finger with increasing abandon. I fed her another digit, murmuring words of nonsense and encouragement as her tight, wet sheath stretched to accommodate me, contracting and squeezing around my fingers. Fuck, she was perfection.

"This okay?" I checked again for good measure.

"Just get my jeans off already." Her free hand scratched down my flank to settle on my ass.

Jesus. I'd won the mating lottery. My composure unraveling, I withdrew my fingers and tugged so hard that I shredded her jeans and panties from her.

"Shit," she exclaimed, her gold-flecked brown eyes wide with alarm as she pulled her mouth from mine. "My jeans."

"I'll get you new ones."

Damn. She looked like she might be pissed.

To reassure her and recover the mood, I conjured jeans for her. Her eyes widened further before flying down to take inventory of the new pair of form-fitting jeans now hugging her luscious curves.

"See?" I said. "Nothing to worry about."

I wasted no time in shredding the second pair as her mouth attacked mine once more. But when I gripped the hem of her tank top, her heart rate spiked and she pulled away again.

"No." Her hand that'd been groping my ass cheek flew to my wrist. "Not the top."

I couldn't decipher the look of apprehension I glimpsed in her eyes. Maybe it was a favorite shirt? Possibly sentimental.

I nodded. "I'll be careful taking it off, okay? I won't rip it. Promise."

"No," she growled, her eyes glowing a defiant yellow that was so hot on her I almost blew my load right then. "It stays on."

I paused. Swallowed. I would find and kill whoever had made her feel self-conscious about her breasts. "I swear to you, your breasts are the most perfect breasts I've ever seen in my entire life. And I've lived a very long time."

Her dry laughter came out sounding like a mini choking fit. "You *know?* You *know* this without seeing them?"

"Yes. Everything about you is perfect."

She gave me a measuring look. "You're serious."

"'Course I am. I wouldn't lie to you."

Her brow furrowed and a lost, faraway expression eclipsed her features. She bit her lip and broke eye contact. "I—I have to go—"

"We'll keep the tank top on," I interjected, fisting her hair and reclaiming her mouth before she could continue with whatever train of thought had made her look so sad.

Half-naked was fine for now. We'd deal with her body image issues later, I assured my wolf. It was more important to appreciate the fact that she'd given us access to her lower half. Because *fuck*—that tight pussy.

That ass!

Wedging my knee between her naked, shapely limbs, I palmed her rear, pulling her into me so that she straddled my upper thigh.

High, tight, and more than generous in size, her ass was everything a man could ever hope for and more. It was the stuff of wet dreams. And I was going to worship it until the end of my days.

Starting now.

I could scarcely breathe just contemplating how gorgeous the view would be when I sank into her from behind. And then she began riding my thigh that she was straddling. Grinding her wet, hot box into me.

I needed inside of her. *Now.*

Slow, I reminded myself.

Name. I needed her name.

I broke our lip-lock. "I'm Alcaeus," I introduced. "Your name?"

There was little hope of me recovering any social finesse at this point. Fortunately, she didn't seem to mind.

"I need this"—her slim fingers wrapped around my dick, squeezing lightly—"inside me."

I groaned and nipped her jaw, nearly blacking out with the effort it took not to come all over her like a twelve-year-old boy.

With superhuman willpower, I made myself pull her hand away. I pushed my thigh higher into her, pressing her up against the door, and drew my head far enough back to look her in the eyes. "Name, sweetheart." I said it with authority this time—as much as I was capable of with my heart and my balls in her hand. "Tell me your name."

She leaned in and tongued my throat. "Mmm, put that big, veiny perfection inside me and I'll sing it."

Aw, shit. I always knew the ancestors favored me. They'd just done a poor job of showing it until now. But this extraordinary woman—this mate of mine—she more than made up for every perceived slight and bad turn of fate I'd ever been dealt in life.

"You're worth the crazy long wait. Don't want to rush it. Don't want to take advantage, honey." The words sounded witless falling from my mouth.

She must've thought so, too, because she giggled breathlessly—*the sweetest sound.* "Take advantage? I've got a gun pointed at your head, and I just told you to put your cock in me."

Fair point. "We're in a public bathroom," I reasoned, brushing my lips against hers—unable to resist the temptation any longer. "It's not good enough for your first time."

"It's not my first time."

It was hardly a surprise, but it was also something I didn't care to think too much about, let alone discuss with her.

"I need your name, honey."

"Okay," she acceded at last, her lips turning up in a shy smile. "It's A—*Cynthia.*"

Huh. That smelled … exactly like a lie.

While the notion of true mates lying to one another wasn't inconceivable, it was a prospect I'd never contemplated in my own mate-bond scenario.

"What?" Her forehead wrinkled as she looked at me, and I realized my own brow had furrowed.

"Nothing," I muttered. Then I shook my head. This was no way to start off a relationship. "It smelled like you lied to me just now," I told her truthfully.

Her jaw unhinged slightly. Her eyes were suddenly wary as she clarified, "It *sounded* like I lied to you?"

"Sure. Sounded like it, too. But mostly it *smelled* like you lied."

Her throat worked. Her frown deepened. "When you say *smelled*, do you mean … figuratively?"

"No. I mean *literally* it smelled like you lied to me." It came out harsher than I wanted it to, but I didn't like it that she seemed eager to hide things from me.

Apprehension filtered into her scent, compounding my frustration.

"Hey, there's nothing to be afraid of," I reassured her, cupping her cheek. "If you're not ready to tell me your name, that's okay." *For now.* "Just … don't lie, all right? It's a scent worse than your fear, and that's killing me already."

Her pupils narrowed, and she visibly paled before my eyes. Her head shook minutely from side to side. "You don't … can't … I'm not—"

"Whoa—easy, there, sweetheart." Damnit. The scent of her panic flooded the bathroom. Her pulse beat wildly in her neck. "It's okay; you have nothing to be afraid of. I'm your mate. I didn't mean to embarrass or upset you."

She kept shaking her head. "I'm already mated." The lie rolled off her lips far too easily. And smelled just as bad.

She was absolutely not mated. She didn't smell as if she'd been with a man in a very long time, in fact. It was a ridiculous bluff that further showcased how young and strangely unversed she was in the ways of her own species if she thought I would buy it.

Still, it called to my predator instinct to claim her— *now*—so that there'd never again be any doubt.

CHAPTER 15

Avery

I REALIZED IT WAS THE WRONG LIE TO TELL WHEN ANY shred of hazel that had been left in his irises succumbed to his wolf's bright golden hue. I'd been too flustered by his assertion that he could scent me to handle the mate bomb he'd laid on me next.

"I mean I *was* mated," I clarified quickly, when in one swift lunge, he'd hauled me up by my ass against the door and was fitting his hips between my spread thighs—positioning the head of his cock to enter me. "*Was*—" I gasped as he thrust forward, penetrating me halfway.

An inhuman sound escaped me as my inner bitch howled in ecstasy. *Oh, God, he was a tight fit.*

I was dripping wet, but it'd been so damn long.

Far, far too long.

I dug my stiletto-heeled ankle boots into his muscled ass, demanding more. With a grunt, he delivered, pushing into me until the base of his cock pressed against my clit.

For a moment, I saw stars. *The good kind.*

I felt him everywhere.

His forehead touched mine and our panted breaths

mingled as I reveled in the sensation of his thick mush-room head seated so deep inside, pulsing against my cervix; his hard, long shaft swelling and straining against my fluttering walls.

He squeezed my ass and ground his pelvis into me, and my body was primed for orgasm already.

"Oh, *yes*, please," I heard myself pant.

"*Mine*," he growled back.

My eyelids opened half-mast to see his inner wolf staring back at me. Something passed—*clicked*—into place between his inner animal and my own then: A silent communion that supplanted human thought and emotion. It was deeper than the recognition of ownership he'd claimed using human words. It was something far more tender. *Sweet*. My she-wolf was already convinced she knew his wolf, that he was trustworthy. She would've followed him anywhere.

I steadied my gun against his temple.

I knew enough about the werewolf concept of true mates to believe I'd never have one. Certainly, I had never wanted one. Werewolf mates were a two-for-one kill in my book. Being bonded with a stranger whose death would theoretically get me killed as well didn't top my bucket list.

No matter how right he felt inside me.

And boy, did he feel right. Dangerously, sinfully so. Like no man had ever felt before.

"*Always* mine," he rumbled, his low, throaty voice taking me closer to the edge.

We held eye contact as he began to rock into me, pulling out just a fraction at first. He looked as if it pained him to do it—as if it required all his focus and willpower to take small, measured strokes rather than drive into me with abandon and fuck me to completion the way my gripping channel was begging him to do.

Slick fluid rushed from my center to lubricate the thick organ penetrating me as he circled his hips and ground the root of his cock hard into my clit.

"Oh, fuck," I moaned. I dug my heels into his ass and tightened my thighs around his waist, arching my upper back against the door to gain the leverage I needed to take him deeper.

"That's it." His hard eyes were as hypnotic as his voice. "Open for me."

He looked less like the sweet, gentlemanly wolf who'd professed a moment ago not to want to rush things or take advantage, and every bit like a caveman on a mission to prove his mate-worthiness.

He was the first werewolf I'd ever been with. I wondered now why I'd waited so long.

Mesmerized, I began to raise and lower myself on his steel shaft, meeting his shallow, rolling thrusts with increasingly jerky, frantic motions.

His jaw tightened and his expression darkened the faster and more feverish my movements became as I worked myself on his length, grunting and panting unabashedly in my efforts.

Big hands groped and spread my ass cheeks. Exploring fingers gathered and distributed my wetness to places it didn't belong.

I could feel how tightly his balls were drawn up each time they rubbed against my slippery folds.

His words of encouragement became garbled, crass demands as he helped raise and lower me by my ass, telling me to fill my cunt and cream on his cock.

And I did.

I so did.

Swept up amid the insanity of an assassination tryst gone far awry, and in our connection that never should have been, I came like a wild thing—clawing at his shoulder as I jerked and writhed and mewled against him.

Fuck, it'd been too long. And my time as an outcast within werewolf society these past ten years had been too intense, apparently, because amid my orgasm an emotional response rushed forth from my wolf that I hadn't counted on.

An overwhelming sense of belonging—of finally finding safety and acceptance with my own kind—ripped a strangled cry from my throat before I could suppress it.

"It's okay. Everything's okay." He was kissing my face. His lips brushed the dampness from my eyes. "I've got you. You're okay now."

Oh, crap. I was crying?

He was still hard. Still rocking into me. But his strokes were slower, gentler, as he cooed words of comfort.

"I'm sorry you've felt alone for so long."

How the fuck—?

"You'll never be alone again. I promise."

Hellfire. I didn't need some big, bad, sexy werelock shoulder to cry on. I was just reacting to a really great fuck after an extended dry spell. Plus, all the stress I'd been under—*for a decade.*

But my wolf was eating his promises up like candy, and my body was climbing toward another release, my inner muscles bearing down on him with every stroke. One more orgasm and then I'd bail, I promised myself, as his mouth reclaimed mine, his tongue stroking a compelling, hedonistic rhythm that once again scuttled my common sense.

His movements, though gentle still, were becoming faster, his hands groping and gripping the flesh of my ass a little more urgently as he pulled me tightly against him, away from the wall, lifting and lowering me on his erection.

I felt every stiff ridge of muscle covering his lower abdomen and groin against my sensitized clit, stimulating me to the brink of unbearable pleasure.

It was too much.

He was too much.

He was too big and too powerful to be fucking me so gently. *So perfectly.* He was too much my mortal enemy to be treating me so sweetly—*after I'd tried to kill him.* Something had to be wrong. The whole scenario was starting to feel like a bizarre dream that I was bound to wake up from, but didn't want to.

"You feel so good," he groaned against my mouth. "Can't hold—*fuck ...*"

He fucked hard into me, releasing his load impossibly deep as my muscles clenched and I reached the precipice of my own explosion.

I'd felt men come inside of me before, but never like this. The sensation of him losing control, of feeling him convulse in orgasm deep within me was so ... authentic. It felt so raw and erotic and primal as his hot cum filled me.

And I lost it. Muttering senseless profanity, my eyes watered again with emotion from how good it felt to come with him coming inside of me. At the same time, my face momentarily heated with embarrassment and confusion at how profoundly I'd been moved by the whole experience—with a stranger who was my enemy.

Yet there was no room for those emotions as my ears rang, my canines extended, and I suddenly felt starved for something I couldn't define as an aching need for this man—superbeast—arose from someplace beyond myself … beyond my wolf. I felt possessed by some innate madness to hold this connection I felt to him forever.

The taste of skin on my tongue was followed by the taste of blood filling my mouth as my canines pierced flesh. Vaguely, it registered that I was biting him, and that I ought to stop.

But I didn't want to.

Beyond blood and flesh, a foreign taste pervaded my mouth. It felt like it came from my canines. The huge cock still jerking within me felt like it got harder the farther I sank my teeth, the muscled arms around me squeezed tighter, the big hands stroking me gripped and soothed everywhere they touched, and a deep voice egged me on and told me to bite deeper when I hesitated, telling me it was okay, this was the right thing to do.

But then another male voice interrupted my bliss, telling me to stop, shouting, *"Alcaeus, what the fuck are you doing?"*

CHAPTER 16

Alcaeus

"**Y**OU DO REALIZE WHAT A HYPOCRITE THIS MAKES YOU," Kai's aghast voice reverberated off the tiled walls as my perfect, beautiful mate startled in my arms and hastily withdrew her mouth from my neck, sending the single greatest moment of my life screeching to a disastrous halt.

Christ, did no one knock anymore?

Words failed me. I could only growl at my best friend as my wolf eyes promised murder.

"Throughout our four-hundred-year friendship, you've acted like *I* was the one afflicted with unhealthy fetishes," Kai's patronizing voice persisted, utterly obliterating the brief taste of heaven I'd basked in just seconds before as the scent of my mate's anxiety filled my nostrils and she scrambled to at once conceal her nudity and climb off of me.

I turned my back to Kai, partially blocking her from his view as I helped her off my painfully stiff cock. I conjured a towel for her to clean up with along with new jeans for her to wear and handed them to her once her heeled boots seemed steady on the floor. Then I conjured a new pair of jeans onto myself, followed by a T-shirt.

A dozen apologies and explanations formed on my tongue, but I was too afraid to speak—for fear of how angry my words might emerge. I needed to calm down. I didn't want to risk making her more distressed than she already was.

"And here I find you ... fornicating with a perfect stranger whose got her canines lodged dangerously deep in your trapezius and a useless gun to your idiot head. Interesting role-play fantasy, Al, I must say."

"What the fuck are you doing here?" I turned and raged at him.

"What am *I* doing here? Let's start with what *you're* doing here. We're supposed to be on a *mission*. You're supposed to be upstairs gathering information about the woman who survived a rogue attack. I've tolerated your endless cavorting for the past decade, turned a blind eye to your insatiable need for meaningless casual sex with random human partners in nightclubs, parked cars, and alleyways. But skipping out on a meeting—a meeting that you insisted I needn't attend—in order to play a kinky game of mate-bond Russian roulette in a basement bar bathroom with some she-werewolf you just met, is a little *too* irresponsible—even for you."

"*Not now,* Kai. I'm ordering you to leave. How did you get here anyway? I ordered you to stay at the hotel. Fuck, never mind; just go."

"Not leaving. Milena sent me."

"What?"

"Milena sensed heightened emotions from you and was worried. She called and asked me to find you and make sure you were okay—overriding your order." His slight smile was smug.

Milena could do that? Sense my emotions? She could override my orders to Kai? *Not great news.* I didn't have time to dwell on it, though. My mate's increasing sense of panic was my current most pressing priority. Her heartbeat had skyrocketed at Kai's mention of Milena sending him to find me. She smelled terribly upset now.

"Milena's not my girlfriend," I projected over my shoulder to reassure her, lest she mistake the situation or my intentions toward her. Kai had done enough damage already by making it sound as if I hooked up with random women in bathrooms every day. "Milena's my sister-in-law. She's just one of those worrying types," I rambled, willing her to scent the truth of my words.

"It's fine," she spoke up from behind me, her voice coming out high-pitched. Nervous. I caught the sound of her jeans zipping up. "Hey, we both got carried away. You don't need to explain anything. I had fun. But I gotta run now, too."

Damnit, she was embarrassed and trying to save face. I glared at my Beta. "Kai, get out of here. Now."

I sensed Alessandra trying to tap my mind to reach me. Jesus, everyone had the worst timing today. I blocked Lessa out.

"Oh, but I'm rather enjoying this," Kai replied, his harassed expression conveying otherwise as a phone vibrated in his pocket. As he fished it out to check it, I turned around to try and calm my mate's growing scent of alarm.

She was fully dressed—albeit looking a disheveled, shell-shocked wreck—and was just strapping on her backpack and adjusting her beanie with trembling fingers. I noticed she was wearing a bulky sweatshirt over her tank top that she hadn't been wearing before. I assumed she'd pulled it from her bag. I was a little disappointed to see her looking so covered up—hiding herself from me.

"I'm really sorry about this," I apologized. "Kai's my Beta. He's also our pack doctor and interminably celibate, so there's no need to be embarrassed about anything he saw. He's not normally this much of an ass. Please don't go, all right? We need to talk." I wasn't about to let her out of my sight. But it was best to phrase it as a request.

"Lessa just texted me," Kai announced to my back, grating on my last nerve. "Have you seen Al?" he read aloud, his speech stilted. "He's blocking me. Is he back from his meeting yet?"

"Tell her I'm busy," I growled over my shoulder. "I'll call her later."

My chest clenched painfully as I watched my mate's gorgeous face go ashen at the mention of yet another woman looking for me. "Lessa's my sister," I quickly explained, forcing my voice to be far gentler than I felt, given my pressing desire to strangle the life from Kai. But my explanation about Lessa only seemed to spike the scent of her panic further.

"It's all good," she said as she gave me a shaky, phony smile. Her heart was racing, her chest heaving up and down like she was struggling for air. "Have to go. My friends are upstairs. Waiting at the bar for me."

She looked so small and fragile. I wanted to wrap her up in my arms and never let go. Her hand reached for the lock on the door. I stopped it, capturing it in my own. "I can't let you go, sweetheart."

"Finally, a shred of common sense prevails. I was waiting to make sure you wouldn't forget to erase her mind of this encounter."

Her eyes widened at Kai's words. I was a breath away from ripping his limbs off.

"Hey, hey—it's okay." I cupped her face in my hand. "He's only joking," I told her, and hoped that I'd adequately masked the scent of that lie. "You're completely safe with me. And that safety extends to my pack. I promise." I raised her hand in mine to my mouth and kissed it.

"Guess I spoke too soon," Kai muttered to himself in that droll tone of his from behind me. "They're waiting upstairs, Al. Just go. I'll handle this."

"You'll handle nothing to do with her." I pulled my mate into my side and turned around to find Kai staring at her with a strangely puzzled expression.

"You put a shield on her?"

"What?"

"Her mind's blocked, Al."

"How—*wait*, what are you doing? Stay out of her head!"

"Al, are you listening? I can't access it. Did you cast a shield? That's a really good one. It doesn't even feel like a shield. How'd you do that?"

"What? *No.* No, I haven't touched her mind."

"Well, someone's blocked it." Kai's eyes on my mate were accusing. "If it wasn't you, then we may have a more serious problem on our hands."

"Don't look at my mate like that."

"Your mate?" His brow rose in disbelief.

I saw red as he eyed my mate up and down like she was something foul. "You don't want to cross this line with me," I warned him.

"You can't be serious. Did you hear what I said? She could be a Salvatella spy for all we know. Role-play time is over."

"She's not a Salvatella spy."

He crossed his arms over his chest. "Try entering her mind and then tell me that."

"I'll do no such thing."

"Then I'm calling Milena."

"You are not calling Mi—"

"Hey, listen," my mate interrupted. "I don't understand what's happening here, but I'm not interested in getting on a call with anyone's girlfriend or wife or … whoever this Milena is—"

"She's not my girlfriend, I swear," I assured her, squeezing her hand in mine. The mention of Milena's name had sent my mate's pulse and panicked scent into overdrive again. Fuck, we were scaring the hell out of her.

"I need to get back to my friends upstairs before they start to worry about me," she reiterated.

"Just humor me, Al," Kai persisted.

"We just met!" I snarled at him. "It's too soon."

"But I thought you two were already mated?" he snarked.

Goddamnit. He wasn't going to drop it.

I turned to my mate. "I apologize for this, but I need to take a quick look around your mind to prove to my Beta that you're not a spy sent by one of our enemies. It won't hurt you, I promise, and I won't read any of your private thoughts. I'll just be in and out. You won't even know that it happened."

She shook her head; her brow creased. "I don't understand."

I stared into her big, brown doe eyes and felt sick over what I was about to do. It occurred to me that she may not have encountered any werelocks prior to me, so she might not be aware of our abilities. *God, I hoped she hadn't met any werelock before me.* The idea of anyone traipsing around in her mind or influencing her thoughts and emotions made me want to commit murder.

"I know you're a young wolf, so you may not have heard of our kind before, but Kai and I … we're part of a werewolf subspecies. We're known as werelocks. Do you know what that is?"

She bit her lip. "Um … I don't think so."

Damn. That smelled like another lie she'd just told me. What the hell?

"Why are you explaining this to her just so you can then erase it?" Kai asked.

I unleashed a growl in his direction. "I'm not erasing anything! I'm satisfying your Salvatella spy curiosity. Shut up or get out of here." I turned my most apologetic eyes on my mate. It was best to just get it over with. "I'm really sorry about this. You feel unconditionally safe with me, sweetheart. Okay?" As I said it, I sought entry to her mind.

And failed.

Not because I sensed a shield, either. It was because there was simply no point of entry. It wasn't blocked off by magic—it just didn't exist.

"See what I mean?" Kai said, accurately reading the confusion that I was sure was written on my face. "That's one powerful shield she's got up."

Meanwhile, my mate was regarding me as if I were nuts. Her eyes flicked back and forth between Kai and me. "Are you guys trying to … Jedi mind trick me or something? Because it's not working."

"*No.*" I shook my head in denial and said with an awkward laugh, "Of course not."

"This is getting creepy," she added, her nose crinkling. "I'm just gonna go back upstairs now."

I gripped her by the elbow when she tried to turn toward the door. "I can explain—"

"What in all that's holy …" Kai murmured, before blurting a frantic, "She's got no scent. Where the hell did you find this one?"

"Kai, just get out of here," I snapped at him. "Go and meet with the pack upstairs."

"I didn't notice it before," he continued, ignoring my order as he eyed my mate with renewed revulsion, "because she's got your scent all over her at present, partially masking it. But she has no underlying scent of her own. *None at all.*"

"Quit scaring her. Can't you hear and smell what your ridiculous accusations are doing to her?"

"Hear, yes. *Smell*—no. Not a bit. That's the fucking problem," he said, his voice raised in anger. "Because she has *no scent.* This is serious, Al. When—*how* did you meet her tonight?"

"Are you insane?" I got in his face. "No scent? She's the best damn thing I've ever scented before. Better than anything in the entire world. She smells like perfection. How can you *not* scent her?"

"If perfection smells like nothing at all, then yes, she's nailed it. Brilliantly."

"Nothing?" I balked. "Kai, she smells like wildflowers. And like fresh, damp earth after a rainstorm when the sun comes out."

"Petrichor?" Kai confirmed with a dubious shake of his head, chuckling drily to himself. "You think you scent *petrichor* on her?"

"*Yes.* And she smells like hardship, struggle, and triumph. Like dignity and rebirth. Like passion, courage, and persistence. And unrelenting tenacity."

I heard her heart skip a beat and then speed up. When I turned my gaze back to my mate, she was staring at me with an unreadable expression. *Well, not completely unreadable.* The scent of her body's arousal—the fierce yearning emanating from her—brought every carnal thought I'd been trying to suppress since Kai interrupted us rushing back to the surface.

I inhaled deeply, relishing the scent of her slick, ready sex. My eyes shifted; my blood rushed south. And I felt a foreign, pulsing ache at the juncture of my neck—where she'd bitten me.

Huh. I reached up, pulled my T-shirt collar aside, and fingered the spot. Holy shit. The bite was tender, and the skin still felt broken where she'd bitten me.

She'd left a mark!

CHAPTER 17

Avery

ALCAEUS'S EYEBROWS SHOT TO HIS HAIRLINE. "You marked me."

His words hit me like a bucket of ice water, instantly clearing my head and checking my runaway heart.

Lust, I corrected myself. This was only lust. My heart had nothing to do with this.

Even if he thought I smelled of petrichor. Even if he truly could scent the strife and triumphs that had made up my life.

I knew that marking another werewolf meant serious business. But I didn't know exactly how it worked. I'd never bitten anyone in a fit of lust before. *Obviously.* I hadn't had any fits of lust since gaining the teeth to bite someone, until now.

There was no way my teeth could've done damage to a werelock where bullets had failed.

His annoying killjoy Beta, Kai, was swearing and freaking out even more now, as he pushed forward to inspect the spot that Alcaeus was palpating.

Kai struck me as the quintessential

brooding Heathcliff type who probably would've tattooed his brand of damage across his fat forehead if only his rapid healing capabilities would've allowed the ink to take. He had dark hair and brown eyes, but his complexion was fairer than Alcaeus's was. He looked more European than Brazilian. If not for the iron poker rod jammed up his ass, he might've been a hottie.

I backed up out of the way—pressing closer to the door.

"By God, it's the real deal," Alcaeus professed, staring at me with a look of wonderment. "She marked me."

It didn't escape me that he genuinely sounded—and smelled—wildly, inexplicably thrilled about it. Which only freaked me out more. Because he wasn't just a powerful werelock and member of the Reinoso pack—he *was* a Reinoso! He'd said that Lessa was his sister, and that Milena was his sister-in-law. He was Alex Reinoso's brother, for fuck's sake. *And I'd just shagged and bitten him in a bar bathroom.*

"Move your hand and let me see it," Kai complained.

"Wait, I wanna see it first," Alcaeus said, moving to the mirror to get a look. Kai followed after him, hovering to get a look as well.

This was my chance.

I spun around and quickly unlocked and yanked the door open, only to look up and find none other than my former pack mate, Chuck—the bad-breathed redneck werewolf—standing on the other side, his knuckles raised in the air as if he'd been on the verge of knocking.

Shit. Could my luck get any worse right now?

His eyes widened in recognition. "You!" His breath hit my face, confirming that his bizarre supernatural halitosis affliction hadn't improved one bit over the years.

Then his eyes traveled above my head, looking past me into the bathroom. "This is her, Alcaeus! This is *Blythe Delacroix,* the abomination we told you about," he declared, giving me away and reminding me that "Cynthia Pressley Blackwood" was hardly the first ridiculous boarding-school-bitch name that Wyatt had ever given me.

There was no time to lie my way out of this—not with two werelocks at my back and six other werewolves upstairs who wanted me dead.

I'd taken the liberty of strapping my gun and a switchblade to my midsection and concealing them under an oversized sweatshirt when Alcaeus's back had been turned to afford me privacy before. I drew the switchblade and threw it straight down into Bad Breath Redneck's right foot as hard and as fast as I could.

When he yelped and immediately pitched forward and down into the open doorway in reaction—rushing to pull the knife from his foot—I wedged my body sideways through the small space between his bent form and the doorframe, grabbed hold of him by his belt where it was looped through the back of his jeans, and hurled him the rest of the way through the doorway and into the bathroom as I scooted out of it—sending his bulky body toppling headfirst into Alcaeus and Kai as they made to follow after me.

I bolted up the stairs.

As I reached the top, I came face to face with yet another former Highlands Ranch pack mate. *Ugh.* This one I shot twice in the leg at point-blank range before shoving him down the stairs—once again, into Alcaeus and Kai, who were bounding up after me.

"Cynthia, wait!" Alcaeus called.

I ran.

I made it to the front door and was just about to push through it, when I was yanked backward—by my stupid backpack.

Damnit, this was why I normally wore a backpack in the front. A backpack became a point of vulnerability when worn in the back, where anyone could easily grab hold and leverage it against you.

Before my arms could squirm their way out of the confines of my bag's shoulder straps, someone knocked my beanie off and grabbed a fistful of my hair. Two hulking male bodies crowded behind me on either side, each grabbing and twisting one of my arms behind my back as they lifted my feet off the ground and hauled me out the front door with my legs kicking in protest.

"Been a long time, Blythe," the nasty voice of Clifton, the Highlands Ranch pack Alpha, said, as he and his Beta, Zeke, quickly carted me down the empty sidewalk and straight into the alley.

"You're making a huge mistake," I told them. "My name's Cynthia."

I suspected that fib might've gone over a bit better if they hadn't just seen me shoot their pack-mate Barry and toss him down a flight of stairs. But that didn't stop me from continuing.

"The big werelock in there is my mate." Damn, where had that lie sprung from?

Too late to turn back now. Probably be more convincing if I called my "mate" by his name, only I wasn't sure if I could pronounce it right. I recalled Wyatt's advice of *'Al' plus 'chaos'* and went for it.

"If you do anything to me, my mate, *Al-chaos*, will kill you," I bluffed.

"Ha!" Zeke mocked. "Right. Well, that's convenient, because he and his friend were very interested in hearing about how you managed to survive a rogue attack as well as your werewolf transformation. I'll enjoy hearing you howl for this 'mate' of yours to save you when we skin your wolf alive. We'll be sure to offer him a front-row seat."

Clifton snorted. "Mated to a werelock. Named *Cynthia*, my ass. It's gonna be standing room only at this bitch's execution."

They were dragging me toward the back parking lot. The good news was I knew they wanted to take me back to their pack and kill me in some grand ceremonial display. They were too dumb to know that ease and efficiency won out every time and that they should always kill an enemy immediately, while they had the chance.

That point was proven a moment later when Zeke and Clifton's meaty paws were ripped from my person and their bodies were sent flying into the side of the old brick building that we'd emerged from.

"Her name *is Cynthia*, and she's my mate."

As I was released, my feet hit the ground, and I stumble-stepped, my body pitching to the side. But Alcaeus's arms came around me a second later, righting me on my feet. Then he did that move again where he cupped my face in his hands like it was totally natural—while being the highlight of his day.

"You okay?" he checked.

I nodded, a little dazed. I'd had my escape plan practically worked out in my head already. This changed everything. Now I had to escape from a bulletproof werelock instead of a bunch of werewolf simpletons.

Alcaeus leaned in and brushed his lips to my ear. "Sorry I took so long. Had to take care of a few things."

That was long?

"That's impossible," Zeke spurned, picking himself up off the asphalt. "She's not your mate. Her name is *Blythe,* and you came to us looking for her. You'd never met her before tonight. She's wanted for crimes against our pack." His wolf eyes glowed an angry orange color. "My house was destroyed by that crazy bitch. Besides that, she has a price on her head. There are rogue hunters who'll pay a monstrous ransom to get their hands on her. We're not letting you walk away with our prize."

"How about we let you live and call it even?" Kai's voice suggested.

Oh, yay, the doctor had come to my rescue, too. *Make that two bulletproof werelocks to escape from now.*

"No deal," Clifton snarled, dusting off the seat of his jeans. "My mate, Patsy, has waited a very long time to see this one's execution." He pointed an accusing finger in my direction.

Right. I'd blown Patsy's prized, tricked-out Range Rover sky-high. I had to cover my mouth with my hand to thwart the sudden onset of church giggles that hit me at the memory of Patsy's keening wail of agony over the loss of that gaudy, new-money-trash ride of hers.

"She burned our entire community to the ground!" Clifton proceeded to rage. "It took years for us to rebuild. And she just attacked members of our pack in the bar tonight. She's *our* captive, and we're taking her back to stand trial before our pack and face the retribution she has coming to her."

Idiots. A trial meant at least a week, if not more, to escape. How did their pack operate like this and manage to survive?

"Is this true, Cynthia?" Alcaeus's stern voice demanded, his glowing wolf eyes shifting from Clifton to me, pinning me in place. He looked shocked by what they had told him. *Check that; he looked furious.* "Did you burn Clifton's pack's entire community to the ground?"

Whoa. That was some hardass Alpha mojo he was throwing off. It shot straight to my lady bits—at what was a really inopportune time to be getting turned on.

"Well?" he prompted, a bit gentler this time.

Oh, geez, what to say here? I thought back to my days of standing human trial and of what Wyatt's dad would've told me to say and went with, "I don't recall."

Alcaeus's lips twitched faintly, but his eyes and mouth were hard once more as they returned to Clifton. "There, you see? Not Blythe. Not guilty."

Dang. I should've tracked down and bitten me a hot werelock ages ago.

I felt a stupid grin break out on my face. *Al-plus-chaos was seriously into me.*

"You challenging us?" Clifton growled at Alcaeus, his claws and fangs extending.

"I believe it's simply implied as an unspoken *threat* when there isn't a challenge to be had," Kai returned. "We're taking her." He turned to Alcaeus. "Shall we?"

Alcaeus looked down at me, then back at Clifton and Zeke. He shook his head and wrapped his fingers around my bicep. For a split second, I thought he'd decided to hand me over to them. But instead, he handed me over to Kai, telling him, "Go. I'll catch up with you."

"So, Doc … about that whole bite thing," I broached. "That mark I made on Al-chaos will heal, right? I mean, I was just going for a little hickey. A love bite, if you will. I didn't mean to do any lasting damage. Is he really single?"

I'd been talking to myself for the past twenty minutes while Kai had restlessly drummed his fingers against the steering wheel of the SUV we were sitting in, waiting for Alcaeus.

Kai had taken hold of my arm and had done that same sick-cool werelock trick that Raul had done with me before—disappearing us from the alley and reappearing us to a parking lot next to the SUV we were presently inside of. I wondered if all werelocks could do that. If so, I was in trouble.

"How old are you?" I tried again to get him to converse with me.

He smelled super-old, like Alcaeus. Werewolf males usually loved to brag about their age. More strength and power came with age, typically. So with male werewolves, I'd learned that it wasn't only about whose wolf balls were bigger; it was also about whose were *older*—as odd and *ew*-worthy as that testosterone competition was.

Kai hadn't said more than "Get inside" to me since *Star Trek*-beaming us here. But I'd get him to crack yet. I needed info. And I could tell he was super-annoyed with my very presence already.

"You and Al-chaos been friends for long?"

Nothing.

"Do you want me to talk for us both? Because I can. Gosh, what should we talk about? The possibilities are endless—"

"Alcaeus's mark will heal," he answered my earlier

question. He didn't look at me as he spoke. His eyes remained cast forward, staring out through the windshield. "I'll make sure of it," he added under his breath.

Yeah ... Heathcliff didn't care for me so much. *At all.*

"Al's not been himself lately," he offered up without prompting. "He's become addicted to ... *consoling* himself ... via random nightly trysts—endless meaningless casual sex."

I got the sense that Kai was the one talking to himself now—trying to ease his own concerns about his friend's behavior toward me, more so than he was attempting to explain anything for my benefit.

And by "for my benefit," I meant he was attempting to insult and degrade me, of course. Too bad he was way out of his league embarking on that cause.

"He lost someone recently," Kai expounded. "He's ... grieving."

I gave his profile a raised, whatever-the-fuck-you-gotta-tell-yourself brow.

"We all lose people," I blurted a bit callously before I could catch myself. "I mean, my sincerest condolences for your friend's loss," I amended. After a pause, I asked, "Was it a woman?"

"Yes."

I nodded, studying him in profile. "You loved her too, huh?"

A strained, faraway look had flashed across his features that had made me suspect that the woman he spoke of had been someone special to him as well. But he seemed startled by the very suggestion for some reason, as slowly, he turned to look at me. *Oh, yeah,* he was supremely irritated with me now, judging from the way a muscle ticked in his jaw and the vein that ran down the centerline of his forehead suddenly pulsed to life.

Oops. Direct hit. *And score.* I shrugged and flashed him a toothy smile. Time to jet before the old dog killed me.

"Want some gum?" I asked, bending down to unzip the backpack at my feet. Werelock or no, one flashbang at close range should do enough damage to give me a decent running head start at least.

My fingers had just wrapped around the very item they were searching for, when I felt a sharp, pinprick stabbing sensation in my thigh.

CHAPTER 18

Avery

I AWOKE FROM A DREAMLESS SLEEP CHAINED TO AN unfamiliar bed.

Never a good sign.

"Good afternoon." It was the surly voice of Kai, the asshole doctor, that greeted me.

An even worse sign. That bastard had needle-roofied me or something. I didn't remember anything beyond the few moments right after he'd stabbed me with an injection.

I breathed a little easier when I opened my eyes and noted the telltale signs that I was in a hotel room—in what looked to be a luxury suite—an unfamiliar-location situation that was likely preferable to any number of other possibilities since it meant close access to the general public, at least. Not that any of them could actually help me to escape from werelocks, but they were useful as a stall tactic in a getaway scenario if I could create a big enough scene.

He'd said it was afternoon. If that was true, it meant he must've hit me with some serious tranq for me to have slept through the night as well as morning.

Daylight streamed in through the windows. I caught

sight of familiar high-and mid-rise buildings that made up the cityscape of downtown Denver and was relieved to know that I hadn't been transported far.

Kai stood next to my bed, appearing as annoyed as the last vision I'd held of him in my memory. I decided it was probably his normal look. My guy Alcaeus didn't seem to be anywhere in sight, which was a disappointment, since he'd been my biggest fan and champion the night before. Perhaps he wasn't that into me after all. Maybe he really did fall in love with strangers in bar bathrooms every day.

Yet I noted that his scent clung to the made-up bedding that I was lying upon—an indication that he might've slept next to me. As foolish as it was, the notion made me smile inside.

I still had all of my clothes on, which was another positive. And my lady parts didn't feel as if they'd been accessed or violated in any manner while I'd been knocked out. As anxious as I was to get away from these Reinoso werelocks and back to Sloane, this was by all accounts as positive as it probably got in a waking-up-after-being-drugged-and-kidnapped scenario.

I'd get out of this one.

Time to see if the doctor was into anything other than having a pole permanently lodged up his ass.

"Wow," I greeted him with a smile. "I knew last night that you were crushin' hard on me. But I didn't realize how desperate you were to play dirty doctor. You could've just asked. Where's my bae? Did you steal me away from him?"

His sour expression curdled further, if that was even possible. "Rest assured, I am not *crushin'* on you."

I had to suppress a giggle at the look of sheer disgust he gave me.

"Ah." I gave him a wink. "Playing for the other team, eh? Thought you might be in love with my bae. Guess that would also explain the drugging and kidnapping. You two been together long? You kinda argue like a married couple."

The smile he gave me was one of pure contempt. "I am not interested in playing games with you, Averhilda."

Damn. Despite my best intentions to remain blasé, my heart rate picked up at the mention of my real name. "You must be confusing me with another bathroom tryst your lover has had recently. My name's Cynthia."

"Cynthia? How interesting. Because your DNA partially matches that of one Averhilda Fatima Haskie, born in 1981."

"How very fascinating," I replied in a mockingly droll tone of voice that mimicked his bored, supercilious one. "I had no idea that 'partially' counted in science, Doc."

"It does when your werewolf DNA wouldn't have been available in the system. Because you weren't always a werewolf, were you, Averhilda?"

"You got me. Cynthia Pressley Blackwood's my werewolf stage name. Rolls off the tongue better, don't you think?" God, I felt like an idiot every time I said it. I cursed Wyatt internally for that stupid name.

The uptight doctor didn't look amused. "Tell me, how does a woman with a Ph.D. in molecular biology from M.I.T. wind up hunting rogue werewolf hunters?"

"What's with the chains?" I yanked on the bonds securing my arms above my head and binding my ankles to the end of the bed, using the opportunity to test the strength of my restraints. "Do they come with the room or do you travel with these? Wouldn't have pegged you as the S&M type, Dr. Kai."

I'd totally pegged him as the S&M type.

His impassive demeanor didn't waver. "On September twenty-second, 2013, Ms. Averhilda Haskie went on a camping trip to the White Mountains with her fiancé and another couple."

"Are we gonna play the fun kind of doctor games or the torture kind here?"

"Averhilda's fiancé and the other couple were attacked and killed during that camping trip"—he raised one distinguished brow at me—"by a pack of wild, rabid wolves"—he paused to study my non-reaction—"according to official reports."

It was getting harder to control my heart rate, but he'd need to do better to get a rise out of me. "So it's a surprise then? Good, I love surprises—especially the torture and kink kind."

"Ms. Haskie, the sole survivor of the unfortunate attack, reported the incident to the authorities. Then she mysteriously disappeared off the face of the planet less than a week later."

"I'm hungry." My eyes flitted about the hotel room. *True statement, actually.* I was famished. "Does this place have room service as well as bed chains? Just a tip"—I craned my neck and pretended to scan the room for signs of food or an in-room dining menu while assessing my situation—"I don't cave well under torture, but *food*—I can be bribed to talk."

"Have you any idea how rare it is for a human to survive the werewolf transformation?"

The irritation in his voice was music to my ears. I shrugged—to the extent I could within my bonds—as my eyes continued to canvass the room. "Most humans aren't like me."

"Most common werewolves aren't like you, either, Avery."

In a blink, the mattress dipped and he was perched next to me on the bed, one hand clamped around my throat while the other yanked my shirt up past my ribs. Any snarky retort about kinky doctor play I'd hoped to deliver was cut short as his fingers tightened around my neck, blocking my airway.

In stark contrast to the hand wrapped around my throat, his other was gentle against the skin of my stomach, warm fingers tracing my abdominal muscles before stroking higher to explore my ribs. Eyes on my face, he found what he was looking for through touch alone. Which meant he'd done some exploring while I'd been knocked out. *Dick.*

My eyes shifted, and I forgot all about controlling my heart rate as I thrashed and yanked against the chains holding me. He squeezed my throat harder in response and leaned in, observing my distress with casual disinterest while my bulging, fuming feral eyes promised vengeance.

"The scars of your former human life will forever give you away, Avery."

Tell me something I didn't know.

He wanted to see me shift. It was the only way out of my bonds and the only chance I had of survival if he kept squeezing, and we both knew it. Why he wanted to see it— what he was looking for or hoping to figure out by this, escaped me. *And made me stubbornly resist shifting.*

"What the fuck are you doing?"

I was released as soon as the door burst open. A great ruckus ensued.

"Why the hell is she chained to the bed?" Alcaeus

demanded. "I wasn't gone for more than fifteen minutes, Kai. How could you do this?"

"She has scars, Al. On her ribs and back. One on the back of her left thigh, too. She was human before. And now she's a werewolf with no scent. She's hiding someth—"

A cracking sound cut the doctor short, and I couldn't help but grin. The big hot werelock with the weird name was still totally into me. And he definitely seemed to be the Alpha in charge.

"You undressed her?"

"*No*—I mean, yes. Come on, Al, I'm a doctor. It was—"
Crack.

I bit my lip to stifle my laughter when the doctor groaned in agony. I hoped it'd been his nuts.

"You chained my mate to the fucking bed!" my savior roared at his friend.

"He strangled me, too," I couldn't resist chiming in to tattle. "And I think he liked it—if ya know what I mean."

More swearing and loud cracking noises ensued while the doctor tried to deny the latter part of my accusation. As satisfying as it was to hear him get his ass beat, I was over being tied up. Upon Alcaeus's arrival, the smell of food had filled the room—food that I was unable to get at while chained to a bed.

"A little help over here maybe?" I called out.

The chains around my wrists and ankles magically broke apart, and Alcaeus was by my side a second later, spouting apologies as he inspected first my wrists and then my neck for injury. But when his concerned hazel eyes dropped to my midsection—where my tank top had ridden up amid Kai's inspection—they widened and flamed bright amber.

"Who did this to you?" His hands went straight to the scars on my ribs.

The blind fury in his eyes was so piercing that I felt momentarily paralyzed. But I quickly snapped out of it.

"Back off," I smacked at his hands as I tried to pull my shirt back down. "I'm over being inspected and manhandled for one day."

He didn't relent as his eyes burned unseeingly down at me. It was as if my words hadn't registered. He even pushed me back down to the bed when I attempted to sit up. So I threw a right hook that connected with his jaw, and that got his attention.

"Ouch!"

"I said back off, Chaos."

His feral yellow eyes blinked. "What'd you just call me?"

His expression was difficult to decipher. I couldn't tell if he looked angry or ... charmed.

"Um ... Chaos. You know, like short for Alcaeus? 'Cause your name sounds like 'Al' plus 'chaos.' It uh ... helps me to remember it."

A slow smile stretched his lips as his bright golden eyes bled to hazel.

Definitely charmed.

"It's a bit more of a 'key' sound than 'kay,' actually. But I like it. *Chaos.*" His grin gave way to a chuckle as he tried it out. "You gave me a pet name," he said softly, his eyes moving over my face. "That's"—he shook his head, gazing at me as if I'd completely enchanted him—"adorable."

My lips twitched of their own volition, and I found myself grinning back. "You're welcome."

"Precious." Kai's harsh voice cut in, breaking the spell of our private moment. "Congratulations, Al. Your 'fated mate' has come up with a mnemonic device to aid her in remembering your name."

Alcaeus's smile faded. "I'm sorry," he apologized, smoothing my tank top down for me. "I didn't mean to lose control like that."

When my shirt was back in place, he laid his palm over my now-covered stomach. His flattened palm and fingers pretty well spanned the width of my waist, warming me straight to my core, making me feel irrationally calm inside as his concerned hazel eyes probed my own and his fingertips slowly stroked over the thin cotton of my shirt, gently palpating where the raised scars on my rib cage lay beneath.

"And I'm truly sorry about Kai's behavior." His eyes became more disconsolate as he continued to gently explore my ribs through the barrier of my tank top. "So deeply sorry."

I wasn't sure why I was still just lying there, allowing him to continue. Or why it was that his apology triggered a sudden burn of tears at the backs of my eyes.

Probably because I knew that he wasn't simply apologizing for Kai. It felt like he was apologizing for the scars on my ribs—something he'd had absolutely nothing to do with.

"I'd give anything to be able to go back in time, so that I could've been with you, and stopped it from happening."

He definitely wasn't talking about Kai's behavior today or last night.

"It was nothing." My voice was a faint whisper. "Your kinky doctor friend doesn't scare me one bit."

My stomach chose that moment to growl its hunger against the palm of his hand.

CHAPTER 19

Alcaeus

I WAS DESPERATE TO HOLD ONTO SOME MEASURE OF CALM. The gurgle of her stomach beneath my palm gave me the excuse I needed to smile in that moment when she started giggling in reaction.

Hers was a nervous laugh that caused more sadness and regret to well up in me at first. But then I saw the true laughter in her brown eyes staring up at me, and an over-whelming sense of pride and gratitude for the fact that she was okay—that she had survived everything that she'd been through in her life up to this point and that she was with me now—overcame me.

She was with me now.

She was whole and perfect. And no one would ever be able to harm her again. I would make certain of it.

But she *had* been hurt in the past. Damaged. She didn't trust me yet. I'd have to be patient with her tendency to lie so easily to me until I earned her trust.

"Are you hungry?" Dumb question.

"*Starved*," she confirmed, her eyes flashing with such excitement that God help me, my dick got hard.

Pushing visions of my cock in her mouth from my mind, I offered her a hand up off the bed and led her to the adjacent living room of the hotel suite, where there was a small dining table and two service carts brimming with food.

"I ordered everything on the menu that I thought you might like from the restaurants downstairs. I got a selection of breakfast, lunch, and dinner foods."

"Wow." She inhaled deeply, eyeing the carts, and moaned. "I think I love you."

Ah, shit. I wasn't going to make it much longer without being inside her again.

I adjusted the bulge in my slacks as she rushed forward to investigate the food, lifting plate covers and taking sample bites as she went, before piling more food than she could possibly fit into her tiny stomach onto a dining plate for herself. When she paused to twist her long black hair into a knot at the back of her head to keep it from getting in the way of her eating, I knew I was going to live happily ever after with this woman.

I pulled up a chair so I could sit and watch her. *And so the bulge in my pants would be less obvious and uncomfortable.*

The sounds of ecstasy that she made while she ate would've tempted a saint. The way her eyes rolled back in her head and she licked her fingers and got all into it kept my mind firmly relegated to the gutter.

"Did you really set Clifton's community ablaze?" I asked, simply in the hope of steering my brain away from the fantasy it'd just latched onto of eating her out atop the dining table. I already knew from the memories I'd collected from Clifton and Zeke's minds that she *had*, in fact, torched it.

"I don't recall," she answered from behind the cover of her hand as she chewed.

Hearing the same answer she'd given me the night before—right in front of her accusers—made me chuckle to myself all over again as I watched her attack a sausage link with her fork. It was all I could do to keep my hands from reaching for her and pulling her onto my lap.

"That's a yes," Kai interjected. "Your 'mate' is quite the seasoned criminal, as a matter of fact. She got an early start at it. You should read her juvenile records."

Her fork slipped and clattered against her plate, but she picked it up and replied casually, "Dr. Kai's just jealous. Thinks I'm your Yoko. He confessed in the car last night how worried he is that I'm gonna break up your touring werelock band." She shot a side-eye glare at him that promised pain. "Right before he stabbed me with a hypodermic syringe."

My smile faded at the last part, and I leveled a censorious glare of my own at my Beta. I never should've left her alone with Kai. I wouldn't be doing it again after what he'd just pulled with chaining her to the bed.

"I'm very sorry about that, Cynthia. It won't happen again, I promise." I hated calling her Cynthia, but it would have to do until she felt comfortable revealing her real name to me.

I couldn't fault her for being wary based on how those werewolves in Clifton's pack had mistreated her. They'd deserved every bit of the damage she'd done to their property years ago and much more, as far as I was concerned.

My mate had accomplished the unthinkable and survived the unsurvivable in her short life: She'd suffered a rogue werewolf attack while she'd been a fragile human!

And then she'd apparently survived her initial werewolf transformation unassisted as well—a feat that historically had been nothing short of impossible. The fact that she was alive at all was a testament to how miraculous she was.

My blood seethed at the knowledge that the first pack my mate had looked to for acceptance and guidance as an innocent new wolf had dared to label her an abomination and had openly persecuted her for her astonishing survival. I'd had zero qualms about the retribution I'd dealt the Highlands Ranch pack last night.

"Are you always this apologetic and hospitable to the women you drug and abduct?"

"Huh? *Never.* I mean, no, I don't drug and abduct women. You're the first." Christ, I was an idiot. It wasn't helping that all the blood in my body settled just below my belt whenever I was near her.

She giggled. "Am I the first because I bit you? Sorry 'bout that, by the way. Dr. Kai says it's going to heal just fine, though."

My eyes cut to Kai, who was pretending to be busy on his laptop. How dare he feed her that lie?

"Dr. Kai is mistaken," I told her carefully, watching closely to gauge her reaction. "You marked me. Permanently. There's no question of it. And no reversing it."

She paused in chewing as her body froze—her fork suspended midair on its way to her mouth.

"Do you know what it means to mark another werewolf?"

Slowly, she shook her head. Foregoing the bite of food on her raised fork, she set it down and reached for her glass of water instead.

"Werewolves mark their mates with a special bite that is permanent. One that will leave a definitive scar, regardless of any supernatural healing abilities."

She set her water glass down and reached for the pot of coffee on the table.

"There's a unique venom that's released from our fangs when we will it—one that is different from the normal venom we release to attack or turn prey. Traditionally, it happens during moments of peak arousal, because the special venom that's required to mark a mate gets released when our inner animal feels profoundly stirred to bind another to us forever."

"One caveat," Kai inserted, "is the recipient of the marking must be in a sufficient state of arousal, and therefore receptive to the one delivering the bite, in order for the mark to take."

Her hands shook as she raised the cup of black coffee she'd just poured for herself to her lips and took a sip. "Interesting," she muttered dazedly. "Must've skipped the day they covered that one in werewolf parochial school."

Shit. She was completely shell-shocked.

I leaned forward, closer to her, resting my elbows on my knees. "Honey, I know you grew up as a human, and that this is all new for you. But I promise, everything's going to be fine. I'm not going to force you to do anything, or push feelings or relationship demands on you before you're ready."

"It just seems so weird," she said after a pause, staring blankly at a spot on the table. "Weird that no one's ever bitten you before me." Her brown eyes lifted to mine. "Exactly how old are you? Is there something wrong with you that I should know about?"

"Ha!" Kai barked out a laugh and mumbled, "Where to start?"

I choked and coughed amid the sudden fit of humor that overcame me as well, before answering, "I was born in 1604. I'll be four hundred nineteen years old in about four months—on November twelfth. There are a lot of things wrong with me that you should probably know about, but I'd prefer it if we took this one step at a time and let you get to know me and figure them out as we go along, if that's all right?"

I gave her what I hoped was my most charming, non-threatening smile. Getting her to accept this as a foregone conclusion was the first step in wearing down the barriers she'd erected.

"And to answer your other question," Kai piped up, much to my chagrin, "being the ancient and powerful werelock that he is, Alcaeus has the ability, if he acts *promptly*"—he shot me a meaningful look—"to block the progress of your simple werewolf mating venom and prevent your mark from becoming permanent."

Asshole.

He crossed his arms over his chest in self-satisfaction as my mate's jaw fell open and her eyes widened at me in accusation. "I was *not* mistaken," Kai asserted. "In fact, it's worked successfully enough in the past whenever a power-hungry, conniving bitch has attempted to lay claim to Al's wolf."

"It's not the same, Kai, and you know it!" I blasted him.

I decided to lay it all out and make my intentions known. She was obviously confused about what was happening between us—about what our mate bond even meant. *As was Kai, apparently,* if he thought that the mark was all that this was about.

"Look, Cynthia, what happened between us yesterday

when we first met was an act of fate. This bond between us—it's predestined. For me, we were mated the moment we saw one another. The marking makes it official, yes, but it's nothing but a formality at this point."

She looked from me to Kai, as if she was unsure of who or what to believe.

"Don't get me wrong; you marking me yesterday was the single greatest moment of my life, and I have absolutely no desire or intention of reversing it." I delivered the last part to Kai. "But this"—I gestured between us—"isn't about a bite."

Her brow furrowed. She looked lost. Looked so small and fragile, the way she had in the bathroom when she'd been so startled that she'd shot at me.

"You can't imagine how awful I feel—how sorry I am that I haven't been there for you for all these years. That I wasn't around to protect you from a rogue attack. That I wasn't there to assist your initial werewolf transformation and keep the pain from you that you undoubtedly experienced."

She pursed her lips, giving nothing away. Then she picked up her fork and started eating again, shutting me out.

I kept talking anyway.

This needed to be said.

"I like to think that to some degree, up until this point, my ancestors have protected you—my predestined mate—in my stead. But I'm here now. The bad things that have happened to you—those scars on your ribs from your human life"—I shook my head, wincing internally at the pain they must've caused her—"nothing like that will ever happen to you again. I swear it on my life, Cynthia."

"Your mate's name is Averhilda, by the way," Kai supplied. "Let me know if you need help coming up with a mnemonic device for it."

CHAPTER 20

Alcaeus

"**A**VERHILDA? *AVERHILDA* IS YOUR REAL NAME?"

She looked like she was getting ready to deny it and lie to me again as she rapidly chewed and swallowed the bite of food in her mouth, so I headed her off.

"Boar-like in battle—it totally suits you," I rushed to say. "I love it!"

She made a face of surprise—or maybe *horror*—like she couldn't believe that I knew what it meant. Either that or it was one of horror that I'd professed to love it.

"It's awful," she said. "I go strictly by Avery. Don't ever call me Averhilda if you want me to answer."

"Got it," I readily agreed. "I love the name Avery even better."

From the corner of my eye, I saw Kai roll his eyes in disgust. I knew that I was probably grinning from ear to ear like a cheeseball, but I didn't care. I didn't give a damn what Kai or anyone else thought of me or of my situation with Avery.

"Do his eyes always twinkle and smile like this?" Avery asked Kai, her mouth half-stuffed with home fries as she jerked her chin in my direction. "Do you constantly feel like you're left out of a private joke whenever you're around him?"

A laugh burst from Kai's chest—a genuine one. His sulky demeanor momentarily cracked and his eyes sparked at Avery's observation. "Yes, actually. I do feel that way most of the time."

She nodded once. "Thought so." She brushed her hands together, dusting the crumbs and salt from her fingertips, before announcing, "I need a shower. Mind if I borrow yours?" she asked me directly.

My cock jumped in response as my imagination ran rampant with visions of showering with Avery—of sliding my hands all over her wet, soapy curves. Of tasting her wet skin in my mouth; of sliding her slick body against my own inside the shower stall; of fucking her against the tiled wall—both from the front and from the rear; of holding her spread thighs open wide between my biceps as I held her high in the air and ate her out—sliding her squirming ass up and down the slippery tiled wall as I licked and sucked and—

"*Wowza!*" Avery's breathy exclamation jarred me back to reality to find her staring at the obvious erection tenting my pants.

"I need a shower, too," I blurted without thinking. My brain was toast.

She shook her head, biting her smiling lip. "I didn't invite you." She stood from the little dining table. "But maybe later." She tilted her head to the side, and her eyes gave me a flirtatious once-over that projected some kind of maddening contradiction between "give me space" and "fuck me senseless."

I was dangerously close to ripping through the seam of my slacks.

Then she did the inconceivable. She grabbed the hem of her tank top and pulled it over her head, exposing the knife scars on her ribs that she'd denied me access to before. I didn't have time to decide between anger and arousal as she unsnapped her bra and tossed it on the floor to join her discarded top.

So I settled on shock.

And awe.

Her breasts were perfect, exquisite mounds. Not precisely symmetrical like the breasts of a female who'd been born a she-werewolf or werelock would've been, but full and natural and—*real.*

Like everything else about her.

The sight of her hard nipples straining for the heavens—beckoning me to devour them—all but sent me to my knees.

I swallowed and nearly choked when she unbuttoned and unzipped her fly, turned her back to me, and pulled her jeans and underwear down. She stepped out of her discarded clothes, then stood and looked back over her shoulder at me.

Whether she did it to make sure that I was still watching her little show, or to see if I'd already come in my pants, I couldn't say.

I didn't have the mental capacity to contemplate it because I was too busy struggling to breathe like I'd only learned how to use my lungs five minutes ago, as my eyes feasted on the stunning sight of her gorgeous naked body, of all that golden-olive skin on display, of her mouthwatering ass—*and of the scars that crisscrossed her back. And the one on her left hamstring that looked like it had been made by a belt buckle.*

I'd never been torn between so many conflicting emotions and corporeal sensations at once before.

"Who? What? *Names,*" I finally demanded, every muscle in my body vibrating, straining against my wolf's urge to shift and go to her—and then to run and kill whoever had left these scars on her. *"Addresses,"* I clipped out.

Hands planted on her hips, she pivoted to face me. "Been there, Chaos. Done that." One corner of her mouth kicked up. "I can only give you cemetery plot numbers."

"W-what?"

"Deceased," she clarified. "Caput. Six feet under."

I felt myself frown. I didn't understand. My brain had stopped working. I tried and failed to do the math.

"You strike me as a guy who might like to overindulge his hero complex. So I just want you to know, I'm good."

"Hero complex?" I shook my head. "I don't have a hero complex."

"Look, I get it," she said with a little smile. "You grew up in ancient times. I appreciate that you want to be chivalrous and protect me from the world. But I didn't grow up in the seventeenth century. And I can't be that damsel for you." She shrugged one shoulder. "Never been wired that way."

There was a long pause as I willed my brain to function to no avail. I just sat there, staring, at a loss, trying to figure out which of my wounded organs was in more distress—my dick or my heart.

"We cool?" she checked.

I didn't respond. I could barely comprehend what the hell had just happened.

Her gaze flicked to Kai, reminding me of the fact that he was still in the room with us.

"Nice boner, Doc," she said as she strutted past him on her way to the bathroom. "Knew you were crushin.'"

Once the bathroom door had shut and locked behind her, Kai said, "You totally have a hero complex."

After I'd worked my jaw off the ground, punched Kai for getting a chubby, and then rubbed my own out in the hotel suite's second bathroom, I was able to assess the situation with restored brain cells and see just how well everything was going already between Avery and me.

My woman was absolute perfection, ideal for me in every way. I was so high in love that there was no coming down.

"Let's examine the contents of her bag, shall we?" Kai's voice droned in my ear, calling my attention back to the "evidence" he'd gathered snooping into Avery's human background—as well as her backpack. "Ah, what's this? *Grenades.* Both the deadly kind and the annoying stun kind. How adorable," he deadpanned. "What's next? Oh, here's a handgun. With a silencer—you know, in case she needs to murder someone without the neighbors hearing."

Despite my mounting irritation with Kai over his disdainful behavior toward my mate, I couldn't quell the shit-eating grin that had broken out on my face as he revealed the awesome contents of Avery's backpack. My mate was the cutest little badass that ever was.

He pulled a ziplock bag of unmarked pill bottles out

next. *"Pills,"* he said with feigned exuberance. "How utterly precious. What could they be, you ask? Oh, just some ovulation suppression hormones, is all. Who has time to go into heat when you've got rogue hunters to slay?"

"Sensible." I gave a thumbs up.

That was the best item he'd pulled out yet. The idea of my mate going into heat without me near her was abhorrent. Thank God she'd had those pills. She wouldn't need them anymore, though.

"I'll take those," I told him, pulling the bag from his hand and chucking them straight into the trashcan in the corner.

He groaned and lectured, "Al, at least dispose of them properly." He walked to the trashcan and retrieved them. "Oh, hey, I'll just take care of it for you." He tossed them into his medical bag. "As usual," he appended under his breath.

I rolled my eyes at his dramatics. Not getting laid in over a century had taken a serious toll on his personality.

Kai pulled several stacks of cash from Avery's backpack next. They looked to be mostly small bills—twenties and fifties. I whistled low and shook my head, busting up laughing. It was all just too cute.

"Getaway funds, perhaps?" Kai said. "Stolen, maybe?" He shrugged. "Who can say for sure? Well, *we* could say for sure—*if* her mind wasn't blocked off by the most intricate mind shield that our kind has ever encountered, right?" He pulled a phone from the side pocket of Avery's backpack. "But let's not worry about that mind block just now. I'm sure there's a perfectly logical explanation for it that is in no way a threat to our lives.

"Let's talk about this instead, shall we?" He held the

phone up for me to see and pressed the button to access its programmed contacts. "There are just two contacts programmed into Avery's phone. And they're both for the same number. One is labeled 'Friend,' and the other is labeled 'Scary Stranger.' No doubt this amounts to more adorableness to you, and you're not the least bit curious, but dare we call the number and see who this contact might be?" He raised a challenging brow.

The better man I wanted to be for Avery would've said no. But I wasn't that man. *Yet.* I grabbed the phone out of Kai's hand and pressed the call button.

CHAPTER 21

Avery

I'D ALWAYS DONE MY BEST THINKING AND MASTURBATING in the shower. But there was no time for the latter now, so I tried to wash Chaos's divine scent off me in an attempt to restore my focus. His musk was too distracting. The man smelled of raw, carnal lust. Of dark, primitive cravings, and a dirty side of original sin.

I couldn't risk shagging him again, though.

How was I going to shake these guys? *Think, Avery. Think.*

I needed to get back to Sloane. To get a message to Azda soon at the very least.

Hmm … Alcaeus had just sworn on his life to never let anything bad happen to me ever again. He'd professed to feel awful about not being there to protect me from the rogue attack or the knife fights I'd been in as a teen.

The rational, intelligent adult in me knew that he had to be full of shit no matter how genuine he seemed. *Either that or he was nuts.* In which case, there was a decent chance I'd be able to leverage that misplaced guilt of his to get my hands on a computer and Internet access. I'd just have to be careful about which online message board I used to communicate in code with Sloane if I did it from any of Alcaeus and Kai's computer equipment.

If the guilt tactic didn't work, maybe I'd claim that the ancestors who'd been looking out for me in Alcaeus's absence all this time said that he should give me Internet access. I chuckled at the notion of actually trying to say that one with a straight face. If all else failed, I could always invent a prophecy about it, I supposed. Superbeasts who put stock in ancestors and predestined mates would definitely be all about prophecies, too.

Supernatural idiosyncrasies aside, Chaos was pretty darn adorable—in a weird, old-school kind of way.

I could admit to it.

I smiled to myself as I recalled the look on his face—*and the bulge in his crotch*—when I'd dropped trou next to the breakfast table.

I definitely wouldn't mind fucking him again. I could admit to that, too.

Eyes closed beneath the shower spray, I was getting ready to shut the heavenly warm water off and go con my "predestined mate" into giving me Internet access, when suddenly I felt a muscled arm materialize around my waist. As it did, a hard, clothed male body squeezed up against me from behind and a palm clamped over my wet mouth before I could let out a scream.

"Why're you helping me again?" I asked over a huge mouthful of my French dip sandwich.

Raul, my mysterious werelock rescuer, had come to my aid yet again—teleporting into the hotel room shower, no less, to whisk me away from Alcaeus and Kai. Upon conjuring clothing for me, he'd casually offered to take me out to eat—*in San Francisco*—as if snatching women from showers and grabbing early dinner with them twelve hundred-some miles away was his normal routine.

As if I really had the option of saying no.

How Raul had been able to pinpoint my exact location in order to "rescue me" was troubling indeed. It was a question he hadn't answered. But we'd started drinking halfway through lunch, and I was hopeful I'd be able to pull it out of him yet.

I was hoping to pull information on Alcaeus out of him as well.

Having finished his sandwich already, Raul had been sitting on the restaurant bench seat next to me looking a bit lost in his own thoughts for the past few minutes. But at my question, that easy surfer grin of his stretched his lips.

"Told you," he said, snagging one of my fries and dipping it in the leftover glob of mayonnaise on his otherwise empty plate. "I'm your friend."

I shook my head as he popped the fry in his mouth. "No, you're not."

He laughed. "I'm still a scary stranger, then? Two daring, dramatic rescues and you don't like me yet?"

"Hey," I whacked his hand hard when he made to grab for another fry. "Get your own, pretty boy."

"Damn, girl," he said, chuckling as he made a show of shaking out his "injured" hand. "You know something? I definitely like you, Avery."

He sounded sincere. And the smile he gave me was

neither predatory nor creepy. So far I hadn't gotten any sexual vibes from him at all, in fact—not even when he'd been pressed up against me in the shower. But judging from the way I'd seen him interact and look at other women in the restaurant, I didn't think he was gay.

I took a liberal gulp of my Jack and Coke, trying to figure him out. He seemed so laid back and easygoing at present, and yet I sensed a frightening intensity lurking beneath the surface—an emotional darkness inherent to him that he didn't readily display. He was like a barely restrained Alpha powerhouse trapped in the guise of a flirty, blasé surfer boy playacting at being a werelock.

"I'll never tell you where my daughter is," I reiterated for the record, stone-faced. "I'll die before I tell you," I stressed, when my first statement caused him to burst out laughing again.

"Duly noted." He nodded easily in accord, still smiling. He signaled to our waiter before shifting his position in his seat so that he was fully facing me, his arm draped behind me high over the bench seat we shared in the back corner of the restaurant—since both of us had insisted upon keeping our backs to the wall. "If you won't allow me to directly protect Sloane, will you at least let me protect you?"

The way he continued to casually drop my daughter's name—as if he knew her somehow—unnerved me. As did the way he'd just invaded my space—even if it wasn't in a way that felt particularly sexual or threatening. I could tell he was trying to draw me in with his Alpha energy. Make me feel safe.

He was wasting his time. I was immune.

I turned to face him, scooting back in the process to put more distance between us. "I don't need you to protect me."

He hummed and bit his lip, his head bobbing slowly up and down, his soft brown eyes holding mine, radiating concern. And frustration. And that strange, hidden pain that seemed so much older than his years should've allowed.

"So you could've gotten away from Kai and Alcaeus on your own back there, then?"

"Yes," I answered. Then sighed and muttered, "Eventually."

He smiled at my admission, and his demeanor shifted once more to his laid-back surfer persona as he mouthed, "You're welcome."

I rolled my eyes. "Oh, fine. Thank you. Thank you for rescuing me, all right? Now how well do you know him? I mean *them*—Alcaeus and Kai?"

"We go back a ways," he evaded.

"Here you go," our server announced as two more Jack and Cokes were placed in front of us on the table.

"Age-old enemies, huh?" I pressed, reaching for my fresh drink.

He shrugged. "Not exactly friends. The last time I faced off with Alcaeus, it took three of the most powerful werelocks in existence to stop him from killing me."

I nearly choked on the large sip I'd taken. It was all Jack with very little Coke this time. "For serious?" I blurted. "Chaos?"

Raul's dark brows reached for his hairline. *"Chaos?"*

My face flushed. "I meant Alcaeus." Crud, why was I blushing? "It's just the way I learned to pronounce his name the first time, so that's how I remember to say it. You know, as in *Al* plus *chaos*." I was rambling.

Raul was looking at me strangely now—like he felt sorry for me.

"Well, that's a relief," he said, reaching for his Jack and Coke. "I was afraid it might be some sort of term of endearment you had for him. And I'd hate to think of you as another notch on that old, arrogant bastard's belt. I know all too well how much pussy that asshole—"

I rammed my fist into his stomach as hard as I could without thinking, prompting him to slosh drink on himself.

Fuck. "I don't know why I did that," I said in a rush as his whole body began to quake. I really didn't. The guy could end me without even laying a finger on my person. And so far he'd only been helpful. What the hell was I thinking?

"I think I'm tipsy … this drink is all Jack …" I ceased my rambled apology when I realized he was shaking with suppressed laughter rather than fury.

I punched him again. "Didn't your mama ever teach you never to refer to a woman as a notch or pussy?" I scolded.

"Oh, *that's* what upset you?" he said with a chuckle. "My apologies. My mom kinda bailed on me when I was eight, so she failed to deliver that lecture."

Well, that explained a piece of his hidden pain. "How about your dad?"

"Never around. My nagging aunt raised me. Dad came back into the picture later on to ruin my senior year, though." He threw back what was left of his drink. "Carted me off to Brazil to let me know he was dying and that I would have to take his place as a human slave to the Reinoso werewolf pack for the rest of my life."

I felt my eyes go wide. This was good intel. "You weren't born a werewolf either? You changed into a werelock later on? How?"

"It's a long story," he evaded once more.

"The best ones usually are. Come on, dish it, surfer boy."

He leaned forward, resting his elbow atop the table, entering my space again. "Buy me a shot to replace the drink you spilled, and maybe I will."

"You rescued me wrapped in a shower curtain, remember? I don't exactly have a purse on me."

He smirked. "I do remember. I'll buy. But you have to have a shot with me. *And* finish your drink. Deal?"

"Are you trying to get me sloppy drunk?"

He shook his head at the ceiling. "Avery, if I wanted to drug and take advantage of you, I'd have done it already. And if I wanted you dead, you'd be dead by now."

I believed him. "You sure know how to charm a girl."

"Not trying to charm you. I just want to talk to you. I like you, Avery. And I don't like many people these days."

~

"Let me get this straight … Kai, Alex, and Alex's sister—who shan't be named because you're still butthurt over her rejection—can all teleport like you. But Chaos can't? Even though he used to be the Alpha of the Reinoso pack?"

"Whoa, I am *not* butthurt over her still," he raised his voice in objection. "I'm angry."

"Anger stems from butthurt," I pointed out as he tossed back his fourth shot.

"She's a royal bitch. You won't like her either."

"I'm going to meet her?" I asked with feigned excitement, craning my neck to survey the restaurant. "Is she joining us for shots?" I was way buzzed.

"Ha ha. You're two shots behind, woman." He jutted his chin at the lineup in front of me.

I tipped one back to appease him. And keep him talking. We'd covered quite a bit of ground about the conflict between the Reinoso and Salvatella packs already, and we'd even touched on some of the prophecy nonsense.

Raul was head Beta of the Salvatella pack, and I got the impression he didn't get along so well with his pack Alpha, Gabriel Salvatella. In fact, my gut said Raul was probably busy politicking and plotting a coup when he wasn't busy rescuing me from showers and alley brawls.

When I slammed my empty shot glass back onto the table, it was to find Raul shaking his head at me, a dejected, tired expression on his handsome face.

"You like Alcaeus; admit it."

His statement caught me off guard. "You're really keeping score. Sure you're not trying to get in my pants?"

He looked away, scrubbing a hand over his face. "You're falling for a man who's a serious danger to your daughter. I don't like it."

Wow. O-*kay.* "You know, I'm six years older than you, Raul. This big brother act is endearing, but not quite working for me."

"Good. Because I'd make a terrible big brother." The eyes he returned to me were sad, despite his smile and jovial tone. "I'd only disappoint you."

His eyes and our line of conversation reminded me of a time and place I preferred not to dwell on—of people I couldn't afford to think about anymore. I shook it off and plastered a smile on my face. "Maybe you're the one in need of a big sister."

He hissed air through his teeth. "Eesh, I dunno. You gonna nag me to death?"

"It's the job."

"Fine. But little bros get a say in who their big sisters date."

"Pssh! Not where I come from."

He looked genuinely puzzled. "But they discuss that sort of thing, right?"

"In what universe?" I huffed. "You're obviously an only child. Look, I'll admit that I don't *dislike* Alcaeus as much as I dislike his friend Kai. But that doesn't equate to me 'falling for him,' okay?"

"Ugh, I knew it. You've bumped uglies already, haven't you?" He made a face. "I knew I smelled him on you." He groaned and snatched up my remaining shot.

I was happy to see him down it, because I didn't think I could keep up with him for much longer and retain my wits about me. It was bad news if he could scent Alcaeus on me. Until he'd said it, I'd nearly convinced myself that it was only in my imagination that I'd been scenting Chaos's lingering aroma since my shower.

"You're totally his type, too," Raul said, shaking his head as his eyes gave me a once-over. "On the surface, at least."

Alcaeus had a type? "Excuse me, but I don't fall into any *type*."

"Not disputing that. I said on the surface. Alcaeus has always been a sucker for a good rescue case. But even that won't be enough to alter his intentions where your daughter's life is concerned."

"Rescue case?" It was the most insulting thing he could've said to me. "I am *not* a rescue case. Just because you crashed my alley fight—which I totally had a handle on, by the way—does not mean—"

"Slow your roll, woman. *I* know that. But we're talking about a guy who took in a homeless sixteen-year-old human once—a girl who had been impregnated by a were-lock who was an enemy to the Reinoso pack."

"Chaos did that? When was this?"

"Let's see"—Raul squinted one eye at the ceiling—"would've been early sixties. In sixty-two or three, I think. Sixty-three," he decided with a nod. "Because Jussara was born in 1964. Lupe was on the run from the baby's father's family, the Salvatella pack."

"Your current pack?"

"One and the same."

"Why was she on the run?"

"Nahuel Salvatella—the werelock who knocked her up—had tried to claim her as his fated mate. When Lupe's parents objected, Nahuel killed them. Right in front of her."

I felt my face crumple in disgust as I deadpanned, "Romantic."

"Yeah." Raul rolled his eyes. "That's a werelock for you—the mating bond can make our kind nuts."

Yay, me.

"But Lupe wasn't about to take it lying down and spend the rest of her life mated to her parents' murderer. She got Nahuel sauced off her daddy's moonshine, and after Nahuel passed out, she took his head off with a machete."

"Yes! Boss move, Lupe," I cheered a little too loudly for our setting. She didn't sound like such a rescue case to me.

"Long story short, Alcaeus gave Lupe shelter for fifty

years at the Reinoso compound in Morumbi. Moved her into his own house and helped her raise her daughter, Jussara."

Wow. "That was … crazy nice of him." And now I needed that last shot Raul had just downed. I signaled our server, holding up two fingers and pointing to our empty lineup of glasses.

Raul made a "hmph" sound. "Lupe and her daughter were collateral to the Reinosos. A prized enemy possession and future bargaining chip if they ever needed one."

"Well, if that's true, then Chaos sounds more like an opportunist than a sucker for rescue cases."

"Eh, not quite. Alex, who was Alpha at the time, was the one who viewed them that way and fixed it so that Lupe and Jussara would have to stay permanently—whether they wanted to or not. Alcaeus fancied himself in love with Lupe. But I think he was more in love with the idea of saving her." He shrugged. "Or maybe just with the idea of being in love."

I felt a weird pang in my heart.

"I was seventeen when my dad brought me to Brazil to serve the Reinoso family," he continued. "Lupe was fif-ty-seven at the time—and aging like a human—and believe me, Alcaeus was still giving her googly eyes, even then."

Where was my damn shot?

"Word is Lupe and Alcaeus never consummated their relationship; they were only ever close friends. But it wasn't for lack of trying on Alcaeus's part. Officially, Lupe was Alcaeus's housekeeper, but he would always bring in other pack members to do the housework so that she didn't have to."

I rubbed my palm against my chest. It was all so

terribly sweet. *And really upsetting to hear about for some reason.*

"Alcaeus went berserk when Lupe was killed during a major blowout confrontation between our packs ten years ago. That's when he tried to kill me."

I gasped. "You killed Lupe?"

"No." He shot me a scowl of utter affront. "Lupe killed herself."

CHAPTER 22

Alcaeus

"ALEX PROMISED ME MORE MEN. HE AGREED TO IT WHEN I agreed to go to Morumbi to visit Milena. I need those soldiers *now*, Remy. I needed them *yesterday*. So line up at least eighty of our best and get them ready to go in the next two minutes, because I'm sending Kai to start teleporting them here. Got it?"

"Ah … okay … Would you put Kai on the phone for a sec—"

"*Now*, Remy! There's no time."

"Right. I hear you, Al. But Alex and Milena aren't back yet, and—"

I hung up the phone and barely restrained myself from crushing it in my palm as I turned and ordered Kai, "Go. Bring back as many as you can at a time."

"Al, you need to calm down before we do anything else. You've already dispatched all of the wolves that we have here in Denver to search for her. We need to think this through and approach it sensibly. She has *no* scent."

"She does so! Stop saying that." I shot a blast of magic that caused the hotel room television console to explode.

When that wasn't enough to calm me, I shot a blast into the uncomfortable, ugly settee in the corner. It was useless anyway.

"Not to anyone but you, she doesn't," Kai snapped. "At best, our soldiers might be able to pick up and track your scent on her if she's still carrying it. But beyond that, all we have are photos of her for them to go on. And we have to face reality: it's not as if she slipped out the front door on foot and couldn't have gotten far. We know Raul teleported her, which means she could literally be anywhere on the planet right now."

I knew he had a point. I just didn't want to hear it. We had to keep moving. The faster I rounded up more were-wolves to search for Avery, the faster I could get out and search for her myself. We couldn't afford to lose any time. I would be out of my mind until I knew that she was safe.

"She's still close by. I can feel it. Besides, she's cunning and resourceful. My mate will find a way to prevent Raul from taking her too far away from me."

"Al, your 'mate' had Raul's number programmed into her phone—a phone with a tracking device," Kai said, his voice rising in exasperation. "This could all be part of a trap that Gabriel and Raul set for us—using her as bait. Have you thought about that? You've just deployed all of our soldiers throughout the city in search for her, leaving us vulnerable. What if that's exactly what Gabriel and Raul were hoping we'd do?"

"I don't care. Let Raul and Weenie Gabe come for me." I pulled Avery's phone from my pocket and redialed "Scary Stranger" for the four hundredth time. For the four hundredth time, it went straight to voicemail. I forced my hands to be gentle as I slipped the offensive little black device back into my pocket for safekeeping, when all I wanted to do was grind it to dust between my fingers.

"I will rip that little shit's throat out when I get my hands on him. I will torture and kill him, Kai," I seethed as I paced the room. "And Milena is not stopping me, either. She gets no say in this when my mate's life is on the line."

"Right." Kai scrubbed a weary hand over his face. "Look, who among us wouldn't relish ripping out Raul's entrails? But the fact is Milena *does* get a say in her brother's torture and execution—and not just because she's the Alpha of our pack and more powerful than the rest of us at this point."

"About that …" I stopped pacing to level my pointer finger at him. "We need to discuss the issue of Milena's power. But later." I resumed pacing. "After we recover Avery. Why are you still here? I need those soldiers."

"Issue?" He crossed his arms over his chest. "Since when is Milena's power an *issue*? Or something that is up for discussion? It's a fact, Al—and a positive one at that. Milena's the best thing that ever happened to our pack."

I nodded and paced. "I don't disagree. But what if we made a mistake ten years ago—in disabling her guilt reflex?"

"We didn't disable it; we *balanced* it."

"What if we balanced it too far in the wrong direction?"

"It's *Milena*," Kai reasoned. "She's the most levelheaded and fair-minded among us. She's fixated on fairness and justice in all things."

I couldn't dispute that either. "Right, but what if in balancing it we accelerated her power development a little too far? Maybe we should've let it balance on its own as she matured? I'm just wondering if—"

"Are you serious? Al, we had to. That was the whole point—to accelerate her ability to honor her own instincts and innate self-preservation faculties that were being thwarted too often by that Catholic-girl predisposition of hers to feel as if everything was always her fault. I disagreed with you at the time, but in hindsight, it's one of the best calls you've ever made."

I nodded, only half-listening as I pulled Avery's phone from my pocket once more. I redialed "Friend" this time as Kai continued to rationalize and justify our interference in Milena's psyche a decade ago.

"Milena might've let Raul guilt-trip and manipulate her forever. She might've been paralyzed by the shame of success and plagued by indecision for decades before she grew out of that habit. She never would've been able to lead our pack, Al. And besides, it was only a subtle shift that Remy and I made. We did the right thing."

"Goddamnit." I threw a blast that incinerated the coffee table when the call went straight to voicemail for the umpteenth time. "This is all my fault. I never should've let Avery shower alone."

CHAPTER 23

Avery

T HREE SHOTS LATER, MY HEART DIDN'T FEEL ANY BETTER about this Lupe development. I couldn't decide if it was jealousy I felt over his fifty-year friendship with his housekeeper or disappointment at the prospect that Alcaeus might only see me as some sort of "rescue case," too. To make matters worse, I'd reached the point of inebriation—which had only happened to me a handful of times since turning into a super-canine. It was hard to accomplish as a werewolf, given our rapid metabolism.

"You're saying that Lupe was the guilty sacrifice part of the stolen eye prophecy?"

"Innocent," Raul corrected me, stifling a yawn. "She was the guilty *innocent* caught between two rival packs whose untimely death was prophesied to spark a war between them. She was the stolen eye—the unforgivable sacrifice."

"Right." I nodded, rubbing my temple. "Makes perfect sense." He yawned again, prompting me to tease, "I thought superbeasts like you never got tired. Is this your polite way of saying you want to call it a night?"

He smiled. "Trust me, I'm not that polite. Just a bit more tired lately."

Raul had explained that Lupe's suicide had been more of a sacrificial act—hence the "unforgivable sacrifice" designation. Lupe had made a deal with a powerful undead female werelock named Maribel—a former member of the Reinoso pack who had been hanging out in the ether for ninety-eight years, stealing just enough life energy to remain in limbo by draining the life force from the terminally ill or the dying in order to sustain herself. *And sometimes just killing people outright, along with consuming the occasional soul when she needed a power boost.*

Raul had been vague about the details of how Lupe had allowed herself to be used as Maribel's medium. He'd said it involved helping Maribel gain access to a defective part of a blood curse that Alpha Milena had been harboring at the time. Lupe had agreed to her role in Maribel's scheme in exchange for Maribel severing Lupe's bond to Nahuel—so that Lupe could die without fear of potentially being tied for all eternity to a man she despised.

Raul had been equally vague about why Maribel had needed the defective part of Milena's blood curse.

"Is it because Nahuel bit her that Lupe was tied to him?"

"Nah, Lupe lopped his head off before he ever had a chance to mark her." Raul pulled his phone out and powered it on. "I think it's just the fact that they were mates from the moment Nahuel saw Lupe. Plus, they obviously consummated their union." He shrugged, distracted by his phone as the screen lit up. "Not really sure how it all works."

Great. This tracked with what Chaos had said about

the two of us being mated from the moment we saw one another. *And we'd also consummated.* "So what exactly does the bite do then?"

Another shrug. "I dunno. I guess it solidifies the bond even more or something."

This shit was depressing. Because a part of me—the part who looked and felt a lot like my inner bitch—was perversely excited about being irrevocably tied to Alcaeus.

"So I should never mate-bite anyone? Is that my take-away?" *Whoops—too late, sucka. Already went there.* I could practically feel my inner she-wolf doing a touch-down dance.

Raul abruptly burst out laughing. He pounded his fist against the table—rattling our empty shot glasses in the process—as he fell into a fit of hysterics over whatever it was he'd just read in his phone messages, it seemed.

"Ah, God, this is priceless." He shook his head at his phone as he flipped through more messages he'd missed while it had been off. When at last he stopped chuckling to himself, he powered the device off again and gave me his full attention. "Your takeaway, Avery, is that Alcaeus isn't your friend. He's not on your side." He grinned. "I am."

We'd come full circle. "Okay, okay, point made: Alcaeus is my enemy. Got it. Will you buy me more fries now? And those fish tacos that woman over there is noshing on look phenom." I pointed to a table about ten feet away. "I need those too. Oh, and by the way, I'll never tell you where my daughter is."

His grin gave way to a sober look of impatience. "Our supernatural world has become firmly divided into two camps at this point—those who want the *Rogue* to prevail because they view the *Rogue* as a savior and liberator of our species, and those who see the *Rogue* as an evil threat bent on destroying humankind—and in attempting to do so, possibly getting our species annihilated," he lectured. "My pack—the Salvatella pack—views the *Rogue* as the former and is eager to find and protect her. The Reinoso pack believes the *Rogue* must be destroyed at any cost."

"Yeah. I think we covered this already. I'm not joining your Salvatella pack."

"What if I'm not asking you to join the Salvatella pack?" He leaned in, scooting closer on the bench seat and invading my space. "What if it was only me and not my pack? What if I went on the run with you and Sloane and we started our own pack?"

My brows pulled together. His proposal was preposterous, and yet he seemed dead serious about it. "No offense, Raul, but I'm just not into you."

He rolled his eyes. "For last time, I'm not hitting on you. I'm trying to save your life and the life of your child."

"That a 'no' to the fries and fish tacos, then?"

"Hunting and destroying the *Rogue* is all Alcaeus has ever preached, Avery." His mouth thinned into a hard line. "His father, Antonio, who was Alpha before him, was crazy dogmatic in his interpretation of the *Rogue* prophecy. Hunting and destroying rogue werewolves—and ultimately destroying the *Rogue* in specific—has been a primary ongoing mission of the Reinoso pack throughout Alcaeus's life. Believe me, I know. My dad participated in their rogue hunting missions in America. It's how he met my mom."

I knew I needed to hear this. Because I needed to get my head knocked back on straight. It didn't make it any less painful to come to grips with the fact that I'd shagged and bitten and was still actively lusting after a man who was possibly the greatest threat to my daughter's existence, though.

"I know you like to work alone. And you've done an admirable job of protecting Sloane up to this point. But your world is about to change—you must realize you're running out of time. The decade of no light has shielded the *Rogue* from both camps. But in a few months, the decade of no light will end."

Shit. This was the piece that Wyatt and I hadn't been able to figure out. I should've asked Raul about it sooner instead of getting distracted by the story of Alcaeus and Lupe.

"Wait—what does that mean?" I asked. "What's it about—this great race to find and eliminate the *Rogue* before the end of the decade of no light? What's going to change?"

His face scrunched up like I'd asked a ridiculous question. "Are you serious? Have you not noticed how fucking obsessed our species is with prophecies, psychics, and the like?"

"Of course I've noticed that, but—"

"Everyone believes that the next generation of seers are bound to start coming into their powers at the decade of no light's end. In a few months, the search will be on for the next great seer—you know, so that he or she can tell us all what's coming next and what to do with ourselves about it," he said with no small measure of sarcasm. "It can amount to bad news and good news on both sides. But either way, for you and Sloane, it means that there may be virtually nowhere that you'll be able to hide anymore."

My mouth went dry. My heart raced. "I'll take my

chances. We'll be fine." I felt suddenly desperate to get home to Sloane.

"Jesus, you don't get it." He slammed his palm down onto the tabletop, rattling our shot glasses once more. "You wanna know why I'm tired? Because Sloane has recurring nightmares, that's why. Did you know that?"

My racing heart stalled for a moment at Raul's words; then I reminded myself that there was no way that he knew. "All kids have nightmares from time to time," I responded carefully.

"Right." He nodded slowly, his throat working. "But Sloane's are bad. Lately, they're always about explosions." His eyes held mine, gauging my reaction. "She has recurring nightmares where she's trapped in a ball of fire that she can't escape from. Doesn't she?"

I couldn't process this. "I don't know what you're talking about," I mumbled, moving to stand.

He grabbed my wrist and jerked me back down to my seat. "I know you think I'm some kind of creep … a supernatural opportunist who is a danger to your daughter." He paused, his eyes lowering to the tabletop. "And, well, maybe I am—or *was*—just that." His brown eyes returned to me, pleading. "But I swear, I only found you because Sloane found me first."

I hadn't a moment to digest what he'd said before he continued quickly, "I can't gain access to Sloane's mind or yours. But somehow Sloane is able to draw *me* into *her* subconscious when she wants to. I don't think she knows who I am, why or how she's doing it, but she's doing it more and more. She does it when she's having nightmares, so I don't think she can control it."

He paused, regarding me anxiously, before he said, "I

think that maybe when she gets scared, she reaches out blindly to those she has an unconscious connection to who she thinks can help her. But if she can do that with me, then she can do it with others, which means you may not even have a few more months that you'll be able to remain hidden. She could inadvertently draw enemies to you sooner."

"Connection to you?" I hissed, my voice barely carrying as I fought to process the horror of what he was claiming. "You sick fuck. My daughter has no connection to you. She's a *child*. And you don't know her!"

I realized I might have shouted the last part loudly enough for the whole restaurant to hear when Raul's hand clamped over my mouth and I was yanked flush against him, all but pulled into his lap.

"You are missing the fucking point," he spoke in my ear. "Focusing on your worst motherly fears while ignoring the greater danger to your daughter. I am not *that* kind of predator."

"You're the insane kind." My words were smothered against his palm, muffled and unintelligible to everyone else in the room but us. "How could anything you're saying possibly be true?"

"Because if you believe that souls are eternal," he spoke calmly in my ear, "then maybe you can believe that Sloane was someone else before she was born as Sloane. And that maybe her spirit knew me before. Maybe ... I was one of the last connections to this world that she had before she left it. Maybe on some level ... she feels that connection to me still—even if she doesn't understand it."

"You're lying. My daughter doesn't connect, you ass," I shouted into his palm. "She's the goddamned *Rogue*. Don't you get it?" I felt tears well up in my eyes.

I willed them away. I was on the brink of hysteria. And I couldn't afford to have a breakdown.

Not now.

He was lying. He had to be. My daughter wouldn't reach out to some stranger in her sleep when she was scared. Our connection might've been fragile, but any connection Sloane felt to anyone, she felt with me.

Me. I was her mother! *I* was her protector. She wouldn't pick some pretty-boy surfer werelock over me to come to her rescue—unconsciously or otherwise—even if he did have greater, cooler powers than I had.

My vision went red. Then it went black as the blood roared in my ears and I confronted the same insidious fear that had taunted me from day one: the fear that I wouldn't be enough to protect my own child. That no matter how strong or clever I was, ultimately, I would never be strong or clever enough to protect Sloane from the world of hunters and opportunists who were destined to seek her.

Even Sloane knew I was so outclassed that I was bound to get myself killed. That's why she kept warning me away.

I heard Raul shushing me and telling me to calm down as he dabbed a cloth to my eyes. I heard a woman's voice asking if I was all right, too. And then I felt Raul press a kiss to my forehead as he responded, "We just got engaged. She's a little emotional."

CHAPTER 24

Alcaeus

Once Kai had teleported to and from Morumbi ten times, returning with a total of twenty soldiers, in addition to Remy, to aid us in our search for Avery, Kai and I went out to look for her ourselves, teleporting all over Denver. We'd canvassed Union Station and every corner of LoDo, LoHi, Wash Park, Cherry Creek, Uptown, RiNo, and Capitol Hill when Remy tapped my mind and said that he had news.

Kai teleported us back to the hotel suite, where Remy had been busy reaching out via phone and videoconference to various contacts across the U.S. that he said he'd gotten from Lessa.

"I just heard from a small pack in North Carolina," Remy announced upon our arrival. "They recognized Avery from the photos I circulated to werewolf packs across America."

"You did what?" I shouted. "What photos? Who told you to circulate my mate's photo to enemy packs? Goddamnit, Remy, I thought you had specific contacts you were working with who we could trust to be discreet about this?"

"Riiight," Remy said in a maddeningly calm, patronizing voice as his green eyes squinted questioningly at me before cutting to Kai.

Fucking Remy and his bullshit touchy-feely empathic powers. He'd been trying to read my emotions and force his calming mojo on me ever since he'd arrived—lecturing me about how all the angry, threatening texts I'd fired off to Raul from Avery's phone would only put her life in more danger. And now he was treating me as if I was the one overreacting, when he'd just put my mate's life in jeopardy by blasting her photo across the Internet to American packs who, like the Highlands Ranch pack, might be out to kill her simply because she'd survived a rogue attack.

"They're not enemy packs," Remy defended evenly. "These are all American packs on the list that Lessa identified as being on our side—at least as far as wanting to destroy the *Rogue*."

That was exactly my fear. The Highlands Ranch pack had been on Lessa's list. "Lessa gave you that list?"

"Well," Remy said with a sheepish shrug, "I kind of swiped it from her computer files when she said she had an emergency of her own to manage and couldn't help us."

"What did the North Carolina pack have to say about Avery, Remy?" Kai interjected.

"The East Lake pack knew Avery as 'Holly Bishop Carmichael,' actually," Remy said, reading from the notes on the pad of paper in his hand. "They said she was nine months pregnant at the time that she came to them, reportedly fleeing from an abusive ex-boyfriend werewolf who had knocked her up."

"Pregnant? What? Who? He's a dead man. Did you get the name of the ex-boyfriend?"

Kai covered his face with his hand and exhaled audibly next to me. "Yes, let's make sure we track down that abusive ex-boyfriend werewolf of hers. I'm sure he's every bit as real as Avery's 'Holly Bishop Carmichael' identity."

"It's not the same thing!" I snapped. "He could very well be real."

"Ah ..." Remy held one finger up as he again referred to his notepad. "You should know, Avery has also been identified as Franchesca Amelia Dupont, Paris Kenya Watterson, Theresa Jane Havensworth, Charlotte Anne Rousseau, Gertrude Katarina York, Arabella Justine DePaul, Camilla Beatrice Ravenscroft, Jacqueline Grey Margot ..." He paused to look up from his notepad. "Shall I continue? There are a few more names that various packs and rogue hunters have assigned to her image."

"No, please don't," Kai said. "When was she with the North Carolina pack?"

Remy glanced back down at his notepad. "She came to them seeking shelter on May seventeenth, 2014, and they helped her give birth to a baby girl on June thirteenth, 2014."

"Fuck," Kai swore. "That puts her date of conception right around September twenty-second, 2013, the same day that Avery miraculously survived a rogue werewolf attack while on a camping trip in the White Mountains with her friends and fiancé."

"Oh, shit," Remy murmured, sharing a look with Kai. "You're not thinking—"

"Wait—Avery has a daughter?" I blurted the obvious aloud, realizing I'd overlooked that bombshell in my anger over the abusive boyfriend.

My mate was a single mother! What an ass I was that I'd

never even thought to ask her if she had any children. I'd just assumed that she didn't when I'd scented that she was single and hadn't been with anyone in a long while.

"What happened with the baby, Remy?" Kai pressed. "Was the child born healthy? Normal?"

"Healthy, yes. Normal—not entirely. The baby girl was born completely scentless, according to the East Lake pack." Remy's eyes flicked from Kai to me. "Stranger yet, they said that the baby's mother, Holly Bish—I mean, Avery—ceased to have a scent as well after the birth."

"She does *so* have a scent!" I raged at Remy. Goddamnit, what was wrong with everyone? "What did that pack do to her? I will kill every last one of them."

Remy's eyes widened. He darted a glance at Kai. "Uh … nothing, really. They're a fairly religious pack, as I understand it. So when Avery's baby girl werewolf was born on Friday, the thirteenth, utterly devoid of scent and having somehow caused Avery, the birth mother, to lose her scent in the process as well, they declared the newborn the spawn of Satan. Avery no doubt sensed that she was no longer welcome or safe there, because she fled their compound that same day with her baby."

I felt my eyes shift and had to focus to stop my claws and fangs from extending as outrage burned and bubbled up within me at the thought of Avery having to flee for her life from every pack that she'd ever tried to join. Envisioning my mate on the run and in hiding with a newborn—alone and completely on her own for so many years—was enough to make me want to tear the whole world apart avenging her.

"I want names," I demanded. "I want a list of every werewolf who has ever threatened or persecuted my mate. Make that every human, too, while you're at it."

I was stomping over to the little bar next to the settee I'd destroyed earlier to pour myself a stiff drink, when the realization hit me. I stopped in my tracks as a huge grin broke across my face. "Oh, my God."

I spun around to face Remy and Kai. Remy was regarding me strangely. Kai was sporting his normal harassed-and-put-out expression. "Guys—I'm a dad! Can you believe it?"

Remy's jaw fell open. Kai's eyes closed as he reached up to pinch the bridge of his nose.

My excitement dwindled, along with my grin, as another thought occurred to me. "Wait. Where's Avery's daughter? We need to find her right away. We have to make sure my daughter is safe, too."

CHAPTER 25

Avery

I FELT A RING MATERIALIZE ON THE FINGER OF MY LEFT hand beneath the table, right before Raul took that same hand in his and raised it up in the air. A feminine gasp and mini squeal of delight followed.

Raul pressed a kiss to my ear and whispered in a sweet voice for me to pull my shit together and get my eyes under control. I realized when he said it that he'd been dabbing a cloth over my eyes not because I'd been crying, but because my eyes had shifted to that of my wolf. I got it under control then.

Pasting a mask of joyous exuberance on my face, I yanked Raul's hand with the cloth from my eyes to find not only one but two excited female servers standing at our table making "aw" eyes at me and my idiot "fiancé."

I endured their congratulatory platitudes with a patience I didn't possess as one of them called two more servers over to see my ring.

All I wanted was to get home to my daughter. And I was drunk in San Francisco with a bulletproof werelock who'd just "poofed" a six-carat diamond engagement ring onto my finger. *A teleporting werelock who'd claimed that my daughter's spirit knew him from a prior life when she was someone else—and that she was pulling him into her nightmares now whenever she was scared and needed help.*

I desperately needed to find a way to kill this guy.

Fellow diners were now flocking over to our table. Jesus, did he have to pick such a huge-ass diamond to go with his white lie and drag this out unnecessarily? I hoped the rock was real. Because I was keeping that shit. And hocking it at the first opportunity.

Raul had relinquished my hand to the fifth gawking restaurant patron to come by—a sweet little old lady with lipstick on her teeth—and he had been busy rapidly texting something on his phone ever since. But once he'd finished and had put his phone away, he interrupted the old lady's chatter by looking her directly in the eyes and telling her, "You're done here, sweetheart. Go back to your seat now."

I was about to apologize to her and flay him for being rude, but the little old lady didn't seem insulted in the least. In fact, she smiled brightly, said, "Okay," and promptly went back to her table where her husband was still hunched over his plate, eating at a snail's pace.

"What the hell was—"

"Not now," he cut me off, his expression stone-cold serious. "We've got company coming. Bad company." His eyes cut to the front of the restaurant.

I followed his line of sight and saw a tall, sophisticated-looking man with dark hair approaching the hostess stand.

"Who is that guy? Why are his eyes that weird shade of blue?"

"He's someone who'd kill his own mother to get his

hands on the *Rogue*," Raul said with a smile plastered on his face.

He lifted his chin and nodded in greeting to the handsome man who was now chatting up the young hostess. Then he turned his smile back to me and whispered through tight lips, "Change of plans. You're gonna have to trust me and play along. Your life and Sloane's life depend on it."

"Why? What's his superpower? Are those colored contacts he's wearing?"

"He's your average petty, sadistic, emotionally rapey, empathic werelock. And he happens to be my boss." He said all of this with the same strained smile on his face, leaning close and talking to me as if we were flirting.

"He'll assume you're human unless he's near you long enough to pick up on your absence of scent. Try and keep your emotions simple if you can," he advised quickly. "Be as uninteresting and even flat-out stupid if you can manage it so that he won't try to read your mind and discover that he can't. I got a bad feeling we're screwed either way, but we gotta give it a shot," he muttered. "Your boy *Chaos* will have to get you out of here if I can't easily dismiss you without arousing Gabe's suspicion. I just texted Alcaeus our location. Let's hope you're more than a notch to him." He planted a palm on either side of my face.

"Wh—"

Raul's lips crashed into mine before I could protest. Instinctively, I struggled at first. My struggling only caused him to pull me in closer, until I was mashed so tightly up against his hard chest I didn't think I'd be able to squeeze a breath into my lungs—assuming I could even disengage from the unforgiving lock his mouth had on mine in order to take one.

When I didn't immediately open my mouth for him, he bit down on my lip, drawing blood and growling, *"Play along,"* as he fisted the back of my hair in a punishing grip.

I did play along then, forcing my body to go limp against his and allowing my mouth to mechanically kiss him back. There was something in the weight of Raul's command that alarmed me—that and the recognition that the desperate urgency with which his tongue invaded my mouth had nothing to do with sexual attraction and everything to do with fear. *Fear of his werelock boss.*

A fear so great that he'd called upon his enemy, Alcaeus, to get me safely away from Gabriel. Not a great indication of what a sweetheart this guy Gabe was likely to be.

When Raul's hand fell to my knee, then moved higher to squeeze my thigh, I figured his boss was probably almost to our table, so I made a fake moaning noise in response— giving it my best ridic porn-star all.

We were all in or nothing at this point, right?

I knew it the moment Raul's Alpha was at our table. Beyond his canine scent, he smelled of old money—that complicated yet classic old-fashioned cologne scent mixed with a hint of antique furniture polish, fresh linen, gold bullion, and stinky cheese that all filthy rich people somehow managed to reek of.

When he cleared his throat to announce himself, I could tell straightaway he was a dick. The guy managed to project how much better than everyone else in the room he thought he was with one simple throat clearing.

Raul tore his mouth from mine and turned his head to greet him. "Gabe! So good of you to join us. Allow me to introduce you to Cynthia, my date. Cynthia, this is Gabriel, a dear friend and coworker of mine."

"Congratulations!" Another woman who'd been seated at a nearby table chose that moment to rush over to ours and wish me well. "Sorry to interrupt," she said with a glance at Gabriel, before turning to address my fake fiancé. "I saw that beautiful ring and heard you tell the waitress that you'd just popped the question." She gave Raul a motherly pat on his shoulder. "Well done, young man. You two make a lovely couple. And the ring is stunning," she said to me.

As the woman flitted back over to her own table, the priceless look on Alpha Gabriel's face threatened to undo whatever thinly held grasp I still had on my unraveling composure—*and sanity*—tonight. I had to casually cover my mouth with my fingers to hide my twitching lips while pretending that I was wiping a nonexistent lipstick smudge from Raul's kiss.

Alpha "Gabe" Salvatella's appearance reminded me of that of an obnoxious trust fund kid I'd gone to college with who'd had such delicate, perfectly symmetrical bone structure that I'd felt compelled to do him the favor of breaking his nose. Like my former classmate, Gabe's features were the sort that crossed the line of pretty boy into straight-up effeminate. And those eyes of his—*yikes!* His eyes were a phony-looking shade of blue that was way creepy. Like alienesque creepy. I wasn't sure if Crayola even made a crayon that shade of blue. The color was reminiscent of a swimming pool that'd been shocked one too many times with chlorine and wasn't safe to swim in.

But beyond the spookiness of his eyes and the unwelcoming, pompous manner that he projected to the world, I couldn't readily gauge what might be so frightening or dangerous about him.

Raul's fingers latched onto my bicep, and he drew me up to an awkward standing position at his side—sandwiched as we both were between the bench seat and the table.

"It's such a pleasure to meet you," I said, automatically extending my hand to him in greeting.

Gabe didn't take it. In fact, he pinned me with a contemptuous look that said he thought I was trash before pulling a chair out for himself and sitting down across from Raul.

Oh, boy. I was well used to rich, snobby people shunning me. I'd experienced it often enough throughout my life. And although I knew it was a good thing to be ignored by this doucher, attempting to snub or insult me was like waving a red flag in front of a bull—just asking for trouble.

"Oh, thank God. You're a germaphobe, too? *Whew,*" I said, promptly withdrawing my hand as Raul and I reclaimed our seats. "Hey, are those colored contacts? You have to tell me where you got those so I can get some for Halloween."

In my head, I rationalized that my ditzy behavior was in keeping with Raul's advice and therefore acceptable.

Gabe frowned from me to Raul just as Raul rushed to shut me up.

"Gabe, hey, I'm real sorry I didn't check in with you sooner," Raul apologized in his carefree surfer way. "Lost track of time. Cynthia and I hit it off, and things just kinda went … well, you know. So, what's up? You need me for something?" Before Gabe could answer, Raul turned to me and said, "Hey, babe, remember when I said I might have to hit the office tonight because of that big account I've got closing this week? I think Gabe needs my help. You understand, right?"

"Oh, sure, sure. Anything for you, pumpkin." I gave his nose a playful tweak.

"Thanks," Raul said, leaning in to give me a peck on the lips as his eyes told me to knock it off and tone it down.

Well, what did he expect when he called me babe?

"I'll just be going so you boys can do your work thing," I announced like the airhead that I was pretending to be as I stood from the table.

"Not so fast."

The first spoken words out of Gabe's mouth were accompanied by a force of gravity that sent my ass sinking back to the bench seat in a manner similar to how Raul had knocked me to the concrete in the parking garage. The difference was my lungs didn't feel compressed this time—my emotions did. That was the only way I could describe the dizzying, confusing sensations I felt. It was like I didn't know what to feel—what I was supposed to feel, rather.

Suddenly, I felt such an uncomfortable sense of self-doubt that I wanted to cry—similar to how I'd felt earlier when Raul had told me that Sloane was reaching out to him for help during her nightmares instead of me. Intuitively, I sensed that Gabe was somehow reading my strongest, most recent emotions. Perhaps pulling them from me somehow?

Either way, as I stared into Gabe's cruelly mesmerizing blue eyes now as if unable to look away, I struggled to recollect what had seemed so funny about them before.

"What. The fuck. Is this?" Gabe's cool gaze shifted to Raul, and I felt a measure of relief from the weird emotional pressure he'd wielded over me. "Who is she, Raul?"

"Gabe, look, we just—"

"I grow weary of you underestimating my intelligence as well as my patience. *Who is she?*"

"We only met a few days ago, but she's already very special to me."

It occurred to me Raul was trying to stick with mostly true statements as much as possible, so that Gabe wouldn't scent a lie from him. Most of the fibbing he'd done thus far to Gabe had been combined with lies that Gabriel would believe Raul had stated in order to fool *me*—such as the big account closing and the two of them needing to hit the office tonight.

"Did you create that shield? How did you do that?"

"I didn't do anything, I swear. I've never touched her mind."

"Well, some powerful werelock clearly has." There was a pregnant pause before Gabe deduced, "And you know who it was ... don't you?"

"No, I don't. I don't know."

Gabe chuckled. "Right. You don't *know*. But you suspect. Don't you?" His lip curled into a sneer. "Really? Do we have to play these childish games every single time? You leave me no choice when you block me from your mind and play word games to avoid telling me what I want to know."

"Come on, man, don't do this. I'm telling the truth. We just met a few—"

"Help! My husband's choking!" the old lady with lipstick on her teeth suddenly shrieked. "Somebody help him. He's choking!"

There was a stir of commotion as waitstaff and patrons rushed to administer the Heimlich on the old man who was soundlessly choking, his eyes wide and frozen with a look of shock and fear.

"Aw, fuck, Gabe, don't do this." Raul dropped his head in his hands. "Why do you have to do this shit?"

"Whatever do you mean?" Gabe said with a serene smile. "People choke to death in restaurants all the time. Especially the elderly."

"It's fucking senseless, and you know it," Raul hissed.

"Is it? I'm not sure I agree. You know I only do it because you care."

Oh, my God. My stomach dropped as I realized Gabe had caused the old man to choke. And from the way Raul was reacting, it seemed as if this was normal behavior for his Alpha. Petty and sadistic, indeed.

"Stop it," I heard myself demand before I could think it through.

Raul kicked me under the table as Gabe's unsettling blue gaze slid back to me.

I heard another woman scream and turned to see a waitress slip on the hardwood floor as she raced to the choking man's aid, her legs flying out from underneath her with such unnatural force that she flipped hard and fast onto her back, her head smacking against the hard floor with a sickeningly loud thwack that instantly rendered her unconscious.

Pandemonium broke out as people rushed to the unconscious waitress on the floor and shouted for someone to call an ambulance. Meanwhile, the old lady began wailing as her husband went limp and lost consciousness despite efforts to dislodge whatever was stuck in his windpipe.

"Humans die from accidental falls all the time, too." Gabe shrugged, looking from me to Raul. "Such fragile creatures. Aren't they, Raul? Speaking of … how is that med student friend of yours? I believe she lives here in San Francisco, doesn't she?"

Raul huffed and shook his head, his Adam's apple

bobbing restlessly in this throat. "She's Milena's friend. Not mine."

It didn't smell like a lie, but Gabe chuckled at Raul's obvious distress at the mention of this woman who was Milena's friend and not Raul's. *Why would Raul care about a friend of Alpha Milena's who wasn't his friend?*

"Of course, of course. You know, I read some interesting things from Mike's mind the other day about your habit of covertly keeping tabs on *Milena's* friend." Gabe tilted his head, his creepy eyes absorbing Raul's mounting distress with great delight as I heard Raul's heart rate spike.

"Is anyone here a doctor?" a male waiter frantically shouted, raising his head from where he was bent over the waitress on the floor. "We need a doctor! She's not breathing, and I can't feel a pulse."

"Shall we go for three tonight? I feel like an aneurism should be next. Or are you ready to tell me who she is and who you *suspect* put that mind shield on her?"

"I'm a doctor," Kai's voice echoed through the restaurant.

I'd never been so happy to see someone I hated before as Kai cut a path straight to the unconscious waitress. But before I could exhale my relief, my airway was blocked off as Gabe materialized on the opposite side of me on the bench seat and wrapped his hand around my throat.

CHAPTER 26

Alcaeus

WHEN A TEXT MESSAGE CAME IN ON AVERY'S PHONE addressed to "Chaos" from Raul, thanking me for my many "love notes" and telling me to get my ass to a specified address in San Francisco because Avery's life was in danger, I thanked all that was holy, even as I feared the worst.

Kai, Remy, and I teleported to the restaurant to find patrons in a panic over humans who were in critical condition, and to see my mate, Avery—who was sandwiched in between Raul and Weenie Gabe on a bench seat at a back table of the restaurant—*with Gabriel's hand wrapped around her throat.*

"Who is she? What happened to her scent?" Gabriel growled at Raul. "Why are *they* here unless she's someone important?"

I was a blink away from shifting as I rushed to her—*human witnesses be damned*—when Raul beat me to it, roaring in anger as he lost his skin to his wolf form while simultaneously throwing a blast of magic at Gabe that knocked him off of Avery and onto the floor.

"Holy shit," Remy muttered beside me.

Raul regained his human form and conjured new clothing onto himself so quickly I might've questioned later whether or not I'd actually seen him shift at all if Remy hadn't been standing next to me at the time to corroborate it.

I had Avery in my arms a second later. "You're okay, you're okay," I told her. Her hands were holding her throat, and she was coughing and gasping for air. "Let me see, honey. It's okay. Get Kai," I ordered Remy as I carried Avery away from Raul and Gabe.

"Kai's a little busy with a head injury right now."

"My husband's not breathing! Where's the ambulance?" an older woman was squealing behind me.

"I got it," Remy announced, rushing off to help.

"Where the hell did that come from?" Gabriel demanded of Raul in a low, angry voice. "You've been concealing more powers from me now, too? On top of everything else? Don't think I don't know you've been forming alliances behind my—"

"You threatened my woman!" Raul thundered back. "And she just became my fiancé tonight," Raul proclaimed, pointing his finger at Avery in my arms. "I have protective instincts that are beyond my ability to control where she's concerned."

What? Raul's words carried the scent of truth. As I looked at Avery's hands around her neck, I saw for the first time the enormous diamond engagement ring she was wearing.

"You said you just met her," Gabe countered.

They were both dead as far as I was concerned.

I stopped listening to their bickering as Avery ceased

coughing and swallowed experimentally, wincing as she did so. "I'm okay," she said in a hoarse whisper. "I'm fine. Put me down."

Hell, no, was that happening. She smelled terrified and distressed. *And like Raul.*

But she still smelled like me, too—although it was faint. *Avery was mine.* She had marked me. Nothing Raul said and no ring on her finger changed that fact.

I bent my head and kissed her forehead, then her eyes, and then all over her face. Her arms reached up around my neck and her fingers sank into my hair, pulling me closer as my lips claimed hers at last.

She claimed mine right back, drawing my tongue deep into her mouth as she moaned and squirmed in my arms and curled against me, yanking on the roots of my hair to draw me closer. The scent of her arousal hit me, calming my wolf's pressing need to kill Raul and Gabriel.

Cheers erupted all around us. I thought they were for me and Avery at first, until I realized that Remy had successfully cleared the elderly man's windpipe when I heard wheezing noises and his wife sob, "You saved him. Thank you! Oh, dear Lord, thank you."

"Anytime, ma'am," Remy responded.

"Then why is your *fiancé* kissing Alcaeus?" Weenie Gabe's voice further grated the haze of my Avery bubble.

"Because we're fighting over her," Raul returned. *"Obviously.* You saw me kissing her ten minutes ago when you came in. She's confused."

My mouth froze against Avery's at the truth I heard in Raul's words.

Unlike his sister, Milena, Raul had always been an excellent liar. He'd learned early on back when he'd been a human pack member with us how to bob and weave and dance around truths, knowing the wolves around him would scent his lies. Raul's powers had obviously grown considerably over the years if he was able to disobey his Alpha, Gabriel, to the point of openly attacking him in defense of Avery's life. While it was possible he'd also learned from Gabriel how to mask the scent of his lies—as many of us werelocks could manage to do on occasion, depending on the lie—I had a bad feeling he was telling the truth about kissing Avery.

It was confirmed when Avery started to shake in my arms and moved to hide her face against my neck, barely smothering a snort as her body was racked by a sudden attack of giggles.

I felt Lessa try to tap my mind, and I forcefully blocked her. *God,* my sister had the worst timing. I'd been trying to tap Lessa's mind for the past hour, and I'd been blocked. I'd stopped trying when she'd finally shot me a frantic, cryptic message through our mind connection to leave her alone because she needed all of her focus for a crisis she was managing.

Avery had quickly gotten her ill-timed fit of amusement under control, when I turned to Raul and Gabriel and declared, "She's not confused, Raul. Avery marked *me.* We're mates. You have no claim on her."

"Who the hell's Avery?" Gabe asked, setting Avery's body shaking anew against my chest as she buried her face in my shoulder.

"Avery is Cynthia's other name, but she prefers that I know her as Cynthia," Raul had the gall to say to his own Alpha. *Once again not a lie, although not quite the truth.*

Another round of applause and cheering erupted

throughout the restaurant as Kai declared the woman with the head injury to be in stable condition.

"She should still go to the hospital for monitoring," Kai told them. "Make sure an ambulance is on its way."

The restaurant staff was thanking Kai, and someone started to ask him what had been in the intravenous push he'd given the woman, but Kai ignored everyone, striding straight over to me and announcing, "We're leaving." He glared at Raul. "It's your mess to clean up from here. See that you do."

"*Wait.*" Avery pushed away from my chest, trying to wriggle down, out of my arms. I held fast. "Chaos, stop; let me down. I'll go with you, I promise." Instinctively, my arms tightened around her, despite her reassuring words. "For serious, I *want* to go with you. But not if you don't let me down this minute."

Reluctantly, I set her on her feet. But I refused to allow her to move outside the circle of my arms as she turned to face Raul and Gabriel.

She raised her chin, smoothed her hair back, and righted her clothing. "Raul, *pumpkin,* you know I like you. But I realized tonight after your boss with the chlorine-shock eyes attempted to strangle me that he's clearly stressed about that big account you two are closing this week. I think you need to head to the office to work on that with him asap."

Raul covered his mouth with his fist and nodded, while Gabriel's "chlorine-shock" eyes glowed blue fire, directing such unmasked violence at my mate that I yanked her closer, pressing her back flush against my front, and barely restrained myself from moving her behind me to shield her from the evil intent in his creepy glare.

"Sooo ..." Avery proceeded, unperturbed—either oblivious or uncaring as to what nature of monster she was taunting. "I'm just gonna hold onto this ring for a little while longer while I consider your offer, mmkay?" She held her left hand up and wiggled her fingers, showing off the offensive rock Raul had apparently gifted her. "'Cause I think I might need to fuck this one"—she jerked her thumb back at me—"a few more times before the Final Rose Ceremony."

CHAPTER 27

Avery

"**C**HLORINE-SHOCK EYES," A MALE VOICE SAID WITH A chuckle, right next to my ear, startling me. "I'm using that from now on."

I turned to find a werelock with brown hair and gorgeous, deep-set green eyes standing directly beside me. He had the kind of bone structure and enviable features that could make a girl jealous at first glance, but unlike Gabe's, this guy's features were assembled in a way that still made him look masculine. It was something in the harder set of his jaw, perhaps, or the subtle hint of "you don't want to fuck with me" that his eyes projected.

"I'm Remy," he introduced himself. "Alcaeus and I are stepbrothers."

Chaos had thrust me behind his back in some hero-complex protective gesture, and he was now holding me against him with one muscled arm wound behind him, shackled around my waist, while he and Kai argued with Raul and Gabriel in Portuguese. Didn't make much logical sense to me—considering Gabriel could probably cause me to choke to death on my own tongue if he wanted to—whether I was standing in front of or behind Alcaeus. But I decided I'd point that out to Chaos later, when he and his wolf were in a more receptive mood.

"You must be Avery," Remy surmised with a smile. He held his hand out to me, and I shook it. His grip was warm and firm, and he held onto my hand a few extra seconds too long—as if he were trying to absorb information about me through our palm connection. "Or is it Cynthia? Or perhaps Blythe? Franchesca, Holly, Paris, Charlotte, Gertrude—"

"You're so funny." I yanked my hand from his.

Damn. Apparently Raul's little shower rescue had resulted in a *lot* more snooping into my past by Kai and company. This was bad news—potentially disastrous—depending on where they'd sourced their intel. In my head, I went back over the names he'd just rattled off and realized that he had, in fact, said Holly. *Not good news at all.*

"Are they really arguing over who's going to Jedi mind trick all of these people?" I asked.

Remy looked surprised. "You speak Portuguese?"

"No, I just know men."

He chuckled. "I have a feeling it'll end up falling to me, anyway. That sort of task usually does. I've spent a great many years researching and dissecting the human brain and psyche."

Interesting. *And unnerving.* Not sure if that was something I'd be so quick to brag about. What did that research and dissection entail when you were a werelock, I wondered?

"Wow. You really don't have a scent," Remy observed aloud. His brow wrinkled as his eyes assessed me in a manner that made me feel as if my life story was scribbled in permanent ink all over my face. "You just might be Al's mate after all," he concluded slowly, "if he can truly scent you when the rest of us can't. Tell me, has anyone else ever been able to scent you before Al?"

"He goes by *Chaos*," I said in retort. "He prefers Chaos as a nickname."

Whoa. Where the hell had that come from? I didn't even know if that was true, and I'd just insisted on it to his own brother.

"Oh?" Remy raised one brow and grinned wide, exposing perfect, white teeth. "Good to know. I wish he'd told me that one hundred and fifty-three years ago when we first met." He shrugged. "Although ... I can't say that I ever would've agreed to call him that."

Yep ... he hated me. I'd just bombed out with the first family member of Chaos's that I'd met.

I gave myself a mental shake. What the hell was I thinking? *Of course* he should hate me! *And why should I care?* Alcaeus's family and entire pack were my enemies, as Raul had said. It's not like our mate bond was real and we were going to live happily ever after together.

And even if it *was* real and Alcaeus *wasn't* my enemy, over my dead body would my daughter and I ever become another "rescue case" for Alcaeus to indulge his ego and hero complex over.

"What did you say to upset her, Remy?" Alcaeus barked suddenly, releasing me just long enough to turn around to face us before mashing me up against his front.

"Nothing," Remy insisted, taken aback.

"She's upset, and you were the only one talking to her just now."

He could sense when I was upset? *But I wasn't*

upset. Well … maybe a tiny bit—although my reasons were irrational.

"I called you 'Al,' and she told me you preferred 'Chaos' as a nickname," Remy said.

"I am not calling you Chaos," Kai halted his banter in Portuguese to interject. *"Ever.* Don't even think to ask it of me."

"Chaos," Raul threw up the shaka hand signal to Alcaeus, prompting both Gabriel and Kai to roll their eyes. "Take care of my girl, 'kay? I'll see you at the Final Rose Ceremony," he taunted, piggybacking on my earlier joke.

With that, Gabriel and Raul vanished, just as I started cracking up and Alcaeus looked ready to lunge at Raul. Surfer-boy werelock was growing on me.

But I still had to find a way to kill him.

"Remy, you got this, right?" Alcaeus told more than asked his stepbrother.

"Of course," Remy responded. He turned to me. "See? What did I tell you?"

༄

Kai was transporting Alcaeus and me back to Denver *Star Trek*-style when something odd happened with the process. Having only been teleported a handful of times, I wasn't exactly a qualified judge of how it was supposed to go, of course, but even I knew that something had gone wrong when instead of a fluid reentry, it was so violent I felt like my innards had rematerialized a fraction of a second before the rest of me had.

The next big tip-off that something had gone terribly

awry was the fact that we'd rematerialized in the woods somewhere. *Not in Denver.* I was pretty sure we were nowhere near Colorado—or even within the United States anymore.

I fell to my hands and knees atop the leaf litter, seriously on the verge of blowing chunks. There was an awful pressure in my head. Having all those shots with Raul was definitely not the brightest decision.

"What in God's name was that, Kai?" Alcaeus demanded. "Are you trying to kill Avery?"

Chaos rushed over to me and knelt at my side. But when he tried to do that face-cupping move on me, I shook my head and pushed him away. We had a smokin' hot chemistry thing going that I didn't want to wreck by projectile-vomiting in his face this early in the hooking-up stage.

"It's not my fault. I don't know what the fuck happened!" The alarm I heard in Kai's voice was not reassuring. "Some force of magic pulled us way off course. I couldn't control it."

"Oh, no …" Alcaeus murmured. "Kai—you know where we are?"

"Yes."

"This is bad."

"I know it's bad!" Kai growled. His heart was galloping. For the first time, I scented fear from Kai.

"Where are we?" I took deep breaths, trying to get my nausea under control.

"The Hoia Baciu Forest," Chaos said.

"Where?"

"It's an ancient forest in Romania that—"

"I know where it is!" I screeched as panic gripped me. I also knew that it was one of the most legendary haunted forests and timeless wonders of the world, renowned for magnetic anomalies and paranormal activity that scientists had tried and failed to explain. How had we been blown this far off course?

Adrenaline pushed my nausea down as I sat back onto my heels and took in my surroundings. I'd always wanted to see the vegetation of the Hoia Baciu Forest—*during daylight hours*. The trees were as I'd seen them in photographs—bizarrely shaped and creepy-looking as fuck. They were of a strange, twisted wood so strong that reportedly it could not be cut with an ax, and the trunks frequently displayed char marks that scientists could not explain. Electronic equipment malfunctioned and failed within the forest, which was also often referred to as the "Romanian Bermuda Triangle."

I knew that the main magnetic, paranormal "hub" within the dark forest was a circular area three hundred meters wide where vegetation would not grow. Countless scientists from around the globe had sampled and studied the soil from this famous "dead zone" and had found no reason for the absence of growth.

The forest was known for everything from ghost and UFO sightings to talking wind and moving balls of light. I recalled reading how people had experienced severe migraines and nausea from being in the forest, and had emerged with unexplainable burn marks and rashes on their skin. Forest travelers had reported being attacked by unseen forces—clawed at and thrown to the ground. There were countless stories of people getting lost and losing track of time and their hold on reality while inside the forest—legends of those who had ventured into these woods and had never returned.

Kai had crouched to the ground and was holding his head in his hands now, muttering curse words and mumbling in Portuguese. Then he began rocking back and forth on his heels, groaning "no" over and over, before falling into a repeated chant of one name: *Maribel.*

I wondered if it was the same Maribel that Raul had told me about. Raul had said that the undead werelock who'd struck the deal with Lupe had been a member of the Reinoso pack.

Alcaeus's scent had grown beyond anxious as he observed Kai's breakdown.

Shit. We'd crash-teleported into the most frightening forest on the planet at night, and our only ride out appeared to be inoperable.

Alcaeus left my side to squat down next to his Beta. "Kai, talk to me. What happened? Was it a vision that threw you off? Was it Maribel? Did you see her?"

"No." Kai shook his bent head. "It wasn't a vision of her that pulled us off course. I never see her anymore when I teleport—not once these past ten years have I seen her."

His voice cracked with emotion, but I couldn't tell from the way he said it if not seeing her was a misery or a relief to him.

"It was *magic*," Kai insisted. "A magnetic force powered by dark magic. I'm pretty certain Gabriel was behind it. He must've drawn on the magnetic energy of the forest dead zone to magnify the effect."

Note to self: Never teleport again.

Kai covered his face with his hands and sobbed, "I can see Maribel's memories, Al. Her final ones—when she tried to teleport back to the wreckage in Madrid that last time."

I remembered now that I'd also read stories of people

entering this forest and experiencing visions and memories of the deceased, or of recalling detailed memories of past lives, only to forget all but vague recollections once they'd exited the forest.

"I can feel her emotions—her initial sense of panic when she couldn't control the teleport; the confusion she felt—how inconceivable it all seemed to her at first. Her absolute denial that any of it could possibly be happening to her—she never made mistakes."

Kai broke down in a fit of sobs again, and Alcaeus put a consoling arm around his friend's shoulders.

I felt a strong vibration of magic shift the air around me. I knew Alcaeus felt it, too, when his head jerked up from where it had been bent over Kai's form. Chaos's heart rate spiked, yet he turned and gave me a casual smile and a "thumbs up" and said, "Don't worry, he's totally fine. This is a great breakthrough moment he's having. Everything's good."

"There was no way in Maribel's mind that Nuriel and Gabe could ever best her," Kai continued to relay. "The final destruction of the Salvatella pack had been prophesied to come by *her hand*—she was smarter, more powerful than the Salvatella brothers could ever hope to be, and she knew it." He shook his head. "She knew it in her last moments that this was all wrong, and she simply couldn't accept defeat." He cried out and yanked on his hair, unraveling. "Oh, God, Al, I can feel her desperate scramble to figure out a way to stop it as she felt her body begin its inevitable separation from her spirit—because she'd been caught in the teleport for too long. And me ... her thoughts of me when ..."

His voice broke as he resumed sobbing, his body curling into a ball on the ground.

I felt my eyes blink with tears as Alcaeus spoke softly to Kai, consoling him. I'd like to say that mine were tears of empathy for Kai and for how he'd obviously suffered over the loss of this Maribel, but it felt more personal than that somehow.

"Kai, man, keep in mind, this place—the spirits here … they do weird things to people's minds," Alcaeus told him. Then he turned and whispered to me with a reassuring smile, "He just needs a minute."

When Kai began growling and clawing at the ground and at himself like a distraught, wounded animal, Alcaeus winced and said, "But, hey, this is all good. You just … go there, man. It's important to finally work this stuff out … after one hundred and eight years …"

Alcaeus turned to me and said, "Maribel was Kai's mate."

My mouth formed an "o," even as I felt my brows draw together.

Alcaeus must have sensed my confusion, because he explained, "Yes, they were true mates—like you and I are. They even marked one another. But when Maribel died, she couldn't accept the idea of Kai dying because of her— because of their mate connection. So she found a way to remain in limbo between worlds for ninety-eight years— unbeknownst to Kai and the rest of us—in order to keep Kai alive."

My mouth fell open. *Jesus*. Talk about dedication. *And for Killjoy Kai?*

"No one knew how Kai had managed to survive his true mate's death. For nearly a century, his survival was an unexplainable anomaly of the werewolf world."

The ground shook beneath me.

Alcaeus felt it, too, because he muttered, "Fuck," before

quickly continuing to explain for my benefit, "Maribel stole life force from the living and consumed souls of the dead who were on their path to crossing over in order to remain in limbo and absorb more power."

When another, stronger vibration of magic pulsed over us like a current, Chaos frowned and looked down at Kai, who remained inconsolable. He was behaving more animal than human now.

To me, Alcaeus said, "What Maribel did was an unprecedented phenomenon that breaks every rule of the cosmos and our species, basically. Eventually, she amassed enough power over time and figured out how to communicate with and forge alliances and agreements with members of the living—those who could be bribed or coerced into helping her—in order to hijack a power source strong enough to sever her mate connection to Kai." The ground shook again. "So that he could live on freely without her. *And be miserable.*"

He'd spoken the very last part under his breath, but I still caught it. *Wow.* Again, that seemed like a Herculean effort just to save one guy who was a total pill to be around. *Then again, it was just possible Maribel had actually done it for herself—so she wouldn't have to spend eternity with Killjoy.*

"Kai, man, I know this is probably a cathartic, super-important emotional breakthrough moment you're having here, and as much as I'd love to camp out in a haunted forest with you tonight discussing this shit, I think your Gabe theory is spot on. This was no accident. It was a set-up—because we're about to be ambushed."

CHAPTER 28

Alcaeus

THERE WERE AT LEAST THIRTEEN WERELOCKS approaching, and twice as many werewolves.

Don't look panicked. Don't act freaked out.

"About to be ambushed" probably hadn't been the best choice of phrasing to use in front of Avery, but I needed to get through to Kai somehow. I'd done a semi-decent job of keeping Avery calm thus far by distracting her with tales of Maribel, the greatest psycho werelock genius of the last century.

I turned back to Avery with what I hoped was a reassuring smile as I frantically tried to tap Lessa's mind yet again. *Blocked.* Damn. If anyone could teleport us out of this, it was Lessa. I knew that it was no small feat trying to teleport out of the Romanian Bermuda Triangle. And Kai had only been teleporting regularly for the past decade— once undead Maribel had *finally* passed on and the disturbing visions of her that had kept him from teleporting previously, ceased.

I could've reached out to Alex for help, of course, but I'd just as soon eat my own liver than give my baby brother something to hold over my head for the next century. And as rude as Kai had been to Avery, that was nothing compared to how Alex was likely to behave toward her given his track record. I wasn't ready to introduce Avery to Alex yet.

"So, sweetheart, when I said 'ambushed,' I didn't mean that in … an overly *bad* sense of the word or anything," I told Avery. She gave me that adorable "what the fuck" face of hers in response. God, she was perfect. I needed to get inside of her and put my mark on her neck, stat. "Just trying to keep the night exciting," I joked. "This is like our second date—time to ratchet things up, right?"

I turned back to Kai and asked, "Any chance you can teleport us out of here?"

He looked as if he was doing better and pulling his shit together. He wasn't sobbing and clawing at himself anymore, at least. Whenever Kai allowed himself to get emotional—*which was rare*—he reverted to his primal nature in a big way.

Which possibly wasn't such a bad thing right now … come to think of it.

Kai shook his head and sat up. His eyes were still his wolf's blue hue, but his claws and fangs had retracted already. "Do you have any idea how hard it is to teleport out of a magnetized paranormal vortex like this, Al?"

Yep, he was mostly back to normal. Crap, that was fast. I'd have to rile him up again.

"Is this all part of the excitement?" Avery asked with a nervous laugh, unsteadily arising to her feet on the forest ground that was now shaking continuously beneath us. "If you tell me right now that you staged all of this, I promise I won't even be mad."

Fuck. She was starting to smell terrified. And yet she was still cracking jokes and being cute with me. We were totally going to live happily ever after.

"Don't worry, honey, we got this."

I pivoted and slapped my palms down onto Kai's shoulders, facing him at eye level. "You want to avenge Maribel? You want to rip Gabriel into tiny pieces for killing your mate? Then we need to get out of this trap alive. I estimate there are about forty werelocks and werewolves coming our way."

"Holy motherfucker, did you say *forty?*" Avery asked, rushing over to us.

"Yeah ... ah ... give or take. Trust me, it *sounds* way worse than it'll be in reality when—when they get here," I faltered. "Kai and I do this sort of thing all the time." I turned my focus back to my best friend. "Listen to me. I *don't* want your head in this, Kai. I *don't* want you to strategize or overthink your battle approach. I need *primal Kai* right now, okay?"

He shook his head.

The sound of paws thumping and crunching through the forest could be heard coming from all directions now.

"*Yes,*" I told him. "I need circa 1618 feral-arctic-beast Kai—the Kai who attacked my father in the wilds of Greenland and tried to take his whole head off in one bite. I need circa 1638 red-haze Kai who gnawed a Portuguese Inquisitor General's body in half in two bites for torturing and raping young girls."

His eyes glowed brighter and he growled at the mention of the inquisitor. I was reaching him. "I need you to kill whatever comes at you as fast as possible. Got it? Just focus on Maribel's final memories, and channel all of that rage and sexual frustration you've built up over the last one hundred and eight years into tearing things apart."

A howl rang out through the trees. Another responded. Then another.

Kai's eyes had taken on that bright, vacant glow they always got when he was about to go full-blown crazed animal.

"Hellfire, we're surrounded," Avery exclaimed. "They're *really* close. Shouldn't we throw a—a flashbang or … something? *Anything?* Can't you guys conjure weapons?"

We already had a weapon. It was just a matter of drawing the White King out. He was nearly foaming at the mouth with rage now, and I hadn't even yanked his biggest trigger yet.

"These werewolves coming for us, Kai, they're the same ones who hunted the arctic werewolf into extinction. They massacred your family—your entire pack. And now they're coming for you. What are you going to do? *Shift!*"

By the time I gave the order, he'd already done it, morphing into the biggest, angriest, *only* pure white arctic werewolf left in existence.

I heard Avery's sharp intake of breath, followed by, "Nice coat!" Drawing my attention to the fact that she was still in human form.

What the hell?

"Was that true?" she asked. "That's not true, right? That was just your pump-up speech I'm guessing."

My Alpha command should have caused her to shift as well. I was seconds away from shifting myself. I turned feral eyes to her and ordered, "*Shift*, Avery."

Her eyes had shifted and her fangs and claws were already out, but she hadn't let her wolf out any further than that. And she didn't so much as twitch at my command.

My eyes flew wide. "Why aren't you shifting?" I was hoping to keep her out of the fighting as much as possible, but she had to be in wolf form, regardless. She was already more fragile, being that she was a common werewolf.

"Oh, don't wait for me; I'm good like this." She gave me a nervous smile and dismissive hand gesture. "I'll shift when I need to."

My jaw fell open. The wolves were nearly upon us. I needed to shift and back up Kai. "You'll shift *now,* Avery. *Now.* It's not safe otherwise."

"No, really, I'm fine." Her fingers gripped and fidgeted with the hem of her T-shirt. "I do my whole 'wolf thing' a little differently than most, but it works for me. You'll see."

What the ever-loving fuck was she talking about? There was only one way to do your "wolf thing"—*as a god-damned wolf.* You were either in wolf form or you weren't.

"This is not up for debate!" I yelled at her, and felt awful for doing it. I promised myself I'd never yell at her again unless her life was in jeopardy—*which it was right now!*

"I said I'm fine as I am, Chaos," she sassed me back, planting her hands on her hips. "I always start out fighting in human form. I shift if I need to. I'm an excellent fighter in human form."

This was utter insanity. What was wrong with her? She was a common werewolf, not a werelock.

I swallowed the shouted retort on the tip of my tongue and tried to get a grip on my mounting anger over her cavalier attitude and carelessness. She was putting her life in danger. And in doing so, she was putting my life and Kai's life in jeopardy.

I had to take a calming breath and remind myself that my mate hadn't grown up as a werewolf, and she had never been accepted for long by any pack. She obviously had a severely limited, faulty frame of reference for how things worked in our world. She seemed to have no respect for wolf pack hierarchy—no basic understanding of what it meant to take orders or to fight as a pack.

Dozens of pairs of wolf eyes could be seen coming through the trees now, rapidly approaching our small clearing. White King Kai didn't wait for them to break the tree line though; he charged right into the trees to meet the first three werewolves closest to him, taking their heads off in seconds flat, and blasting their bodies into the path of other wolves charging forward as a welcome message.

This was going to be epic. Kai was at his most fun whenever he let his wolf go full-blown off-the-chain savage.

"Dang," Avery murmured. "Wasn't expecting that from the doc."

Most didn't. But most didn't know that Kai was a werewolf who'd been reared in reverse. All werewolves were born human and shifted for the first time at puberty. *Except for Kai.*

Kai had existed solely in his wolf form out in the wild among common *wolves*, not werewolves, for the first sixteen years of his life. He'd had to learn fairly late into his development how to shift into and remain in human form—not to mention how to behave like a human. To this day, Kai often came across as overly controlled and stiff in human form, because his first and true form would always be that of a wolf.

I was reluctant to leave Avery unguarded, but the sooner I started killing, the safer she would be. "Steer clear

of the werelocks," I ordered her before shifting and running to join Kai.

We were down to five werelocks and seven werewolves.
Much to my irritation and ongoing disquiet, Avery still
hadn't shifted.

While she hadn't attempted to fight any werelocks
yet, thank God, I had endured witnessing Avery kill and
kick the shit out of several werewolves while in her human
form. And her methods were downright dangerous, to say
the least. They were clumsy. Unorthodox. Dirty. *And surprisingly effective.*

She would feign injuries. She'd act afraid, cower, and
pretend to surrender, and then when the wolves pounced
at her—mistaking her for an easy kill—she'd spring up and
punch them in the nuts or claw their eyes. She'd latch onto
tails and throw wolves into trees and other werewolves.
I'd watched in fascination and horror as she'd jumped and
wrestled a werewolf to the ground, put him in a chokehold,
and snapped his neck.

I couldn't believe that this was how she'd been fighting
werewolves for all this time. And that she was still alive!

Because there were so many of them, eventually the
werewolves caught on to her ruse and she was forced to
rely on her fighting skills alone. Multiple times, I stopped
fighting, shifted to my human form, and ordered Avery to
shift. But my commands continued to have zero effect on
her.

Once Kai's initial primal killing haze had calmed

enough for him to take notice of what Avery was doing, he'd been horrified as well. He had shifted to human form to try and order Avery to shift, too, to no avail.

A few times it had looked as if she intended to shift at last, because she'd stop and remove an article of clothing— before continuing to fight. I was quick to reassure her that I would conjure new clothing for her. Kai did the same.

I lost an arm—albeit temporarily—while battling two werelocks at one point because my focus got thrown off as I was worrying about Avery when it appeared as if she was trying to sneak off and find cover behind some trees in order to shift in private of all absurd things.

Kai really lost his shit then, shouting, "Bloody Christ, woman, do you need a fucking phone booth like Superman? Shift, goddamnit! *Shift!*"

Kai took to teleporting Avery out of harm's way in order to keep her safe and to help keep me focused on fighting. He would only teleport her ten-to twenty-yard distances at a time, gaining a better and better sense of how to navigate the magnetic pull of the forest each time he did. And while it was an annoyance and distraction for him to be doing it—as evidenced by his constant screaming at her to shift—I was thankful as hell that he was looking out for Avery. She'd become the enemy's prize target with her odd behavior and bizarre fighting style.

We were down to only three werelocks left to kill, and I'd just pulled one werelock's heart out and blasted it across the forest out of his reach, when White King Kai's fuse finally blew beyond control in his annoyance with my mate.

"If you don't shift this goddamn second, I swear I'll kill you myself!" he roared before shifting into his wolf form and charging straight at her.

Avery screamed obscenities at him, but her body finally gave way to her inner animal at long last in what was the most stilted, awkward, spastic, unnecessarily prolonged, and painful-looking shift that I'd ever witnessed in my four centuries.

I was so staggered by it that I lost an arm once more to one of the two remaining werelocks standing. I probably would've lost my head next if Kai hadn't teleported me—and my arm—out of harm's reach and over to Avery's side in that moment.

Eager to unleash his fury over Avery's outrageous behavior, Kai raced off in wolf form to shred every vital organ he could from the final two werelocks.

I probably should have helped him, but I simply stood there next to Avery, staring in a state of disbelief as I feasted my eyes on my mate's gorgeous red-golden coat of fur.

By God, the fates had mated me to a ginger!

CHAPTER 29

Avery

"**Y**OU WANT TO TELL US WHAT THE HELL THAT WAS about back there?" Kai snarled. He slammed his palm against the stone accent wall of the entry foyer we'd teleported to, before proceeding to angrily punch a code into an outdated-looking security system keypad in the wall next to where he'd struck. It looked like he was deactivating a motion detection sensor.

I crossed my arms over my chest and assumed a nonchalant expression, hoping beyond hope that he wasn't referring to what I feared *(knew)* he was. "What are you talking about?"

"Your shift, Avery." Alcaeus's deep voice echoed in the sparsely furnished, dimly lit entryway, making his words sound harsh. As he turned to face me, I was sure I caught both horror and disgust in his features, confirming what I'd been dreading most. "That was—Jesus, what the fuck *was* that back there?"

Warmth flooded my cheeks. I wasn't much of a blusher, which made my reaction all the more embarrassing. I pressed the tip of my tongue to the roof of my mouth to stem the irrational tide of emotion that rushed forth at his criticism. It was a stupid, petty thing to be embarrassed about. I told myself I was just feeling emotional from the adrenaline rush letdown.

"What? You know I don't have the luxury of disappearing and conjuring my clothing like you guys can," I said defensively. "If it's not practical or convenient to change and preserve my clothes, I avoid shifting for fights unless it's an emergency and I absolutely have to. Otherwise, I'd waste most of my life running around naked and stealing clothes to wear." It sounded rational and plausible enough to me.

"We said we'd conjure new clothes for you," Kai inserted snidely, like the dick that he was. "Multiple times. And for future reference, an attack by forty-some Romanian werelocks and werewolves against the two and a *half* of us constitutes a fucking emergency."

"I'm not a *half*, asshole. I'm an excellent fighter in human form!" My shouted retort sounded painfully loud to my own ears as my words bounced and echoed. I flicked my eyes from Chaos's concerned ones to glance around at the marble entryway walls and floors surrounding us before landing a glare at Kai. "Where are we?"

I turned to look behind me when I realized my words were still echoing there, and found an enormous, darkened room with massive floor-to-ceiling windows overlooking a great expanse of a familiar city's nighttime skyline that was most definitely *not* Denver's.

"Welcome to Al's penthouse in Tribeca."

I spun back around. "You teleported me to New York?"

Kai physically recoiled as my volume reached a hysterical level.

"I need to be in Colorado. Send me back right now."

Kai gave me that bland, patronizing smile I'd come to despise so well in the past two days. "Good luck with that."

"Kai, leave us," Alcaeus ordered.

"But it's just getting good," he protested with a dry laugh that was entirely at my expense. "Ms. Haskie is about to explain why she shifts like an epileptic."

"Kai."

"I'm hoping her explanation includes how she managed to survive a rogue werewolf attack as well as her initial transformation, given the fact she was a human with zero family history of any werewolf DNA. No doubt this shifting seizure defect is related."

"That's enough, Kai."

"I don't need to explain anything to you, and I give zero fucks what you think of me, my DNA, or my shifting ability." I knew I shouldn't let Kai rattle me. But the expanding pity and resignation I glimpsed in Alcaeus's eyes hurt worse than the horror and disgust I'd convinced myself had been there a moment before.

"You don't need to explain anything to Kai. But you are going to explain it to me." Alcaeus's low voice had taken on an angry, imperious Alpha quality that sent an unbidden shiver through me. "Leave us, Kai."

For the first time, I wasn't sure I wanted Kai to leave me alone with Chaos.

"I didn't sign up for this, Al. Either she learns to take orders and to shift like a normal wolf or I let her die the next time we're ambushed like that."

"There won't be a next time." Alcaeus's calm, cold words rang with such finality that for a paranoid moment I wondered if he meant to kill me himself.

"She's a handicap enough as it is in a fight being a common werewolf. We don't need the added distraction of her trying to fight in human form like a flashing neon target getting us both killed."

"I said it won't happen again. Leave us."

"Gladly." Kai's eyes passed over me with unmasked scorn. "I'll go report the incident to Milena."

"*No*. You'll go upstairs, get cleaned up, and report to no one," Alcaeus told him.

Geez, this place had an upstairs?

Kai appeared stunned by Alcaeus's quiet command. His mouth opened and closed like a fish before sputtering, "But the pack needs to be informed of the attack. Milena and Alex just met with the Vasile pack a month ago. They formed an alliance. Yet they're obviously in league with Gabriel. This ambush tonight means war."

"We'll inform them later."

"But they could be—"

"*Later.*"

As he made to storm past Alcaeus, Kai stopped and leaned in to his friend, hissing just loudly enough for me to hear, "Fuck her, bite her, fucking strangle her for all I care. Bring her to heel or get her the hell out of your fucking system, Al. Because it's going to come down to her or me."

After Kai's departure, Chaos and I stood and stared at one another as a glacial two minutes ticked by on the antique grandfather clock adorning the foyer.

"Your best friend is a dick." It was probably the wrong thing to say to break the silence, but I needed to get it off my chest. And Alcaeus's uncharacteristically quiet, cool demeanor was making me anxious.

His nostrils flared. "That dick saved your life tonight."

I swallowed the childish retort I yearned to speak. "You're right." It burned like acid in my throat to admit it, but I knew it was true. "I owe you both for saving my life. T-thank you," I managed to force out.

He shook his head, his gaze falling to the floor between us. "You owe Kai. Not me. I couldn't have saved you with that many werelocks attacking at once. You'd have been dead without Kai's ability to fight and to teleport you out of harm's way."

Great. I'd damaged his male ego as well as his hero-complex pride, strained his relationship with his long-time friend and Beta to the breaking point, and almost gotten him killed tonight. I was on a roll.

I was also dirty, exhausted, and emotionally spent. But lashing out at Kai had been the wrong call. I needed to get back to Sloane. And that was best accomplished by appeasing the werelocks presently holding me captive—particularly the one upstairs who hated me and wanted me gone. *Who also happened to have the ability to teleport me back to Denver in a pinch.*

"I—I feel terrible about all this," I announced with what I thought passed fairly well for sincerity. "I should go apologize and thank Kai," I suggested, moving swiftly in the same direction Kai had gone.

"No." Alcaeus's hand shot out and imprisoned my wrist.

Oh, boy.

"You and I are far from done here."

He led me from the foyer past the main room with all the windows, down a hallway, and into a fancy, open sitting room. Soft lighting gradually illuminated the space upon our entry.

"Sit." He released my wrist and pointed to a modern, minimalist-looking, dark leather tufted sofa.

I sat.

He walked over to a little standing bar shelf in the corner and poured himself a full glass of caramel-colored liquid from an unmarked crystal decanter. He downed it like a shot in one gulp then chased it with another before refilling the same glass, walking over, and extending it to me in offering. I happily snatched it from his hand and drank it down in one pull before he could even tell me what it was.

I gasped and coughed as the liquid burned a hole straight to my stomach. "That's not scotch! What the hell is that?"

"*Werelock* scotch."

"You trying to kill me?"

The sound of his soft laughter made me instantly feel better. There was something so natural about the way Chaos laughed. His angry, cool demeanor in the foyer had felt all wrong.

"I'm trying to get you relaxed enough to let me teach you how to shift," he admitted.

"Nice buzzkill. In that case, you'd better bring the whole bottle over."

Ten minutes and another two glasses of "werelock scotch" later, my vision had gone a little blurry and I couldn't quite feel my face anymore as I sat slumped sideways on the sofa next to Alcaeus, blatantly staring at his lips as he explained how my inner wolf was supposed to lead the shift, not me.

"I suspect what's happening is that you're overthinking things, honey."

I liked when he called me honey—*although I'd never admit it.*

"See, you're trying to control each stage of the shift with your human mind"—he pressed his fore and middle finger gently to my temple—"rather than giving in to your wolf's instincts and letting her shift freely."

I leaned into his touch as his fingers stroked downward, tucking my hair behind my ear. He was disheveled and dirty from our battle with the Romanian wolves, and still he smelled divine.

"So you're making it harder than it needs to be, understand? But it's not your fault or anything to be embarrassed about. Oftentimes young werewolves will pick up and cling to ineffectual habits that they learn early on. It's especially problematic when there's not a reliable elder in a pack to assist new wolves their first time shifting."

My eyelids fluttered shut as his fingers curled behind my neck and began to rub back and forth. *Oh, that felt nice.*

"Avery, honey, will you talk to me about what happened the first time you shifted?"

What would it hurt to share just a little? I needed his help. It was essential to my daughter's survival that I learn how to shift right. How would I teach Sloane how to shift one day when her time came if I didn't know how to do it right myself?

"Well, I was in a cage in a basement. I had my only friend—a human guy I've known for years—watch from outside the cage with a tranq gun aimed at me in case I went berserk."

"Jesus." His fingers stilled against my neck.

"We made the most of it … 'cause I didn't really think I'd live through it. He told me stories about comic book superheroes and villains to pass the time before things got intense. Oh, and we had a tripod with a video camera set up … you know, to record the transformation for scientific research purposes and all."

"Are you fucking kidding me?"

I cracked one lazy eye open, then the other, and sighed at the look on his face. "You're disgusted by me again."

"No, I'm not." His jaw was taut; lines of stress marred his forehead. "What do you mean by *again?* I have never been disgusted by you, Avery, and I never will be. I'm upset and disgusted by the circumstances surrounding your first shift. You really didn't have any werewolf assist you your first time? Just some human who didn't know any more than you did about what was going to happen next?"

"Yeah."

"I'm so sorry." His big hand cupped my jaw as troubled hazel eyes roamed my face. "I can't believe—can't imagine—how you survived that. It's unheard of, honey."

I swallowed and shrugged it off as I told myself he was more than concerned. *He was suspicious.* And he was still my enemy. "Wasn't your fault; it all worked out okay."

His eyes on me were intense. "Go on. Please?"

"Keep massaging my neck," I ordered, hoping to lighten the mood.

He cracked a weak smile and resumed his ministrations.

"Not much else to tell. The last three days were the worst—where it felt like my bones were melting and my organs were exploding. And then the actual transformation was pretty fucking gross. Wyatt threw up a few times during the final stages," I recounted with a humorless chuckle. "He's never done well with blood and gore. But he stuck by me the whole time."

Alcaeus made a subtle "hmph" sound and mumbled sarcastically, "Sounds like how a guy named 'Wyatt' might handle it."

Hellfire. I'd slipped up and said Wyatt's name. That werelock scotch was straight-up moonshine.

I was beating myself up while simultaneously reassuring myself that it wasn't as if I'd dropped Wyatt's last name—there were far too many guys named Wyatt in the world for Alcaeus to ever connect it to my Wyatt—when suddenly, Alcaeus's fingers froze against my neck. His whole body went stiff as a board and his heart rate accelerated. And he smelled …

Upset.

Really upset.

"Ah, God." He withdrew his hand and stood up. He began pacing. "Oh, my God, I'm an idiot." He crossed to the bar shelf, poured himself another drink, and downed it.

He resumed pacing.

"You tried to kill me," he said more to himself than to me. "You came into the bathroom to kill me. Your gun was already aimed at me when I first turned around and saw you."

What? *The hell?* Was he just realizing this *now?*

After all that had happened between us since, *now* he was upset that I'd shot him five times?

CHAPTER 30

Avery

"**Y**OU DON'T FOLLOW ORDERS," ALCAEUS CONTINUED talking to himself, tugging at the back of his neck. "It's like your wolf can't even feel my commands."

"It's nothing personal."

He shook his head. "You have no pack. You've been run off by every pack you've ever tried to join."

I didn't like where this line of revelation appeared to be headed. I shrugged, even as my breath quickened. "I've always been a loner-*ish* type."

"But you're not a rogue." His hazel eyes caught mine. "You *can* connect." He licked his bottom lip. "Really, *really* well in fact." His voice lowered and his eyes darkened as he said it. "And you bit me." He took a step toward me. "Your wolf claimed mine."

Where was he going with this? His behavior was making me nervous. I was too tired to deal. *And suddenly very horny.*

"I—I think I should go upstairs now and apologize to Kai," I announced, standing up from the couch. "I need to shower, too. I'll just go do that as well." *And masturbate.*

"Sit down."

I sat.

He came to stand directly in front of me. A certain hardness and determination had settled over his features, raising my hackles. "Kai says that you're on multiple rogue hunters' hit lists throughout the U.S. because you've been tracking and assassinating rogue hunters for the past decade. Is that true?"

He was throwing off that hardass Alpha mojo of his again. It hit me like a sucker punch to my clit.

"I haven't killed *that* many," I said with a huff.

He nodded slowly, his expression stern as his eyes traveled over me. I couldn't tell if he was gearing up to lecture me or fuck me.

"And you survived a rogue attack. That's how you were infected with werewolf venom, correct?"

I nodded. There was no point in denying it. I knew he'd heard it from Clifton and the Highlands Ranch pack already. Kai had gathered more than enough information on me to confirm it as well. And there was little to no chance Kai hadn't already shared that information with Chaos.

"I need to know how you survived the rogue attack."

I swallowed. "Um, well, there were four of us. I managed to grab a rifle while the rogue attacked the other three campers. I got lucky."

"Why'd you just do that?"

"What? Grab a rifle?"

"No. Lie to me."

"I didn—"

"I can smell it loud and clear when you lie, Avery. You aren't adept at masking the scent of it. *At all.*"

Well, I'd never had to worry about it before.

"And why did you refer to them as 'campers' a moment ago," he continued to interrogate me, "as if they were strangers who happened to be at the same campsite as you?"

Yep. Kai had told him plenty.

"Because people who *camp* are called *campers,*" I returned tartly. "In fact, the police report, park ranger report, and all the newspapers referred to them as 'campers,' too. The headlines literally read: 'Three campers found mauled to death in the White Mountains.' "

"But they were your friends who died. Your fiancé."

The last part seemed harder for him to say.

"And they were also *campers.*" I contended. "Labeling them 'campers' doesn't marginalize them in my heart, Chaos. Sure, maybe it compartmentalizes them a bit. Maybe I do it to avoid the innate emotional response tied to words like 'fiancé' and 'best friend,' but that doesn't mean I'm pretending to myself that they weren't important to me, or that I love them any less today than I did that day that I lost them."

"I didn't say that." In one fluid movement, he'd invaded my space and was leaning over me—a hand braced on either side of me against the back of the couch—his muscular frame and delicious masculine scent scrambling my senses all over again.

"You didn't have to." I pushed my palm against his rock-solid chest, trying to put more distance between us. But his huge, hard form didn't budge.

Fuck, the man was hot. And confusing. Why did he have to poke at me like this?

"Look, I don't know what you're getting at here, or what you expect me to say. I'm not perfect, all right? My shifting skills aren't the most pretty or graceful. But I'm not broken. Stop looking for ways to fix me."

"That's not what I'm doing, Avery."

"Yes, you are. Know how I know?" *Crap.* My voice had gone breathy.

"How?" His tongue swept his generous bottom lip as his hungry eyes feasted on my own mouth. His nostrils flared, and I knew he scented how wet I'd become.

"Because I know all about trying to fix people," I continued with a brittle laugh. "I know all about trying to save people, too. And just so we're clear, fixing and rescuing other people is a *you* problem."

"I know it is, honey."

"I mean it's a *me* problem. *And* a *you* problem. Whatever. You get what I mean." I was nervous-rambling now.

He looked like he was about to kiss me.

"I do," he agreed with a hint of a smile. "We're both fixers. It's a shared problem."

"Don't look so pleased about it. It's a bad thing."

"If you say so."

Just when I was sure he was going to kiss me, he pushed off the back of the couch, moving out of my space as he stood upright—leaving me feeling flustered and bereft at the loss.

My disappointment was short-lived, however, because he reached one hand behind his thick neck, grabbed his shirt collar, and pulled his T-shirt over his head and off in one sexy move.

I saw my mark at the juncture of his neck and shoulder, and my mouth watered at the sight.

It was still there. He hadn't blocked the progress of my

werewolf mating venom to prevent it from becoming permanent, as Kai had said that he was capable of doing.

He reached for the button fly of his jeans next, and my stomach flip-flopped.

My inner wolf did a happy dance.

He could have easily vanished his clothing. But it was as if he wanted me to watch him strip naked—knowing full well what it was doing to me. And there was no hiding what it was doing to me.

He pulled his jeans down next.

He wasn't wearing any briefs.

He bent at the waist as he removed his pants at the ankles, one long, powerfully muscled leg at a time.

With his jeans discarded, he casually straightened to his full height again, unabashedly displaying just how virile a man-slash-superbeast he was.

Damn.

I forced my eyes up to his face when I realized that he'd asked me a question.

"Huh?"

"I said, how did you get bitten by the rogue if you had the rifle and shot him?"

What?

Who the hell strips down to their birthday suit to ask *that* question?

"Are you kidding?" My voice sounded every bit as annoyed and sexually frustrated as I felt. "It takes multiple shots." I waved my hand around, struggling to regain my composure as the scent of his sex grew stronger in the air—calling to weaker parts of me. "He charged me and got a bite in somewhere between the fourth and sixth bullet."

"So he got close enough to bite you—bite you hard and

long enough to release his venom—but you managed to keep the rifle in your hands and continue shooting him?"

He'd begun casually stroking the length of his erection as he asked the question, throwing me off kilter even more with his bizarre behavior.

What the—?

"Are you getting off hearing about this?" I balked. "About my rogue attack? Is this some kind of freaky kinky shit you're into? Because I am *not* down with—"

"*No.* No—not at all." His eyes widened at me in disbelief before rolling away, and he began to pace—*while still stroking his dick.* "I'm using physical sensation to try and keep my wolf—and myself—calm as we discuss things that I know I'm going to have a hard time hearing about. Because I need to understand how you were infected and how you survived."

He stopped pacing and planted his hands on his hips, confronting me head on—with his giant dong pointed in the air. "And so far, Avery, I have to tell you, your story doesn't check out. If you were pumping bullets into an attacking rogue, he'd have been so crazed that he would have bitten to kill, not just infect. In the situation you've described, you'd have been more likely to bleed out from a wound by an angry, unstable rogue."

He reached down and cupped and rolled his balls in the palm of his hand briefly before resuming slow, measured strokes up and down his shaft as he awaited my response.

I decided this was the most bizarrely staged exchange I'd ever had with someone. Even for *my* life it was odd—which was saying something.

God, we probably were true mates.

I shrugged and muttered the only snarky excuse I could think of. "Maybe he didn't like the taste of me."

"Where did he bite you?"

"In the woods, by our campsite."

"This isn't a joke, Avery."

That werelock cock of his pointing straight up to the sky taunting me was no joke either.

"He bit my throat," I admitted.

"There's no scar on your throat."

"It healed after I turned." I was grasping at straws.

"But none of your other scars did."

"The others were old scars. The neck wound was still fresh when I turned werewolf."

He raised a sardonic brow. "Ah, that how it works then?"

I pursed my lips. I didn't know how it worked, and he knew it.

He filled the silence. "The wound would've been a week old by the time you shifted. Old enough that it would've left a scar despite your new healing capacity. Unless someone with extraordinary healing capability—such as a werelock—intervened to heal your neck wound and assist your first shift."

"No werelock helped me," I insisted, popping up off the couch in my anger and frustration at his striptease in-terrogation tactics. *How was I supposed to focus with him naked and stroking his cock in front of me?*

"When you went to the police to report the attack," he calmly relayed, "there were no abrasions on your neck or anywhere else. You were dirty and your clothing was torn and bloodied, but there were no physical injuries any-where on your body that they could see—which is what initially landed you on rogue hunters' hit lists when they looked into the incident and read human law enforcement's 'unofficial' record of your account of the attack."

Hellfire.

I walked to the bar shelf and poured myself a glass of water. With my back to him, I said, "Look, I got lucky, okay? What the hell do you want from me? I thought you saw me as your perfect, predestined mate that your ancestors had protected on your behalf all this time. Now you're sorry that I managed to somehow survive the unsurvivable?"

I took a long gulp to soothe the dryness in my throat. *And the panic in my heart.* Then I took another to delay turning around to face him.

"No," he responded from behind me. "I'm sorry that you still feel the need to lie to me. That you can't trust me yet—can't sense how much I adore you. How loyal and devoted to you my wolf and I are already."

I closed my eyes at his words.

I felt his tempting warmth stealing up behind me. Before he could get too close, I turned and sidestepped, holding my water in front of me—as if the cool glass could shield my heart and keep distance between us.

His brow wrinkled. "Don't you know I'm on your side, Avery? That I'll do anything to protect you—no matter who your enemy is?" His hazel eyes on me were searching. Intent.

And his words ... they felt pure—in my heart.

But when he went in for his face-cupping move, I took a step back, challenging, "Why would I know that, Chaos? Trust is something that takes time."

"I agree, honey. But you were smart and courageous

enough to make it this far—to survive for this long keep-ing your daughter's identity a secret from our world."

My heart punch-started and fluttered violently in my chest at his revelation.

He knew.

"And I know you're smart enough to understand that we won't have the luxury of time much longer where your daughter's life is concerned. So I hope you can find the courage to take a leap of faith and trust me."

With every word, he confirmed it: *He knew about Sloane.* How much he knew, I wasn't sure. It sounded like he knew enough.

My heart pounded. The crazy part was it didn't feel so much like terror and panic gripping the organ beating like a wild drum in my chest anymore. It felt like excitement. Maybe even relief.

"Trust that I'll protect your daughter with my life just as I'll protect you."

I didn't stop him or step out of the way when he went in for his face-cupping move a second time.

He knew my daughter was the *Rogue* that he'd been hunting so many years for. *And he wanted to protect her.*

I swallowed. "I don't understand."

His smiling eyes beamed back at me. "I'm all in, Avery. Forever."

His palms were warm on my cheeks as his long fin-gers slipped into the hair behind my ears to rub in sooth-ing circles against my scalp. He sighed gently and pressed his forehead to mine, and that strange sense of familiarity washed over me again—like we'd done this a million times before.

Or maybe it was the sense that we were going to do

this a million times again. *The intuition that we were meant to.*

And I knew in that moment that I wanted us to. More than I'd ever dared hope for such a thing before.

I wanted *him*—the big hot werelock with the weird name who for serious was totally into me despite all the obvious obstacles to our union.

My glass flew out of my hand and shattered somewhere as I reached for him—*for the massive erection between us that curved the right way.*

My clothing evaporated as he groaned and lifted me off the floor, our mouths fusing in a messy convergence of hope and fear, cemented by primal lust as we invaded one another, body and soul.

My hands were frantic to touch him everywhere; my legs locked around his waist. He fisted my hair and his tongue overpowered mine in a kiss that was as exquisite as it was rough. Consuming.

All in.

My back hit the wall. Something crashed to the ground nearby as he shoved inside of me, filling me to perfection.

My claws extended and scored down his back as he thrust hard. *Deep.* Withdrawing and slamming into me with a grunting force that was all animal, his hips rolling and pumping into my slick center that was swollen with need and gripping onto his invading organ as if fearing it might not return each time he pulled it away.

But it did. Returning again and again with a blinding passion that said it'd always be back for more.

He fucked me like his cock was claiming me—because it was.

He was.

CHAPTER 31

Alcaeus

HELD MY WOLF IN CHECK FOR AS LONG AS I COULD. BUT when the first orgasm hit her—her pussy squeezing, fluttering, and clenching around me as her body tightened and then melted in ecstasy against mine—I lost control and sank my canines into her throat.

Mine.

She cried out in surprise and her nails dug into my shoulders.

I paused just long enough to inhale deeply as I pulled my hips from the cradle of her spread thighs, withdrawing a few inches from the heaven of her gripping wet heat. When I scented no fear or pain from her, I growled and thrust my hips forward, biting down until my canines were lodged deep within the muscle tissue of her neck.

Mine forever.

She cried out again.

I didn't pause this time. Because her cry was accompanied by a rush of hot liquid at the base of my cock as her pussy flooded me with heat, her arousal coating my balls as I drew back and rammed deep, again and again, circling my hips and grinding against her to ensure a direct hit to her little button every single time.

Mating venom dripped from my fangs. I released so much of it that the taste flooded my mouth.

Still, I bit down harder—anger and primal protective instincts fueling me as my hands stroked and squeezed her ass and thighs and my fingers found the scar on the back of her left hamstring—wanting to make sure that my mark would take. So that there could never be any doubt to anyone that she was mine.

We were a mated pair. I wanted the world to know that if anyone dared to harm her, they were asking for hell on earth, for fire and brimstone, from me.

When she came a second time, I joined her, filling her with my cum as I released even more venom into her neck.

I bent her over the couch and took her from behind next. The view was everything I'd known it would be, and more.

While the scars on her back that were directly in my line of sight from this angle still enraged me, it was hard to stay angry at the ghosts from Avery's past who had caused those scars amid the sight and sensation of my dick gliding in and out of her wet pink folds. And equally difficult to find room for emotions like regret or sorrow when my mate was moaning and undulating in front of me, arching her back and raising her fucktastic ass in the air, her hips pushing back to meet my strokes as her pussy swallowed my cock, over and over again.

After round six in my sitting room, Avery's tiny stomach began growling.

I brought her to the kitchen to feed her, and wound up feeding myself—spreading her delectable body across the island countertop and eating her to orgasm three times. She returned the favor, dropping to her knees on the floor in the kitchen and devouring my cock with such enthusiasm and skill, I broke down and told her that I loved her.

Seven times.

I'd been trying to hold back, not wanting to freak her out by saying it too soon, but I figured a blowjob love confession was as safe a way to go as any for the first time.

After briefly breaking our sex marathon to eat real food, we found ourselves engaging in shower sex—some of which proved rather acrobatic—for two hours next, followed by a relaxing soak in the whirlpool tub. Avery actually fell asleep curled against my chest for a full thirty minutes inside the tub before my wandering hands made their way between her thighs, rousing her.

Ultimately, we christened every room in the penthouse but the one that Kai was holed up sulking in, before finally doing it classic missionary-style in my bed. We collapsed shortly thereafter from exhaustion.

I was awakened by the sensation of Avery's mouth sucking my cock.

"I love you."

Damn. I'd said it again.

She giggled and hummed around me in response, and my dick jerked, leaking precum into her warm mouth.

I opened my eyes to watch her.

Jesus. She'd twisted her long black hair into a knot at

the top of her head to keep it from getting in the way of her sucking my cock. I could see my mark on her neck. I was in heaven. Her lips were swollen and puffy as they worked me into a state of total idiocy.

I decided she'd never looked so beautiful before as she did with her mouth full of my dick. When she released me with a pop to lick my balls, I decided we'd get married in the morning at whatever church opened earliest.

I think I also said it out loud, because she giggled again as she sucked the head of my cock inside her mouth once more, twirling her tongue all around it before pressing the pointed tip of her tongue into the slit in my glans, prompting me to swear in Portuguese and reach for the knot of hair she'd secured at the top of her head as my hips jerked up into her mouth, filling it to the back of her throat.

Her fingers wrapped around the base of my dick, stroking and pumping the lower half as I rolled and jerked my hips up like a desperate, horny teenager, coming embarrassingly fast inside her mouth.

I was still muttering to myself in Portuguese as she finished me off, licking me clean once she'd sucked me dry, and then pressing a sweet kiss to my dick before hopping off the bed.

"I need a computer," she announced gaily. "And Internet access."

"Take anything you want," I told her with a groan of satisfaction. "Anything in here is yours. I'll put your name on the deed to the whole place right after we get married this morning."

"Right." She laughed and began to explore the room. Naked.

God, she was a sight.

"Am I getting warmer?" she asked as she searched the teak bureau next to my antique writing desk.

"Hot as sin, sweetheart."

She pulled out a razor-thin laptop and held it up in the air. "This one?"

"Any of 'em," I said, stifling a yawn. "I mean it. You're welcome to whatever you want." I rolled over and looked at the clock by the bed. It was a little after three in the morning. We'd barely slept at all.

Before she'd nodded off in the whirlpool earlier, I'd gotten her to confide quite a bit to me about her daughter, Sloane. She'd said that she needed to get a message to Sloane and her caretaker, Azda, and I'd assured her that I'd get her a computer and Internet access right after we got out of the tub.

Of course, that promise had been forgotten the moment I'd been balls deep inside of her again.

"Password?" she asked. She'd set up the laptop at my writing desk and was logging on.

"Bento1482," I answered quickly as I felt Lessa tapping my mind. I hesitated for a second before blocking her.

I really did need to talk to Lessa. But now wasn't the best time.

Right now I just wanted to enjoy being in Avery's presence for a while longer—to bask in this beautiful state of normalcy that we were experiencing. It was so rare in our world. Plus, I was ass-tired, and I needed to have all my wits about me before I started trying to explain to family members about my new *Rogue* daughter, Sloane.

A phone started ringing somewhere—*everywhere*—throughout the house. *I had a house phone here?* Oh, yeah, I guess I did.

I didn't have to look at the caller ID to know that it was Lessa. My sister was a damn bloodhound.

"Sorry. I gotta take this real quick," I told Avery before snatching up the receiver on the nightstand and walking into the adjoining master bathroom for privacy.

"Hey, Lessa," I greeted, then went straight into ditching her. "Now's not a great time. I meant to call you after the meeting in Denver, but I've been kind of busy with—"

"Never mind about that," she cut me off. "I already heard the whole thing was a bust. That's not why I'm calling."

"What? Wait—what whole thing was a bust?"

"When I didn't hear from you, I contacted Clifton, the Highlands Ranch pack Alpha you were supposed to have the meeting with," she relayed at breakneck speed. "He told me they weren't able to make it to the meeting with you because there was some terrible attack on his pack that night."

"Oh, yeah?" I asked nonchalantly, fighting to keep the smile on my face out of my voice.

"Yeah, someone burned their whole gated community down. They don't know who or why."

"Wow. Tough break. Hey, listen, I gotta jet—"

"Alcaeus, wait! I have an emergency, and I need your help."

"I'm listening."

"Wyatt's gone missing."

"What?"

"*Wyatt's missing!*" she screamed into the receiver.

"Lessa, calm down. How can he be missing? Just enter his mind and find his location. I thought you practically lived inside his head already, constantly rearranging his memories and impressions of you."

"This isn't a joke!" she shrieked. "His mind is *blocked*. He hasn't been to any of his homes in the past twenty-four hours, nor has he been to his office. I have tracking devices on all of his cars as well as his shoes, and they're all accounted for. There's been no activity on any of his credit cards, and his cell phone tracking has been disabled."

Yikes. My sister was more than a bloodhound. She had all the stalker bases covered. *And then some.*

"And I've checked the surveillance activity for all the hidden cameras I set up in his homes and his cars and office," she continued, "and there's nothing, Al. *Nothing.* No sign whatsoever of what happened to him. My mate has vanished off the face of the earth. You have to help me find him."

"Okay, okay, when did you last see or speak with him?" I cast my eyes to the ceiling. "Or track him on any one of the many hundreds of tracking devices that you have on him in a given day?"

"About two days ago. I spoke to him in the afternoon on the day of the Denver meeting. Al, I know something's not right. I'm not going crazy or being paranoid. As much as it terrifies me to believe it, a powerful werelock had to have blocked his mind from me. It's the only explanation."

Fuck. Humans didn't just disappear like that—*certainly not when my sister was responsible for stalking them.* And Lessa was right: the most disturbing part was Wyatt's mind being blocked. If Wyatt had been taken hostage by an enemy werelock, it was a threat not only to my sister's life but also to Avery's life, as well as to her daughter's, given how much information Wyatt had about them.

I had a bad feeling I knew just the werelock who was behind this, too.

"Okay. Try and stay calm, Lessa, and keep trying to tap his mind. I'm going to do a little investigating myself. I'll call you back."

After I hung up the phone with Lessa, I immediately dialed the number for "Scary Stranger" that I had memorized yesterday.

Following my initial blowjob love confession to Avery in the kitchen last night, I'd gently grilled her over sandwiches about her relationship with Raul. She'd laughed and reassured me that she was "not into Raul like that" and had explained that she didn't think Raul was actually into her in that way either—that she thought he'd only staged a phony engagement between them in the restaurant just prior to Gabriel's surprise arrival in order to throw the Salvatella Alpha off and help her get away from Gabriel quickly.

She'd also insisted that she'd only met Raul the day before she'd met me. I'd scented no lie in any of it.

And the fact that Raul had disobeyed Gabe, his own Alpha, in order to defend Avery's life last night was significant—I just wasn't sure what it meant or what Raul's game was this time. He was obviously eager to get his hands on Sloane. Yet Avery had said that Raul had offered to go on the run with her and Sloane, rather than try to convince her to join the Salvatella pack.

"Chaos," Raul greeted me in a sleep-roughened voice the third time I redialed his number. "What the fuck, brah? It's five in the morning here."

"Congratulations. It's three in the morning here."

A two-hour time difference likely placed him in Bariloche, the location of one of the Salvatella pack's main strongholds. The fact that he knew that it was me calling from an unlisted number in New York City meant he was either stalking me Lessa-style or he'd only given this particular number to Avery.

"How's my girl?"

I ignored his taunt and got to the point. "What do you want this time, Raul?"

"What the hell? *You* called *me,* dude."

"Drop the surfer-boy shtick. I'm serious."

He laughed. After a pause, he said, "I want an agreement from the Reinoso pack that Avery and her daughter Sloane are off-limits. I want Milena to call off her hunt for the *Rogue,* and I want her to quit lobbying and rallying other packs against the *Rogue* as well."

He didn't sound at all sleepy or surfer-boy blasé as he said it. In fact, he sounded like an Alpha—which was even scarier. Because it was Raul. *And because he was Milena's brother.* Raul had inherited his werelock blood power from the same source that Milena had. And Milena's powers had grown by leaps and bounds over the past decade.

On top of that, Raul had also inherited Nuriel Salvatella's werelock powers—which was the only reason he could teleport. Milena had never gained that ability.

Undead Maribel had transferred Nuriel's powers directly to Raul ten years ago after she'd used Lupe's form as a channel through which to direct her power from the ether and destroy Nuriel in a rather gruesome—albeit well-deserved—display of violence.

Upon his death, Nuriel's powers should have rightfully transferred to his brother, Gabriel, as was the natural law of the werelock species.

My siblings and I had never quite understood why Maribel, a former member of our Reinoso pack, had chosen to rig the system in Raul's favor in this regard. Why hadn't Maribel gifted Nuriel's power to her beloved Kai? Or to Lessa, who had been Maribel's best friend in life? Or even to Alex, who had served as Maribel's Alpha?

We'd been anxious at first about what it would mean as far as Raul's power accumulation and development, but we'd more or less ceased fretting over it when several years passed and Raul's powers hadn't seemed to have changed or developed any further—as far as we knew—and when he remained in his position as Gabriel's head Beta, whereas Milena had already become the Alpha of our pack.

"Are you still there?" Raul asked. "I'm about to hang up and go back to sleep."

"Avery's my mate, Raul. No one in my pack will ever harm my mate or my daughter, Sloane."

He chuckled. "Wow. That's good to hear. I had my doubts about your intentions, but after seeing you and Avery together yesterday, I was almost convinced that you two might actually be true mates."

"We *are* true mates, Raul. There's no question about it. And we've both been marked now."

"Well, congrats, man." He paused. "And you've told Milena? And she's agreed to back off and accept the *Rogue* as her adopted niece?"

When I didn't answer right away, he continued. "Let me guess: that's a no, you haven't told Milena yet? That's what I thought. So look, I'll just hold onto my collateral while you sort things out with Milena and Alex and get me the agreement I want from your pack."

"What collateral?"

"Oh, I think you know, Chaos, or you wouldn't be calling me at this hour."

Little shit. I could hear the smirk on his face through the phone line. *Fuck.* He definitely had Wyatt.

"No, I don't know, Raul," I denied.

"Well, then, you'll find out soon enough. Give my regards to your sister while you still can. And don't fuck this up," he said in warning just before the line went dead.

CHAPTER 32

Alcaeus

AFTER RAUL HUNG UP ON ME, I IMMEDIATELY DIALED LESSA. She answered on the first ring.

"Bad news," I told her. "Raul has Wyatt." There was no time to mince words.

I moved the phone away from my ear as screams of profanity and crashing noises sounded from the other end of the line. Finally, she regained her composure enough to snarl, "What does that bastard want?"

"He wants an agreement from our pack that we'll back off from hunting the *Rogue* and from petitioning other packs to hunt it."

"That conniving sonofa—"

"Just listen, Lessa. He wants an agreement from Milena that Wyatt's friend—Avery, the *Rogue's* mother—and her daughter, Sloane, are off-limits." I cleared my throat and went for it. "Which, by the way, kinda works out well for me. Because um … since I last saw you, I've mated with the *Rogue's* mom, Avery. We're marked and everything. It's a done deal. She's really amazing, and you're totally going to get along with her way better than you do Milena—I promise."

There was dead silence on the line.

"Lessa? Are you still there?" She didn't answer, but I continued anyway. "So we're getting married, and I'm adopting her daughter, Sloane. I know she's supposedly the *Rogue* and all, but c'mon, how much harder could it be to raise the *Rogue* than it was for us to raise Alex?"

When she finally answered, based on her numb, shell-shocked reaction to the multiple bombs I'd just dropped on her at once, I couldn't tell whether or not Lessa believed me that Avery was my true mate. But ultimately, it really didn't matter. The fact that Raul was holding Wyatt hostage was enough to get my sister on board with the plan of protecting Avery and Sloane and backing me up when I went to break the news to Alex and Milena about everything.

I reasoned to her that this all worked in her favor as well—assuming things went as planned and we recovered Wyatt safely. Lessa had been anxious about how Wyatt would handle her betrayal when he inevitably found out that she had used him to try and set up Avery and capture Sloane. But if she switched to team protect-the-*Rogue* now, then at least she could try and spin it to Wyatt that she'd betrayed him because she was trying to capture Sloane in order to protect her, not kill her.

She balked that it was a ludicrous spin, but really, why not? Based on what she'd told me about the level of tinkering she'd already been up to in Wyatt's head, the guy didn't sound all that astute.

I returned to my bedroom to find Avery still completely naked, sitting at my writing desk. I knew it was a visual that would stay with me and that I'd probably never again be able to get any work done at that desk.

She'd just finished up whatever she'd been doing on my computer and was taking measures to erase her recent activity as I stepped up behind her, placing my hands on her shoulders. I bent my head to kiss the mark I'd made last night on her neck.

"Sorry that took so long."

"Hmm?" she responded distractedly, intent on her task.

I didn't know how I was going to break the news to her about Wyatt. And I still needed more information from her about how she'd survived the rogue attack and her initial transformation before I could present the facts to Milena and Alex.

Maybe I could just tell her about Wyatt *after* we recovered him safely?

"Do these hurt?" I asked without thinking as my fingertips traced the scars on her upper back. "I mean *bother*—do they bother you?" I amended awkwardly. Personally, I was anxious to remove them—to heal them permanently with my magic—but I didn't know how to present the option to her in a way that wouldn't offend her. "You know, as a reminder of … stuff."

Stuff that she hadn't shared with me when I'd asked her about her scars in the shower, and then again in the bathtub last night.

She chuckled softly to herself and shook her head as she powered off the laptop. "Nope. Do they bother you?" she countered, before amending in a wry tone, "I mean *hurt*—do they *hurt* you? You know, as a reminder of stuff you weren't around to save me from?"

As she pushed away from my writing desk, I backed up to allow her space. I was still trying to process what she'd just said as she stood and turned to face me. I couldn't read her expression. And I couldn't sense her emotions well enough in that moment to know whether I'd upset or insulted her.

She sighed. "Chaos, the scars"—she shook her head—"you're going to have to get over them."

"Over them? I don't even know how you got them yet. How am I supposed to get over them?"

"Because they're *not relevant*. These scars on me … they're like stamps in an old, expired passport book. They only hint at the places I've been before. They don't tell the story of what those places made of me—of the things that I learned along the way. They can't tell you where I am today, or where I might be going next. They're simply not relevant anymore."

"Then why can't you tell me about how you got them?"

"Because there are better things for us to talk about," she said with a shrug. "More important things—like the things about me that matter *now*." She reached up and cupped my cheek. "You don't need to know the details of all the bad things that have happened in my past to know who I am. Who I am is right in front of you. The things that happen to us in life—that's just circumstance. What we make of them … that's who we are."

She dropped her hand, making a "pfft" sound. "Hellfire, if you don't know that yet after four centuries, then I don't know what you've been doing for all this time."

She crossed to my closet, disappearing inside.

"Of course I know that," I said defensively.

I followed her and found her rifling through my clothes.

Wait—was she upset or not upset? She didn't smell upset, but I wasn't sure. I couldn't figure it out. And I couldn't stop staring at her ass.

"I need something to wear," she muttered as she searched.

She didn't sound upset.

"Are you going to help me by conjuring women's clothing for me, or do I have to try and find something of yours that I can make fit?"

I preferred to keep her naked for as long as possible. Was that an option? I was still naked. Why did she need to be dressed?

I avoided the clothing question altogether and asked, "You're not upset?"

She giggled. "No. But I can tell already that your hero complex is going to get on my last nerve if you don't get it under control soon."

I crossed my arms over my chest. "This isn't about a hero complex. I need to know things about you, Avery. I'm just trying to get to know you better. If I'm going to be able to convince my brother and Milena that Sloane isn't the threat that they believe she is, then I need to know some basic things about you both—and that includes your past."

"Okay, fine," she relented. "I get it. So ask me something more relevant to now. To Sloane."

Wow, sometimes I impressed myself with my ability to pivot and spin shit. I took a deep breath and went in for the big ones.

"Well, you still haven't fully explained to me how you

survived a rogue attack or your initial transformation." I held my hand up to halt her when she opened her mouth to deny it. "I know you said you got lucky, but Alex and Milena will definitely ask about both, and they won't believe that no werelock helped you or that it was luck."

She pursed her lips and remained silent.

So I asked the question I least wanted to hear an answer to next. "And I need to know the identity of Sloane's birth father. Was it your fiancé who was killed by the rogue?"

Please say yes. Please say yes.

She shook her head. "No."

Fuck. *Breathe. Don't look upset.*

After hearing the information Remy had gathered from the North Carolina pack on Avery's "Holly Bishop Carmichael" identity, Kai had been convinced, based on Sloane's date of birth, that Avery had been raped and impregnated by the rogue werewolf who had attacked her.

"So … Kai thinks that … well, he says that based on the birthdate the North Carolina pack gave us for Sloane, your date of conception would likely be …" I paused to swallow. I had been mentally preparing myself for this ever since I'd first heard about Holly Bishop Carmichael. It was best to just push it out and get it over with. "He thinks you were raped and impregnated by the rogue who attacked you."

Proud brown eyes met mine directly, daring me to show pity, as she nodded and replied simply, "Yep. That'd be right."

Fuck.

Breathe.

Think before you talk and react.

Damnit to hell, what exactly was a fucking hero complex anyway? What could I say to her now that wouldn't sound like whatever that complex was that she kept accusing me of? *Shit.* It was all such confusing, uncharted territory I was attempting—when all I wanted to do was go out and kill something right now.

I'd been staring at her for too long without saying anything. I had to say something. I decided to just be myself and handle it how I normally would, while making a mental note to ask Remy what a hero complex was the next time we spoke.

"Avery, I'm really sorry that happened to you. And I just want you to know that you don't have to act so tough about everything all the time. It's okay to be vulnerable with me—"

"Wrong." She held up a silencing palm.

Gah! *Fuck.* I'd blown it right out of the gates!

"You're still not hearing me, Chaos. This has nothing to do with being *tough*. What I'm doing is giving that incident the emotional significance and space within the story of my life that it deserves. That's the difference between being a victim while being victimized, and playing the role of a victim in perpetuity." She planted her hands on her hips. "I'm sorry if your previous rescue cases never grasped that distinction, but I'm not interested in having you try and use my pain to make your dick feel bigger, so get over it."

I was catching serious flies now. It occurred to me that I probably should've been offended by what she was saying to me. I was pretty sure she'd just called me out for being some kind of dinosaur chauvinist.

But my dick—*the dinosaur chauvinist that he was*—didn't get that memo, because he was standing straight up at attention now, looking for the fastest route to getting himself buried between her shapely, naked thighs again.

I took a step forward, planting a concerned expression on my face as I reminded myself not to glance down at her breasts that were jiggling in my peripheral vision when she was lecturing me like this.

She continued, "That rogue attack: circumstance. The daughter I have as a result of that rogue attack—that's the story of who I am. *Today.* You want to see me vulnerable? Talk to me about my child. Don't talk to me about something that happened nearly ten years ago that amounted to a blip of time in the grand scheme of my life."

I nodded and took another step. "You're right." Those two words had always worked with my sister whenever she was upset and lecturing me about something.

Avery's eyes narrowed. "What am I right about?"

Damn.

If I went with "everything," she'd know that I was full of shit and think I hadn't been listening to her at all. The truth was I had been listening. But I could only remain so focused when she was naked and acting all badass like she was right now when all my blood was in my cock.

"You're right that I'm a dinosaur chauvinist from the seventeenth century who has spent several centuries um … rescuing … too many damsels."

Her brows went up.

Score. I totally had this. "But I think I can change that. With time and … hero complex … therapy."

I winced as the last words left my mouth, knowing I'd taken it too far.

She bit her twitching lip, confirming it.

Yeah. *Too far.* Her shoulders were shaking with laughter now.

I'd get better at this.

CHAPTER 33

Avery

WE ENDED UP HAVING SEX IN CHAOS'S WALK-IN CLOSET, then twice more in the bedroom, before he finally conjured suitable clothing for me. The man—*my mate*—was too damn adorable and sexy to resist. Particularly when he walked around sporting monster wood and talking about going to hero complex therapy for me.

While snuggling in his bed in a state of postcoital bliss, I finally broke down and shared the truth with him about how I actually had *not* survived a rogue attack—about how I'd died and come back to life again, my wounds from the attack healing themselves in the process.

Chaos listened intently as I told him about the dark orb that I'd seen and connected with in the ether ... and brought back with me. I told him I believed the soul of my daughter had somehow healed me and that perhaps she had also prevented me from dying when I'd shifted into a werewolf for the first time.

I didn't really know for sure how I'd managed to survive it. That was the truth. I'd definitely felt as if I was dying during that horrible transformation. No one and nothing had helped to hold the pain from me; that much was certain.

Alcaeus said it was important that he meet with Sloane before talking to his brother and Milena about her. I'd wanted Kai to teleport us only as far as Denver, telling Alcaeus that he and I could drive the rest of the way down to Durango. But it was a long drive at six hours, and Chaos insisted we didn't have time.

I didn't trust Killjoy Kai. He'd been giving me the stink eye all morning, and he and Alcaeus had barely spoken since last night. But ultimately I agreed to let Kai teleport us directly to Durango, on the condition that he not come anywhere near Sloane.

As promised, Alcaeus ordered him to wait outside, at a safe distance from the little house I'd rented at the end of a sparsely populated street.

I'd sent a message to Azda and Sloane a few hours earlier through one of the online message forums I used to communicate with Sloane in code, letting her know that I was on my way and that I was bringing a friend with me. The only friend of mine that Sloane knew about was Wyatt. And she had only met him on a few occasions, and always in public settings, never in any of the homes we'd rented.

I knew right away as Alcaeus and I entered the house that they'd gotten my message, because Azda was sitting in her rocking chair dressed in her best housedress, wearing really poorly applied make-up.

As Chaos crossed the threshold behind me, I suddenly felt the blood drain from my face and bile rise up in my throat at the magnitude of what I'd just done in bringing him here. He must have sensed my inner turmoil because he gave my shoulders a reassuring squeeze and stepped forward to introduce himself to Azda.

He had her charmed in seconds flat. Once the initial introductions were made in English, Alcaeus said something to her in another language, and she responded in kind. As I got my breathing and heart rate under control, I realized they were conversing in Navajo.

Tears stung my eyes and I released an internal sigh of relief when Alcaeus chuckled abruptly at whatever it was that Azda had said to him. I gave myself a mental shake and yanked my heightened emotions under control, before quietly excusing myself and heading down the hallway to Sloane's bedroom.

I found her growling and hum-talking to herself, sitting on the floor in the corner, facing the wall.

My eyes flew wide as I took in the destruction that had occurred in the three days since I'd last been here. Her bed was a total loss, as was her dresser. Ashes and scorched remains were all that was left of most of the furnishings that had been in the room. Used fire extinguishers were everywhere I looked. Black char marks marred the walls and the ceiling. And the floor—the carpeting in the room had been burned through to the gypcrete subflooring that lay beneath. Whatever small sections that hadn't fully burned away had melted to the subfloor.

The only thing left in the room that seemed to still be intact and undamaged was her Disney suitcase with the image of Elsa and Anna from *Frozen*. She really did like that movie.

This was bad. Although I'd confessed to Chaos last night that Sloane had recently begun telekinetically setting things ablaze, I might've downplayed just how out of hand that habit of hers had quickly become.

I knocked twice on the doorframe to get her attention. She didn't turn around to acknowledge me, but after about another two minutes, she stopped hum-talking to the wall and issued her usual greeting.

"I was hoping you wouldn't come back this time, Avery."

"I know." I nodded at the back of her head and took a few steps into the room. "But here I am—still living to disappoint you," I teased lightheartedly. "It's a mom's job."

"Your scent's changed," she observed without emotion.

"Yeah." I guessed it had. It occurred to me that I might permanently carry Alcaeus's scent now that he'd marked me. "Um … I brought a friend here with me to meet you."

"I know."

"He's a werewolf, like I am. But he's got special powers, like you do. Do you think you might be up for meeting him? I think you'd like him." When she didn't respond, I added, "*I* really like him. He's … fun. Kinda goofy, actually."

"I can't have fun, Avery," she said over her shoulder before turning around to face me, drawing her knees up to her chest. "I can only do bad things. The voices say—"

"Whoa!" Alcaeus exclaimed, startling me as he suddenly came up behind me and put his arm around my waist. "This is *awesome.* Can this be my room?"

I turned and pushed hard against his chest, walking him backward out of the room as I scolded in a hushed tone of voice, "You can't just do that kind of thing with her. You can't just—"

"Yes," Sloane answered him. "I'm finished with it."

Alcaeus started laughing, and he whispered, "Don't worry," to me before taking my hand and walking us back into the room.

"Wow, that is super-generous of you, Sloane," he told her. "I gotta tell you, your mom is even cooler than I already thought she was if she lets you decorate your own room like this. My mom never would've let me do this." He whistled low. "This is amazing."

"Her name's Avery," Sloane told him, her expression stoic. "Everyone calls her Avery."

"Oh, okay," he agreed, shooting a glance at me. I nodded. "I'll call her Avery, too, then. My name is Alcaeus. But your mom—I mean, *Avery*—likes to call me Chaos. That's cute, right? You can call me Chaos, too, if you want to."

She didn't answer. I could tell she was taking him in, though—doing that thing where she looked through people more so than looked at their exterior.

Chaos took a step closer to Sloane, but I held him back when he made to take another one.

"I was supposed to stay dead," she said to him conversationally at last, like it was a normal getting-to-know-you thing to say. "It was a mistake when I was born again."

That she was talking to him at all and connecting so much already was a really good sign. I prayed she hadn't stumped him with her morbid declaration when he didn't respond right away.

But after a beat, he nodded and said, "O-kay, then. Thank goodness for mistakes, right?"

"You're with the others," she assessed.

Oh, shit.

He cocked his head. "Others?"

"The ones coming for me. The ones who kill Avery."

Hellfire. How to explain that one?

He frowned. "Um … I'm sorry, what did—"

"No one's going to kill me, Sloane," I interrupted. "I'm

always coming home. That's what moms do." I smiled and pulled on Alcaeus's hand, dragging him out the door with me as I told Sloane, "We'll just be in the living room chatting with Azda if you need us, baby."

Once we were far enough down the hallway and mostly out of Sloane's hearing range, Chaos pulled me to a stop and cupped my face in his hands.

My voice was an anxious whisper as I rushed to defend the situation he'd just witnessed. "I swear, that's the first time she's ever burned her whole room like th—"

My words were smothered by an open-mouthed kiss as his body pressed mine up against the wall. I was dizzy with arousal by the time we came up for air.

"She's adorable," he proclaimed with such absolute conviction and enthusiasm, I almost started to cry.

"You really think so?" I squeaked. "I mean, *I* know so—but I'm biased, as her mother and all. I think she's perfect, of course. And she can connect, right? You saw that, didn't you? She totally connected with you in there."

"Totally."

"Oh, my God, this is great." *Hallelujah.* Everything was going so much better than I'd ever imagined it could.

"We need to talk about Azda, though," he said.

"That's right. You really speak the Navajo language, too?"

"Yeah, a little bit. So listen, I—"

"That's so amazing," I gushed.

"Well, you know, I've been alive for a while. I've had time to learn a few languages at this point." He tugged nervously at the back of his neck.

He was so hot when he got all cute and modest. I tilted my head to the side. "So ... you speak every language on the planet, pretty much?"

"Nah. C'mon, there are over seven thousand spoken languages. Give me a break; I'm not *that* old." A faint tinge of pink colored his cheeks as he smiled back at me, and my heart had never felt so light and full of hope before.

I wasn't only in desperate lust with Chaos; I was in love. Seeing him with Sloane had cinched it.

"So listen"—his smile fell away and his eyes grew serious—"we need to talk about Azda."

"Yeah?" I smoothed the goofy grin from my face and straightened my posture. "Sure. What's up?"

"Well, did you know that Azda was close friends with your paternal grandmother?"

"Ah … yeah, Azda speaks English, Chaos. And she's lived with me for nearly eight years now."

He nodded. "Okay, but did she tell you that your grandmother was a powerful seer?"

An unsettling feeling came over me. "No. She never mentioned it." *Why* hadn't she mentioned it?

"Well, she was. And she was able to foresee her own demise and the beginning of the decade of no light. She saw glimpses of the dark spirit who was prophesied to enter into the world, and she accurately surmised that this spirit would kill off all of the seers prior to its birth—herself included—which, by the way, is something my own pack's supernatural seers failed to see coming."

"What are you saying?"

"Well, I'm saying your grandmother had to have been a pretty badass seer." He shook his head. "But that's beside the point. She saw you—her long-lost granddaughter—in her visions, too, and she saw how your future would be tied to the birth of the *Rogue*. Her visions of you and Sloane were so vivid that she was able to give Azda a street address and a date for where and when she'd be able to find you."

"Oh, my God. That's how Azda was able to find us when supernatural hunters had failed?" Why hadn't Azda ever told me this herself?

"Yeah. So your grandmother told all this to Azda, and she asked Azda to do her a massive favor in order to protect you—the granddaughter she'd never known about. She felt as if she'd already failed you, because she'd found out too late about your existence. Understand?"

I felt myself frown. "What are you getting at? What did she ask Azda to do?"

"Is this true, Azda?" I confronted her where she sat in her rocking chair. "My grandmother asked you to find and murder my only child?"

She nodded solemnly. "She was hoping to protect you."

"Oh, my God. Azda, I can't believe this. How could you? All this time? How—*why*? I don't understand. But— you didn't do it. Wait. Why didn't you?"

She shrugged. "I changed my mind."

I couldn't even.

"That's it?" I tossed my hands up. "You just changed your mind?"

Alcaeus sat down on the ruined couch while I proceeded to pace nervously in front of it, trying to process the bomb of this alternate reality and side of Azda that I'd somehow been blind to. "This is insane. We can never let Sloane know about this."

"She knows," Azda said.

"What?" I stopped and spun around to face her. "Sloane knows? You told her?"

"No. She figured it out a while ago." Azda smiled and then chuckled softly to herself. "Sometimes, when you're not around, she gives me grief about it. She'll say she's still waiting for me to kill her, and she'll ask me what's taking so long."

My eyes bugged out. "Azda! That's horrible."

"*Bah*," She threw a dismissive hand my way. "You don't get it. It's her best and only joke—aside from calling me the old blind spot. I laugh myself silly every time."

Alcaeus started snickering then, and I shot him a death glare. "This isn't funny."

He covered his mouth with his hand, nodded, and mumbled an apology, but I could see that he and Azda were still sharing in the humor of this supposed "joke" that Sloane apparently made about her own murder by her caregiver. *The caregiver I'd been leaving her with for eight years.* I saw now how the "old blind spot" nickname that Sloane had given her was more of a crack at *me* than it was at Azda.

Azda had been *my* blind spot. I was the worst mother ever.

"I can't handle this. I can't believe that this has been happening right under my nose. All this time. *Why*, Azda? Why did you change your mind?"

"Because I saw that you were harboring a power even greater than the power within the *Rogue*."

Say what? I stopped pacing. "Are you suggesting that *I* have some hidden supernatural power that has yet to emerge? Something that my grandmother foresaw?"

She rolled her milky eyes, and Alcaeus started chuckling again.

"The skinwalker gets it," Azda remarked with a snort.

"What is so funny?"

Chaos laughed harder at her skinwalker label, grabbed my hand, and pulled me down into his lap on the charred sofa.

"Well?" I punched him in the shoulder. "Is someone going to let me in on the joke?"

"You have something better than a hidden supernatural power, Avery," Azda said with a smile. "It's the same superpower you've always had, even when you were human. *Strong will.*"

"Strong will?" I huffed. *"Strong will?* You get me all excited that I might be getting a cool new superpower and then let me down with an afterschool special message? You're saying you didn't kill Sloane because I have a *strong will?* That makes no sense."

"Does so." She raised her chin. "Special talents and superpowers can only carry a being so far. Strong will prevails when powers fail; it trumps all in the end. And a good sheep-herder can make all the difference."

"Makes perfect sense to me," Alcaeus inserted.

I didn't know whether to laugh or to smack my palm to my forehead. To think that for all this time that I'd been out slaying rogue hunters in an effort to protect my baby, I'd left her alone with a seemingly harmless old lady whose sole motivation in entering our lives had been to kill her.

"Also," Azda continued, "I realized that the darkness in Sloane could never be destroyed. It can only be moderated. *Curbed.* Killing the child solves nothing." She leveled her gaze on Alcaeus. "Your tribe is wrong in your approach. Eliminating Sloane will not save the human race."

I felt Alcaeus's arms band tighter around me, although he said nothing in reply.

"Darkness will always find a way to live on," Azda asserted. "Perhaps even through Sloane's reborn soul, if she is killed. The world has a better chance of stopping the prophecy of the *Rogue* not by killing it, but by understanding it. By accepting its nature. By helping it to cope with its own darkness and by finding commonality within its deviances. This is the only way.

"Sloane is strong-willed, too, like her mother. And there *is* light in her. There is a chance that Sloane may master her own darkness yet. But she needs time. And she needs a strong, loving sheep-herder." Azda's not-so-blind eyes cut meaningfully to Chaos. "Perhaps two."

CHAPTER 34

Alcaeus

"**W**HO ARE ELSA AND ANNA?" I WHISPERED TO AVERY AS she passed me where I stood just within the doorway of Sloane's bedroom. "Are they friends of hers that she plays with?"

I'd heard Sloane mention the names a few times amid her internal dialogue.

Avery gave me a restrained version of her "what the fuck" face and covertly shook her head, before walking farther into the room to set a tray carrying a glass of milk and a grilled cheese sandwich down on the floor about four feet from where Sloane was growling and arguing with herself.

I'd lost track of time standing in the doorway of the decimated bedroom, observing little Sloane growl and make humming noises. While she displayed some classic rogue-like characteristics, there was nothing common about her. At times she seemed overly refined, highly intelligent, wise beyond her years. Other times she came across as feral and demented. Any way I looked at it, the girl had the makings of a supernatural savant. She was clearly a genius and very special.

And she was going to be a werelock powerhouse to be reckoned with when she hit puberty in a few short years and shifted for the first time.

Sloane seemed to spend most of her time having conversations—or arguments—with herself as well as with … others. Who the "others" were remained the question. Sometimes she seemed to have control over the forces at play in her mind, and other times, those forces seemed to control her.

I wanted to believe that they were outside of her, but in talking with Azda, who had perhaps spent the most time alone with Sloane, I had a feeling the old woman's intuition was right in that the greater darkness was *within* Sloane. It was a part of her and not something that could ever be separated.

The repetitive things the little girl said—whenever she did connect with the people around her—were disturbing. She talked about dying a lot in general. Of dying, of trying to stay dead, and of how she wasn't supposed to have been born. It was a recurring theme with her. She also told me that she could only do bad things in the world—that the "voices" told her so.

None of this behavior made her an easy case to plead to Alex and Milena. Neither did the fact that Sloane possessed no scent. *None whatsoever.*

But for the times when Sloane didn't look as if her head might start spinning in 360-degree rotations atop her shoulders, she was an exceptionally adorable child. A precocious little beauty who resembled her mother. Except for her eyes—which were a vibrant shade of violet.

Avery took hold of my arm and walked me out into the hallway before whispering in my ear, "She doesn't have friends, Chaos. Elsa and Anna are from the animated Disney movie, *Frozen*. Her favorite. It's the only movie she'll watch."

I nodded, my chest tightening at Avery's confirmation of what should have been apparent: of course little Sloane didn't have any friends to play with.

"Sorry," I told Avery, wrapping my arms around her. "I should've realized."

She smiled and shook her head. "You're doing great."

"Eh, I'm a little rusty, but I'll catch on."

As soon as I settled things with Alex and Milena, I was going to watch that Disney flick. And then I'd find lots of werelock kids to be friends with Sloane.

"Hey, know what I was thinking?" I pressed a kiss to Avery's forehead. "I was thinking I'd throw Sloane another ninth birthday party to make up for the one I missed out on last month." Her eyes widened. "We can rent a bunch of those big bounce houses and some giant trampolines and invite all the—"

"*Whoa.* Too much—*too soon*," Avery said, looking at me like I was nuts. "She doesn't like to be around very many people."

"Okay, what if we go with just two bounce houses and limit the guest list to—"

"Chaos, she's the *Rogue*," Avery interjected quietly. "She does connect somewhat, but it's relative, and it takes time. It's not in the way that people expect. I know you mean well, but you're going to need to be patient with her."

I nodded and gave her an apologetic smile. "Right. Sorry. I tend to get carried away when I get excited about stuff."

She stared at me, her expression unreadable. Assessing.

"You're really not freaked?" she asked. "I mean, because her behavior is so … different? And the fact that she can start fires with—"

"Are you kidding me? *Nah*. I told you last night I raised my little half-brother, Alex. He burned my house down five times. This is nothing. Sloane is a sweetheart compared to how Alex was as a kid."

"Really?" Her brown doe eyes were bright with unshed tears. "You really mean it? You think her behavior's not so far off the normal range that we'll be able to convince your family?"

"Of course we'll convince them," I told her with confidence. "Look, as seriously as Milena takes the *Rogue* prophecy and her role as Alpha, my sister-in-law is a born softie—the sweetest, most kind-hearted soul you'll ever meet. She's all about fairness and doing the right thing, protecting the weak and subjugated—you know, all the classic do-gooder stuff. I mean, she *does* get a little self-righteous and hall-monitor-ish at times, but eh … our pack needed a little more of that. My brother Alex definitely needed it to balance him out."

Avery still looked skeptical.

"Honey, Sloane's just a child," I stressed. A beautiful, *gifted* child. Who could possibly dislike her? Besides, we were expecting the *Rogue* to be an adult. I think every pack was. No one is prepared to exterminate a *child Rogue*, trust me—least of all Milena. And even if my pack were so inclined, they can't, because it's against our Reinoso pack law to persecute minors. Believe me, there's no way Milena would ever harm your—*our*—daughter."

I'd just gotten Avery's scent and heart rate calmed when a blood-curdling scream came from Sloane in her bedroom.

310   HETTIE IVERS

Avery yanked my arm to hold me back when I made to bolt into Sloane's bedroom. "*No.* Stay outside the door," she directed. "She doesn't like anyone to touch her or get too close when she's upset," she explained before rushing into the room herself.

Avery stopped and dropped to her knees when she was about five feet from her daughter.

She began talking to Sloane, keeping her voice level and calm despite the shrill, piercing wails that continued to flow from her child.

Regardless of Avery's warning, I took a step forward into the room, listening with a heavy heart as my mate said things to try and soothe her distraught daughter—while Sloane shook her head rapidly from side to side.

If anything, Sloane might've been screaming louder now. It was hard to tell with the way my eardrums were ringing. Yet it didn't seem to phase Avery.

Jesus. Was this their normal routine? How often did this happen?

I felt powerless as I stood there watching them—not being able to help. Not knowing *how* to help. I'd never felt so mortal before.

I took another two steps into the room, just as Sloane finally stopped wailing, and I caught the sound of muffled voices coming from behind me down the hallway.

I heard Azda saying, "You can't go back there," as I felt Kai's presence approaching, and I realized that in my intense study of Sloane, I'd forgotten how long I'd been inside Avery's house—how long Kai had been waiting for us outside.

"What the devil is going on in here, Al? Is everything okay?"

No sooner had the words left Kai's mouth as he entered the room than Sloane screamed bloody murder again, and Kai was suddenly set on fire—his whole being flaming like a torch from head to toe.

Avery's screams joined Sloane's as she saw it.

Kai shouted obscenities, using his magic to put out the fireball that was encompassing him.

"Good God!" Remy's unexpected voice exclaimed from behind me, just as Azda rushed forward into the room and doused Kai with a fire extinguisher, coating his now-half-naked, disheveled, but otherwise unharmed body in frothy white foam.

"Damnit, stop that," Kai ordered Azda. "It's out. Stop. I don't require your assistance."

"What are you doing in here, Kai?" I demanded, then turned to my stepbrother. "Remy? Why the hell are you here? How'd you get here?"

"Kai … brought me," Remy answered distractedly, his eyes on Sloane where she huddled in the corner. She'd ceased screaming again and was now hum-talk-arguing with herself. "Oh, my God," he murmured. "Those eyes … they're … she's …"

"*Adorable.*" I finished for him. "She's fucking adorable, and that's final."

"Language, Chaos," Avery scolded, her head snapping up from where she was crouched on the floor no more than three feet from Sloane now, attempting to get the little girl to engage with her.

"Sorry," I apologized to Avery, before turning back to Kai and Remy. "Get out of here. Both of you. You've caused enough damage."

"*We* have?" Kai's harassed expression turned

incredulous. "I just walked into a room and was literally lit on fire simply for asking if everything was okay."

"Because you startled her," I accused.

"I did no such thing," he rebuffed. "Al, you've let this mating bond with that woman warp your mind. You've completely lost touch with reality. That child isn't right. She's not normal. Remy and I are fairly certain she's the *Rogue,* Al. We have to bring Milena and Alex into this."

"If she's the *Rogue,* then every seer was wrong about the *Rogue,* because this child—*my child*—is perfect. And she *can* connect. Quit looking at her like that," I reprimanded when Kai and Remy continued to stare from me to Sloane, aghast. "What is wrong with everyone? She's just a child! An adorable, precocious little girl who relates to the world a bit differently than other kids."

Remy shook his head, glancing around the destroyed room. "I'd argue it's a bit more complicated than that. The darkness craves her, Al. I can feel it. *Sense* it. Can't you guys feel that?" He looked from me to Kai, his eyes anxious.

"I feel it," Azda piped up, nodding and raising her hand in the air from where she was crouched next to Avery's side now, close to Sloane. "All day, every day," she said with a sigh.

"Afternoon," Remy greeted with an awkward smile and a little wave in her direction. He turned to me and continued, "The darkness ... it's like it runs to her—flows to and from her. It *seeks* her. As if it wants her to embrace it— to lead it. My God, this is just like—" His eyes cut to Kai, then to Sloane. "It's exactly like it was with ..." He looked at Kai again, then me, before frowning and looking back to Sloane. "Maribel."

"*What?*" Kai balked, his eyes suddenly feral and

fuming. "Have you gone mad? How *dare* you compare this unfortunate ... *creature* to—to my mate—to my Maribel?"

"Yeah, Remy," I rushed to attack him as well. "How *dare* you compare my perfectly beautiful little daughter to that warped and demented *murdering psycho*"—I swiveled my head to shout the last words at Kai—"who drained the life force from the living and consumed souls in the name of true love?"

Remy held his hands up, recoiling, as Avery joined in and yelled, *"Ew, hell no*—take that back! My daughter is her own person. She's a *child*—a child with a clean slate and her whole life in front of her. Don't you dare try to saddle her with the sins of some creepy dead soul's baggage."

"Exactly," I chimed in. "What she said."

"And furthermore," Avery lectured, "even if by some bizarre metaphysical possibility she *were* the reincarnation of someone who'd walked this earth before, let me assure you that no daughter of mine would *ever* be desperate enough to get paired with mister constipation fucking personified over there." She jutted her chin at Kai.

"Language, Avery," I reminded her.

"Fine, *fine.*" Remy threw his hands up with an angry huff. "It was a wild theory. An intuition that struck me when I walked in and first saw her based on the energy flow I felt surrounding her and the fact that Sloane's eyes are *exactly* the same remarkable shade as our Maribel's were. Never mind the fact that Sloane's conception date was shortly after the time that Maribel's soul supposedly finally, *finally* departed from the ether at long last—*carrying a beast of a revenge-greedy, defective blood curse with her.*"

Remy shrugged dramatically. "But what the fuck do I know? It's not like I guess these things right every goddamn time before everyone else and yet no one ever seems to remember or give me credit for anything."

"*Language,*" I snapped at him. "Watch your language around my daughter, Remy. And don't try and turn this around and make it somehow all about you and your Jan Brady complex like you always do. We don't have time for that."

"This Maribel person," Azda asked, looking in Remy's general direction, "did she kill off all the seers ten years ago?"

"Yes," Remy answered. "She did."

Azda nodded. "I think the good-looking werelock's theory is sound: Sloane may be this Maribel."

"She is not," Kai vehemently denied. "It's preposterous; an utter disgrace to Maribel's memory to dare compare the two."

Avery and I chimed in, supporting Kai's denial of Sloane being the reincarnated Maribel.

Remy ignored us, sighing as he turned to Azda. He gave her a polite smile and said, "Thank you, dear lady. And thank you for the compliment as well."

"Her name's Azda," Avery told him flatly. "And she's legally blind, just so you know."

Remy's brows shot up. "Ah, well, then," he said with a dry, humorless chuckle. "Your mate's a peach, Al. My congratulations to you both. Please do let me know when you're bringing your new family to Morumbi so that Jussara and I can have enough fire extinguishers at the ready throughout—"

Kai noisily cleared his throat, cutting Remy's irritated rant short just a few spoken words too late.

"What did you just say?" I asked, my blood igniting

in anger. I *knew* there'd been something going on between Jussara and Remy.

Remy's eyes widened a fraction in alarm, but he quickly recovered enough to mask his horror over his own careless revelation. *But not his scent.*

"Throughout the compound," he fibbed. "Jussara and I—we're in charge of fire safety for the whole place now. It's a thing Milena started. She set up fire preparedness … teams."

Kai pinched the bridge of his nose and shook his head at the ceiling as Remy continued.

"We're on … rotation. Fire safety team rotation. We do weekly fire drills and everything …"

"For God's sake," Kai exploded. "You and Jussara aren't doing anything wrong, Remy. You're both consenting adults who don't need Al's permission. For the record, I don't approve of you and Jussara, and I never will. But it's none of my business. What *is* my business is Al's relationship to the mother of the *Rogue*—an aberration of nature prophesied to destroy us all."

It took all my self-control not to change into my wolf and attack them both. "How long have you been sleeping with Jussara?" I demanded of Remy.

Kai growled—loud and long—silencing the room before telling me, "Remy and Jussara's relationship is not up for discussion right now. Neither is the fact that we are turning this *Rogue* situation over to Milena, Al. You are not of sound mind at present. You've lost all perspective regarding this mission."

"I am still in charge here," I growled in his face, even as realization hit: Kai had already betrayed me to Milena. That's why Remy was here. "What the hell have you done, Kai?"

"I *had* to report the Vasile pack ambush to Milena, Al. And I had to report this situation with the *Rogue* as well. Milena's been worried about you for some time. Worried that you were losing focus on the mission and going off the rails in your grief over Lupe." His features were as hard as his voice, his wolf eyes glowing, as he stood his ground—against me. "I won't apologize for doing the right thing. For protecting the greater good—the good of our pack, not to mention the future of our race as well as the human race. I chose to make the responsible choices that you have refused to make, again and again."

My first reaction was blind fury over Kai's betrayal. But it lasted only a fraction of a second as I scented Avery's fear—so sharp and pungent I felt as if I had been stabbed through the heart—not only in the back—by my best friend and Beta.

I had to get Avery and Sloane somewhere safe while I worked this situation out with Milena.

Never until this moment in my life had I felt so vulnerable and resentful of the fact that I couldn't teleport. I forced my emotions under control and asked with a calm that I was nowhere close to feeling, "What have you told Milena?"

Kai exhaled. "Everything."

I nodded. "You're dead to me."

"Al, you're not thinking—"

Before I could even process what I was doing, I'd already grabbed Kai by his shredded, burnt clothing and thrown him from Sloane's room, clear down the hallway.

Sloane started screaming again. Avery and Azda did, too. I realized that the hallway had caught on fire, as well as most of Sloane's room, and I moved quickly to help Remy, who was trying to put it all out and keep the flames from Azda and Avery.

Amid the mayhem of Sloane's wailing and of fires blazing to life right and left throughout the house, four Salvatella werelocks teleported into the hallway outside of Sloane's bedroom, along with the lead Beta who had brought them.

"I told you not to fuck this up, Alcaeus," Raul said to me as he waltzed right into the bedroom and crouched down beside Sloane.

When I moved to stop him, he blasted me aside. Then he did the unthinkable—*the impossible:* he picked little Sloane up.

Not only did Sloane let him do it; she immediately stopped screaming. And all the fires around us went out.

CHAPTER 35

Alcaeus

THERE HAD BEEN MANY MOMENTS THROUGHOUT MY LIFE when I'd wondered: How the fuck did I get here? Where did I go wrong? What the hell was I thinking?

But as I sat inside of a holding cell in my own pack's—*my own family's*—estate home in Salvador, I pondered such questions harder than I ever had before.

Of course, this was after I'd expended all of my energy and every shred of magical ability I possessed first trying to escape, then threatening and bargaining with any guard within hearing range, and finally destroying anything and everything within my cell.

Goddamnit, I resented not possessing the ability to tele-port right now. Short of bribing or manipulating a guard, there was no other way out. And Milena and Alex had already blocked all of the guards' minds from me.

I'd personally had a hand in conceiving and rein-venting our holding cells here at the Reinoso pack estate in Salvador after Raul had managed to escape and lay destruction to an entire wing of the place a decade ago. *Talk about irony.* I was trapped within my own invention:

stone-and steel-constructed walls too thick to break or blast through with magic—*that were also reinforced by magic.* Convenient.

Never would I forgive Kai for this.

Never would I forgive any of them.

My own family had stood before me as a united front—*against me*—when Kai, Remy, and I had teleported back to Brazil and I had sought their help in recovering Avery and Sloane from Raul.

Before I had known that they intended to betray me, I had warned them that Raul had changed—that he'd disobeyed his Alpha Gabriel to save Avery, arguing that his power development had to be greater than what we knew it to be at this point—greater than what Raul displayed to the world, at least.

Raul. That conniving sonofabitch always managed to have some secret that he was keeping from everyone and unlimited tricks up his sleeve. As much as I hated him for the way he had waltzed into Avery's home and plucked little Sloane up in his arms like it was no big deal, as much as I resented him for teleporting both Avery and my daughter away from me, I also knew that he was possibly the only hope I had left—the only protection there might be for Avery and Sloane from Gabriel now that my own family had betrayed me and locked me away like I was the enemy.

Locked me up "for my own good," they'd claimed.

My own good? To prevent me from protecting my own mate and her child!

They all thought I'd gone mad. But they were the ones who were crazy.

And they were all dead to me.

I still couldn't believe how my whole world had gone

to shit in a matter of minutes within the four burnt walls of Sloane's bedroom. It had been easier for Raul to calm Sloane than it had been for him to subdue her mother. Avery had flipped out at his initial intrusion, her motherly protective instincts kicking into high gear when Raul blasted me out of the way and snatched up Sloane.

Yet Raul had still managed to convince Avery to come with him. *Willingly,* she'd agreed—right in front of me. Even after Raul had confessed to having switched the cell phone her friend Wyatt had given her for one with a tracking device days ago when they'd first met; confessed to have been watching the house ever since that day in order to make sure that she and Sloane were safe.

My mate had ultimately believed in Raul—*trusted* that Raul could keep her safer than I would when I'd tried to convince her not to go with him. I'd foolishly begged her to come with me instead—to bring her daughter to Brazil so we could convince Milena and Alex that Sloane wasn't the *Rogue* threat the prophesies perceived her to be.

Avery had whispered that she was sorry, had told me with tears in her eyes that she couldn't come with me—because she didn't trust my family; she didn't trust Kai.

And she had been smart not to. *Wiser than I had been.*

Raul had already saved Avery from Gabriel once. I fervently prayed he would do it again in my absence now. I had no other options.

Looking back on my four centuries, I realized now that mine had been a very privileged existence. Too much had come far too easily.

Avery was right about me: I did have a hero complex— *to the extent that I accurately grasped what that was.* And that hero complex had made me stupid.

Because I'd been so wrapped up enjoying a life where I'd long been top dog, spoiled and arrogant from centuries of besting every opponent, of overcoming every obstacle thrown at me, of always getting the final word in and having the last laugh, that my pride had prevented me from accepting the truth of Lupe's situation all those years ago when I'd been faced with it.

For decades, I'd chosen to deny the reality of Lupe's connection to Nahuel, because it was easier than accepting that I would never truly be able to save her—no matter how long she lived or remained under my protection. That I couldn't *fix it*, as Lupe had reminded me on more than one occasion.

It was a shameful moment of realization now to see all of the ways that I had spent the better part of the past decade nursing my own ego as much as I had mourning the loss of a woman I'd loved so dearly.

Worse yet to admit that same stubborn ego had caused me to grossly underestimate my former best friend's level of frustration with me; and had prevented me from fully acknowledging his and the rest of the pack's increasing respect for and loyalty to Milena.

Milena had been weepy and apologetic about having to lock me up—moments before she'd knocked me out cold with a lightning bolt to the back of my skull.

She'd doled out every assurance that no one would ever harm Avery, promising me that my mate would be recovered safely from the Salvatellas and brought to me here. She couldn't say the same for Sloane, though—not until she'd witnessed the *Rogue's* behavior firsthand, she said.

And they'd all stood by Milena in agreement with this decision: my own brothers as well as Kai and Jussara. Even

Lessa had taken their side and said it was best to recover Wyatt by other means rather than negotiate with a pack that had never been honorable.

Alessandra caving and abandoning me at my darkest hour had cut the worst of all.

But then again, I should have seen that one coming, too. Ever since our baby brother was born, Lessa had sided with Alex over me. And I knew of only one time that she'd been able to disobey his direct order when he'd been Alpha.

I hadn't eaten any of the food they'd brought to my cell. I hadn't slept a wink in the past twenty-eight hours and forty-three minutes since I'd been away from Avery. I wasn't sure how I ever would again until I had her back safely with me.

I was curled up in the corner in my wolf form, revisiting all the ways I'd let my ego blind me and cause me to put my mate's life in danger, when I caught the sound of Lessa's voice on the other side of the thick cell door.

Then it stopped, and I dismissed it as my ears playing tricks on me.

Alex and Milena had forbidden Remy, Jussara, and Alessandra from coming to Salvador to visit me until everything was resolved with Raul. I'd heard them give the order.

And they were all likely on their way to meet with Raul by now. I had informed them of Raul's demands in exchange for Wyatt's safe return.

My ears perked up again as I heard the door bolts in the floor slip out of place, one at a time. No one had opened the door since I'd been in here. Food was provided through the smaller portal in the wall.

Were they letting me out already?

Had they recovered Avery?

I didn't expect so. Not enough time had elapsed. And Avery's energy still felt so far away from me.

And so sad.

A side bolt slipped out, then another.

The door swung open, and Lessa walked in—*not* dressed like a schoolteacher. She was wearing red-heeled combat boots and skinny jeans.

She threw a blast at every surveillance camera throughout the room, before turning her attention to me. "You look like shit."

Lessa had come back for me! She'd disobeyed both Milena and Alex's direct orders.

She could do that?

"You waiting for an invitation?" She stomped over and snapped her fingers in front of my muzzle. "Put some clothes on and get your head in the game, Al. We've got mates to rescue and a pack to take back."

CHAPTER 36

Avery

"**A**RE YOU SERIOUSLY ON FACEBOOK RIGHT NOW? WAIT, who is—oh, my God, is that like your catfish profile? Lemme see."

Raul jerked his iPad from my line of sight, locked the screen, and set it aside. "Finish your steak, Avery. We're leaving in twenty minutes."

I took another bite and went through the motions of chewing and swallowing as I again tried to distract myself with something—*anything*—to pretend that I wasn't close to having a full-blown emotional meltdown as Sloane and I sat beside one another, eating steak for lunch.

We were seated across from Raul at a dining room table in the house we'd spent the night in with Raul and about twenty or so other werelocks. I wasn't sure how many there were, really, because Raul had the other were-locks steer clear of Sloane and me for the most part. Azda had stayed back at the house in Durango.

I'd caught some of the werelocks talking in Portuguese, others in Spanish, and more than a few had spoken on their phones in French. I wasn't entirely sure they were all part of Raul's Salvatella pack, either. Because it seemed like some of them were just meeting one another for the first time.

I also hadn't been able to figure out where we were staying. We'd teleported to wherever we were, and there was no indication anywhere in the house as to where that might be. The view outside our windows didn't reveal much, either. There was nothing to see but dense woods stretching in all directions.

Since coming here with Raul, Sloane hadn't had a single bad episode. She hadn't had a screaming fit or set anything on fire, and she'd slept through the night without any indication of suffering nightmares. She was acting so passably normal it felt like we'd teleported into an alternate reality.

I, on the other hand, hadn't slept a wink. I was a fucking wreck.

I missed Chaos. My heart hurt whenever I remembered the look of devastation on his handsome face as I'd told him that Sloane and I were going with Raul instead of with him.

"So who's the hot blonde?" I teased the werelock who was now the only hope my daughter and I had of living to see dinnertime. "The one you were stalking just now on Facebook?"

"No one, Avery," Raul said, shutting me down again as he wiped his mouth with his napkin and pushed his finished plate aside. He was upset about something. And he'd been fine only a minute ago—before he'd gone on Facebook.

Weirdo. He'd been friendly and goofing off around Sloane all morning—doing his best to engage her. And he'd been utterly nonchalant about the upcoming meeting with Alpha Milena and her pack, yet someone's status update on Facebook had put him in a foul mood?

"I ate all of my steak," Sloane announced, her violet eyes trained on Raul.

I swore my heart stopped and I nearly fell sideways out of my chair.

She'd said it without emotion, as usual, but her eyes remained fixed on Raul—looking to him for something.

Acknowledgement.

Approval. *Connection.*

Raul's eyes leveled on hers, and he smiled and said, "Awesome. You want another one?" He extended his fist across the table to her. He'd been trying to teach her to fist bump all morning. "Come on, Sloane, don't leave me hanging, girl."

She didn't extend her fist to bump his, but I could've sworn I saw her eyes warm just a fraction as she stared stoically back at him, and a hint of emotion—*amusement* even—softened her little pink lips.

I could've cried.

How the hell did he do that? What was it between them?

It still disturbed me on some level—this sense that Raul and my daughter were strangers who seemed to share some cosmic link beyond rational comprehension—but since seeing him interact with Sloane, I was comfortable now that he wasn't *that* kind of predator.

Sloane rarely allowed me to pick her up without throwing a fit. The fact that she'd allowed Raul—a perfect stranger—to pick her up and hold her yesterday was unprecedented. The fact that she'd ceased screaming and torching things as soon as he'd done so was miraculous.

My daughter felt safe with Raul for some reason. I had to trust her instincts on this and believe that he could protect us.

Raul teleported us to a vacant swath of desert in Round Rock, Arizona: a small community on the Navajo Nation where we'd agreed to meet with Milena and her pack. Raul had told me that he had a bargaining chip to offer in exchange for the Reinoso pack agreeing to back off from hunting my daughter. But he'd yet to tell me what it was.

I'd more or less assumed that all the other werelocks who'd been at the house in the woods with us would be coming to the meeting with the Reinoso pack as well, so I was a bit flustered when Raul said it'd just be the three of us going.

"It starts to look desperate when you bring too many soldiers to a simple negotiation," he said. "We don't want to go in overgunned—looking like we're nervous or something."

But I was nervous.

As I stood there beside Raul, who was holding Sloane again, I scanned the horizon and spotted a gathering of what looked to be at least twenty-some people about three hundred yards or more away, standing closer to the rock formations the area was known for.

"I don't feel overgunned." I felt decidedly undergunned, in fact. "We're one werelock, a werewolf, and a child, Raul."

"Don't worry," he told me with a smile. "Sloane and I

got this." He set Sloane down on her feet in between us. "Right, Sloane?"

I still couldn't get over the fact that she let him hold her so easily. Or that she hadn't hum-talked to herself since early morning.

"Are we going to teleport closer, or do we have to walk all the way over there?" I joked anxiously.

Why was he so calm? Did he have some grand master plan? Or was he just an idiot?

"Neither. We're gonna wait right here and make them come to us." Raul crouched down so that he was at Sloane's eye level. "You remember me from your dreams, right?"

She didn't respond, but Raul continued as if she had, telling her, "I used to get really scared sometimes. And when the darkness closing in around me became tough to handle, you used to tell me that no one ever found daybreak by avoiding night—only by passing through it. Do you remember that?"

What was he jabbering about? *Dear Lord, please let this surfer werelock saying bizarre, unsettling things to my child about dream encounters have an actual plan for today's confrontation of superbeasts.*

The gathering of werelocks was on the move now, walking swiftly in our direction. "Wow, they really are coming to us," I announced to myself as my heart rate kicked up. "And they don't look happy about it. Particularly … Alpha Milena."

A willowy brunette with long, wavy hair was leading the charge—and she looked pissed. I suspected that had to be Milena, judging from the beefy hotties flanking her and the Brazilian god at her side who, at a distance, strongly resembled the photos of Alex Reinoso that Wyatt had shown me.

"Milena can't teleport," Raul commented. "I might be rubbing it in."

I studied the werelock group approaching, hoping to spy the tall, gorgeous werelock I missed most among them. I spotted Killjoy Kai, and then Remy. I didn't see Chaos anywhere, though. Why wouldn't he have come? Was he all right?

Clouds rolled over the band of werelocks marching closer to us, partially blocking out the afternoon sun.

"Yes," Sloane answered Raul's previous question, her voice carrying a surprising measure of excitement. "I remember," she said. Then she repeated, "No one ever found daybreak by avoiding night."

Thunder cracked in the sky.

I felt myself frown. "Wait a minute ... are they—"

"That's right," Raul confirmed enthusiastically to Sloane. "You do remember!"

"You said that to me," Sloane told him, causing me to glance away from the sky and down at my daughter. For a split second, I thought I almost saw her smile as she said, "That's what you say to me."

Holy shit. She never smiled.

"That's true," Raul said with a laugh. "But *you* said it to *me* first. I'm just borrowing your cool lines."

"Would you like to be her nanny?" I blurted. How was he so good with my kid? "Hey, are they somehow ... *causing* this sudden weather change I'm witnessing? I know that sounds crazy, but it kinda seems as if—"

"Calm down, Avery. Your heart rate's all over the place," Raul said to me before telling Sloane, "I need you to stay close to your mom while I talk to the Blind Warrior about some stuff. Okay? Hold her hand and try not to set anything on fire. Keep your cool, and just think: What would Queen Elsa do? Think you can do that?"

"I can," she agreed.

Blind Warrior?

Sloane reached for my hand, and I gratefully gave it, grasping her small one in mine. It was rare that she let me hold her hand. Was it some kind of Alpha pull that Raul had on my child?

Raul stood and faced me. "They believe you're Alcaeus's mate. Even if they don't like you or want to accept you, they won't harm you. But still, keep your head down as much as possible if shit goes to hell fast, and try to remember that you're not a werelock."

I nodded and turned to watch the Reinoso pack as they came to a stop about twenty yards away, bringing the first drops of rain from the sky with them. Along with loud, rolling thunder—*and more lightning than was at all normal for any flash storm.*

I squeezed Sloane's hand tighter as bolts of lightning illuminated the sky and smaller ones fell to singe the ground around us.

Hellfire. Alpha Milena wasn't the Burning Man flunkie I'd pegged her to be.

When the angry sound of thunder finally quieted, Raul leaned into me. "So there's something I meant to mention to you sooner about Milena."

If side-eye could kill. "Such as the fact that she's capable of electrokinesis?" I whisper-screamed through clenched teeth.

"Nah, not that," he whispered back. "Don't worry. She's just trying to intimidate us. She's all bark. And actually, she's got full-on powers of empathic meteorokinesis or something, from what I hear. Not sure. We haven't interacted much—*at all*—for about um ... ten years or so."

"*What?*" I gasped. "You said you were the only one capable of stopping her! You've put my daughter's life on the line with a werelock you've never fought before?"

"It's complicated," he muttered out of the side of his mouth. "We should talk about it another time."

"You mean if we're still alive?" If the Alpha bitch didn't kill him, I'd find a way to do it.

"Where's your keeper, Raul?" Milena hollered in greeting to us, stepping forward. "I was counting on seeing Gabriel today."

She looked every bit the waifish hippie she'd appeared to be in Wyatt's photos, but her voice was far stronger—a lot more confident—than I'd imagined it would be. It rang with authority.

"Don't worry, I got this," Raul spoke quietly to me before shouting back to her in acknowledgement, "Miles!" He gave her a jubilant grin and threw up the shaka hand sign in classic surfer salute. "S'up, Sis?"

Oh. My. God.

"Milena's your sister?" I hissed under my breath. "She's your fucking sister?" I repeated, incredulous. All this while, I'd assumed he was an only child, given his relationship cluelessness. This could only prove to be a disastrous development.

He waved me off and took several steps forward, proceeding to project his voice conversationally across the barren desert that stretched between him and my daughter's executioner, "Hey, so listen, I know it's been a while, and this might not be the greatest timing, but I feel like we need to talk about some stuff. Like ... Mom." He paused. When there was no reaction from Milena, he added, "Probably Aunt Cely, too." Another pause. "Maybe even … Mateus?"

My eyes rolled to the heavens, and I prayed for a miracle. He'd said the last one like it was a question—as if he was just tossing out family issues she might have with him to see which would stick—because he had no idea what his sister's beef with him was.

I'd known our situation was grim when Milena's mate, Alex, who was standing to the side a few paces behind her, had visibly cringed in reaction to Raul's "S'up, Sis?" opener. But when Alex started making not-so-subtle throat-cutting gestures behind his own wife's back to her clueless brother to get him to shut the hell up, it was a dire sign that I'd bet it all on the wrong horse.

I'd unknowingly pitted my daughter's life against the mother of all supernatural sibling rivalries. *Major parenting fail, Avery.*

After what seemed like an interminable minute of awkward silence, Milena finally responded to her estranged brother. Her cold, glowing green eyes failed to mask the disgust that she managed to keep from her voice as she calmly told him, "Alcaeus was mistaken. You haven't changed."

The ground shook beneath my feet. I felt Sloane tug my hand as she took a step back. I stepped backward as well when I felt a great gust of wind and saw the dry, dusty earth kick up and circle around Raul's feet.

"Aw, come on, Miles!" Raul shouted in complaint as the makings of a windstorm the size of a small tornado brewed to life around him—encircling and encapsulating him in its unnatural vortex. "This is over the top. We can work things out."

Sloane tugged my hand again, and we both stole another step back—away from the supernatural ass-whooping about to take place.

I was desperate to pick Sloane up and hold her. But this was the longest she'd ever let me hold her hand before. My daughter never wanted me to pick her up. I couldn't risk attempting it now and sparking a meltdown that might further betray her true *Rogue* nature that we'd come here in an attempt to deny.

"I know this one," Sloane said, tugging my hand for a third time.

I glanced down and saw that her little forefinger was pointed at Milena and the gathering of Reinoso pack werelocks.

"Who?" I asked. "The Alpha? Milena?"

She shook her head.

I tried to follow the line of her finger, to see which one she was pointing to, but she kept redirecting it, as if she was following a moving target. An invisible moving target, I realized, when she said, "The one who's coming."

Shit. Raul had warned me that Gabriel was among the few werelocks capable of teleportation.

I scanned the group of Reinoso werelocks. If any of them had sensed the arrival of whoever it was that Sloane saw coming, it wasn't apparent. They all seemed too engrossed in watching the spectacle of Raul, who'd just been launched at least two hundred feet into the air.

Milena's face was tilted up to the clouds, along with everyone else's, as Raul shouted down from his personal twister in the sky, "Is this about the time I kidnapped Bethany?"

Even though he'd pretty well screamed the question,

his tone had still managed to sound surfer-boy blasé some-how. I had to hand it to him: He was something else, the big idiot.

My intuition was that Raul's comment about the Bethany kidnapping hadn't been the smartest one to make when I saw Remy cover his face with his hand.

"I know this one," Sloane said again.

I tried to pay attention to where her moving finger was pointing, but a crack of thunder rolled through the sky above, and I watched in horror as a bolt of lightning struck Raul. Followed by another one. And then a third!

This was bad.

Worse yet, Raul seemed to be trying to antagonize his sister now, as he burst out laughing and taunted from his cyclone in the sky, "I'm telling Aunt Cely that you hit me first!"

When the earth rocked beneath us a second time and Sloane actually grabbed onto my leg momentarily in order to keep her little body upright, I could no longer suppress my maternal instincts. I picked her up.

Bad call. "It's just so you don't fall, okay?" I told her when she immediately protested and flailed her limbs, struggling against me, wanting to be put down.

She growled and tossed her head from side to side, looking like she was on the verge of screaming bloody murder.

Please don't do this now.

Please not now.

"Sloane, honey, it's okay," I tried to calm her. "I'll put you down in a minute ... just as soon as the ground is steadier."

My daughter wasn't having it, though, and she started screaming. *Loudly.*

"Put her down," an arrogant, cultured voice demanded as Alpha Gabriel materialized next to me, bringing the offensive scent of furniture polish, gold bullion, and stinky cheese with him.

Oh, fuck.

I squeezed Sloane's squirming, kicking, screaming little body closer to mine, hanging onto her for dear life as the sadistic, chlorine-shock-eyed werelock proceeded to lecture me on my own child.

"You don't even understand her," he spat with disdain. "She doesn't need you—doesn't want to be held or coddled by you. Can't you see that?"

My claws came out before I could stop them. My canines did too. And I growled like the devil in his direction.

"This child is the true *Rogue* of rogues," he proclaimed. "She's the future of our species—the deliverer of our race. You were never anything but a host to her, and she has no use for you anymore."

Somewhere deep down, I recognized that he was baiting me. Using his special brand of emotional rapey skills to yank on my darkest, most insidious parenting fears—and trigger my greatest handicap. But knowing it was intentional didn't make it any easier for me to ignore.

Because it still felt true.

"You're nothing but a common werewolf—a defective one at that. There's nothing you can teach her. You can't even protect her."

Sloane was screaming louder and thrashing about in my arms. I saw the earth catch fire around us, felt flames lick my feet and legs. But it was nothing compared to the fire that raged within me as I set my daughter down behind me.

You can't even protect her.

I remembered Chaos's words of advice to me about shutting my human mind off when I shifted, and I gave in to my wolf's instincts completely this time: *the instinct to protect, to defend, to kill.*

"Avery, don't!"

I heard Raul's order. But it didn't stop me. My body was already shifting—morphing with brilliant speed into the form of my wolf in the smoothest, most graceful transformation I'd ever accomplished.

And I attacked—going straight for Alpha Gabriel's throat.

I didn't get far, though. Not even close.

I was knocked on my ass with a blast of magic before I'd so much as gotten a claw swipe at him.

That had never deterred me before. And it didn't now.

I went back for more.

Raul teleported in between me and my target just in time to take the blast that Gabriel had intended for me next.

Sloane was still screaming—and setting the desert earth ablaze around us.

All hell broke loose as more werelocks rushed to the scene and Sloane reacted by lighting them on fire whenever they got too close.

Soon there were blasts of magic flying right and left. I circled around my daughter, guarding her like the mad mama boar I was inside.

The sky opened up and torrential rains descended. I heard Alpha Milena shouting orders as more werelocks encroached upon us from all sides of the desert—seemingly from different packs.

Another ambush?

I heard Milena yell, "Alex, get Avery out of there."

I'd known that I was in way over my head before Milena said it. I'd known it the moment that Raul and Gabriel had stopped trying to kill one another and had started fighting as a team against the new wolves attacking.

I should've kept my head down and backed off then. Still, I didn't stop when I should have. Not even when a blast took my left hind leg out and I felt jaws sink through my shoulder.

Because this was the story of my life.

It was a lesson I'd failed to accept on the playground, and I'd carried it too far into adulthood. Some kids went down from a single hit and stayed down. And some of us never learned when to stop getting back up again.

Until the choice was made for us—because we couldn't.

CHAPTER 37

Alcaeus

I FELT THE BLAST THAT STOPPED AVERY'S HEART AS LESSA and I teleported into the melee at Round Rock. My senses absorbed a million critically unimportant things at once then as the world that I had always known ceased to hold any further significance.

In an instant.

As I surveyed the chaotic desert landscape before me, I saw my family. I saw the pack that I'd helped to build with my father, and with Lessa, Kai, Remy, and Alex. I saw packs from around the globe that I had known over my four centuries—some of them allies, some foes—all fighting. Attacking one another over the *Rogue* prophecy.

Fighting over a foretelling that I had spent a lifetime preaching about—of propagating fear of throughout our supernatural world.

And I knew in that moment that none of it had ever mattered at all.

Nothing that was happening around me now mattered anymore either. It was all over.

This world held nothing for me.

Even the anger that had so fueled and propelled me moments ago was gone. Evaporated. That, too, was pointless.

Everything that had once seemed so important was reduced to scattered white noise—extraneous background static.

Yet I still took it in—absorbed it all: The look of realization on Alex's face as he lifted Avery's lifeless wolf in his arms and our eyes met. Lessa's howl of agony next to me. The horror in Kai's wolf's eyes as he, too, understood in that moment that I had arrived at my end. The sight of Raul as he sank to his knees next to Sloane—his glassy eyes wild with pain and disbelief—as Alex teleported my mate away from the daughter she had lived and died for.

I was cognizant of Remy comforting a wailing Jussara, of Milena's tears prompting a sudden downpour that promised to flood the desert.

I sensed my family's devastation, their regret, their incomparable sorrow—even as they channeled their misguided righteous fury into felling the "enemies" they still battled.

But I didn't *feel* any of it. Didn't claim it as my own.

My father had survived his true mate—Alex and Remy's mother, Renata—by a little more than a week. I remembered how I had prayed for more time with him. And only now did I realize how cruel and selfish a prayer it had been.

Already, I had no more desire to be here. But for whatever time I was forced to remain, I would spend it with Sloane. I would spend it protecting Avery's daughter and doing whatever was in my power to secure her future safety after I was gone.

"I was hoping Avery would stop coming back. I knew that she'd die when they came for me."

There was no emotion in Sloane's violet eyes as she said it. But neither was there confusion. She knew what death was. She knew her mother was gone.

"I can't have fun. I can only do bad things. The voices know." Sloane repeated her mantra that I'd become familiar with in the brief time I'd spent with her.

The fighting had subsided after Milena's tears from heaven had turned the desert landscape into a muddy pond that was too inconvenient of a battleground. The end of physical fighting had given way to arguing over the *Rogue* as representatives from various packs deliberated over what Sloane's continued existence might mean for our species—for our world, and the future of humankind.

I sat sprawled in a heap on the ground, holding my mate's lifeless human body in my arms, with little Sloane seated at my side, as strangers debated whether Avery's daughter could connect. Whether or not she could ever love, ever learn to feel empathy.

As if it wasn't obvious that she already had.

The irony of a bunch of supernatural predators arguing over the great risk they might all be taking in allowing a super-cute little girl with wicked-cool pyrokinesis skills to live—it pretty well topped the charts. I was prepared to speak my piece, but Raul had been busy speaking it for me—saying nearly everything I would have said in defense of Avery and Sloane's strong mother-daughter connection.

And I was already feeling far too weak. Thirty minutes after Avery's passing, and I felt like a dead man walking—an empty shell of the man that I'd been. I wasn't sure if I'd survive the night.

Raul and Gabriel had stacked the votes in Sloane's favor as far as the packs that were present—which was hardly an accident. The only pack representatives who were still lobbying hard for the *Rogue's* destruction were those from the Alsace and Istanbul packs—the ones Milena had invited as backup for her cause. Lessa had been late in rescuing me because she had been helping Kai and Alex to teleport the two packs' representatives here for the "negotiation" with Raul.

Given my imminent demise and the fact that Lessa's mate's life was on the line, I knew Milena and Alex wouldn't openly vote against Raul and Gabriel on this. But that didn't mean I trusted them not to hunt my daughter later.

Gabriel—*the great sadist-empath that he was*—had been lobbying hard that he should take Sloane with him and assimilate her into the Salvatella pack, arguing that he and he alone had the touchy-feely skills necessary to "reform" Sloane's *Rogue* ways.

Yeah, right.

I knew Gabe saw Sloane's potential to be an emotionless werelock killing machine as her greatest asset.

When I'd first carried Avery's body over to sit next to Sloane, she had been in Raul's arms. Raul had left Sloane with me shortly thereafter to go join Gabriel's cause in arguing for the Salvatella pack to have custody of her. But before he'd done so, he'd leaned close to my ear and sworn on his life that he would kill Gabriel before daybreak, saying that he had already set such plans in motion and had no intention of allowing Gabriel any prolonged contact with Sloane.

I believed him. Raul was the only one present, besides Sloane and me, who mourned the loss of Avery. He was the only other person present who had any sense of the amazing woman and mother she'd been. And for whatever reason, Sloane trusted him.

I didn't actually believe that Raul intended to harm Avery's longtime friend Wyatt anymore, either, which reassured me greatly for Lessa's sake. But there was no way I was letting my family know that and give away Raul's best leverage with them where Sloane's life was concerned—even if it meant distressing my sister for a little while longer.

Sloane was hum-talking to herself when the compromise was reached that she would go with the Salvatella pack for now while the supernatural world waited for the next great seers to emerge and tell them what the future held for the *Rogue*.

Typical.

I felt Sloane's little hand land on my forearm, and she whispered to me, "I know this one." I followed the line of her sight to see her staring at Gabriel. Then she said, "I remember this one."

I wasn't sure what she meant—where she was saying that she remembered him from—but I got the sense she didn't remember him in a positive way.

When Raul and Gabriel approached Sloane to take her from me, I felt my dying wolf stir—felt him attempt to rise just once more—*to bite the head off that fucking Weenie Gabe*. But he couldn't. Because I didn't have the strength to shift. Not even one last time.

My own family members, along with the heads of the other packs, surrounded me now as I held Avery.

Lessa had been keeping Alex and Milena, as well as Kai and Remy, away from me as best she could—for which I was grateful. Because if any of them said "sorry" to me one more time, I wasn't sure what I'd do. I didn't want their apologies. I didn't need to feel their guilty consciences.

I wouldn't make eye contact with any of them. I couldn't forgive them for this corner they'd backed me into with Sloane—leaving me no choice but to endorse handing my mate's only child over to Gabriel Salvatella because Sloane was safer with that evil bastard right now than she was with my own family.

When I heard Gabe talking to Sloane about her mother, expressing how sorry he was for her loss, and saying that he would do everything in his power to look after her now in Avery's place, I couldn't bear it.

I bent my head and pressed my lips again and again to Avery's peaceful face, whispering that I was sorry, before pressing a kiss to her unmoving mouth.

"You would take the place of her?"

I raised my head as I heard Sloane's impassive tone of voice ask the innocent question of Gabriel.

Weenie Gabe's slight smile as he nodded down at Sloane—the conniving sense of triumph in his creepy blue eyes as he feigned a look of concern—was my undoing. Even knowing that it would be temporary and knowing what Raul had promised me, it killed me to let Gabriel take her.

There had to be another way.

"Sloane," my voice was weak, beseeching. My eyes filled with tears. "You're more than the prophecy foretold you to be. You reached for the light before … when you chose Avery for your mom. Don't reach for darkness now."

Sloane's amethyst eyes cut to mine and held. They were still dry. Still vacant. Emotionless. Her expression was blank as her gaze traveled from me to her mother to Gabriel and back to me again. Her voice was equally devoid of feeling as she responded flatly, "The old blind spot says the darkness is my instrument. My conduit. And I must learn to shepherd it if I am to change the rules."

She looked down at her mother once more before shutting her eyes and turning away from me as she raised her small hand up to Gabriel. He reached for it without hesitation, and my heart broke for Avery all over again.

But as her little hand was engulfed in Gabriel's, a shock of magic rippled through the air, and it dawned on me the meaning of what Sloane had just said.

Weenie Gabe's mortal scream of horror in the next second was the tip-off that cinched it, evoking memories that had haunted me for a decade, as Sloane's eyes reopened and glowed the same vibrant, iridescent violet hue that in my nightmares I'd come to despise.

Gabriel's body shook as it was lit from within—burning a bright violet-blue color like the inner core of a flame—as his body began to incinerate from the inside, just as his brother Nuriel's had ten years ago in our Morumbi estate dining hall when Maribel had used Lupe to kill him.

Jussara screamed. Milena ordered everyone to step back as Gabriel proceeded to melt before our very eyes—in the same manner his brother had.

I heard Lessa begin murmuring "Maribel" over and over again, like a prayer.

I hadn't wanted to accept that Sloane could be the

reincarnation of Maribel's departed soul, as Remy had claimed. But there was no denying the truth of it now. And never would I have imagined feeling as overjoyed as I did in this very moment to welcome back the soul of a werelock I'd so despised, as I was when Sloane's free hand reached back and clasped onto Avery's lifeless one.

Because I knew ... I just *knew* that if any being—alive or dead—was capable of twisting and reshaping the laws of the universe to suit her means, it was our Maribel.

Maribel had stolen the precious life of Lupe from me. But she'd also restored Avery to life once already. She'd altered the laws of our world before when she'd severed her mate connection to Kai, and then again when she'd transferred Nuriel's powers directly to Raul upon Nuriel's demise, when rightfully they should've transferred to Nuriel's surviving brother, Gabriel.

There was no telling what a reincarnated version of Maribel might be capable of, but as I clutched Avery's body in my arms, I prayed that her little daughter Sloane—*Maribel 2.0*—would deliver nothing short of a miracle.

I felt life force flowing into Avery—strong and powerful—as if it was flowing into me as well as Sloane drained the life energy and werelock powers from a shrieking, melting Weenie Gabe and passed it to her mother.

CHAPTER 38

Alcaeus

AVERY'S BROWN EYES BLINKED OPEN SUDDENLY. HER confused gaze shifted restlessly from me to Sloane to Raul and back to me.

"Shit. Did I die again? How long was I out?"

I laughed through the tears clouding my sight, thanking fate and every ancestor I could remember, along with every deity I'd ever considered worshipping, as I told her, "Yes. You did. Don't ever do that again, please."

I bent my head and crushed my mouth to hers. She kissed me back this time, her warm, full lips matching the passion and urgency of my own as I squeezed her living, breathing body to me so tightly it felt like I could merge us as one.

Her slender arms squeezed me back; her fingers slid through my hair and her nails scratched against my scalp, and I had never felt so alive, so strong and full of purpose before in my four hundred and nineteen years of life.

I felt like I could do anything; overcome any challenge or obstacle that came my way. As long as I had this unbelievably courageous, tenacious woman who smelled of petrichor at my side, I'd never lack for anything again. She was all I ever wanted. All I needed for the rest of my life.

When our lips eventually parted, she said, "I feel like I could fly."

"I know the feeling."

"Sloane brought me back to life again?" she asked.

I nodded. Swallowed. "I'm sorry I got here too late. I'm so sorry I couldn't save—"

She placed a silencing forefinger over my lips. The corner of her mouth hitched. "I'm not. Never been one of those little girls who dreamed of a man coming to her rescue. Let's let Sloane flex her hero complex for a little bit."

I nodded.

"Damn, I feel really great," she announced, her rich brown eyes bright, shining with love and life as she sat upright in my lap to face the audience of shell-shocked werelocks surrounding us. "Crazy alive. Like I drank Molly mixed with my coffee this morning."

Raul busted out laughing. I looked up to find him wiping a tear from his eye. "Damn, woman. You really don't know when to quit, do you?" He extended his fist, and Avery bumped it with hers.

"Never did. Thanks for having my back, surfer boy."

"Aw, come on, you." Raul swooped down and plucked Avery up out of my arms before I'd guessed his intentions.

How could I have? Who the fuck was idiot enough to grab someone's mate from his arms after that mate had just died and come back to life again? *Only Raul Morales, that's who.* I rolled my eyes and resisted the compulsion to punch him as he hugged Avery tight and twirled her in a circle off the ground while she squealed with laughter.

"Hey." I scooted closer to Sloane, who was watching

Raul twirl Avery. "What do you say? Wanna try it? You and me?"

She shook her head, not looking at me.

"How about just a hug?"

She shook her head again.

"Okay, how about a handshake?"

"No."

"Secret pinky shake?"

Her little brow wrinkled, and her gaze shifted to me. "What's that?"

I held my pinky up. "It's where you just link pinky fingers and shake on something instead of using your whole hand."

"I'll think about it," she told me after a beat.

Avery rushed back over and dropped to her knees in front of us.

"You died," Sloane told her plainly. "I told you that you would."

Avery nodded. "You did. You were right."

"I couldn't stop it. Just like in my dreams. I knew it would happen."

Tears flooded Avery's eyes as she nodded. "It's okay, baby." She reached a tentative hand out and brushed her fingertips against Sloane's cheek. "You brought me back to life again." Her tears flowed freely as she said, "Thank you."

Lessa crouched beside me, throwing her arms around my neck and sobbing. "She's Maribel. Oh, my God, she's Maribel come back to life. She's come back to us, Al!"

"I told you guys she was Maribel!" Remy's annoyed voice exclaimed as everyone began to crowd around.

"When did you say that, Remy?" Alex refuted. "You never said that."

I assessed each of their reactions as they expressed joy and relief at my life being saved, and shock and confusion over the Maribel 2.0 development, and I reflected on what we were going to do next—on where Avery, Sloane, and I would go from here.

Where would we be safest now that Sloane had been identified as both the *Rogue* and the reincarnation of Maribel?

Representatives from multiple packs had just witnessed little Sloane incinerate a powerful Alpha from the inside—witnessed her steal the life force and werelock powers from him and transfer them to her mother. They had seen a child *Rogue* who hadn't even shifted for the first time literally raise the dead. In truth, I saw now that most of them appeared to be trying to hide how terrified they were of the small girl next to me.

They were smart to be terrified. And they were quickly scrambling to switch sides. *Because who in their right mind would openly vote against a child with the ability to suck the werelock powers right out of you?* Already the Alsace pack representative was singing a different tune to Alex, as I overheard him change his position and state that his pack was now in favor of protecting the *Rogue*.

Word would spread fast of this throughout the supernatural community. That much was certain. Sloane—*Maribel 2.0*—had changed the rules of our world. *Again.*

I noted that Milena looked deeply troubled as she observed Sloane with her mother. She also kept casting concerned glances at Kai, who was standing at her side.

I had avoided looking at Kai before, but as I did so now, I saw that he appeared more than troubled. He looked lost. Confused. *Shattered.*

I could tell that he was in denial of what he'd witnessed—overthinking things as he always did. He stared at Sloane, rubbing his chest, muttering to Milena that Sloane couldn't be Maribel, that he didn't feel anything, that there was no way she could be his departed mate come back to life—because he felt no connection to her.

Well, thank fuck for that mating bond being severed. Because as much as the idea of Remy and Jussara shacking up had disgusted and infuriated me, that was nothing compared to how I felt about the notion of my daughter Sloane ever being mated to Kai.

"Sloane, you were amazing," Raul told her.

"I did what Queen Elsa would do," Sloane said with a shrug.

Raul laughed and said, "You sure did," making me feel even more left out of their inside joke.

I needed to watch that movie right away.

"I want to go now," Sloane said to Raul, rather than to her mother or me.

As Avery and I shared a look, I knew where we were going next had already been decided for us. Sloane trusted Raul. Avery did too. It would take a lot longer—hopefully not more than a few centuries—for me to trust Raul, of course, but I was willing to give it a go. I'd go anywhere Avery wanted to. Join whatever pack she wanted to be a part of.

Avery turned to Raul and asked, "Got room for three more in your crew?"

He beamed. "Now more than ever."

With Gabriel gone, Raul was now the Alpha of the Salvatella pack. I knew that the Salvatella pack was *not* going to embrace me with open arms, given the history of bad blood between our packs. But with Raul in charge and Sloane in our corner, we weren't giving them a choice.

And while I suspected this coup was something that Raul had been plotting and campaigning for all along ever since he'd joined the enemy pack of his ancestors, he would still need help with the transition. *A whole fucking lot of it, most likely.*

Internally, I rolled my eyes as I got to my feet and wrapped my arms around Avery. We had our work cut out for us with two dangerous kids to parent now.

Best to negotiate my terms at the outset.

"We'll join your pack, but with conditions, Raul," I told him. "The first is that you return Wyatt safely to Alessandra. Immediately. We're not going anywhere until I see Lessa reunited with her mate."

At my proclamation, everyone around me began talking all at once as my family flipped out over the announcement that I was joining the ranks of the Salvatella pack—our longtime enemy. Meanwhile, Avery struggled to digest the revelation that my sister and Avery's best friend, Wyatt, were fated mates, as well as the revelation that Raul had kidnapped and used Wyatt's life as collateral with my family to bargain for hers and Sloane's.

Then Raul dropped another bomb: Wyatt had been infected with werewolf venom—allegedly at Wyatt's request—and would soon be joining the ranks of the Salvatella pack as well.

To his credit, Raul took it in stride when Avery delivered a punch to his face that sent him flying forty-some feet when she inadvertently put magic behind it—unaware as she was of her new werelock capabilities.

Yep, my mate was badass. Together, we could handle parenting our new Alpha.

But when Lessa declared that she was joining the Salvatella pack as well, and Raul flat out refused to accept her, I was the one who stepped up, ready to sock him.

"Just hear me out," Raul appealed. "I am not an Alpha without compassion, as you well know," he professed to Avery and me, placing his palm over his heart—*laying it on thick.* "But the thing is, Wyatt joined my pack first. And when I figured Lessa might ask to join as well, I did the honorable thing and checked with Wyatt to make sure he would be okay with that." He grinned wide at my sister, and I had a bad feeling I knew where this was headed. I wondered if I'd last a week without killing my new Alpha.

Raul continued, "The facts are, Lessa betrayed her own mate. And not just a little bit," he reported to the crowd with relish. "Not only did Lessa lie to Wyatt about essentially everything about herself, manipulate his mind on count-less—and I mean *countless*—occasions, tap every one of his phone lines, plant tracking devices on nearly everything he owned, and follow him on surveillance cameras twenty-four-seven, she also set up his best friend Avery to be attacked on numerous occasions and was plotting to capture and kill both Avery and Sloane."

He shrugged at my sister and raised his hands in the air, palms up. "I think you can guess which way Wyatt voted. But hey, in case you don't believe me, I've got a video record-ing of Wyatt expressing his feelings on the matter himself that he wanted me to deliver to you. I'll just send you the YouTube link."

Raul ended up pulling up the video on his own phone and playing it for all to see and completely destroying my sister.

As furious as I was over the way Wyatt had chosen to reject Lessa, I could admit that he had made valid, rational points in the video regarding her level of deception. *Maybe he wasn't as dumb as I'd thought he was.* I promised Lessa that I would smooth things over with Wyatt when I saw him, reassuring her that he wouldn't be able to resist the mating bond pull for long and would soon change his mind.

I gave Lessa a hug goodbye, as well as Jussara. Despite Jussara's deception regarding Remy and the fact that she'd sided against me in favor of Milena, there was little I couldn't forgive and overlook where Lupe's daughter was concerned. It had always been that way for me with Jussara.

But as for the rest of them, they could all go fuck themselves.

While Jussara and I were saying our goodbyes, Sloane surprised everyone by breaking away from Raul's side and approaching Lessa, who was seated on the ground crying, with Alex and Remy flanking her, attempting to comfort her.

"No one ever found daybreak by avoiding night," Sloane stoically told my sister. "Only by passing through it." Then she raced back over to Raul's side, and he promptly picked her up.

Avery, who was standing next to Raul, gasped and covered her mouth with her hand as she witnessed the exchange. When our eyes met, she said, "Oh, my God, Chaos. She just—I think she just tried to comfort your sister."

Lessa looked equally shocked and charmed as she sobbed, "She really is Maribel. She's *Maribel*—"

"That's *my* line," Kai, who had been silently standing

next to Milena, suddenly proclaimed, his eyes wide with alarm. "By God, that's my line!" he shouted. "That's what I used to tell Maribel. She's quoting *me*. She—oh, fuck. Fuck … My God, she really could be—"

"*No*," Avery growled, pinning feral eyes on Kai. "That's *Sloane's* line—one that she shares with Raul. It's their bonding thing. It has nothing to do with you or anything you used to say to your dead mate. My daughter is *not* the reincarnation of a murderous, lovesick nutjob who drained the life force from the living and consumed souls in the name of twisted love for you, Killjoy Kai!"

I winced internally and decided to hold my tongue. I was certain that Sloane was indeed the reincarnated Maribel, but as there was really no way to ever prove or disprove it, it was best to let Avery think that she wasn't.

After all, Avery was right when she'd argued before that Sloane was a child with a clean slate—a child with her whole life ahead of her. Why saddle her with Maribel's baggage? The fates had already done that by bringing her back as the *Rogue*.

"I'm sorry to say that Sloane most likely *is* Maribel," Milena spoke up, gently contradicting my mate as she stepped forward and addressed all of us, her Alpha tone somber, her blue eyes sad yet severe.

"As most everyone here knows, I was the last one to see Maribel in the ether." As she spoke, Milena's gaze connected with Alex's, before seeking mine, and finally Kai's. "And she told me that this *might* come to pass. Maribel said that if she'd miscalculated the timing, misjudged her ability to fully drag the hideous dark power—the defect attached to and driving my blood curse—to the other side and remain dead, that she might be reborn as the *Rogue* of rogues. Reborn as an unholy beast filled with and controlled by darkness; a supernatural powerhouse bent on destruction and revenge."

Well, I'll be damned.

I'd always known that Milena kept her cards close to her chest. In this, she and Raul were more alike than most probably recognized.

Raul turned to Avery next to him and transferred Sloane to Avery's arms, instructing, "Take her for a walk."

"But I—"

"She doesn't need to hear this."

Avery looked ready to argue with Raul. But then it seemed to dawn on her that Sloane wasn't resisting being held, and Avery beamed with happiness as she did as requested, walking our daughter out of earshot.

"The truth is," Milena continued, her apologetic eyes on Kai, "Maribel knew that all of this was a possibility when she absorbed the dark magic of my blood curse into her soul and used it to sever her mate connection to Kai. She knew that what she was doing was something that was unnatural to our kind—that not only could it permanently warp her, but that it might endanger the future of our entire species. *But she did it anyway,*" Milena stressed, the blue in her eyes bleeding into angry, bright green.

To Kai, she said, "She did it even though I begged and pleaded with her not to. And then," Milena revealed with a humorless laugh, "she reminded me that she'd killed my mother and Mateus, and had taken my only brother from me"—her green eyes cut to Raul—"before threatening to kill my best friend Bethany if I didn't agree to go along with her scheme. Oh, and on top of that, she informed me that *if* she should come back as the *Rogue*, it would be *my* job to end her before the decade of no light's end."

I'd been in the dark after all. Milena had kept us all in the dark. I understood why she'd done it with Lessa and the others. And I was eternally grateful now that she'd done it with me as well. Because I, too, had felt the anger and resentment that Milena still harbored for Maribel. I had harbored it myself. And I might've acted on it had I come across Sloane before I'd met Avery. Avery had given me the ability to see the *Rogue* from a perspective I never had before.

"So that's what your beef is then?" Raul had the nerve to ask his sister.

"You think this is funny?" she hissed at him. "You think I wanted this responsibility? You think I want to kill a child, Raul? A child!"

"No. I don't."

"You have no idea what it's been like for me these past ten years, knowing this day might come. Knowing that she had made this my burden. She told me that I was the world's only hope. That it would be *my* responsibility to kill her if she failed to stay dead and was reborn as the *Rogue*. Do you have any idea how conflicted I've been over this? Any inkling of the pain I've felt in my heart knowing that—"

"*Yes*, goddamnit," Raul said, cutting his sister off with an eye-roll. "Yes, I do know."

Milena frowned. "She told you?" She paused, then gasped. "Oh, my God, she told you, too, that I would have to be the one to end her if she—"

"No," Raul interrupted her again. "She told me that *I* would have to be the one to end her if she was reborn as the *Rogue*."

Milena's jaw fell open. "*What?*"

"Maribel didn't think you'd be able to do it when the time came," Raul confessed. "She feared you were too much of a Pollyanna to pull it off. She was afraid you might go soft, wind up feeling sorry for a child *Rogue,* and fall into some misguided mission to protect rather than destroy the *Rogue* as she had asked of you.

"So she made me her backup destroyer. In exchange, she transferred Nuriel's powers to me so that I'd have enough power to best you if it came down to it—if you failed in the mission she'd given you."

Jesus. So Azda wasn't the only one who'd changed her mind. As horrifying as Raul's confession was—the notion that Avery and Sloane might've had *both* Raul and Milena out to exterminate them these past ten years—I felt myself getting teary-eyed as I grinned with pride, of all idiotic things. *My daughter was so damn adorable she turned her killers into protectors and nannies.*

Milena's nostrils flared. "*What?* She ... she told you, too? *She asked you, too?* Then—what are you doing? You'd betray a dying woman's wish to end her soul's misery?"

Raul rolled his eyes. "Look, sometimes it's not what people *say* that carries the most meaning, Miles. It's what they *do.* Let's examine the evidence. She chose Avery for a mother—a woman who doesn't know when to quit. A woman who would gladly die protecting her. Not exactly the best choice for a soul looking for destruction. Then there's the fact that she was born scentless, and somehow managed to extend that ability to her mother as well, masking Avery's scent to all but her mate. Again, not the actions of a soul looking to be discovered and destroyed."

"But she didn't *want this*, Raul," Milena objected. "She didn't *want* to come back as some demented, fractured being attached to a dark curse. Don't you see? This is her worst nightmare—a purgatory worse than even the one she imposed on herself for all those years in the ether. That's why she asked us both to destroy her! Raul, she said that if I didn't—"

"It doesn't matter what she *said,* Miles," Raul's voice rose in anger. "The whole world doesn't see in black and white and deal in absolutes simply because you do. I *know* what Maribel *said* that she wanted. I don't need you to remind me. She says nearly the same things now as Sloane—because she lives attached to a dark energy that makes her feel terrible about herself, that tells her she can only do bad things in the world. She says she shouldn't be here. That she was supposed to stay dead. But that's not what she wants."

"How do you know that?" Milena shouted. "How can you be so arrogant as to interpret that what she wants is other than what she so clearly told us both?"

"Because I just *can,*" he growled. "Because I just know, okay? She came back. She picked Avery. She found me before I ever found her. She pulls me into her nightmares when she gets scared—that's how I found her. And I know that she wants what any soul wants. She wants redemption. She wants a second chance. And I'm going to see that she gets it. I'm not letting you or anyone else take that away from her."

It was a lucky thing after all that I hadn't killed Raul that fateful day in the dining hall ten years ago. After over four centuries, it seems I could still be surprised.

I'd just been yanked back from death's clutches by the two people I'd wanted to exact retribution from the most throughout the past decade. And for the first time ever, I felt fully alive.

Once Raul had stormed off, I'd been left to rebuff another round of empty apologies that spewed forth from my family and former pack members. They were still apologizing for failing to protect my mate. Apologizing to me for Avery's death—*which they were only sorry about because it had nearly caused my death.*

They didn't get it. Hopefully one day they would.

I knew Milena's heart was in the right place regarding her position on the *Rogue*. I had never known Milena to *not* have only the best of intentions. And that's what scared me the most about her now.

History was full of terrible events borne of the best intentions. Raul was right. Milena did see the world in black and white. And Sloane was grey, uncharted territory—dangerous and unknown. Which made it almost hard to fault Milena for her stance. Seeing the world in black and white could make any great warrior blind.

EPILOGUE

Avery

Six months later in Bariloche, Argentina

"**O**H, *FUUUCK*, CHAOS—"

My hips shot up off the mattress as Alcaeus's fingers replaced his tongue inside of me, finding my G-spot with the ease of a natural-born predator who'd spent the better part of four centuries indulging in the study of the female anatomy.

His tongue licked higher, circling and tormenting my throbbing clit, as he hummed happily, pausing every so often to tell me what a gorgeous cunt I had.

Somehow he always managed to sound so sweet while at the same time like a filthy bastard.

He stimulated my G-spot to the point of unbearable pleasure, before withdrawing his fingers and licking them clean. Leaving me hanging—my body painfully primed and on edge.

Holding my thighs spread wide, he rubbed his scruff-covered jawline over my sensitized lower lips, making me moan and writhe as I yanked against the chains securing my arms above my head.

"Chaos, *please* …"

He alternated between sucking, blowing, licking, and straight-up devouring my most sensitive parts until I was begging him to finish me off.

He raked his teeth gently over my swollen bit of flesh then, causing me to buck and shriek. Then he sucked the whole thing into his mouth.

Oh, my God, how did he do that?

I swear it felt like he had my entire pussy in his mouth at times. The suction on my clit felt otherworldly.

I was on the verge of coming, when he stopped.

I groaned in frustration as he held my spread thighs immobilized against the mattress and blew lightly on my drenched, needy slit.

"Who needs to be rescued?" he taunted in that sexy bass of his.

"I do." I panted. *"I do,* you fucking sonofabitch."

He chuckled and slowly kissed his way up my belly. "Such a sweet, sexy damsel in distress," he murmured against my skin.

He licked the length of each scar on my ribs, kissed and nibbled my breasts, and sucked each of my nipples into his mouth, one at a time, rubbing his scratchy facial hair along the valley of skin between my breasts as his mouth traveled back and forth between their pebbled peaks, tormenting me.

"So helpless all chained up like this. Desperate and begging to be fucked …"

His fingers slid down between my folds—teasing, but not satisfying. "So wet and needy for cock …"

I moaned and pleaded, *"Yes.* Please, just save me, now. *Please* rescue me. *Fuck me,* already."

He licked and sucked his way up my neck. I felt the blunt tip of his erection nudge against my inner thigh, and I began begging him to fix me, to fill the ache in me, as he threaded his fingers through my hair and turned my head to the side.

I sensed his inner animal emerging. I knew he was on the verge of breaking as his tongue found and laved the mating mark he'd made on my neck. That mark always set me off, too. So I told him I'd die if he didn't fuck me hard and fill me with his cum.

He growled and snapped his hips forward, penetrating me with one forceful thrust, then filling me to bursting with the second.

He held himself over me, leaning up on one elbow as he hooked his other arm under my bent knee and raised it up toward my shoulder, as he withdrew and slowly penetrated me again.

And again.

With slow, measured strokes that made me want it to go on forever because it felt so good—and made me want to kill him when he settled in and paused, his entire length lodged deep.

"*Chaos.* If you don't save me right this fucking minute, I'll break these chains and strangle you wi—"

He smothered my mouth with his, stroking his tongue that tasted of my sex in and out between my lips as his hips did the same between my thighs, rolling and thrusting, harder and faster, as he sent me over the edge at last, my inner muscles gripping and squeezing and convulsing in the most brutal, beautiful ecstasy, as he emptied inside of me.

"You're terrible at this," he told me, the breath bursting

from his lungs as he collapsed on top of me. "Worst damsel in distress ever."

The chains fell away from my wrists, and I immediately brought my right palm down onto his taut ass cheek with a thwack.

"Hey now," he said with a laugh. "That's it. I'm chaining you up face down, ass up, and starting all over again. We're going to keep doing these therapy sessions until you get better at letting me use your sexual torment and distress to make my dick feel bigger."

"Oh, no, not again," I protested weakly in my best breathy rescue-case voice.

Chaos laughed. "Oh, yes." His lips brushed against mine. "You're going to endure being rescued as many times as it takes, honey."

I felt Raul trying to tap my mind and groaned. *Damn.*

"Therapy time is over," I announced. "Raul and Sloane are headed back."

"Aw, come on! He's had her for an hour," Chaos complained, sounding like a big child himself. "Tell him to suck it up and watch *Frozen* again."

"It's been at least two hours," I pointed out. "Hang on, let me talk to him and tell him to give us five minutes."

"*Five?* Tell him to give us sixty. And tell him I said to stay the fuck out of my wife's head."

I answered Raul through our mind connection and asked him to walk Sloane along the scenic route from the main house so that Chaos and I would have at least ten minutes to straighten ourselves up. Since I'd gained my werelock capabilities, Raul, Alcaeus, and I had figured out how to get around the mind shield that Sloane had constructed.

Raul responded back that he and Sloane were

teleporting over in the next two minutes, before quickly breaking our connection.

"Ugh. He says they'll be here in two. They're teleporting." I patted his back as Chaos buried his face in the crook of my neck, cursing and making pouting noises. Sometimes he was worse than Sloane. "Come on, big guy, get off me so I can get up."

Chaos, Sloane, and I had relocated to the Salvatella pack's stronghold in Bariloche, Argentina. Known as the Switzerland of South America, it was like something out of a fairytale. Nestled between the Andes Mountains and a glacial lake, it was the most picturesque place I'd ever seen.

Alcaeus had insisted upon building us our own private residence within the walls of the Salvatella compound—a modest home for just the three of us, situated a short distance away from the main estate. I had a sense it was because he still didn't quite trust every member of the Salvatella pack. And I couldn't blame him—given the long history of deceit, violence, and bloodshed between the Salvatellas and the Reinosos.

But Chaos insisted that he'd done it so that Sloane could have more space and privacy as she got acclimated to her new environment. *And also so that I would feel comfortable screaming for help as loudly as Chaos wanted me to during our hero-complex therapy sessions.*

Wyatt had been in Bariloche for the first few months that we'd been here. But following Wyatt's initial werewolf introduction and pack-life assimilation, Raul had sent him to the Salvatella pack's estate in Puerto Iguazú, saying he needed his help with something there for a few months. I was sorry to see Wyatt go, but it had been for the best. Things had been very strained between Wyatt and Alcaeus as a result of Wyatt's rejection of Alcaeus's sister, Lessa. And it was difficult for me being caught in the middle.

Azda hadn't moved with us to Bariloche, choosing instead to relocate back to her community on the Navajo reservation. I don't think she liked the idea of living abroad amongst so many skinwalkers. And it seemed clear she felt that Alcaeus and I needed to get used to parenting Sloane on our own.

Raul was now our main help and childcare backup in Bariloche—the only person who could babysit Sloane for us when we wanted time alone as a couple. Sloane adored Raul in a way I'd never seen her take to anyone else. She liked Alcaeus well enough, and was warming up to tolerating him more every day, but she had a kind of hero-worship for Raul, our new Alpha.

Sloane was still pulling Raul into her nightmares. It bothered me less now than it bothered Alcaeus. In truth, I sensed there was probably a bit of a rivalry brewing between the two men when it came to winning Sloane's affection—mostly on Alcaeus's side.

"Why can't they walk? It's barely a hundred yards. Who teleports that short of a distance?" Alcaeus was still complaining and grumbling to himself as he pulled pants on and stowed our bed chains away. "Raul's such a lazy shit."

I teleported from the upstairs level of our house to the downstairs level when Alcaeus wasn't around, actually. I told myself I was doing it for practice, but really, it was because that shit was fun.

I'd just gotten my clothes on and was heading down the stairs when Raul teleported into our living room with Sloane in his arms.

I gasped and nearly squealed at the sight of them, before slapping my hand over my mouth.

"Don't even say it," Raul warned in his Alpha voice, his eyes hard on me as he set my daughter down on her feet next to him. "Not one word."

While it still amazed me to witness Sloane allow someone to pick her up and hold her the way that she did with Raul, that wasn't what had me struggling to contain my shock and laughter now.

"*No one* in the pack hears about this," Raul ordered me as he straightened to his full height, adjusting the hot pink, satiny Princess Anna costume cloak draped awkwardly around his broad shoulders.

I shook my head, still covering my mouth, as tears of laughter welled in my eyes.

Sloane was wearing her ice blue Queen Elsa gown and sparkly cape, along with her tiara.

"*Hol-y* sh—*shirt-cape,*" Alcaeus said as he bounded down the stairs behind me. He was still struggling not to swear around my daughter. "You girls look stunning!" he managed to say to Raul and Sloane without choking on the laughter he was attempting to keep in check. "I need a photo."

"*No,*" Raul immediately declined, while Sloane responded with a stoic, "Yes."

~

"Hey, so as you know, Mike's had some of our guys tailing Kai and his crew for a while," Raul confided to me in the kitchen as I poured myself a cup of coffee. Raul was absent his hot pink cape now, dressed simply in his standard, casual surfer-boy attire.

Because Chaos was now wearing the cloak in the other room—trying to prove to Sloane that he made a better Princess Anna to her Queen Elsa than Raul did.

I nodded. Kai had gone back to the States after returning briefly to Brazil, taking a smaller team of men than what he and Alcaeus had on their original *Rogue* mission. Mike, who'd been tracking Kai's activities, was a higher-ranking Beta within the Salvatella pack and more or less Raul's head of security detail. Beyond that, Raul and Mike were close friends, and I knew that Raul trusted him.

"Mike thinks that Kai may have found one of the next great seers," Raul said, lowering his voice and leaning in to me where we stood next to one another at the kitchen counter. "There's a college-aged woman that Kai has been … well, *stalking* is the word Mike used."

Technically, Alcaeus was Raul's head Beta, not me, but often Raul and I vetted and formed strategies on matters related to Chaos's family members and former pack mates prior to discussing them with Chaos.

Alcaeus's family's betrayal was still too raw of a subject for him. And Chaos often became enraged at the mere mention of Kai's name. So we felt that there was no sense in poking that tiger until we needed to.

"Stalking?" *Interesting.* I raised my coffee mug to my lips and took a sip.

"Yeah. Mike says Kai's behavior has been a bit *off* lately—all over the place, actually—ever since Kai began tracking this coed twenty-four-seven. And most recently, a few weeks ago, Kai dismissed all of the men he had with him in America." Raul raised his palms in the air. "Ordered every single one of them back to Brazil for no apparent reason."

"Wow. So he's gone rogue now?" I said with a wry, embittered chuckle. "Irony of ironies."

"Don't know. From what Mike tells me, it sounds as if he might just be going off the rails. He's attacked the last three guys that this coed had dates with. Attacked them in wolf form," Raul appended meaningfully with a raised brow. "All three of the guys survived, but ended up transferring to other schools. And he's been remaining in his wolf form for longer and longer stretches at a time to the point that he's in wolf form more than he is his human form."

Fascinating. I recalled the version of Kai I'd witnessed in the Hoia Baciu Forest. Perhaps he was reverting to his feral nature—but why? What vision had he seen from this coed's mind, I wondered?

I tapped my fingernails against the rim of my ceramic mug. "What do you suppose all this bizarre behavior means? Has Mike gotten inside the coed's head to see whether she's the next great seer?"

"He has been in her head. And he says he's not positive. He says she has abilities, but she seems clueless—or confused—by them for the most part. She largely just ignores her dreams and visions. And even the spirit voices that she hears—pretending not to hear them the greater percentage of the time."

"Huh. Can't blame her. Probably how I'd handle it."

Raul chuckled. "Right. Says the one who connected with a lost-looking dark soul in the ether and came back to life with it in her womb."

I elbowed him in the ribs. "So, does Mike think Kai's

interest in this potential seer could be personal? Or does he think it's something that Kai has seen in her mind that's freaked him out?"

"It's well out of character for Kai to take a personal interest in any woman, but yes, that's exactly what Mike thinks might be happening. Or maybe a bit of both."

The next great seer's visions of the *Rogue's* future impact on our world were critical. And whatever the visions were, Raul and I knew we had to stay one step ahead of the game in order to manipulate how those visions were interpreted and spread throughout our supernatural society.

And if we couldn't manipulate them, we were going to start slaying some seers.

"Feel like taking a trip to America to check it out?" Raul asked.

I nodded. "Ready whenever you are."

He grinned and extended his fist. I bumped it with my free one as I took another sip of my coffee.

I had a special bone to pick with Killjoy Kai. And by "bone to pick," I meant that I had a personal interest in breaking every last bone in his werelock body, ripping his heart out, and dancing on his grave.

"Hey, who's up for watching *Frozen* again?" Chaos shouted excitedly from the living room.

"Oooh! Me, me, me!" I hollered back as Raul groaned quietly at my side. I turned to him and amended my earlier reply. "But let's leave after we watch *Frozen* again, okay?"

THE END
(For now)

JUST LIKE ANIMALS

Werelock Evolution, Book 5

Bloody hell, I'd bitten her!

She spun around to face me, her hand clutching the side of her neck. Pink hit her cheeks the moment her startled eyes met mine, and she gasped. "Holy baby Jesus in a filthy fucking manger."

Despite the seriousness of the situation, my lips twitched helplessly at her outburst. "I'm so sorry"—I cleared my throat to keep from laughing—"I don't know what came over me, Bethany."

"Raul. Wow. Wow, oh, wow." She shook her head continuously, staring as if she couldn't fathom that it was me. "Holy shit. Oh, my God. Oh, my Gawwwd. Wow. I didn't know you were *you* … and you … didn't know that I was *me*," she explained it aloud to herself. "I mean—obviously. Because I never would've—and you never would've—I mean—we, *we* never would've …"

Damn. She was cute all flustered, gesticulating wildly with her hands as she rambled on.

"I'm sure what you experienced was a moment of shock. Panic? Exactly," she confirmed to herself. "Panic. It was reflexive. Instinctual. A PTSD response. Yes." She snapped her fingers as if she'd found the explanation for it all. "I read about how this happens to individuals who are orally fixated. I read it in a medical journal somewhere. I think. God, I don't normally get myself off on strangers' hands … in uh … ahhm … pub"—she trailed off as she watched me suck my fingers into my mouth, tasting her—"lic."

Fuck me. That taste. Definitely not letting her go. I hummed and nodded. Her jaw fell open. I took advantage of the opportunity, pulling my fingers from my mouth and slipping them into hers before she could object. I used her moment of stunned inaction to lower my head closer to her shoulder and assess the damage I'd done to her neck, whispering, "You taste delicious, Bethy," next to her ear on the way down.

I was no expert in mating bond bites by any stretch, but her neck didn't appear to be as bad off as I'd initially feared when I'd tasted her blood in my mouth. Certainly not the way I imagined a mating bond bite would look. Huh. Maybe it hadn't been deep enough to be damaging or significant? Somehow I felt disappointment at this rather than relief. I was sick.

I licked over her broken skin a few times, partially healing it with my saliva. Then I kissed the spot. "I didn't mean to hurt you." I pulled back to look at her. "You were just so hot. I got carried away."

Her eyes were dazed, her pupils wide. Her lips had closed over my fingers. When her tongue moved tentatively against them, I feared I might bust a nut in my pants. I vowed that I would come in her mouth before the night was through.

"I'm afraid you're going to have a hickey for a few days," I advised.

Or a few weeks. *Or maybe a lifetime?* Best guess was one of the three.

Her hand reached up and lightly grasped my wrist. Slowly, she pulled my fingers from her mouth, giving them a timid, parting suck as they passed between her plump lips. I was absolutely coming in her mouth before the night was through.

"It's late. I should go."

Hell to the no. "Of course. I understand. But maybe you could buy me a drink first? So I don't go home feeling cheap and used."

Her eyes widened and she turned so red I thought she might pass out.

"Kidding, Bethy." I held up both palms. "A joke to lighten the mood. But I am serious that we should have a drink and catch up a bit."

She looked unsure. And entirely too sober all of the sudden. I couldn't have her overthinking this.

"Look, if we try and ignore what just happened, it'll only be more awkward the next time we run into each other, don't you think?" I reasoned. "C'mon, we're old friends. We can handle this like two responsible adults, can't we?"

"Hi, Bethany's friend," a slurred female voice broke in, bringing too much perfume with her into our personal space. Great.

I endured introductions to several tipsy girlfriends. To my annoyance, Bethany introduced me as her "best friend's brother" every time. It shouldn't have bothered me. It's what I was to her. It's what I would always be to her.

Unless I'd bitten her too hard.

We got drinks and found a quieter spot tucked away from the dance floor. She was still flustered, but she put up a good front, plastered on a bright smile, and proceeded to catch me up on her life, confirming mostly facts that I already knew.

"So I'm finishing my residency, and I'll be opening my own gynecology practice next year."

"That's amazing. Congratulations." The reminder that

she stuck her fingers inside of other women's pussies for a living wasn't helpful when I was still struggling to get my mind off of hers.

"I adopted a rescue puppy last week, I'm getting married in three months, and I just couldn't be happier," she concluded.

"Wonderful. Where's the fiancé tonight?"

"Who?"

"Your fiancé." My eyes slid to the giant princess cut diamond on her finger in indication.

"Oh!" Her eyes lit with understanding. "Oh, you mean Gregg? That fiancé?"

I frowned. Nodded. "There more than one?"

She broke into high-pitched, nervous laughter. "No, no, it's just the one," she confirmed, punching me playfully in the arm. "God, you were always so funny." She sighed and took a sip of her drink. Then she took another sip that turned into a chug as she downed the remains of the glass.

"Gregg's cheating on me," she announced with the next release of air that escaped her. "Not that it's an excuse for me using your hand to masturbate myself on a dance floor or anything."

"I see." They were the only words I managed as conflicting emotions and a million thoughts jumbled through me. How hard had I really bitten her? Could I get away with killing Gregg without upsetting her? Would I be able to resist biting her again if she continued to make reference to coming on my hand?

"It's just—you were touching my breasts," she continued in a rush. "And I'm really into nipple play, and your hands felt so good on me that I had this mad impulse to come on them. And I always preach that women should follow their sexual instincts. So I did. Would you excuse me a moment?" She didn't wait for my reply before jumping up from her seat and bolting in the direction of the bathroom.

Jesus. She was the same Bethany I remembered. Adorably quirky. Strong-willed. Unconventional. Sexy as hell.

And I was fucking her tonight. Off-limits be damned.

THANK YOU, dear readers!

Thank you for reading *No Light (Werelock Evolution, Book 4).* If you enjoyed reading this story, I hope that you will consider leaving a few words in a review to help other readers discover it. Every review is very much appreciated!

If you'd like to check out other books that I've written, please feel free to visit my website at www.hettieivers.com, sign up for my Newsletter, or friend me on Facebook to keep in touch.

Warmest Regards,
Hettie

ACKNOWLEDGMENTS

To my awesome professional editor big sis, thank you for taking time out from reviewing and editing critical life-saving medical publications in order to remind me when Alcaeus was walking around pantless for too long in this manuscript. I feel like my ability to recognize when I'm dangling modifiers grew by leaps and bounds this werelock installment. You are the best, and I love you dearly!

To my amazing husband with the smiling eyes, thank you for always being so supportive of my writing hobby and for beta-reading stories in genres that I'm sure you would otherwise never in this lifetime choose to pick up. Thank you for inspiring certain characters and hilarious relationship dynamics in this book in particular. Both parenting a rogue and being married to a rogue must get tough at times. Good thing you have all those private jokes happening in your head 24-7 to keep you amused.

To my awesome friends Sheena, Joan, Shanel, Becky, Chelsea, Jessica, Lauren, Melody, and Rachel: Thank you for being early readers/beta testers/bouncers-of-ideas at various points in this process for me. I am so thankful for your honest feedback and your kind encouragement for this story. A special thanks to Sheena for tirelessly spreading my name, banners, and covers all over Facebook on a daily basis. I don't know what I did to deserve your support, but you're beyond amazing, and I really appreciate you!

To my SOAM sisters, thank you for your ongoing friendship and support, and for the countless hours of fun, laughter, and fantastic female camaraderie.

Have you read Alex and Milena's enemies-to-lovers tale?
Werelock Evolution: The Complete Trilogy **is the story that started it all.**

Werelock Evolution: The Complete Trilogy

He's a spoiled Alpha used to getting whatever he wants. She's a stubborn eighteen-year-old determined to disappoint him.

Finding love at first sight with your fated soul mate sounds so romantic. *Unless*, of course, that "mate" happens to be your brother's sworn enemy and the overbearing Alpha werewolf-warlock who has taken you hostage.

Things get complicated in this twisty enemies-to-lovers trilogy about an American girl who stumbles upon forbidding paranormal circumstances when she travels to Brazil and finds herself at the center of a blood feud between rival South American werewolf packs.

The task of taming a formidable, drop-dead sexy werelock has never been so hard. And so hot.

Excerpt from SLIP OF FATE
(Werelock Evolution, Book 1)

I wasn't sure what I'd expected to find when we approached the foyer, but the scene we came upon was far worse than any I could've envisioned.

There were more people gathered in the semi-cylindrical receiving area than before. We entered the open room, and Alessandra deposited me on my feet in time to see Felix suspended by his throat against a wall, his feet dangling at least a foot off the ground, his broken arms hanging uselessly at his sides.

A tall, dark-haired, formidable man in a tuxedo was holding him up by the neck with just one hand. Felix's eyes bugged out in horror and his face went from red to purple to blue while the cruel man, whose face was turned from me, proceeded to mercilessly crush his windpipe.

My first instinct was to scream at the faceless, heartless man to stop and let him go, but the words died in my throat and ice coursed through my veins as he leaned in closer to my dying abductor and rasped, "No deal, Felix. I've no need of Raul's worthless sister. Not as bait, as a trade for your son, or otherwise."

He spoke in a forbidding, deep whisper, presumably meant for Felix's dying ears, yet the words were clearly heard by everyone in the otherwise silent hall as they resonated off the stone walls.

"Raul's dead," he hissed. "I saw to it myself days ago. And thanks to you, his sister will be dead soon, too."

Time and space ceased to exist as I sought to reconcile the meaning of his words. Raul was dead?

"So you've wasted your time," he sneered, "forfeited four lives, and shortened your son's allotted time left by coming here and interrupting my dinner."

He'd died just days ago?

Raul was dead?

I'd never borne witness to much violence in my lifetime, let alone seen a man murdered right before my eyes, and yet I barely registered the visual of Felix's eyes rolling back and becoming lifeless as the final vestiges of his very being were squeezed from him.

I don't know how long I stood stock-still, my own eyes wide and glazed over with terror, before the dark-haired devil whom I knew had to be the infamous Alex turned away from his fresh kill to visibly sniff in my direction like some depraved, wild animal honing in on his next unfortunate prey.

As his cold, dark eyes alighted upon me, they widened perceptibly. Felix's dead body was dropped like a sack of trash a millisecond later as the dinner party host I'd so erroneously assumed would be civilized turned his imposing frame in my direction.

He was darkly handsome like Alcaeus, with facial features that more closely resembled Remy's, but with none of the playfulness or boyishness of either of the two men. And his eyes were unlike any of his siblings'. They were a deep, dark shade of brown. His jet-black hair was cropped short, and he was expertly groomed and outfitted as if he'd stepped off the pages of *GQ*.

On the surface, he appeared the perfect male specimen. I was certain many of the girls I'd gone to school with would've fallen all over themselves just to gain a moment of his attention. But beneath his polished veneer, I knew he was just a monster. A brute who had murdered my brother. And never before in my life had I wished more horrific, fatal harm upon another human being as I now fervently hoped to befall him.

As he breathed deeply in and out, audibly inhaling as if to suggest he could actually smell me from across the foyer, he seemed to regard me much like Alessandra first had—as if he was encountering an apparition.

Then his eyes widened further, and I could've sworn the most unfathomable expression of pure elation and inconceivable rapture transformed his confused, horrified features for the briefest of moments.

Strangely, it reminded me of the expression on the face of this lost little boy I'd helped once at the mall—his look upon laying eyes on his mother when they were at last reunited. It was an odd amalgamation of unmitigated joy mixed with relief juxtaposed against the profound terror of realizing one's own supreme vulnerability for the very first time. The face of one who'd just been saved but would never be the same again for that rescue.

Only in this case, the man before me still appeared hopelessly lost. And judging from the way his expression swiftly morphed into that of unadulterated rage, I wasn't sure he'd wanted to be found at all—much less saved.

"Fuck," Alessandra swore under her breath at my side.

Fuck was right. I was sure if eyes could spit fire, Alex's would have charred me alive already.

And then they did. Either I was going completely mad or his irises had turned a bright golden yellow color as they glowered wildly at me.

Alessandra whisper-swore again as every single pair of eyes in the room seemed to fixate upon me in marked disbelief.

Alex's lips pulled back into a snarl, and a deep, unearthly growl vibrated up from his chest and ricocheted off the walls.

"*No,*" he ground out in a low, deathly grim rumble that sounded more animal than human. "Not mine!"

I hadn't a clue what he'd meant by that proclamation, but I was pretty sure any small chance I'd had of surviving the night had just evaporated.

"This … can't be happening," Alessandra stammered cryptically. "You're … human … you're Raul's sister … "

"Fuck me sideways!" I heard Alcaeus's voice buoyantly exclaim. "No wonder she smells so good and I feel so protective."

My eyes darted to where Alcaeus stood a few feet from Alex. He was grinning from ear to ear like a man who'd just won the lottery. Earlier he'd wanted to save me from Alex. And now, right as I was about to be murdered in cold blood, he looked ready to celebrate.

"Well, isn't this just a juicy slice of poetic justice?" He chuckled, slapping a thoroughly unamused Alex on the back.

"Alex, please meet Raul's little sister and my new best friend, Milena," Alcaeus introduced with a flourish.

"She's injured," he added happily to the otherwise silent, tension-saturated room. "Head trauma," he informed the incensed-looking Alex with glee. "You might want to get right on that, in fact, because Remy and I weren't able to get her to cooperate long enough to heal it."

"Alcaeus, please stop?" Remy's distressed voice implored. He was standing on the other side of the room. He didn't seem to find the situation as funny as Alcaeus did. "This is not the time to antagonize him. Think of Milena."

My eyes darted back and forth across the room from Remy to Alcaeus to Alex. Remy was right. Whatever Alcaeus was doing seemed to be exacerbating the situation and escalating Alex's level of ire. His face was flushed and he'd begun growling at the mention of Remy and Alcaeus's failed attempt to heal my head injury. But Alcaeus waved off Remy's warning.

"I mean, sure," Alcaeus broadcast to the room as he absorbed Alex's every strained reaction with relish, "she enjoyed me licking her inner thighs all right, and she most definitely enjoyed Remy kissing her," he said with a mischievous wink in Remy's direction, "but in general she doesn't much care for warlocks creeping around inside her head. Isn't that right, my dear?" He looked to me for confirmation.

I shook my head in bewilderment. Alessandra was now swearing like a sailor next to me. Alex hadn't ceased growling; his unearthly yellow eyes raked over me as he fisted his hair and his whole body shook with barely suppressed fury—the personification of a geyser ready to blow.

"Alex, please?" Remy beseeched, "I beg you, please don't hurt her. None of this is her fault. Take your anger out on me."

Alcaeus snorted. "He's not going to hurt her. He might be a stubborn, bitter asshole, but he's never been stupid."

I didn't know what the deuce was happening or what they were talking about. All I knew was that Alex had begun cursing a blue streak and yanking at his tie until he'd torn it to shreds in frustration from his neck. He'd just managed to shrug out of his fancy tuxedo jacket when suddenly with an angry roar he burst from his own skin before my very eyes!

Buttons went flying and expensive-looking fabric was torn to shreds as an enormous, viciously snarling black and grey wolf took the place of the enraged man faster than I could blink.

Werewolf!

Almost all the other occupants in the room parted and backed away, bowing their heads in deference to the beast and affording him greater space as with hackles raised he took his first horrifying step forward in my direction.

My mouth fell open and I instinctively took a miniscule step backward. Alessandra's hand shot out and captured my wrist.

"No! Don't move," she warned.

The beast increased his growling and snarling the moment she grabbed me, prompting Alessandra to swear and release my wrist.

"Don't make any sudden movement," she cautioned, speaking slowly and clearly, her voice never rising above a whisper as she began to sidestep away from me.

"And no matter what, do … not … run," she stressed. "When he comes at you, don't panic, okay? Please, *please,* listen to me, Milena?" she appealed. "Alex won't hurt you; just let him scent you."

She didn't want me to run from him? *Wouldn't hurt me?*

He'd just announced to the whole room that I was dead meat next!

Not only had he freely claimed credit for the murder of the only family member I had left, but I'd just witnessed him crush a man's throat with his bare hand after heartlessly denying Felix's dying request to spare his son's life.

What's more, now that the room had cleared, I noted

that Felix's compadres seemed to have suffered even worse fates, as their bodies lay lifeless on the marble floor, their chests torn open and their un-beating, bloody hearts strewn thoughtlessly beside them.

And now, when Alex was snarling at me in his true monster nature form—that of a vicious, oversized, super-natural killer dog—Alessandra expected I wouldn't run? If she thought I was going to stick around and let some cross between Cujo and Hannibal Lecter get close enough to sniff and lick my hand, she was out of her goddamned mind.

I didn't run. I pivoted on my heel and flew!

Ready for Remy & Jussara's enemies-to-lovers tale?
THE REMEDY is coming…

His throat worked. Awareness slowly broke across his features. It only made Jussara's pulse beat faster. "My God," he murmured, more to himself than to her. "I should've …"

He should've realized.

He should have known.

His hands dropped from the fencing on either side of her. Rather than feel relief as he took a step back, affording her space, Jussara's stomach knotted and her cheeks flushed with a different kind of heat as Remy's brows pulled together and his jewel-green eyes assessed her with an emotion she'd never wanted to see from him: *pity.*

"It was never about disdain for your own species," he said, his gaze uncompromising. "It wasn't so much blind arrogance that your mother instilled in you as it was …"

It was fear.

He didn't need to say it. So he didn't. He could scarcely believe what an idiot he'd been. *For all this time.* It was so obvious. And he was supposed to be an empath!

But Jussara had been such a raging spitfire bitch for as long as Remy had known her. Even now, as he watched, her emotions shuttered—while her irises flashed a warning yellow.

Remy's fists clenched at his sides as he fought a mad urge to reach out and comfort the woman who looked as if she was about to hiss and swipe at him like a cornered animal. He saw now that Jussara must've lived her whole life feeling cornered and on the defensive within their pack.

He tamped down the crazy impulse to take her in his arms and swear to her that she had always been safe here—that no one in their pack had ever meant her harm. Because it was a lie. And Jussara was hardly naïve or stupid enough to believe it.

Remy himself had lobbied to snuff out Jussara's life before she'd been born. Her lineage had marked her as an enemy within their pack from day one. Even now, when she was arguably more accepted than she had ever been, Alex had asked Remy to spy on Jussara's emotions—because Alex still didn't fully trust in her loyalty.

And Remy didn't trust himself at present not to do something he'd regret as the scent of Jussara's heat cycle mingled with that of her rising anger … and underlying fear. She intoxicated him—with her savage yet regal beauty and her stormy emotions.

She was an empath's wet dream. She was also pure poison. *And he wanted to suck and fuck every last deadly drop of her.*

"I'll walk you back," he offered instead.

"I'll walk myself." She planted her palm against his chest and shoved as she pushed off the fence behind her.

He staggered back several paces, but quickly regained his balance, and his hand instinctively latched onto Jussara's wrist as she made to pull away and run off in the direction of her house. Remy questioned whether his sanity had finally snapped when he found himself twisting Jussara's wrist behind her back and leveraging his body weight to pin her front against the iron fence.

She growled and lashed out at him with her free hand, drawing blood as she raked her nails across his face. If anything, it made his giant erection that was pressed against her jean-encased ass even harder.

He obviously had a death wish, because he had no intention of backing down and walking away now.

It took longer for him to capture and pin her second wrist behind her back to join the first as Jussara's true panic set in, causing her to twist and thrash wildly against him. He narrowly dodged a crack to the nose when she reared back and attempted to head-butt his face with the back of her skull.

He sensed the moment she intended to shift into her wolf form to aid her escape, and he didn't hesitate to use his superior rank within the pack to his advantage. "You may *not* shift, Jussara," he ordered. "You will remain in human form until I say otherwise."

He didn't command her submission, though. Didn't so much as suggest she stop fighting him. And she didn't. She managed to head-butt the underside of his jaw, stomp on his instep several painful times, and land multiple kicks to his shins that would've shattered the bones of a human man— all while throwing profanity and death threats at him.

Remy welcomed the abuse. Perhaps, because he felt guilty for his recent spying on her. *Guilty for how he'd behaved toward her and her late mother since the moment he'd first learned of their arrival in Morumbi.*

But more than that, he welcomed the abuse from her because he understood her need to deliver it. Remy knew no matter how imperative it was that Jussara allow herself to be vulnerable with someone right now, she couldn't actually handle the thought of being vulnerable.

If he was going to seduce her, he'd have to make her feel that she had control over the situation. *And God help him, he was going to seduce her.* Even if it meant Alcaeus killing him.

The fight didn't leave her until finally he wedged his free hand between her body and the iron fence to cup her sex through her jean shorts.

She froze—her entire body going rigid as immediately she recognized that if she continued to struggle, squirm, and kick, it would cause her overly sensitized, throbbing clit to rub against his hand. And then she might truly lose it—in an entirely different way.

Remy had smelled how wet she was before. Now he could feel it through the fabric of her shorts. He waited, listening intently as her heart rate sprinted and her labored breathing became even more erratic.

"I'll tell Alcaeus," she threatened breathlessly at last.

Predictable.

Desperate.

Delightful.

It took effort to keep the smile that broke on his face from his voice as he tightened his grip on her wrists pinned to her back and asked, "Will you?" He rolled his hips—and his erection—against her ass. His mouth dipped to graze the shell of her ear. "And then what will happen, Juju?"

He'd never called her Juju before. Had never planned to—not until a few nights ago when he'd entered her sex dream and had witnessed the way she'd responded to her dream version of him addressing her by the pet name. When he heard her breath catch and felt her pelvis unconsciously tilt into his hand, he knew he'd made the right move in using it now.

"He'll kill you for touching me." Her voice was shaky, despite the underlying confidence in her words.

"Probably," he agreed. "Suppose I don't care?" He pressed a kiss to the side of her head, pausing to inhale the earthy sweet fragrance of her hair. "What if I think that helping you through your heat cycle tonight would be worth facing Al's wrath?"

Her swallow was audible. "You're not thinking clearly. You're reacting to my scent."

A chuckle escaped him. "I do believe you're worried for my safety. That's quite touching."

"I don't give a fuck about—"

"I'll make you a deal." His fingers flexed lightly against the seam of her shorts, causing her to mewl. "What if I promise to let you use me however you want through your heat cycle—just as you would one of those random human men in town that you intended to pick up and fuck tonight?"

ABOUT THE AUTHOR

Hettie Ivers is an accidental romance author who likes to escape the stress of her workweek with a good dirty book—preferably one that's also funny. Her current career does not allow much time for creative smut writing, but she loves to write after hours and on weekends and strives to publish one to two books per year, as life permits.

To learn more about Hettie and the books she has written, please feel free to visit her website at www.hettieivers.com, sign up for her Newsletter, friend her on Facebook, or join her Facebook Group to keep in touch.

Please feel free to follow/connect with Hettie via any of these platforms as well:

Website: www.hettieivers.com

Amazon: www.amazon.com/author/hettieivers

Goodreads: www.goodreads.com/author/show/15044336. Hettie_Ivers

BookBub: www.bookbub.com/authors/hettie-ivers

Facebook Page: www.facebook.com/hettieivers

Facebook Group: bit.ly/HettieIversReaders

Instagram: www.instagram.com/hettieivers

Twitter: www.twitter.com/hettie_ivers